WAR ANTHEM

For Linda,

I'm so proud to present my work to you.

WAR
ANTHEM

I hope you enjoy!

KEITH ANDREW PERRY

In loving memory of my parents, Andrew and Etoile Ashton Perry; fiercely proud native Washingtonians.

viii

"...Like men we'll face the murderous, cowardly pack,
Pressed to the wall, dying, but fighting back!"

Claude McKay

"In years to come, I'll earn my people's adoration. For only gentle feelings, my lure did awake. For freedom did I praise in time of tribulation. And mercy ask for fallen heroes sake."

Alexander Pushkin

"And I will plant them upon their land and they shall no more be pulled up out of their land which I have given them, saith the Lord thy God"

The Book of Amos 9:15

x

PROLOGUE

In my native land, there are no wanderers, though many lose their way, only errant souls condemned by their own misdeeds. If absence from the body is presence with God then what is the converse: the body existing in alienation from the soul, resulting in a corporeal gentrification. Desolation. Fire in the streets, hell on earth.

From *The Journal of Jason Diggs*
October 7, 2038

I knew two things about it. No, maybe a little bit more; but in the end, they were the things to know. I knew that the business of Washington is power; its acquisition, exercise and loss and I knew that there was not one Washington but three.

A tourist city, gleaming white and resplendent with flowers—an elaborate subterfuge hiding the ill intent of the second city and the darkness of the third; a political city of mahogany conference rooms, dimly lit restaurants and hotel suites, where the debauchery of the powerful is made manifest; and a *Chocolate City*, beautiful in it's suffering,

1

proud of its improbable ascendance, defiant in its fall.

Washington straddles the North and South, but it is neither. Within its complex divisions, the city has always been segregated. From its infancy there were slave quarters, which persisted even after the city's early emancipation. By the 1970s and 80s the divisions were so complete that Blacks could go for days without encountering whites unless they wanted to. Most were disinclined.

The millennium brought a resurgence of ancient hostilities. Power continued to concede nothing, as it always has; demands went unheard, as they usually are. In the city, it was a season of ice; it was the eve of war.

BOOK ONE

ONE

White Linen

"Quod me nutrit me destruit."
That which nourishes me destroys me.

Latin Proverb

I have always hated winter. It reappeared in April that year killing the cherry blossoms before they could bloom. The Daffodils, unfortunate early risers, sported crowns of frost atop their regal trumpets, which made them look in death like ice princesses.

A ghostly gray shroud embraced the city, veils of frozen tears descended in unplowed streets and the world appeared encased in crystal. The revelation was stunning; the configurations of tragedy can be glorious.

I wasn't vigilant. If I had been paying attention, perhaps I might have realized that the end had already begun, announced by the peculiarities of the day. But I never saw it coming. None of us did.

It was still early when Kelleye's voice crackled through the intercom. "Jason Diggs, you have a visitor!"

It was 2001 and the dawn of a new millennium but her tone was raw and punishing, like the tough old dames who played telephone operators in black & white movies. She spoke from a pall of hate, making her words feel like shrapnel ripping through me, shutting down my vital organs. Killing me, but not so softly.

I entered the reception area in my shirtsleeves, feeling the chill but shrugging it off. I was obedient to the first rule of politics and the jungle. Show no weakness.

I expected to find one of the lobbyists who roamed the halls of Congress like hyena, in search of some offending legislation or staffer to devour. Instead, it was Valor Abernathy sitting there demurely, her knees delicately touching and her toes pointing in sweetly, like a young girl's.

Valor's ferocious reputation as an advocate was well deserved, and if she was there on business I was prepared to back her off with my own array of weaponry. But she instead disarmed me with a smile, which worked for me. It was too early for a fight—I hadn't had my coffee yet.

"Good morning beautiful," she said gently removing a yellow Hermes scarf from her neck. I instinctively checked the status of the shine on my Ferragamo shoes. It had taken more than the usual number of passes with a cloth to rescue the gloss from the morning's slush, but I was satisfied. Women notice shoes.

"What's up girlie? This is a surprise."

I looked at Kelleye with disapproval. Throughout my career in government, I'd become accustomed to having my visitors announced by name, but in her anger, Kelleye no longer afforded me such courtesies. She glowered back with pursed lips and rolled her eyes for emphasis.

I hadn't seen Valor in weeks; it worked like that, the staccato pace and guiltless low expectations of relationships in Washington. We all stayed so busy then, saving the world.

We walked the short distance to my office through a chaotic mess of file cabinets, haphazardly stacked committee reports and ramshackle rows of wooden bookcases. It was 9 a.m. and the workspaces, which usually convulsed in exquisite pandemonium stood silent, pierced only by the unpredictable outcries of office machines.

The threat of more snow, an ambitious legislative agenda and a battlefield promotion had given me three simultaneous subcommittee hearings to manage that morning. The staff was in full deployment for the first time since my appointment in January, as Deputy Counsel to the United States Senate Judiciary Committee.

I didn't know why Valor was there. She wasn't on the schedule and I briefly wondered whether I'd forgotten another lunch date, but quickly dismissed the thought—we hadn't made any plans in over a month and on

7

that day, I'd be lucky if I got some *Senate Bean Soup* in a Styrofoam cup for lunch.

I lived for days like that.

"So you're alive huh," said Valor. "You haven't called me or sent any emails so I just finally decided to come up here to see *you!*"

I responded tersely, my usual style when confronted with Valor's nonsense. "I'm glad you did." I was. Her face had secretly held many of my most cherished memories.

Over the years, Valor had become my best female friend and possessed a window into my soul like no other—except for my mother. It might have been the sheer longevity of our association that accounted for this, but her ability to grasp issues directly and without fanfare had clearly played a decisive role. Like my father, I didn't suffer fools gladly.

Valor's attire was confusing. Over night, the snow had given way to ice and yet Valor had dressed herself in a stylish but noticeably short sky blue trench coat, which she wore buttoned full to the neck. Her legs, always her best feature, had been exposed to the bitter cold, making her look singularly out of place on a day when topcoats reemerged from mothballs, becoming the garments of choice. She had inexplicably dressed for a warmer day and the boots she wore barley mattered.

"You must be cold," I said.

"Yeah, but I'm cute."

I studied her in detail, the way old lovers do; her carefully applied lipstick, her freshly appointed mascara and rouge, her delicate features framed by gold hoop earrings. The office was wonderfully fragrant now that she was there, displacing Kelleye's sour rage. The *White Linen* perfume that Valor preferred was a potent brew which had long ago become intertwined with her in my thoughts.

Tightly linked memories of Valor romping playfully in her panties after late night study sessions, red wine slowly savored before our sexual adventures. The pleasures of motionless slow dragging to music from her collection: *Con Funk Shun (Make it last), The Commodores (Zoom)* and *The S.O.S Band* (she'd adopted Weekend Girl as a personal anthem); or *Nancy Wilson* (Guess Who I Saw Today) and *Johnny Hartman and John Coltrane (Lush Life)* — from mine, exploded powerfully inside my brain, like sap in a burning log.

"What's this?" Said Valor.

"A little light reading."

Amid the wreckage of papers on my desk, she had found my most recent piece of political research, a book on Bobby Kennedy's fateful Presidential campaign that I had hoped to snatch a few moments to read during the chaos of the day (if only during bathroom breaks).

"Light reading? You still have time for books?"

"I make the time for important things. Books are always important."

"I see," she said, her eyes furtively dancing around the room. I'd offended her.

Giving her my undivided attention seemed the judicious course of action at the moment—I generally endeavored to limit the number of women angry with me at any given time. I had already developed one nemesis (at the reception desk) and that was really quite enough.

I decided to indulge her, give her slightly more time than I'd originally intended. I was headed toward the door to arrange just that, when Valor grabbed my arm. Her grip was impressive. For a petite woman, she was surprisingly strong.

"Scare you off?" She said. Her eyes taunted me, as they always seemed to.

"No, just buying us a little time with the receptionist. I'm running the office today and things are going to get hectic later."

"You just started here and you're running the Committee during the session?"

"Our Chief Counsel stayed home with her kids because of the snow—you know how those Northern Virginia Counties close the schools if there's even half a flake. The Chairman didn't want to postpone any hearings, since all the witnesses were already here so he gave me the go ahead. It's what I would have done, we're kindred sprits."

"How does *that* work?"

"We both drink bourbon and smoke cigars."

"Really?" I could tell she was confused.

"My father says you can tell a lot about a man by how he takes his liquor and even more by what he smokes."

"Alright?" Her eyes invited additional explanation.

"Okay, take smoking for example. Non-smokers can be arrogant and dictatorial. They don't smoke and then they demand that you refrain from smoking around them. You *know* Hitler didn't smoke. Didn't drink either."

"So they're fascists?"

"You know, there's a strong argument for that!"

"Continue."

"Weed smokers are damaged. They self medicate but then fallaciously attribute their habit to some notion of intrinsic coolness or they identify it as some ethereal expression of spiritual enlightenment or they simply represent it as an ideological position that they've taken, like a form of social radicalism. Either way, they operate like they're Louis Armstrong, Bob Marley, Abbie Hoffman or somebody!"

"You seem pretty animated about this. Did you have a bad experience with a pothead or something?"

"No, but I do think it's ridiculous when people get all pompous and self-righteous about marijuana when all they're really doing is getting fucked up. I'm just saying, they're channeling Rick James not Rosa Parks."

She laughed. "I know there's more."

"Cigarette smokers are nervous and possess a flighty disposition; you've got to be worried about nervous people in a fight. They're unpredictable."

"So, let me guess; cigar smokers are the chosen ones?"

"Not exactly, but we are strategic, patient and relaxed. Think about it, you have to have patience to smoke a cigar. They take a lot of time to finish, thirty minutes to an hour at least."

"That's quite a theory."

"It's my father's actually. He's got it all figured out. You should hear what he has to say about pipe smokers, like himself."

"So you and the Chairman *strategically* and *patiently* decided that you should run the committee today?"

"Yes and I might be offered the position permanently. My boss is leaving during the Christmas recess to become a partner in one of the K Street lobbying shops."

"You're kidding."

"No, the Chairman just scheduled a meeting with me for next week to talk about the job. It's not exactly an interview but it's likely to turn into one."

"How'd you work that? It's only been a few months."

"You've known me how long?"

"But it's Senate Judiciary!"

"Too bad I can't take it. That's a nice resume entry. Chief Counsel, Senate Judiciary Committee? I could get a law partnership at any firm in America after that."

"I still want to know how you wired this Jason?"

"I'm *that* good," I announced and then left for the reception area.

"Damn." It was only a whisper, but I heard her clearly in the silence. I'd impressed her and Valor Abernathy was not a woman that was easily impressed.

I walked back through the spectral maze of cubicles and shelves on full alert. Kelleye had been more insufferable than usual that morning and I expected to be met with even more hostility when I reached her desk.

I had it all worked out. I was going to tell her that my meeting with Ms. Abernathy from the NAACP was going a lot longer than expected and that I needed about an hour, without interruption. I would attribute it to *ongoing sensitive negotiations* and a *heightened need for discretion*.

It was a good excuse. Since I joined the Committee staff, Valor had only been to my office once, about a month after I started. It had been an official visit and she had accompanied her boss, the Director of the NAACP's Washington Bureau, to begin discussions on the reauthorization of the Voting Rights Act.

Valor had hit the committee pretty hard during the discussion. She used phrases like "indefensible foot dragging and political cowardice" requiring me to respond in kind with "legislatively untenable" and "fatally naïve"; making the sex we had later that night even sweeter. As we lay naked in her bed, we laughed at our poses of professional stoicism during the meeting and at how clever we'd been at hiding our status as friends and lovers.

Kelleye was on the phone when I reached her desk and against my better judgment, I waited for her to end the conversation. She chose not to.

I had no time. Valor was waiting patiently in my office and the demands of the day were swiftly encroaching upon me. So I decided to act.

I stood at Kelleye's desk, with its dark wood lightly brushing the front of my trousers. *She can't ignore me now*, I thought, and I was right. She did begrudge me an impertinent glance before continuing with her conversation.

I didn't dare call her from my office. Who knew what she might say and what Valor might hear. It was important to nurture the silence that conspiracy demanded.

Despite the implacable expression that she wore on her face, Kelleye's ebony skin, red lipstick and short-cropped blond hair made her a woman of great chromatic interest. Visitors to the Committee, staffers and even Senators gawked at her as a matter of routine—as I had done when I first arrived.

V-neck sweaters were a central element of her appeal. When leaning forward at her desk, her breasts cascaded into fathomless canyons of cleavage, which attracted even the most recalcitrant eyes. But, as she leaned back in her ergonomic chair, Kelleye's bosoms jutted out professionally and without even a trace of lewdness.

A muted television hung above the reception desk and as my wait dragged on into what seemed to be an eternity, the words scrolled along the bottom of the screen. I could see that Senator Levi Milton was speaking from the floor on the Church-burning bill. Closed captioning was garbling his stately Indiana delivery and my words had become confused.

It was a common problem, but how many busy, multitasking Americans with their televisions on mute, thought that their Senators were being unclear when faulty closed captioning was the culprit. *Too much is at stake! People need to pay attention and take their government off mute*, I thought.

As a Howard Law School graduate, I was a by-product of the same Houstonian Jurisprudence that brought down *Jim Crow*. I was *a social engineer, a mouthpiece of the weak*. By graduation, the professors had us all believing that we were legal superheroes, heirs to a storied past. We were.

Thurgood Marshall had himself graduated from Howard Law. He'd been lead counsel on the Brown v. Board of Education case, later sitting as the first African American on the Supreme Court. I now worked on Supreme Court confirmations, added vigor to the statements of statesmen. I was confident that greater things awaited me.

The fact that I was the anonymous wordsmith to grey haired old white men did nothing to minimize my optimism. I was determined to be the *mouthpiece of the weak,* even if, in the initial stages, I had to borrow somebody else's mouth to do it.

Kelleye's conversation continued and I remain convinced that she extended it for my benefit. (There were too many *yeah child's,* and *I know that's right's,* for it to have been related to any crucial matters of state) I took matters into my own hands, shouting: "I NEED YOU TO HOLD MY CALLS FOR ABOUT AN HOUR!" Her smirking red mouth, comically raised eyebrows and loud exhales did nothing to disguise her feelings.

I walked away with Kelleye glaring spitefully at my back, through her preposterous grey contact lenses. As I rounded the corner, she finally answered.

"Okay beautiful, I gotcha boo."

She'd been waiting for her opportunity and no doubt had deduced, only that morning, that Valor had bested her in a battle for my affections. It was a miscalculation; Valor had always been there.

But, Kelleye *had* gotten something right. She had seen through our well-constructed artifice and seemed to know, in the way that women just seem to know.

I angrily shoved my hands in my pockets fingering their contents: an engraved Zippo lighter that my father had given me, a bulky assemblage of keys, an indeterminate amount of change and all the linty matter that collects in men's trousers. I was furious at myself for having had sex with Kelleye during my first week on the job.

†

The day of the indiscretion had been almost implausibly warm for February. Nearly seventy degrees; hot enough to get the pollen flowing.

At lunchtime, I watched as one of the newest curiosities in Washington began to unfold. The grassy areas nearest the Capitol, from pocket parks to office building lawns, filled from end to end with white female staffers foraging for suntans.

There seemed to be a science to it. They hiked their skirts and dresses shamelessly above their thighs with panty hose discarded and midriffs bared. During summer, the larger Capitol Hill parks (Stanton and Lincoln Parks most notably) would fill to capacity with even more sun worshippers, who exposed themselves in all their bikini-clad entitlement. The overflow areas included storefronts and public sidewalks.

Those uninitiated to the new custom scoffed. "They ought to be ashamed of themselves, the common hussies," growled the old Black ladies from their aluminum porch gliders. But if the sunbathers heard the complaints, they couldn't have understood the outrage and wouldn't have acknowledged its legitimacy.

At the close of my first week as Deputy Counsel, eight of the thirty staffers of the Senate Judiciary Committee, assembled under the green awning at Armand's Pizzeria, which abuts the blandly menacing edifice of the Heritage Foundation. Unofficially, the gathering was billed as the kind of pizza and beer happy fueled hour that is customary among hill staffers on an unexpectedly warm day. Officially, it was a rite of passage, my welcome to the office; *lets see how the new black guy operates under the influence of ridiculous amounts of alcohol party.*

I had seen it before in television comedies. Obnoxious office workers subjecting their new colleagues to outrageously malign pranks; such as announcing the wrong time for staff meetings (invariably an hour or more later than the actual time), publishing the arrival and departure times of colleagues and other petty schemes designed to create workplace anxiety.

I was terribly annoyed when I discovered that such rituals were alive and well in the highest reaches of American government but I went along for the ride anyway; curious as to what form my torture might take.

They ordered twenty pitchers of beer for the eight of us, college level foolishness. But I had followed my father him into a Black Fraternity, which was as renown for the stunning achievements of its members, as it was for its rock ribbed drinking habits; and like other aspects of my political tradecraft, I'd practiced drinking under my father's direction and learned to hold my liquor like a New Orleans barkeep. But I still had weaknesses that could be exploited.

18

Kelleye had taken the subway to work from her home in Prince Georges County, Maryland. At half past ten, as the group broke up for the evening, she complained that she was afraid to collect her car from the Metro parking lot so late in the evening. "It's dark back there, I may have to leave it until tomorrow." She claimed.

When everyone ran for the exits pleading long drives or Metro rides to Fairfax, Virginia or Bethesda, Maryland, I offered to drive Kelleye to her car. It was a predictably chivalrous move; she'd played her card well.

I lowered the top on my SAAB and drove along East Capitol Street, past RFK Stadium, and through the darkest provinces of Washington. During the drive, Kelley shared her considerable knowledge about the Judiciary Committee and its staff with me. Her five years on the job had given her a commanding grasp of the players and their secrets. As the only two African-Americans working for the Committee at that time, an ancient code required that we support each other.

At the beginning of the 21st century, many African-American's were deeply mired in a nonsensical haze of post-racialism and no longer gave credence to the utility of a racially specific code of affinity. But when Kelleye volunteered that she too had grown up in the city, I understood; native Washingtonians are the unrivaled masters of *the hookup* and *the* hookup is central to the code—communal self-reliance at its best.

I liked *the hookup,* benefited from it and even enjoyed it. I'd gotten free bus rides, free cigars and free food through *the hookup,* just because I was in the right place at the right time. *The hookup* had been good to me.

I was in the midst of Kelleye's *hookup* inspired information dump, when I noticed the Capitol View Towers in our sights. A hulking monstrosity on East Capitol Street at the D.C./Maryland line, the *Towers* formerly housed thousands of poor, Black and elderly citizens of Southeast Washington. They were people largely forgotten by society and placed in storage in the *Towers.*

As it was near my old high school, I was accustomed to seeing the gargantuan building, its bleak façade glowing dimly with the interior lights of its residents. Now, I found it devoid of its windows and doors and counted thirteen exposed light bulbs, radiating in the vain hope that the former inhabitants might return.

When we arrived at the Metro Station, Kelleye invited me to her apartment for a shot of cognac. I agreed despite my longstanding plans to celebrate my new job with old friends. One drink and I could still be on U Street in thirty minutes; the rooftop at *Tabaq* would be jumping on such a warm clear night.

True to her word, Kelleye had a sealed bottle of Hennessy on hand, which she presented to me with a tiny printed snifter from a wedding or a prom. With its purple lettering mostly chipped and faded, I couldn't determine which.

I accepted the cognac graciously, fully intending to drink it quickly and depart. I didn't leave Kelleye's white shag carpeted apartment until nearly 8:30 the next morning.

Kelleye announced that she wanted to "get out of these work clothes and relax," which she did, while I sipped my caustic drink and watched Sports Center. She returned in a microscopic white nightie, which represented clothing in only the most procedural sense. The brightness of the lingerie set garishly against the rich matte of her skin and smacked somehow of ghetto fetishism but *I couldn't look away.*

"Oh I'm sorry Jason," she giggled. "I usually don't wear much around here after work. I hope it's okay?"

"It's fine, I just need to make a call and reschedule something." I said.

The morning was awkward as hell. The army of white stuffed animals bivouacked in Kelleye's bedroom were confusing so early in the morning and I couldn't find my pants.

"You're gonna call me, right baby?" She said, handing me her home number on the back of a crumpled Shoppers Food Warehouse receipt. I noticed that she had an unusual fondness for canned peaches.

"Um, I'm really busy this weekend; family stuff. I'll see you on Monday." I offered, as I rushed through the door.

"You don't want to take a little *slick leave* with me on Monday? We can snuggle up right here."

"I'll see you *at work* on Monday." I said.

Kelleye waved from her third floor balcony as she watched me pull out of her parking lot. The temperature had dropped significantly overnight and it was once again below freezing. Yet, there she stood, braving the cold.

My well-practiced approach after such indiscretions was to behave as if they never happened. It never failed and I was very often able to revive casual friendships with the women; but Kelleye's attitude following the events of that night proved that I had fallen into the most untenable of circumstances. I had a scorned woman on my hands.

TWO
The Sweet Betrayer

"Politics have no relations to morals."
Niccolo Machiavelli

As I walked to my office, the phrase *"—but I'm cute,"* Valor's little quip, was stuck in my mind; running around in there like a mouse in a maze searching for an exit. I'd definitely heard it before. As I reached my office door, I suddenly remembered that they were Kelleye's last words as I left her apartment.

It had come to me that I'd told Kelleye to close her door, that morning as I left her apartment, because in her open, sheer robe she was sure to catch cold. My true motive was escape.

Kelleye clutched herself and bounced in bare feet at the edge of her white shag rug. Her rubenesque body, which I had so vigorously explored the previous night, was clearly visible, punctuating my guilt. She was a much larger woman by daylight, quite robust to put it kindly, but I couldn't escape the fact that I had enjoyed her. She was a big girl but remarkably self-assured and that had made all the difference.

"Mr. Dii-igggs," Kelleye chanted. "I might be *cold…*but *I'm cute!*"

I entered my office disgusted with myself, only to find Valor's trench coat and dress draped dramatically across a chair and Valor perched mischievously upon my desk. She was wearing a bright red lace bra and thong—it was pornography.

My office was a relatively Spartan affair, festooned in minimalist fashion by my law degree and a drab assemblage of office furniture. There was A P.C. on a side table near my desk, three chairs, a bookcase and a large color television, which rested upon a perpetually dusty Watergate era credenza.

The bookcase held a set of the United States Code, which was still in the bubble wrap and an assortment of speechwriting talismans; including a writer's thesaurus, a dictionary, a Bible and dog-eared book of quotations that I'd owned since college. The presence of my law degree was the only thing, which identified the office as mine.

My office was a utilitarian workspace; a means to an end and its bland appearance was intended to send a clear message. The Judiciary Committee was but a way station: *I was already dreaming beyond those walls.*

As I closed and locked the door, Valor's familiar lures both beckoned and unnerved me. Once again I was on the familiar fault line between desire and destruction.

"Surprised?" said Valor.

"You could say that."

"So what do you think?"

"I think you're a beautiful lunatic!"

"There's a complement buried in there somewhere."

"You, um—look great."

"Is that all you can say? Men are so visual. Are you actually at a loss for words?"

"Not a loss for words girlie, only a judicious use of them."

"Part of your strategic nature?"

"Common sense."

"Whatever. I know I surprised you. I was so excited coming over here, I couldn't stop grinning."

"Okay, I'm duly surprised and I can see what I've been missing. That was your point, right?

"Not entirely."

"Well I certainly appreciate your good intentions. Now would you please put your clothes on? This is a federal building and my place of business.

"I'm not ready to do that yet."

"Look, I can come over tonight and cook. How about mussels, sautéed in fresh basil, crushed tomatoes and garlic? I'll toss in some linguini. We'll have a nice New Zealand,

Sauvignon Blanc and then I'll have you for desert."

I amused myself by devising the menu so quickly because with each word I spoke, I was breaking a long anticipated first date with the lovely Adanech Makonnen, M.D. a shapely Ethiopian second year resident at Howard University Hospital. Adanech's doe eyes and coke bottle figure would have to wait. Valor's gambit changed everything.

She was right; men *are* visual. Even Kelleye, with her blue-collar sensibilities knew that. *Lingerie is my undoing,* I thought.

"Come here sweets," she said, with her smoky Georgia contralto echoing all the painful ecstasies of a fine single malt scotch. She looked at me possessively, in a way that I had regarded women in countless encounters. It was an expression of carnal presumption.

Valor had never before been so direct. Her tactics in such matters, like most middle class Black women, were veiled, like the note Miles Davis chose *not* to play or a word elegantly omitted from a sentence but understood. Over the years, I had come to depend on Valor's regal subtlety, but on that day my own experience betrayed me. I was the victim of a perfectly executed head fake.

"You've been working out," I said impassively. *Change the subject and try to feign indifference,* I thought.

"Yeah," she shot back, hands on hips, "I got myself a personal trainer; apparently there's this clock thing. I finally had to concede that I am not getting any younger."

There was a subtext to her remark but as I had never viewed her as a potential mate, I refused to acknowledge it. She was too irascible and pushy for my tastes. I thought she'd end up in some bohemian relationship, beyond the boundaries of legal obligation. But I was still captivated.

Her body though petite, was curvaceous. Her mind was a rapier and her humor irreverent. But the craggy cliffs of her personality were confusing and segregated. She was not one person but three; none of them integrated into a catholic whole but a troika forced to share her body out of convenience.

We'd been friends since our first year in law school and in the main; our relationship had been without complication. We held no claims on each other because we understood that a romance between us would be difficult to sustain but we knew the sweet satisfaction of mutual respect.

We used sex as an apparatus, as a bridge over our frenzied, incongruent lives. We crossed when in need of affirmation. Yet, history aside, I couldn't understand why she was standing in my office in lingerie and boots.

"Stop stalling Jason!" Valor ordered. "Isn't it clear what I want?" She rose in her black boots and perused me as she would a prime cut of meat. "You've never refused me before."

"I think you should get dressed. I'm not up for a scandal today, perhaps next week? Let's compare schedules."

It failed as a joke but I had meant it as a deterrent. She knew as well as I did that the situation could ruin both of our professional careers and still carry enough destructive force to eviscerate my political ambitions.

"You're not really going to make me wait are you? Look at me!"

Hell, I *was* looking at her, I couldn't stop looking at her; she was a beautiful woman, sexy, desirable. Her ass was round, high and tight. Her nipples were engorged and erect and fully visible through the lace of her bra. But, I still reached for her dress.

"It doesn't have to take that long," she whispered. All in one motion she snatched the dress from my hand and laid it neatly back across the chair. "Let's face it, you're not exactly a marathon man anyway."

"I don't recall hearing any complaints. Especially from you!"

Valor smiled and I chuckled but as I did, I could visualize how this thing she wanted might be accomplished.

I'd walk over to her and she'd unzip me, my trousers falling to the floor. I'd neatly lay them across the chair and pull off her thong; gently leaning her across my desk. It wouldn't be difficult. Bills, amendments and legal memoranda would crackle like kindling under the weight as I pressed my body on to hers.

Then I'd remember that Kelleye was in the outer office and I'd fumble for the remote to allow the audio from C-SPAN to drown out our transgressions. Valor, always prepared, would produce a condom and we would open it together as she always liked to do—me ripping, she pulling, with the Presiding Officer and Clerk of the Senate providing appropriate commentary:

The clerk will call the roll.

Mr. Johnson?

Mr. Johnson, Aye.

It would be a passionate but brief encounter, as she'd already released me from any obligation to the contrary; but before our joy was broken, her eyes, vaguely moist with tears, would appear a perfect praise song of honesty. Somehow we'd crossed over, transcended the false constraints and bitter oppressions of the world. We'd become simply a man and a woman in a tender embrace, fellow travelers in life's perilous journey—two who shared both the beauty and the burden of darker hue and more spirited souls.

Like most men, I had difficulty subduing the sexual impulse; and while these phantom images aroused me, they were also cautionary. I couldn't do it.

"We're not going to do this," I said as I held her. Valor resisted at first, but then slowly relaxed in my arms. With my fantasy's memory still fresh, I rocked her back and forth. We remained like that, sweet and comfortable, for a while.

Finally, she said, "Jason, thank you for stopping us. That wouldn't have been right."

"Don't worry about it girlie," I offered, "we have time."

Valor gathered up her things, dressed and without missing a beat said, "Jason, before I go, I need to speak with you about

Project Kujichagulia—oh and would you mind zipping me up?"

"Nice try, but you know I don't have the time to talk about that. We can try to air out this office before the staff comes back though."

"Air it out? All you smell is my perfume."

"There's much more to smell here than perfume girlie. Don't lie, you were ready."

"What?" she protested, her eyebrows furrowing into deep trenches.

"You know, that sweet sticky thing; those natural elixirs, which when combined with your *White Linen*, is reeking havoc up in here."

She could see that I was joking and began to smile. "You're *sooo* silly!"

"No, really, it's the pheromones, its like you've just detonated a biological weapon or something…damn. It's odorless, colorless and tasteless but if it ever escaped into the ventilation system, you're liable to have people doing each other all over the Capitol. They wouldn't know what hit 'em."

Valor smirked as I zipped her into her slate blue Ann Taylor dress. I'd never seen it before but it was as business like and sedate an affair as her lingerie was explicit. *It really suits her*, I thought—*fire and ice*.

"We still need a Chairman!" she protested. "I don't know anyone who could lead a committee on community self-determination the way you could."

"I'm flattered Valor, but this isn't the time, we both need to get back to work. I'm actually *at* work, if you haven't noticed."

"So, you're not worried about what gentrification is doing to this city? To the people?"

"I'm concerned, but I have my own strategy on that issue."

"*Strategy? Issue?* People are getting run up outta here like roaches when the lights come on Jason...and they're clueless about how to stop it. We have to fight this."

"Look girlie, you know I'm running next year and I can't just focus on one issue, not even one as important as this. The city is changing fast, which means that this is likely to be my only chance. I'm disinclined to fuck up that chance by raving on and on about gentrification, like some mudcloth wearing radical."

"Jason, you know how I feel about your campaign. No one deserves to win as much as you; but I wouldn't have asked if I didn't think you'd do this for me."

Her eyes were soft again, gentle almond truffles that made me briefly rethink my earlier decision. But there would be plenty of time for that.

"I said that I couldn't and I can't. I have a sick mother, a full time job, a campaign to organize and I don't have enough time to do everything as it is."

"But you're a Diggs—you ought to be more concerned about the displacement of Black folk in D.C. than *I* am. This is *your* political base we're talking about and I *know* you don't expect those *Boers* to vote for you!"

Valor regarded me angrily, with a glare that belied the remarkable intimacy we'd almost shared. She was actually trying to intimidate me.

If Valor was likening the whites that were relocating to the city in droves to the Europeans that invaded South Africa, what the hell did she think I could do about it? Even the mighty Chaka Zulu couldn't repel the Dutch and British with only spears at his disposal.

I believed that for all of its intended moxie, the efforts of a ragtag committee of neighborhood activists, even one bearing the culturally significant name of *Kujichagulia* (self-determination, the second of the Nguzo Saba or seven principles of Kwanzaa), would end up ringing hollow against the powerful forces arrayed against it. A committee was an empty gesture; it was a rhetorical spear.

Thinking all of this, I turned and stood at my window, determined not to let Valor aggravate me. A massive snowball fight had begun in the park across from Columbus Circle and despite the gloom; I could still make out Union Station and the icy traffic circle before it.

People were traveling to and from Washington by train as they had for over a century and the freakish snowstorm had not slowed the pace. Life goes on, even in harsh weather.

I reigned in my emotions at the window, watching all the people scurrying in the snow. I vowed that Valor wasn't going to get to me this time; she was well intentioned but ultimately misguided.

She came from Southwest Atlanta, an idyllic enclave covered in azaleas, Georgia Pine and Black people. She was smart and empathetic to a fault, truly desirous of affecting change but like all transplants to Washington, she never quite grasped the nuances.

Beyond federal Washington lies a secret city, which has clandestinely bred and nurtured a strain of Black people unique in the world. For Black native Washingtonians, equality was never the goal; domination was their only objective.

Native Washingtonians are endowed with a justifiable conceit, a confident swagger unlike the sooty crassness of the Northeast, the quiet smugness of the industrial Midwest or the haughty self-aggrandizements of Southern California. Washingtonians simply feel vested and sure.

"It's in the tap water," my father always said, "newcomers always find it difficult to stomach." The sudden run on bottled water after a citywide lead pipe scare during the late 1990s seemed to prove his point.

Native Washingtonians grow up hard by the memorials to the rise of American power but astride the postcard images stand symbols to the establishment of Black identity. Howard University and the homes of Frederick Douglass, Carter G. Woodson and Mary McLeod Bethune stand among them and some believe that the invincibility that these icons convey has leeched inexorably into their souls.

To lead a group with such a messianic belief system isn't for the feint of heart and has always made political organizing in D.C. a dangerous enterprise. The people are stubborn in their pride and there are precious few followers among them.

As confused as she was, Valor's reference to my family's political reputation struck home. It was known to most that I was the culmination of my father's Black dynastic dreams, the fulfillment of the hope of thirty years and as such, I was fully cognizant of the implications of my policy positions. The city and I had linked destinies.

I had a progressive pedigree but become a raging pragmatist after a lifetime under my father's tutelage. More than half of those years were spent engaged in active urban political warfare. I had learned that one never runs screaming into a firefight, telegraphing your position as you go, when stealth and deception are available options.

I'd calmed myself and it felt like hours had passed before I turned to Valor and responded. "The loss of Black population is troubling to me and the long-term political implications are obvious. The Black vote was a base twenty years ago, but it just isn't anymore."

"I don't believe that just came out f your mouth." She said.

"This may shock you but I can win some of the white vote, *the Boers* as you call them. It's about convergence of interest."

"How do you figure that?"

"Look at Barry in '78, Gordon in '88 or even Al Canada's race in '96. Those campaigns represented classic coalition politics. Policy prescriptions don't matter if you're not in power—you have to get elected to effect change."

"I don't see how you can get white folks to support policies that are so clearly against their interests."

"Nixon went to China and remember the Reagan Democrats? Clinton, the so-called progressive, ended welfare, as we know it. Locally, look at Terwilliger in '98 and how many left-wing supporters he had even after he'd already fired half the government?"

Valor had a mouth on her and I knew I was in for it. Once she had her mind made up, she locked on like a Cane Corso and wouldn't let go. The fragile could be ripped to shreds.

"Don't get me started about Terwilliger, Gordon and Canada—they're a bunch of sellouts; and yeah Barry did get the white vote his first time out, but honey, damn if they didn't regret *that* for the next twelve years and you know what happened to him after that. Both Barry and Gordon had a lot of poor Black folks at the core of their base, despite the support they received from west of the park, Kennedy Center Progressives."

"Valor, are you lecturing *me* on D.C. politics? Don't forget who taught you this stuff."

Valor always demanded attention for herself, but she could relate to others with withering indifference. She hadn't even bothered to breathe as she went on impugning my commitment to Black liberation and self-determination for D.C. residents.

Her assault had just moved into overdrive when she uttered a terse, "—you listening?" My only safe answer was in the affirmative; I didn't want matters to get worse.

"Well, your only real shot is to *win out* in the Black precincts and not get blown out in the white ones. Black folk are not voting for a *pawn* anymore. That's over."

"That's enough!" I backed away from her, crossed the room and reached for the doorknob. "If you think I sold out then why are you here?"

"Don't try to blame this one me, she said rolling her eyes disparagingly, "so many of you, what's your oh so inoffensive term for them, *multigenerational Washingtonians*, have already sold out. Otherwise, the Boers wouldn't be nearly finished taking the city.

Where are all your third, fourth and fifth generation Washingtonians? You know, the ones that can trace their ancestry back to when great-great grandma Bertha was a slave at the White House. I'll tell you—the poor ones either have parole jackets with Court Services, or they're still locked down.

The low-income folks are stuck in what's left of those creepy orange low-rise projects ya'll have up here, like at Potomac Gardens just walking distance from the Capitol. Then, there are the ones who were forced out years ago, in the first wave and live in slum apartments out in Seat Pleasant, Landover and Capital Heights."

I thought of Kelleye and the shag carpeted, Capitol Heights stuffed animal farm that she called an apartment. I hoped to God she couldn't hear our conversation, I was in enough trouble with her already.

"Would you mind lowering your voice a little Valor, this is getting loud." I pleaded.

"Alright," she said quietly, "but my question is where are all the Black folk with money? You know, the non-threatening ones with the keen features? (Some would say that without her dreadlocks, she might fit that description)

I never had a chance. Valor was filibustering like a Dixicrat on civil rights.

"I'll tell you where they've gone. Some of them are still up 16th Street, in Crestwood and Shepherd Park, but a lot of them high tailed their butt's to the suburbs the minute they got the chance. The selfish bastards took their legal retainers, medical practice profits and D.C. government contracts out to Woodmore, Ft. Washington and Bethesda."

She had a point, the *Black Bourgeoisie had* largely abandoned the city; but I couldn't admit it for fear of encouraging her further. They put contracts on prefab mini mansions in invented subdivisions with nonsensical names like *The Meadow of Raspberry Vines* and *The Courses at Trevelyan Glen*. Sadly, some of these developments were named for plantations or confederate luminaries or both, adding further to the shame of bougie abandonment—*The Plantings of General Beauregard.*

These neighborhoods had houses that came in three or four floor plans with a few variations in carpet style. People had purchased pre-construction for deep discounts and thus as a result of clever semantics, had their homes *built*. It was farcical, but now these gated communities were the new indicia of success, safe havens for the Black elite to count and re-count their thirty pieces of silver.

It was then that I heard a chorus of garbled conversations through the walls. The heavy oak door, nearly a half a century old, was no bar against the sound of hill staffers emerging from hearings. They had been on the dais for three hours, quietly riding shotgun in the jump seats behind the members and now their voices, like steam in a kettle, needed release.

It was time to end the discussion, there was nothing to be gained, but Valor wasn't finished. "I have one more thing to say," she announced. "This is *The Plan,* the end of Chocolate City and all you're going to do about it is run in a 60% white district?"

"It's actually more like 46 percent."

"Not on election day. We don't show up, they do; and yes—you taught me that."

"Look, this isn't a exclusively racial issue, it's mostly economic. I'm no Martin Luther King, I'm not trying to lead some epic movement here—I'm just running for a City Council seat."

"I seem to remember a first year law student about 12 years ago, who thought he *was* Martin Luther King."

"I never came off like that."

She was disgusted and her face was contorted into what was for her, a remarkably grotesque scowl. She leered at me in the way only a Black woman can, hand on hip, head swiveling on an impossible axis and lips pursed in angry distain. After so much back and forth, her message had been delivered without uttering a word. To her, I was full of shit.

"Martin Luther King," she began, "wasn't even Martin Luther King, until he got up off his black ass and did something. You have a gift and you ought to use it by writing and speaking out strongly on those issues that are important to us. We need you to lead instead of catering to the egos of demagogues and fools."

Now I was pissed. "What the hell are you talking about? I've been a senior advisor to Councilmembers, Mayors, Senators, I've written—"

"—You've just made my point. I've heard these people both before and after you've finished with them and you make them sound like they actually speak English and have a little integrity. Especially that last Councilman you worked for before you came here, the one with all the cars and that boat that he somehow bought on a Councilman's salary. What was his name? Abed Marshall?"

"It's Ahmed Mitchell, and stop playing, you know his name. Anyway, I was his Chief of Staff, not his C.P.A."

"I know you don't want to talk about it but it's grimy Jason. People are dying in the streets, being forced from their homes and this asshole is feathering his own nest."

Valor wasn't the first to ask questions about Mitchell. No one could understand how a man who didn't come from money, didn't give speeches for honoraria, didn't have another job, and had a stay at home wife, had come by five luxury cars and at least one boat on a ninety-six thousand dollar Council salary. I wondered too, but since the Washington Post, the Office of Campaign Finance, and the U.S. Attorney hadn't exposed anything untoward, who was I to bring it up?

"Valor, I'll get around to all the writing and speaking you want me to do after I'm elected. It's actually a good idea, it'll be great supplementary income with which to buy cars and boats and such; but not now."

"This is no time for jokes. This city is being taken away from us."

I wasn't joking. I had plenty of time to write books, supported by riveting speeches delivered to standing room only assemblies at a few Historically Black Colleges and Universities. The books themselves would likely have an even longer half-life, as they luxuriated on the *remainder rack Riviera* for a dollar seventy-five, following what promised to be a polite and painfully local frenzy of interest. I was up on this stuff. I'd seen weighty, impactful books by such leonine figures as Cornel West, Henry Louis Gates and my own father come to such an inglorious end.

"Black socio-political commentary, no matter how incisive, is just not flying off the shelves anymore in America. Black people don't even read it. They don't read anything without a salacious title anymore anyway, that's why *a mainstream press would never publish Black Bourgeoisie and The Miseducation of the Negro* today. People want to feel good about their inadequacies and you know, get their literary freak on. Nobody likes a scold."

She just looked at me, so I continued.

"What do you think about this for a title? *The Politics of Punany: How the Welfare State Got It's Groove Back* or what about *Gerrymandering on the Down Low: Why Majorities Back Door Minorities*."

"*You* need to stop Jason, this is serious. Don't you want to do something meaningful?"

"Let's see, I'm the first African-American Deputy Counsel to the Senate Judiciary Committee and I'm preparing to run next year for the D.C. City Council. You tell me whether that's meaningful."

"I think I've already explained how that's likely to end up," she said dryly.

I sidestepped the insult and continued. "*When* I win, people will have a voice in D.C. government again. I'm going to force a conversation about the next phase of our agenda and I'll tell you this, if 2003 rolls around and I'm marching around *outside* city hall with a dashiki on, then I've failed."

"No, honey, let's not get it twisted, I'm not trying to take you out of your bespoke suits and monogrammed shirts, you *know* you look *good*. You're a brilliant, beautiful Black man. All I'm saying is, we need more than style from our leaders today, more than good looking, voices of moderation. We need a little courage."

"Valor you know as well as I do that these housing trends have been building for twenty years. People *were* forced out but many left on their own. Some of my own family members are in that predicament and now they can't even get back in.

Leading some weak ass protest won't turn it around. It's like Chaka Zulu trying to fight the British army with spears or the Wampanoag Indians on Martha's Vineyard trying to run the colonists out with their arrows against English cannon. There's too much skin in the game, too much money to be made. It's got to be done another way."

She took in my words and they went down hard. She was angry but for the first time in my memory she had no response.

She calmed down just in time too. I heard the frenetic buzz of staffers outside my door and according to Kelleye they liked to eavesdrop.

"Alright girlie, where's that toughness that I so love and cherish?"

"Toughness in the face of failure is stupid. And as for love, we're a little dysfunctional in that department don't you think?"

"But all you do is argue with me." I placed my hand on her shoulder and pulled her close. "You know I'll help you figure this out; I just can't take an official role. I have too many other things to do."

"I hoped that you might be interested in helping me save my job."

"I didn't realize things had gotten that bad."

"Well, they have."

Her eyes fell to the floor and I could see that she was in trouble. I felt compelled to offer her something.

"When I come over tonight, I'll help you come up with a plan."

"Promise?"

"You have my word my dear."

"Please Jason, they're *going to* fire me if a steering committee isn't in place by the end of the year and they won't abide any broken down old civic association types either. All those folk ever want is lunch and then they nod off in the meeting."

I laughed. I had known many such people in my life; individuals so hyped up on the trappings and implied status of community activism that real results often took a back seat. They took pictures with the powerful, went to conventions and wore silly hats. *I had also seen them fall asleep after lunch.*

I continued to laugh while visualizing the dozing, corpulent faces of the only people that Valor would ever be likely to recruit.

Everyone else that she might approach had careers to consider. Especially me.

"I told you, its not funny. We need fierce brothers and sisters ready to break a foot off in somebody's ass."

I doubted many such people existed anymore. We had largely tired as a people after centuries of constant struggle.

"I'm only laughing about the civic association folks. Don't worry. I will help you."

"If you can't, the Board may give it to a PR firm."

"They're outsourcing civil rights?"

"Sounds crazy but that's exactly what they're prepared to do. Just imagine what'll happen when the media finds out that we couldn't even recruit ten righteous people to fight gentrification in Washington, D.C."

"It'll be alright. They're out there. We'll find them."

Valor began preparing herself for the elements. I helped her into her nearly weightless trench coat, which she promptly buttoned to the top, wrapping her scarf snugly around her neck. Lastly and with great ceremony, she produced a yellow beret and positioned it rakishly on her head. Her shoulder length dreadlocks flowed bravely behind her like chocolate lightning bolts.

"Jason, you're sweet for doing this. I'll see you tonight and I hope you're ready for me." We kissed for several moments and I knew that the night would be memorable.

I reached for the door. It was more than slightly ajar; an oddity which I tried to ignore. As I walked Valor through the office and past the reception area, I felt fortunate for having avoided a potentially embarrassing encounter with Kelleye.

We said our goodbyes and Valor disappeared down the long marble corridor, her boots clicking in martial quarter notes. I was somewhat disappointed in myself for lying to her so convincingly but it was a necessary betrayal.

Valor was still an outsider and no matter my personal sentiments I'd been taught to never collaborate with outsiders. No matter my feelings, no matter how beautiful or brilliant. It had been driven into me like the Lord's Prayer: *Extending our influence over the city requires sacrifice.* In the long history of war, countless others have betrayed much more for far less a purpose.

THREE
Indigestion

"Don't cry because it's over. Smile because it happened."

Dr. Seuss

My lie had been smooth and the feeling was unnaturally gratifying; so much so that I barely noticed the telephone ringing. I answered it just before it went to voicemail and heard a ravaged version of my father's voice on the other end.

"Come home son."

"I'm kind of busy here Pop. What's the problem?"

I didn't want to hear his admonitions about scheduling meetings with Ministers or Advisory Neighborhood Commissioners. My plan didn't include cozying up to many of those types; they represented the old politics, steeped in racialism and ancient enmities.

"Just come home, I need you."

"Pop, I'm managing the Committee today."

"Come home—*now* son."

For years my father's lectures, in the political science department at Howard University, had been a showcase for his eloquence. In the seventies, he was noted for his monthly radio commentaries on the Daily Drum news program. Progressives throughout the city sought him out for his political wisdom. Yet, all he said was *come home*.

In matters of protocol, my father was a traditionalist and he considered it bad form to announce grave news over the telephone. For him, to do so would be an *infamnia*. I had to go.

"I'm on my way Pop."

"Get here!"

I hung up, grabbed my jacket, my overcoat and the black Borsalino fedora that my mother had ordered from J&J Hat Center in New York. "You have my father's head Jason. Such a nicely shaped head deserves a stylish hat," she'd informed me the previous Christmas. I recall laughing as I leaned down to the bed to hug her.

On a clear day, it would have taken twenty minutes to make my way across the Anacostia River to my parents' home in Hillcrest but in bad weather, incompetent Virginia drivers, the bane of my existence, clogged traffic badly enough to double the time. I prepared for a long trip.

I went into the hall muttering vaguely about my family emergency. I quickly appointed a proxy from among the fungible bunch and rushed out into the snow. Constitution Avenue was heavily clogged with taxicabs and limousines, which were stacked two abreast as they released their mismatched cargo of natty K Street lobbyists and scruffy constituents from the provinces.

Adding to my frustration were the hordes of pimpled kids from the flyover states, rudely dressed and simple, who darted in front of my car in soggy sneakers. Like most native Washingtonians, I hated tourists for the persistent inconvenience they presented. With their maps and rustic attitudes they were always in the way, slowing the city's rhythm, failing to yield. Fortunately, I knew short cuts.

The Anacostia River, that brown sludgy waterway, which flows beneath the John Phillip Sousa Bridge, was as nasty and forbidding as ever; more so on that frozen day. The river bisects the southeastern part of the city and forms a natural border between the privilege of Washington and the struggles of D.C.

Once known as the eastern branch of the Potomac, the Anacostia River is east of every college and university in the city, east of the tony salons, restaurants and art galleries for which the city is renown, east of any supermarket worthy of the name and east of the corridors of power from which the world is ruled. The city is asymmetrically arranged and even the diamond that forms its borders is incomplete.

Responding to my father's call, I drove past the railroad tracks, past the dingy old Animal Hospital where many of my childhood pets had died and beyond the run down shops that marked the farthest reaches of Pennsylvania Avenue. Then, I passed the gas stations and the dank old strip mall that loomed in front of Mario's Pizza, a carryout once known for its Sicilian pizza and which since my childhood, had changed ownership (from Italian, to Black to Korean) without changing its appearance (except for the acrylic package receivers, cash slots and bullet proof glass).

I suppressed tears as the street rose toward the impressive tree line of Branch Avenue. It wasn't time. Such tears can only be shed once in a man's life.

When I arrived, I launched the car into the driveway, my tires cutting deep ruts into the snow. I thought about how in my day the kids would have made it all disappear for a measly ten dollars; and how at that very hour, in my Capitol Hill neighborhood, the task had fallen to fortyish Black men who competed for such work as their only sources of income. Things had changed.

I ran up the front stairs, which wound along the front of the house, bulldozing the untouched snow with my feet and fumbling for the key that my father gave me when I was nine years old. Upon entering the house, I knew everything. It was as if all the molecules had frozen in place, time mercifully stopping to give my mother a point of embarkation.

As I went up the steps and down the long corridor, I saw my father trying to compose himself near my mother's closed bedroom door. *It was never closed.*

The hallway walls were covered with ancestral photographs dating back several generations and although I had lived with the sepia images all of my life, they were somehow more forbidding on that that day. Scurlock, D.C.'s own, was a genius with light and I saw myself in those people—the dimpled cheeks and mischievous eyes of the Grafton clan, the high forehead and thin mustache of the Diggs men; my hair a nearly untamable mixture of elegant Grafton waves and sturdy Diggs bristle. I imagined these ancestors passing judgment, over my suitability as their heir and I was uneasy as to their conclusions.

"She's gone son." My father groaned his words in the same decimated voice that I had heard on the phone and it chilled me in a way that I couldn't shake off. I rushed passed him and into my mother's sickroom—which had now become something else.

The stillness was no longer the most impressive thing. There was the medicinal smell that always attended that room; and an unnatural tint to the light, opaqueness that should have been more brilliant through her bedroom window on what was gradually becoming a sunny day. In that milky half-light, my mother's dead eyes were focused upon something beyond the visual, fixed, I decided, on what was next.

That morning, I had spoken with my mother as I always did and she knew that I'd returned from Atlanta, where I'd been prospecting among old college friends for commitments for campaign funds.

I could take solace in that at least. My mother died knowing that I was home safe. Perhaps she had waited.

50

I had lost so much of her in the years before. Mobility, independence and in the end, continence were no longer to be taken for granted—but nothing can prepare you for death.

Parkinson's is a hard disease; it cheats you because the mind is still there. Her wit, her searing intelligence and a love so deep that it could only come from God—all there. So you continue to hope the vain hopes of all who wish to outmaneuver death and in the end, you come face to face with the futility of your cause. My mother was dead and I allowed myself to cry the tears that I had grimly reserved. It was the proper time.

What was her last moment like? I had planned to visit after work as I always did and by habit, I would have procrastinated before going in to see her; reading the mail that I still randomly received there, pirating a shot or two from my father's well stocked liquor cabinet, steeling myself for that day's cruel manifestations of her ailment.

I joined my father in the hall and for the first time in years we hugged, amid the stalwart images of our ancestors. My mother was now safely among them.

The events that followed were a litany of the horrible. The calls were made and soon the ambulance gave way to the medical examiner. The body bag is a cruel device for a family to see employed—a loved one reduced to the moral equivalent of potatoes, or onions, or dog food, or any other such commodity that is best transported in a bag.

The sullen grey men from the medical examiner's office looked so industrial in their blue jumpsuits and boots wet from the snow. They brought my mother's body down the winding stairs and through the living room toward our rounded Tudor door.

My father was inconsolable, which unnerved me. There was a time, 25 years before, when the hopes of the entire city had been discreetly carried on his shoulders, but even his titanic visage could not withstand the coldness of that day.

There is no accurate way to report how I felt as they carried her into their dull white van; a vehicle that had carried thousands, who had succumbed to gunshots and AIDS and tuberculosis and stabbings and blunt trauma to the head; my mother cold and dead in black vinyl. Gone.

She should have been borne high on a bed of rose petals with sprigs of baby's breath in her hair. A mass choir should have attended her on our snowy sloping lawn, singing mournful spirituals to ease her transition to God—a fitting departure worthy of her station. But reality is raw and my emotions had no sway. This was how it was done: Royalty reduced to rubbish, nobility to nothingness, a body in a bag.

My mother, Rachel Grafton Diggs was mentor, friend and Svengali. She dreamed me into existence long before she birthed me. She shaped my understanding of the world and fiercely guarded my place in it until I could make a way for myself.

I remember the life that we shared before the illness that began to steal her from us in my teenaged years. I protected the memory of it, like a happy dream that I dared not forget.

My parents' strange energy begot me at a time in their marriage when hopes for a child were no longer maintained. The notion was so improbable that I was thought to be a terrible case of indigestion until a doctor's examination confirmed that I was not.

At 39, my mother had quietly abandoned the notion that she would ever bear children and busied herself, in her dignified little way, with her marriage, her career and serving as doting aunt to the dozens of nieces and nephews that she considered it her blessing to have. The shock of my conception reverberated through my mother's world and added new purpose to an already mighty calling.

On October 7, 1963 I was born at school, that is, my mother gave birth to me on her old wooden desk at Payne Elementary School. Apparently, she had failed to realize that the pains she was experiencing as she taught her Sixth grade English class were *the* pains, so focused was she on teaching her favorite module on gerunds. By the time the water broke, her emphatic desire to share knowledge became the focal point that eased her labor pains and made birthing me, in her words, "as much as a surprise, as was the fact that I was pregnant at all." The children that were hastily ushered out of the classroom by the Assistant Principal, as the school nurse was delivering me, learned an important lesson in Biology along with their English that day.

I was born during the only chapter of African-American history when a Eurocentric orientation could suspicions. For a century it had been considered the only way up from slavery and into the mainstream of American life. Now, this second Black renaissance swept through Black communities everywhere in the 1960s, redefining the essential question of Blackness.

My father wanted to name me *Vladimir* after Lenin or *Nkrumah* after Kwame, "they're strong names and send an even stronger message," he told my mother, but my mother was doggedly mainstream and refused to name me after some "mysterious African" or "communist bomb thrower" whose names she felt were "nearly unpronounceable." My father even considered naming me *Che,* after Guevara, to which Mother asked, "Where's the rest of the name?"

A brilliant woman, she was fully aware of the lofty reputations of my potential namesakes but used her often-withering sarcasm to win the debate on points. My father laughed through his pipe, when he later explained that my Mother didn't want people calling me *Na-cru-may* or the inevitable and rather unfortunate bastardization, *Macramé.* "He'll have to fight every day at school with a name like that," mother said. "Then he'll learn karate," my father responded flatly.

But my father relented and I became Jason. He was an uncompromising devotee of

Dubois and Senghor and was incredulous as to why in 1963 anyone would name a Black boy after a character from Greek mythology. Such was the quixotic nature of Black life in America and of my parents' philosophically mixed marriage.

The power to speak a name into existence is the heart of self-determination. In the heady years before my birth, my people had already been officially labeled as *Colored*, *Negro* and *Afro-American*. Later, *Black* was starting to make its own bid for supremacy; but *nigger* had sadly never gone out of style. It was a word so charged with power that like the Frankenstein monster, it had its own strange immortality.

Then there was the procedural, but nonetheless, psychically relevant matter of capitalization. Entire elements of the early civil rights struggle were devoted to pressuring newspapers to capitalize the N in *Negro* in the course of their reporting and even achieving reluctant compliance with that modest request was considered a victory.

Soon after my birth, Baldwin was saying, "to be Black and conscious in America is to be in a constant state of rage." Men I later met, Stokely Carmichael and Willie "Mukasa" Ricks, dared voice the rallying cry of the late sixties "Black Power!" Riots had people burn baby burning all over America.

White people were terrified across the whole of America and in the District of Columbia; the Presidentially appointed Board of Commissioners, in an effort to head off a confrontation, summoned my father to make a scholarly presentation on the roots of Black urban violence. My father seethed at the notion that anything needed explaining and instead delivered a brief statement for the record, which concluded with:

"Gentlemen, consider the roots of Bunker Hill or Gettysburg. There's your answer! No reinterpretation was required of D Day, Dresden or Hiroshima. Burn baby burn is a universal anthem. When people consider their existence threatened, they tend to fight with all available means."

Then he added improbably, "Can you dig that Man," shocking the Commissioners and electrifying the packed chamber of students and African attired protesters.

It was during the tumult of that time, that my father taught budding revolutionaries at Howard University while my Mother taught the next generation of public school teachers at D.C. Teacher's College, chairing the English department after the merger that created the University of the District of Columbia. Amid this pedagogical effulgence, I lived a charmed life.

"Jason, you are the smartest, strongest, cutest little boy in the whole world," Mother would say. "You will do great things." It was an oft-repeated mantra, which dominated my early consciousness and endowed me with the confidence and the ambition to make her sweet incantation manifest. She guided my hand as I made the perfectly formed letters that only a teacher can bequeath to her child. *Love letters.*

On weekends we would catch green and white D.C. Transit buses from our row house near RFK Stadium and soon, I would find myself in another world. A world where reality was what you made it, even if in the more garish regions of the land, state sponsored limitations on reality were the order of the day for my melanin filled clan.

In the District of Columbia of the 1960s, the museums, galleries and monuments were at your disposal and my mother and I were so disposed. Every week I lived with the mercury capsule, dinosaurs and a real life Model T. It was the pilot light that ignited my already vivid imagination.

A highlight of these explorations was our visits to the Blue Mirror diner on F Street, downtown. The specialties of the house were open-faced hot roast beef sandwiches with mashed potatoes and gravy and there was fresh baked strawberry shortcake for dessert. To my small eyes, this was fine dining at its best and nothing conjured up in Lyndon Johnson's White House could ever be so magnificent. I was in the first generation of Black children to enjoy these delicacies, as the Blue Mirror had only recently ended its soft up-south segregation.

In my mother's later bedridden years, her brown eyes sparkling despite her discomfort, she talked effusively about those days. She'd regale friends and family with tales of how the crowds would gather in Woodward & Lothrop, Kann's or Lansburg's department stores, because I was carrying on adult level conversations with her at 4 years old!

"Jason," she'd say, "you were so uninhibited as a young child. You would sing your nursery rhymes on the bus at the top of your lungs, *Twinkle, twinkle, little star*! Without the slightest hint of modesty."

The body bag bearing my mother was being maneuvered into the van and I understood how death changes both the future and our understanding of the past. Gray images flashed before me of mother's heroism during her illness and I considered the vacuum she was leaving behind. Had I been a weaker man, I might have passed through this time immune to my suffering, spared by some fit of grief induced amnesia; but like my mother, it was my privilege to consciously endure.

FOUR

Sun Up

"For his anger endureth but a moment; in his favour is life: weeping may endure for a night, but joy cometh in the morning."

Psalm 30:5

My parents met as Howard University students while in line for breakfast at the Florida Avenue Grill, but it took ten years of often rigorous hazing, from her father and brothers, for my father to deign to marry her. An added obstacle was my mother's determination, being a thoroughly modern woman, to complete school and begin her career before entertaining his proposal.

The Grafton's were just the kind of middle class Black family that made D.C. unique during the days of segregation. They were also of the class of Black folk that my father was working furiously to undermine.

He considered them, with their quiet and steady upward mobility, to be somehow complicit with their own oppression. "Lowercase n–grows," he called them, "people satisfied in their marginalization."

But they were far from that. Like W.E.B. Dubois, Horace Mann Bond, Ida B. Wells and Mordecai Wyatt Johnson, they saw education as the key to their future equality, even as my father's own family had suffered and sacrificed in the hope that one of them might somehow make it over the wall.

My grandfather, Rev. E.D. Grafton, was born just outside Washington in Falls Church, Virginia only twenty years after the Civil War. While a student at Howard Divinity School, he met his future bride while preaching his trial sermon at Ebenezer Methodist Episcopal Church.

The church was situated in Capitol Hill's historic Black neighborhood and its basement served as the first public school for *colored* children in the Nation's Capitol. Rose Taylor was the pastor's daughter and during a massive celebratory feast in honor of the successful trial sermon, eager eyes locked across the crowded table, and after a highly supervised, gas lit evening stroll, love began to spark.

Rose's light brown skin, high cheekbones and long coal black hair revealed the imprint of her mother's Cherokee heritage, born as she was on the Smoketown reservation near Woodbridge, Virginia. (A haven for Black Indians, the sturdy products of intermarriages between the Northern Cherokee and both runaway slaves and free people of color.)

Rose's striking beauty, quick wit and intelligence bowled him over and my grandfather was immediately smitten. A year later in the very church where they met and courted under watchful but approving eyes, they were married. My Grandfather was 24, my Grandmother was 19, and along with a wife, he received the assistant pastorate of the grand old church.

Twelve years later, Grandfather was teaching at Howard Divinity School and had taken over as pastor of Ebenezer. Five healthy and inquisitive boys had already been born to my grandparents' union, but on a sunny day in May, my mother was born.

My mother was instantly the princess of the household and my grandfather dotted on her constantly. Brilliant, she skipped fourth and fifth grades and vowed to become a schoolteacher.

My father's hardscrabble life could not have been more different, as he rose from the dirty streets of Southwest D.C., long before the neighborhood was raised, in the 1950s, to make way for what the government called urban renewal. In characteristic form, the colored folks called it by the more precise, *Negro removal* as the neighborhood was wiped from the face of the earth, only to be replaced by overwrought monuments to a squalid and decadent modernity.

But when my father was a child, poverty was the norm in Southwest and the only way out was a job as a Pullman porter, a government clerk or in service to a rich merchant or high-ranking official. For most, collage and the professions were simply out of the question.

My father reserved comment about his father, due to what I believe to be embarrassment over his general ignorance about the man. The only information that I ever got out of him was that my grandfather was probably an illiterate laborer. It was a time when the higher paying skilled jobs only went to Caucasians—illiterate or not. Even newly arrived Irish and Italians could get jobs, as masons and carpenters when the sons and grandsons of the Black men who built the White House and the Capitol could not.

Grandfather Diggs hauled lumber and bricks to the sites and removed the debris of a day's construction. He and his fellows were the first to arrive and the last to leave and had the poorest compensation. Often they'd work twelve hours for a dollar but somehow, raised families, built Churches and Masonic temples. These men made lives and though denied the opportunity to erect buildings, they laid the foundation for the achievements of their descendants.

One thing was almost universal. These men died young. The harshness of their lives contributed to stress in their households. Many drank themselves to death or succumbed to the violence of street life. Others, motivated by the need to provide for growing families took multiple jobs, as waiters, cooks, porters, butlers and stride piano players in alley borne juke joints. The life was hard; but unearned suffering, the saying goes, is redemptive. *It lasts but a night, but joy cometh in the morning.*

I've often wondered whether in church on Sunday, these men would think, *"but Pastor, does joy contribute anything to what's in my cupboard today? Me, I would like to have some of that there joy, before that 'ole sun come up!"*

In any case, they say that Grandfather Diggs's body just gave out one day. Six children, thousands of loads and hundreds of job sites later, George Diggs died at thirty-five years old. In those days, a cold could kill you.

My father was the second oldest of the Diggs children and was spared as his mother and eldest brother Carter, led the family out of crisis. Carter dropped out of high school and took up where his father left off in the pits, first as a runner and later as a loader and hauler himself. The noblese oblige of the company's management clearly knowing no bounds.

Throughout the 1930s, Grandmother had been a seamstress for one of the large department stores where no member of her shade could dream of shopping until just a few years before my birth. Together, mother and son tried to insulate the younger children from the difficulty of their situation. They were heroic but not unique. The depression was in full swing and while the nation suffered, Black America, as with all of the nation's historic catastrophes, was in familiar territory.

Institutions that had guided the way out of slavery now supported an entire race. The church was central and grandmother's family, the Calverts, probably descended from Maryland slaves, were the leading force in establishing Douglass Memorial, a small African Methodist Episcopal church on New

Jersey Avenue in Shaw. Named for Frederick Douglass, the church split from the prestigious Metropolitan A.M.E. where Douglass actually attended until his death.

Douglass Memorial acted as a surrogate father for the Diggs family and soon sufficient food, clothing and rent money flowed from fellow parishioners, who due to their own battles with the beast of American racism, were not that much better off themselves. *In the modern age of the gospel of the dollar almighty, my father's family might have starved on the streets, if the congregation's largess was needed to fuel the Pastor's private jet. The cross-emblazoned tail section would not have provided hope and the flight crew of four would not have served them dinner.*

Somehow, my father thrived in these dire conditions, like an oak seedling spouting from a cracked sidewalk. Like Paul Robeson (his childhood hero), he became a four-letter man, in football, baseball, track and basketball and at 18, his athletic prowess coupled with his nearly perfect grade point average, landed him a scholarship to Harvard.

Negroes were occasionally given an opportunity at Harvard then, but so as not offend their hosts, there were very few that fell beyond the acceptable range in the paper bag test. For many colleges, even elite black students were automatically excluded if they weren't *high yellow* or at least lighter in skin tone to a brown paper bag. To be clear, Steppenwolf Diggs wasn't a very dark man, but he was far from the kind of pale that earned one status in a color based society. My father's exceptionalism made him an aberration.

Despite the disadvantage of race and color and having come from "the only commercial high school in the United States for Negroes," as Cardozo High School's 1940 yearbook proclaimed, my father marched proudly onto Harvard's campus in 1944, when if he could have scrounged up the money, he might have stayed at home to attend Minor Teacher's College, or Howard University, or marched into the Pacific theater during the final push of World War II.

It's the unexpected that changes things most profoundly and while attempting one of the acrobatic catches that made him an all Ivy end the year before, my father shattered his knee in the season opener against Princeton. He was clipped by a linebacker, whom he always swore was yelling, *"kill that nigger,"* as he hit him low and from behind. The Princeton player, who later became a Dixicrat Congressman from Georgia, was not flagged on the play.

That was football then. It was the risk a Negro player took in the days before integration, before Jackie Robinson, before the inevitable Black dominance of American sports. My father never played again and despite having an academic scholarship, he soon found himself without that too. The quid had evaporated and with it, the quo.

I have always been interested in what propels people forward in the absence of hope. My father's life was an inspiration to me, but for years I could never grasp what hidden force was the catalyst for his steely attitude during such a fearsome stretch.

I had ignored the obvious. He had his mother's example and what propelled her was a force beyond hope, beyond anything tangible. It was that inexplicable thing known as faith.

Unable to come up with tuition, he returned to Washington to find a job. His injury kept him out of the war; about which he always said, "that knee injury saved me from either running around with a little brown ball, while my people suffered or with a big brown rifle, while I did."

He was determined to get an education, to be of use, to be as the Harvard men called him when they showed him the door, *a credit to his race.* His mother always said, "an education is the only thing they can't take away from you," which motivated him. He'd been radicalized by his experience at Harvard and by hearing Dubois and Robeson speak at a rally in Harlem, which he'd hopped off a Washington bound train to attend.

After years of working as a clerk for the NAACP, waiting tables and driving cabs at night, my father finally resumed his studies at Howard. He was twenty-four years old and sporting for a fight.

I am still amazed that with their disparate backgrounds, my parents got together at all; she with her proper Methodist upbringing and strict adherence to her fathers code of conduct and my father, the bold creation of cruel circumstances, charitable hearts and seething rage.

66

Pictures don't lie. In the fifties, my mother looked like a slightly browner version of Dorothy Dandridge. Her cinematic beauty, good humor, poise and brains made her a popular co-ed on the Howard campus. My father was possessed of a Harvard arrogance and vocabulary, with but with the anger unique to those who have come face to face with the lie of full black opportunity in America.

He pledged a fraternity during his junior year because the lads in crimson and cream were leaders on campus and above all, my father considered himself a leader. "I'd been wearing crimson for the white man on a football field, I could damn well wear it for myself, he explained.

As a senior, he was a magnetic and popular figure in his horn rimmed glasses, fraternity sweater, pipe and beret—a big, dashing Dizzy Gillespie type figure, walking my mother to class. My mother loved his contradictory nature, which was expressed most clearly by his angry masculinity, his gentility to women and his potent mind, but to her, his eyes were illuminations, twin beacons of knowledge and understanding. He could heal her with his eyes.

Between days of grueling classes at Howard and evenings bopping to Charlie Parker and Miles Davis, at the Lincoln Colonnade or Bohemian Caverns on U Street, my parents fell in love. After eight years of dating amid the cruel and nearly constant harassment of my grandfather, they married at a small chapel in New York after Ma's gradation from NYU with her PhD.

67

Rev. Grafton echoing the classism that plagued the race, thought my father to be beneath my mother, despite their identical academic achievements. But it seemed my parents' marriage had a touch of the inevitable. She was the only person that had ever been able to soften my father's anger and my mother had never met anyone that was his like.

FIVE
Chocolate City

*"We didn't get our forty acres and a mule
But we did get you, CC, heh, yeah."*

Parliament Funkadelic

B y the time of my birth, D.C. had become as Mary Church Terrell foretold in 1906, "the Colored man's paradise." It was a promised land with all the grandeur and possibility of a latter day Constantinople.

A rifle shell tore into the neck of Martin Luther King and a gaping wound was opened in America. Many of the notable civil rights soldiers found their way to the Nation's Capitol to join an advance guard led by the likes of the young Marion Barry and Stokely Carmichael, the first of these young radicals to sense the city's potential. Their survival during the movement depended largely on perfect political pitch and they collectively viewed D.C. as the next frontier. Violent acts have changed history since the beginning of the world.

Instantly, we had a political class, battle hardened agents of progressive change who knew how to organize and register the teeming masses of black folk to vote. They had the ability to give the kind of stirring oratory that could raise the floorboards. They germinated seeds of hope in desperate hearts.

The city possessed a gritty elegance then, a revolutionary aura that ran counter to its status, as the capital of a western democracy and when I imagine Santiago under Allende, or Nairobi under Kenyatta, I do so through the prism of childhood remembrances. Scattered images of tanks on city streets, burned out stores and the unbearable scent of tear gas linger warily along side the Jefferson Memorial and Washington Monument as the dominant icons of my early childhood. They are *all* happy memories.

Understanding D.C. means listening to the music of Marvin Gaye. The city is alive in his soulful shouts, joyous shrieks and politically charged polemics, his haunting, bittersweet lamentations. At the bottom, there is always the funky suggestion of sex.

The neighborhoods defined D.C. then and Marvin, a son of the city, embodied then reinterpreted the vitality of the community in universal terms. Listen to *Trouble Man* and you can feel the Far Northeast streets from which he emerged. Benning Road alleys strewn with broken glass and in the stifling summers, Deanwood children playing bare in streets flooded over by spraying fire hydrants as retired couples on porches rocked majestically in gliders. In Marvin's music, you can almost hear the old Chesapeake and Potomac Telephone Company trucks and D.C. Transit buses smoking up the winding hills, and middle aged men in wife beaters, sporting two days growth, sitting on steps eating Pappy Parker's Chicken, slowly savoring the accompanying hot biscuits drowned in butter and honey. Oh, yes! D.C. was that sweet.

Then there were the perfumed young women fresh from the beauty parlor, sexy even to my immature eyes, that switched up the block in their colorful mini dresses and pastel colored lipstick, off no doubt, to meet an *Afro'd* beau at one of the corner bars.

Those were the days when ice cream trucks played nonsensical tunes as they patrolled the streets, offering a simple menu of soft chocolate or vanilla ice cream on cake cones. Daily rations were conveniently obtained at the ubiquitous corner stores that capped each block like exclamation points.

Large rambling families inhabited the city's boundaries and commemorated their ancestral ties with elaborate barbeques and crab feasts staged in riotous backyards or within the sprawling urban parks like Rock Creek and Fort Davis, which pepper the urban landscape. It seemed everyone was Black and we *were* beautiful.

The epicenter of this world was the corner of 14th & U, which for years smelled like a dubious combination of soot, half smokes from *Ben's Chili Bowl* and hastily dispatched urine from the heroin fiends who stood clustered and moaning on that corner like ghouls in a George Romero film. U Street, the cradle of Ellington was burdened by its 1968 rebellion but it was made inviolate by its legacy. This was the D.C. that Marvin knew and the one that I would inherit.

Petey Greene shouted prideful riffs over the radio as he played *Where Have All the Flowers Gone* for the swaying dashiki'd masses, and the city was set to vote for its first elected city council and Mayor. It was Black Power! For a boy paying attention, events of historic import were afoot, events that foretold the future.

⸸

The names of Black children have long been of mysterious provenance. After slavery and motivated perhaps by some congenital *Africanness*, the labels given by mostly illiterate and downtrodden freedmen, always seemed to reach for something far greater than their circumstances. More than names, they were generational prayers for freedom.

Millions named their children and even renamed themselves after Presidents of the United States, biblical icons or classical heroes. And while my own name, might have been recrudesced from that time, my father's clearly was. Steppenwolf Diggs was a name that belied race and background and dared him to evolve into the bold, iconoclastic man that he became.

My father's fight for home rule was an essential part of both family and city lore. As policy strategist and speechwriter for many of those who were destined for political leadership in D.C., he became known as *the Minister of Propaganda.*

Following the city's riots in 1968, my mother facilitated a family move. Our Capitol

East neighborhood had suddenly become dangerous in the aftermath of Dr. King's murder. It seemed to trigger a rash of Black on Black crime that had been virtually unknown among the flowerpots and row houses. Nihilism had descended on Black America and some now believed that absent King's dream, we should all live a nightmare.

So we moved in 1970 and our new house in Hillcrest, near the Prince Georges County Maryland line served as the headquarters for the strategy sessions, which led to home rule. Since many of the principals were already on the radar screen of the Congress, FBI and the press, they chose the home of a humble college professor as the location for small groups to gather and strategize. They mocked the American security apparatus; we lived down the street from the stately former residence of J. Edgar Hoover.

The protective bubble of Hillcrest shielded me from the increasingly scarred landscape that dominated the rest of Southeast, which as a result of flawed urban policies made it the most dangerous part of the city. The Federal government, in its insight, had located much of the city's public housing on the city's eastern edge.

Within a few years, rolling hills and bucolic meadows had been transformed into hard ghetto and Hillcrest became a white flight neighborhood. Black professionals ran in droves to claim the former homes of frightened Caucasians who'd high stepped like Black College drum majors, in a desperate parade out of town.

They called the gatherings *Poker Games*, which was a ruse. These veterans of civil rights battles, in the deep dangerous south, knew the value of hiding their true intentions from an aggressive and potentially violent enemy. The regulars became legends and in addition to my father were led by Rev. Wilson Dent, who later represented D.C. in Congress and the unforgettable Edmund "Lock" Smith.

Lock Smith was an astonishingly short, balding man with skin the color of a Hershey bar. His girth gave him the appearance of being just as broad as he was tall. He had noticeably small hands and feet and the light of a searing intelligence was evident in his eyes. To my young mind, he looked like one of Santa's elves might have, had Mr. Kringle been required to enact an affirmative action policy.

Lock got his nickname from a young schoolteacher named Elaine Whitfield who ran for a school board seat in the first such election. She came out of nowhere to defeat several better-known and better-financed opponents.

On election night, in a fit of shear joy, she gave Eddie Smith, as he was known then, the nickname *Lock*. "Ladies and gentlemen," she said, "in this election, they said the doors would be closed to real people but this is our Lock-Smith!"

It had been Lock's field strategy, which included a relentless door knocking campaign that had *locked up* the precincts that secured her victory. My father had written all of her speeches and brochures.

The men drank cognac when they came to our house, except for Lock, who was fond of scotch and milk. They were my earliest heroes because by the sheer force of their imaginations they willed our body politic into existence using techniques honed and perfected in the trenches of the civil rights movement.

They infused in our people a dream of a city governed fairly, democratically and openly, perhaps more so than any city in America had ever dared. It was radical thinking for a city that had been ruled by segregationist Congressmen and corporate interests, for more than a century and it represented the initial stirrings of a dynasty.

I learned to keep secrets early. Some of my earliest memories are of men in dark suits and dashikis coming to my house late on school nights, as I got ready for bed. Occasionally, they'd bring their young wives or girlfriends to keep my mother company, a practice, which encouraged my frequent intrusions to show off my blue corduroy slippers and favorite batman pajamas. "Look they glow in the dark."

"Now Jason, you are not to share what goes on in our house with anyone. Do you understand?"

"Yes, Mommy."

"If someone asks who visits your father, what are you going to say?"

"I am going to say my father's kinda mean and doesn't have any friends. People only come here to see you."

My mother smiled and then gave me a hug and a kiss. "I like that very much Jason, you're such a smart little boy."

I heard the voices as they bounded down the narrow wooden staircase to my father's knotty pine den. I remember the deep and constant murmur after they closed the basement door. It was on these nights that I was lulled to sleep by the stern music of committed men.

Thursday nights were the designated meeting nights of the *Poker Game* and these conclaves would continue late into the evening. The relentless debates over suitable candidates and editorial sessions over press statements always included a hearty buffet catered by one of the great Afro-American restaurants in the city.

On one night it would be fried chicken and potato salad, green beans and peach cobbler from Ed Murphy's Supper Club, on another it might be fried fish, corn on the cob and collard greens from Morgan's Seafood. This always gave way to friendly banter over liquor, Kools cigarettes and my father's cigars. Sometimes, the brilliant, rowdy bunch would actually play a hand or two of low stakes poker just to keep Reverend Dent honest.

In a world where children are more often alienated from their fathers than not, I cherished those nights of youthful anticipation, when the sounds of men bonded by struggle, spirited beneath my door and braced my ears with the sounds of a war room. I didn't know it yet, but I was already in the embrace of the path I would travel.

You might say that politics is a disease. I'd been made susceptible by witnessing my parents' frequent dinner table debates, my father's activities with the *Poker Game* and a constant steam of politicos flowing through our house. Yet, I had not been completely ensnared by it due to tender years. Six is young for politics.

At ten and having already gone through the natural progression of career goals: Fireman, Police officer, Veterinarian, Doctor, Preacher (I was a Black child); I settled on being a lawyer—which is historically a gateway drug to politics. This single-minded focus was my greatest gift and most vicious malediction.

A chance meeting in 1974 set my life's course when quite by accident I met Randall John Reilly as he ran for Mayor during that first home rule election. Hillcrest was a grand neighborhood situated amid old trees, on a peak in the southeastern sky. Azaleas and manicured lawns adorned every block and the stately brick homes equipped with hardwood floors and fireplaces gave the area the feel of suburbia in one of the nation's most populous cities.

Hillcrest was situated in the newly designated seventh Ward of the city and Reilly's motorcade had cut across the river to garner votes. You had to admire his guts, it was enemy territory and his patrician bearing was out of place among the largely working class neighborhoods of Fort Dupont and Deanwood. Things were slightly better for him in upwardly mobile Hillcrest.

It was one of those insanely beautiful spring days in Washington when Reilly encountered me riding my bright red *no speed* bike. He looked me in the eye, shook my hand and asked me to support him for Mayor. "But I'm too young to vote," I said predictably, but he would have none of it. His response was gallant, "Yes, you are young man, but you can ask your parents to vote for me. I care about older people too."

Obviously this had not been my first experience with aspiring politicians. I grew up with them encamped in my parent's house, their ears bending to my father's sage advice. I played with their children during the social gatherings, which added balance to political ambition. But, my random meeting of Reilly was the first time that I had ever encountered a politico on my own terms.

There was something about the selflessness of Reilly's actions that cemented my love of politics. Stopping a fifty-car motorcade to speak with a kid on a *no speed* bike would normally be considered ludicrous, unless it was within the sightlines of cameras or earshot of reporters.

"How are you fairing in school and how's life in the recreation centers for you and your friends?" He continued. Such kindnesses are not easily forgotten; my father rarely asked such questions. He was of the old school and left such matters to my mother.

"That's nice son," my father said, after I rode home to tell him as fast as my gear challenged bike would allow. "He'll go back to practicing law soon enough," my father continued. "Maybe he'll give you a clerkship one day, that is, if you still want to be a lawyer," he clucked.

It was over before it started and Reilly lost badly. I still remember his beautiful daughters crying behind him on television. Unbeknownst to me, my father, Lock and the *Poker Game* were on the other side, which was instantly dispositive of the matter. It was the birth of Chocolate City.

By the mid 1970s my father was the leader of the best political operation in a city, which had been deprived of local politics for almost a century. Schooled in the trenches of social protest and highly skilled in covert organization in a jurisdiction, where the opposition consisted of majordomos and dowagers of civic association and social club fame—the *Poker Game* was invincible.

In those formative days, I learned in practical terms what I had heard my father say so often when visiting his classroom on days off from school. "My dear young men and women," he would begin, his basso voice vibrating the wooden podium, "according to me, democracy in its purest form is an expression of common will and a civic extension of collective spiritual or moral purpose. It is not, despite overwhelming evidence to the contrary, an exercise of extra-civic power on popular resources for individual or factional gain—that is an oligarchy masquerading as democracy."

It was his—a mostly original thought of vaguely *Rousseauiste* inspiration, which invalidated on ethical grounds, all political systems that fouled the purity of the public will by attempting to influence communal instincts and moral impulses in the exercise of governmental purpose. He'd written three books and dozens of scholarly works on it.

My father believed that since the Declaration of Independence states that, as a matter of agreement by the rebelling colonies, "All men were created equal and endowed by their creator with certain inalienable rights..."—then, in his oft repeated words,

"Slavery could and should have been immediately abolished in America as a founding national principle. The bitter two centuries that followed the revolution, were preordained by the impure system that was artificially sustained due to an amoral, fallacious and commercially inspired manipulation of public will." In short, slavery and the profit motive, hijacked democracy. As he put it "This nation was born deformed."

Meeting Randall Reilly cemented my interest in politics in a way that having a political genius in the house could not. There is often a wary distance between fathers and sons, which may be largely born of sameness, a manifestation of the notion that distance is useful in gaining perspective on proximal things.

SIX

The Spirit Of Heroes

For what is it to die, but to stand in the sun and melt into the wind?
Kahlil Gibran

T he house teemed with relatives, friends and strangers. A week had passed since we lost my mother and after a proper Methodist funeral, we returned to Hillcrest for the traditional repast. The attendees ate fried chicken and potato salad and drank champagne—a combination my mother favored. I ate nothing. My repast took liquid form.

The Grafton's were delicate, short-lived people and only a few distant Grafton relatives remained to morn my mother's passing. But, my father's siblings had all produced massive, boisterous, 19th century style families and they descended upon our house that day like a mass of penitents at a church revival. The cold snap had ended and most of them retreated to the backyard to escape the crush of mourners in the house, smoke their Newports and play Bid Whist. I retreated also, to my favorite room in the house, the knotty pine basement from which our city's revolution was launched all those years ago.

The basement's worn out furniture had been removed for space and folding chairs had been thoughtfully arranged around the walls to accommodate guests who now happily eschewed them for standing room on the grass. I was grateful for the privacy.

After putting away an entire bottle of *Veuve*, I wanted a real drink and found the *Louis Trey* that my father always kept well hidden, in his bookshelf, behind his prized, signed first edition of *Invisible Man*. I knew the book's inscription well, *"To The Wolf,"* it read, *"keep lighting those candles in the dark, Fondly, Ellison."*

I always felt safer in isolation but as the liquor and I bonded, the gangly legs I saw descending the stairs suggested that my tranquility was over. I carefully slid the baccarat bottle under my chair.

"I've been looking for you young man. I just wanted to express my condolences. Rachel was a quite *beautiful—ah*, remarkable woman."

I didn't like the way the man's eyes looked when he said the word *beautiful* in reference to my deceased mother. It felt inappropriate in some way, almost lustful. I resisted the urge that I felt to curse him out. It would be imprudent to disclose my family's universal disdain for his ass.

"Thank you Dr. Cole," I said wearily. I took a large swig from the snifter to steel myself against the coming onslaught.

"I just spoke to your father. He's putting up a brave front but you should watch over him tonight. He's pretty low right now and it's going take some time."

"I appreciate that," I said.

"Time heals all wounds Jason."

"I'm not sure this one will ever heal."

"She'd want you to move on. She was sick for so long, she'd wanted you to be happy."

This dirty bastard, I thought. It's one thing to console and to gaze off into the distance with inappropriate eyes, but to presume to tell us how long to grieve? Fuck him.

The irony was that my mother hated Cole. As chair of my father's department, he had been elevated more on the strength of good campus politics than on scholarship. My father's years as a public intellectual, traveling to other cities and exporting the strategy that won us D.C. had oddly hurt his chances at the post.

My mother considered Cole a third-rate intellect, complemented only by first-rate arrogance. At 65, he was one of those people that thought that playing the regular Joe, dying his thinning straight hair and wearing ridiculously trendy clothes was an adequate disguise for his particular brand of conservatism. His feigned humility completed the ruse.

On that day, he was wearing a black pinstripe FUBU suit, a lavender shirt and a purple Windsor knotted tie that was almost the size of an ascot. He was somehow unaware that he looked like a clown.

He was a man accustomed to being catered to, but usually introduced himself as "an instructor at Howard," when everybody knew that he was chair of the Political Science Department. It was as ridiculous as if Rev. Jesse Jackson went around introducing himself as just a preacher.

Cole certainly had his votaries— sycophantic fools, but I wasn't impressed. The man was a fraud.

"If you would excuse me Dr. Cole," I said standing and finishing off my snifter. "I need a refill."

"I understand Jason. Godspeed to you and your family."

I chose not to respond and left him standing there, his beak like nose tilted skyward, nostrils fixed in a dazzling display of hauteur. It was only later that I realized I had left the baccarat bottle under the chair—in the basement, with him.

I went looking for my father. If Cole had disturbed me so thoroughly, I knew my father was deliberating the merits of killing the motherfucker. Instead, at the top of the stairs, I found our long time family friend and physician, Dr. Louis Thurman eager to talk politics. A kindly old gentleman, with wavy salt and pepper hair, Dr. Thurman fancied himself an amateur political consultant. He had given hundreds of political fundraisers over the years in his fabulous platinum coast home on Kalmia Road and through his membership, in the *Boule*—that vaunted inner circle of the Black elite, he had been highly successful in raising the crucial cash the *Poker Game* needed for it's victories.

Dr. Thurman knew that I had been planning a campaign—everybody did, and he was already lined up to do my first event. My eventual entrance into the fray as a candidate had been my father's driving ambition since I finished High School.

Dr. Thurman leaned into me as if sharing a secret and began to speak in his high-pitched, elfin squeak. "Jason, D.C. has changed and the old way of life in our fair city is passing from the scene. Someone will have to rise to the occasion that not only has a history with the previous order but an understanding of the new one. We need a representative, if you like, that will negotiate the best terms for the people left behind in all this change. Perhaps the most appropriate term for such a person might be *transitional leader*."

Caretaker was what it sounded like to me, but even if Dr. Thurman was no Fred Hampton, I knew he meant well. Still, I had no interest in running a losing protest candidacy, or appeasing the development interests that were hell bent on displacement.

I couldn't stomach the idea of pleading for amenities for gentrifying neighborhoods that would turn over in a year or two no matter what I did. No political anesthesia for a dying community for me, it would be *save the patient* or let her die while you're trying.

Despite what Valor thought of me I was enough of a student of history to understand the legacy that I had inherited. But she was right about one thing, time was not on my side—Chocolate City was in her death throws. We were losing hundreds of people every day.

I thanked Dr. Thurman for his well-intentioned insights and left him graciously. I had to keep him on board for his fundraising prowess but I wasn't ready to reengage in politics. I'd just buried my mother. Public life could wait.

I found my father in the kitchen being swarmed by mourners. He seemed fine; still the broad shouldered dreadnaught of a man than I had always known. At 74, despite his slight limp, he still had the carriage of an athlete. He looked as if he could still run a perfect hook route or knock an opposing outside linebacker into oblivion.

Yet, on that day, he appeared diminished somehow. *Might grief actually shrink the size of your spirit?*

I knew he wanted the mourners out of his house, but tradition governed the day; a last brave face before the world and then a heavy dose of reality. We discussed the arrangements the day after Ma died and quietly negotiated which of us would write the obituary or *family paper*, as the old folks called it.

In the Diggs household, everything was a negotiation. The presence of two academics at the helm of the family necessitated an orderly process of decision-making in order to avoid gridlock.

In our family, a typical discussion might have just as easily been a colloquy on the Senate floor, instead of a conversation over where to buy lawn furniture. I learned the subtleties early.

I never recognized our family in the usual television or film representations of Black folks, where domestic flare-ups, the daily beating of children and drill sergeant like parental aggression were considered a normal part of life. I had no idea what government cheese was. My mother bought our cheese from the kindly Scandinavian man at Eastern Market, so there was no need to federalize the matter.

Sensible, rational arguments won the day in the Diggs household and emotional outbursts were to be avoided like some form of medieval pestilence. After an hour of intense deliberation, it was decided that the orator would write the paper. As a practical matter, familiarity would lend itself to a smoother delivery.

In the end it was concluded that I would make the presentation. In my father's words, "I can no longer vouch for my composure, I'm leaving it to you."

I couldn't vouch for mine either, but having seen my father falter on the morning of my mother's death, I was ill prepared to witness what might happen to him on what promised to be an even more glacial day. Diggs pride was at stake and the unspoken words between us were as present in the room, as either of us.

My mother's constant edict when coaching college forensics was, "be brief, be bold, be brilliant and be gone." There was no room for emotional surprises. For the speaker, tears were not allowed.

With the speaker decided, we went on to discuss the program and the repast. My father made it clear that he did not want a house full of people. "I would rather let the simple elegance of the service suffice," he said.

"What about Aunt Sara and Uncle Joe," I said. "What about the folks from the Universities, I'm sure they'll want to come over and—"

"—And what?" He interrupted, "fawn over us, cry, and speak their meaningless platitudes? Later, of course, they'll succumb to their actual motives, eating, drinking and partying. I will not have those gluttonous sons of bitches dancing on her grave."

"Nobody's going to dance Pop."

"It's hyperbole son," he said quietly. "I believe I'm allowed *that* on a day like today."

My father had become more and more irascible over the years but mother's death left him nastier than I had never seen him. My mother used to say that he was reverting to his earlier, less refined self, as a result of her illness.

I could see it. The steely temperament, which allowed my father to battle out of the muddy ground of Southwest Washington and into the Ivy League, had been submerged as he set his mind to winning my mother's hand and establishing himself as a giant in politics and academia.

Now he was resurrecting its formidable power to grapple with my mother's illness. The irony was that he appeared to reserve his most vicious displays for her, as Freudian payback, for her illness and for denying him the peace of mind that he would pass on before her.

Then, there were the murders. In battles over turf and profits, nearly two thousand souls perished in D.C. in just half a decade. My father took this personally.

Homegrown drug crews, with Rayful Edmunds at the helm, were at war with Jamaican gangs from New York (Christopher Wallace among them) and The Nation's Capitol instantly became Beirut. With the violence oddly limited to the darker provinces, only Black people seemed to die.

Every night, my father would watch *City Under Siege*, the television chronicle of the death toll and grumble angrily to himself, at the carnage. After weeks of this I remember looking to my mother for answers.

"He's devastated," she said. "He was responsible for nurturing the political class in this town. He feels like he failed."

"But he's not in office Ma. It's not fair that he's taking it out on you."

"His people are in office, remember that. We mustn't let this momentary crisis break us apart. This family stands, no matter what. It's stronger than any one of us because it represents all of us. Remember, this family has always had a higher calling."

Steppenwolf Diggs, *The Wolfman, The Wolf, The Professor, The Doctor, The Minister of Propaganda* had made these several names for himself electing the leadership class that had, proven itself incapable of ending the crisis. While the city was literally dying on their watch, it wasn't entirely their fault. It was obvious that stemming the tide of drugs in Black communities was beyond the capacity of local officials. The Feds were either asleep at the switch, *(JUST SAY NO!)* or according to the conspiracy minded, deeply complicit in the matter.

The ultimate tragedy was that the *Poker Game* vowed never to relinquish the power that came with controlling the capitol city, but the Black middle class had a mind of its own. By fleeing the killing zone and dissipating D.C.'s famous African-American voting block, all that the *Poker Game* had built was at risk.

My father always told me, "The District is unique in world history, Jason. Nowhere else have colonized people of color grabbed power in such an awe inspiring way—actually controlling the capital of the colonizer." No wonder the heads of third world governments flew in for consultations not only with the President, but also with the Mayor of D.C.

This is what the middle class so foolishly abandoned. This was the *crack,* which formed in a formally impenetrable wall, an opening to be exploited by the cunning. And exploited it was.

90

By the day of my mother's funeral in 2001, nearly twenty-five percent of the Black population had been lost. Soon, of the thirteen members of the Council, eight were Caucasian. There was much to be concerned about, if you were an old style Black politico.

The Mayor, Alvin Terwilliger, though nominally African-American, was what my father called a "colonial administrator," and one of the white Councilmembers, Dexter Callahan, was widely considered the be the first white person with a legitimate shot at becoming Mayor. At the time of my mother's death, all of this took its toll on my father. I worried that it might end him too.

It was late afternoon, people were leaving the repast and I heard laughter in the living room. *Pop was right; they really couldn't maintain the sanctity of the day.*

I rounded the corner only to find number eighty-five of the Los Angeles Rockstars holding court. AJ "Jet" Johnson had found his public.

An all pro NFL receiver and newly minted actor back at home for a funeral was bound to cause a stir. I actually believe some people showed up just to see him.

I was upset by the display of hero worship throughout the day but I must admit, his presence was reassuring. My friendship with him had endured through the years, though time and distance had intervened.

"*Howyadoin?*" said AJ, who had somehow managed to maintain a suggestion of his old New York accent.

"I'm doing about as well as can be expected," I said.

"Come on and sit with us then. Want a refill?"

"Got it downstairs. I just came in to see what the commotion was all about."

I was not surprised to find that the room was full of fawning overly perfumed women that I didn't know.

"Ladies have you met my boy Jason, Dr. Diggs' son, said AJ.

The little one spoke first. "We only met once, remember? It was at the party your frat brothers had about eight years ago, at the Reeves Center." I did remember, we danced to a few go-go songs, but when she told me that she had been one of my mother's TA's I thanked her for the dance and went for a Jack and Coke.

She was cute and just about my type but I never, ever, dated my mother's students and there was an added impediment, the relationship that I was in at the time. I did have *some* boundaries.

It was odd that I'd never seen her around until then. Within our highly stratified social circle, we were always running into the same people in clubs, restaurants and bars.

"Sure, I remember. You're the one that dances so well, I said. She smiled at my gratuitous flattery, dimples deep and impressive, on her eager face. *I could have her*, I thought and I noted to myself that the old constraints no longer applied.

The three other women in the room had all mumbled nearly inaudible responses in the negative to AJ's question, but they also never looked away from him to acknowledge me. They were the groupies, and little Renee, she of the dimples, was clearly their somewhat reluctant leader.

"AJ was just telling us the story of how he stole Rashawn Muhammad's jock strap and filled it with Icy Hot during mini camp this year," said Renee.

"Got to welcome them rookies drafted to take your spot properly," said AJ. Renee and her friends all giggled like schoolgirls in response.

After nearly 20 years at the top of his profession, AJ had just announced that he was retiring at the end of the upcoming season to concentrate on what had been up to that point, a lackluster *direct to video* acting career. His most memorable line up to that point had been in his 10 minutes on screen as Corporal Beauvoir in a *Dirty Dozen* knock off set in the first Gulf War called *Hard Way To Go.*

The line, *"sand is like an evil woman, it rubs me the wrong way,"* was delivered with a more than credible New Orleans accent *and* became a minor catch phrase among southern white fraternities the year the movie came out.

"Well if you guys could keep it down a little, my father is in the kitchen and he is not exactly in a jovial mood." The sarcasm nearly welled in pools at my feet. *My mother would have been proud. Valor too.*

"Oh my bad Jason," AJ replied. "You know *me* dog."

I certainly did.

I never felt as though I fit in my neighborhood as a child but few were aware of it. I was highly skilled at making other kids comfortable with me despite my discomfort with them.

While they were aficionados of the usual fare of basketball, go-carts and BB guns, I was a far more interested in reading and watching Star Trek after school. Orwell and Roddenberry were my heroes then, with a brotherly head nod to Richard Wright.

Tackle street football was my only concession to what was expected of me by peers and I was the second best wide receiver in the neighborhood. As one of the fastest boys in my neighborhood, I enjoyed a special distinction within our pre-pubescent society. Despite possessing certain qualities that might have pushed me to the corners, my speed made me a part of the elite.

I held back in most conversations with my friends in order to be understood. I became so adept at this charade that I once avoided a fight with a much larger kid by telling him that my name was Publius and quoting from what I considered a relevant section of Federalist Paper Number eight, *"The history of war... is no longer a history of nations subdued and empires overturned, but of towns taken and retaken; of battles that decide nothing; of retreats more beneficial than victories; of much effort and little acquisition."*

The boy, who had obviously paid no attention in 8th grade civics, was fully convinced that I had lost my mind. The confrontation ended nonviolently, and he was so befuddled by the encounter that he backed away hands up in resignation, muttering, "I don't mess with no crazy mothafukas and believe me, *that mothafuka, is* crazy."

At eleven, like most boys my age, girls were the nemesis. The problem was that I loved them, all of them. Round ones, skinny ones, it did not matter to me. They were rare and special and alien to everything that I understood. My popularity with my rag tag group didn't seem to extend to girls and I was hopelessly frozen at the platonic stage with every one of them I liked.

A few girls ultimately found me as attractive as my mother always said I was, but they seemed quite incapable of understanding me. I was forced to continue my charade by slouching thuggishly and suspending my knowledge of the English language (*so like um show-ti, can I get dem seb'um digits? You kinda fine right?*) thereby reducing myself to a manageable level for them.

I hated the deception. *Why,* I asked myself, *should I have to shrink my personality, my mind, my spirit, myself, in order to have a girlfriend? But the answer was simple—the alternative was loneliness.*

I was constantly frustrated. The concept of having a girlfriend didn't seem to elude my friends, all of whom seemed to have them and quite pretty ones at that. But I wasn't like those guys, any of them.

There were several variables at play. I watched public television and read weird books, by my friends' standards. Jack London and Frank Herbert and Tolkien.

By eleven, I was even writing a book of my own, a *Battlestar Galactica* knockoff, that I called *Return of the Graftonians* (after my mother's family). The plot was decent enough. A space ship lands in Rock Creek Park and the space men, all Black, destroy the earth when they find out what has happened to Black people.

The story concludes when all the Black people on earth are transported to the planet before the explosion. They are greeted as returning royalty because, as the book reveals, all Black people on earth were descendants of a forgotten and highly advanced African civilization in Tanzania that went to space with solar powered starships colonizing the planet *Graftonia* over two thousand years before.

I guess I had to shrink myself because even at eleven, I seemed destined for greater things than saccharine playground romances, elicit French kissing in church closets and the pathetic dry humping sorties that my friends ran on living room sofas throughout the neighborhood. With masturbation my dearest friend and my poster of a *Phaser* packing Nichelle Nichols, the object of my desire, I bloomed late in the ways of romance and prepared for greatness, endlessly obsessing over girls that I wouldn't shrink myself to have.

Growing up in a neighborhood like mine you had to have a buddy and Alphonzo

Juan Johnson or AJ was mine. He was fast, so fast that we never knew who would win our weekly races for neighborhood supremacy. In high school, he could beat me convincingly, displaying the talent that would ultimately make him a pro, but by then, social stratification hinged on more meaningful criteria.

Growing up, we were the most coveted pair of wide receivers in all of Southeast D.C. pick up football. We were unstoppable. If you double covered one of us, there being no zone defenses in street ball, the other would simply run a fly pattern, which always resulted in a touchdown.

Popularity translated into invitations to the best parties, having pretty girls around and never walking in fear of being jumped by the roguish few who garnered self worth from such adventures. We were privileged.

While it seems inconceivable, my relationship with AJ did not begin in stellar fashion. He'd moved to the neighborhood, from Sunset Park, Brooklyn, New York, after many of us had already lived in Hillcrest for four or five years.

When I first saw him at the large brick house on the corner of 34th and Camden, we were both approaching twelve years old. The For Sale sign hadn't been there long because when Mr. Larsen, the last white man on the block, died the month before, his daughters had quickly sold the house.

My father and Mr. Larsen shared something of an intellectual kinship and my father liked to spend time playing chess and smoking cigars with the old man. On thick summer nights, my mother supplied them with iced tea, as they played on one patio or another until the lightning bugs came out. So it had been sad to see the truck hauling away the lifetime of memorabilia from the former Justice Department official's house.

"Why does Daddy have to play chess with Mr. Larson all the time?" I asked my mother, when I was about nine years old. I was angry that I was not being taken to visit my cousin's house, where I'd stay up late watching *Creature Feature* on WDCA Channel 20 and roughhousing until morning.

"Your father likes Mr. Larsen because he's a hero."

"A hero?" I said, skeptically, because at that age, my notions of heroism required colorful, ornate regalia, which minimally consisted of tights and a cape. Certainly not the baggy gray chinos and frayed Penguin shirts that were Mr. Larson's daily uniform.

"Yes, he's a hero. He was a lawyer for the government before he retired and he volunteered to go to Alabama to protect the civil rights workers that your Daddy helped before you were born. He was beaten by a mob for saving a young Howard student from being attacked and he almost died to save her. Yes, Jason, he's a hero."

I had new respect for Mr. Larsen and never again complained about being inconvenienced. After that, I understood that not all heroes wore capes.

AJ was bouncing a basketball and talking to some of the neighborhood boys who had gone over to Mr. Larsen's house to investigate the moving van that was awkwardly slanted in the driveway. The encounter began bizarrely, like all childhood conflicts.

"What are you man?" said Larry Montgomery, who due to his brutish size and massive Afro was the unofficial enforcer of the group.

"You ain't that *light skinned*, but you kinda got good hair," Antoine Jones declared.

"I seen your Daddy earlier. He Black! Where your mama at? She ain't white is she?" Tyrone Barnette added.

AJ just kept bouncing that ball—*phutd, phutd, phutd*. Then he answered.

"I'm ghetto mixed with Spanish. I'm from Brooklyn, you southern pricks!"

I hated him immediately. First of all he talked funny, in a mash up of *Spanish patios and ebonics* and he wore a constant smirk on his face, denoting an air of superiority. He was from the fast-paced playgrounds of New York City and was just the kind of kid that the tougher fellows felt needed his ass kicked.

"You lil, funny talkin', ball bouncin', wavy hair brushin', halfway wannabe pretty boy looking motherfucker" said Larry. We called it *joanin'*, the adults called it playing the dozens and they were the most viciously ad hominem of ad hominem attacks;

intentionally cruel and designed for maximum comedic effect. We all laughed on cue.

"Chupa mi huevos, maricon!" AJ fired back. None of us knew what AJ had said but his body language and the look of utter contempt on his face was enough. We knew that Larry had been bested in someway in the battle of polemics and we knew that the war would have to be won by more conventional means. It was hard to *joan* on a kid who could do it in another language.

We soon found out that AJ was much too fast for the big lumbering haymaker throwers among us, like Larry and Tyrone and too strong for the stick and move experts like Antoine and me. AJ would just absorb punishment and then counter attack with a barrage of blistering overhand lefts and rights until he moved in with punishing body blows. Then, he would haul ass into the house realizing that no one could catch him. He'd perfectly mastered the *Rope a Dope* used by Muhammad Ali, in the *Rumble in the Jungle* the previous year.

After weeks of vain attempts to subdue him, we simply gave up, claiming that he had been properly initiated into the fellowship of the block. Sometimes I laugh with amazement at the primal logic that we displayed. Welcoming AJ to our clan was quite simply to our advantage, in him, we would have a potent new weapon to deploy in our low intensity conflicts with other neighborhoods.

Back then we had such wide latitude to make mistakes, without the burden of permanent consequences. I still long for the extended childhoods we enjoyed, when the absolute worst were busted lips, a few stitches or a broken bone; the obligatory aches and pains of childhood. Today, to offend in the wrong neighborhood is often fatal and too often, the offense is simply being there at all.

AJ was the kind of strange cultural amalgam that is commonplace in New York and almost no place else. His mother was a Dominican immigrant and his father was an African-American Vietnam vet from D.C. by way of North Carolina. After two tours as an MP, Mr. Johnson had become an NYPD beat cop. AJ told me that when his mother died tragically of ovarian cancer at only thirty-three, his heartbroken father made the easy decision to return to the D.C. area. *"Mi Papi, he sayd tha he never want to see New York again, he sayd he kep seein her everywhere he wen."*

AJ's father had some kind of connection and was allowed to take the detectives exam for D.C.'s Metropolitan Police Department. He scored at the top of the list enabling him to start investigating major crimes immediately upon his arrival. After a brief stay with relatives, he bought Mr. Larsen's house.

Naturally, my Mother frowned on my friendship with AJ, he was not the cultured, mannerly little boy of which my mother generally approved; but my father provided the balance that would ensure a continuation of the alliance. "That boy just lost his mother, Rachel and now he's 250 miles from home. Did you ever consider that Jason might be a positive influence on *him*?" My father told her.

He wanted to make sure that his only child and the heir to his exceptional brand of Black manhood, did not grow up to be effete and insipid like so many of the people he encountered in academia; like Cole. My father's insistence on personal toughness, academic excellence and social breadth gave me access to a world that I could never have glimpsed under my mother's protective gaze.

As my mother feared, in the weeks and years that followed, AJ was the one that helped me to shatter the hothouse that was my sheltered life. Watching Black exploitation films, popping bubble gum, throwing soda bottles with no other end in mind than to see them shatter and hours of brazen girl watching (of the construction worker variety) were some of the pastimes that AJ introduced to me.

It was AJ that pulled me off the last white boy in the neighborhood after I jumped the poor kid, after watching the second episode of Roots.

"Don't *killim Yase-on,* you have *jour* whole life to get some payback."

I'd never been so angry in my life and was looking for some form of reparations for Lavar Burton's misfortune. When my father found out, he just smiled knowingly, while my mother grounded me for a week.

"That boy didn't do anything to you Jason. I'm not raising a thug!" She said.

When I wasn't locked inside, AJ and I would explore the neighborhood together. It seemed to take hours to walk down the long wooded expanses of Branch and Pennsylvania

Avenues, toward the old Randall Theater. It became our secular sanctuary.

For three dollars and an eager mind, Bruce Lee, Richard Roundtree and Steve McQueen would lead services that widened our imaginations and provided endless fodder for recess recapitulations and lunchtime reenactments. Afterwards, dozens of *Little Tavern* hamburgers would fuel our journey home.

I was thinking wistfully of these happy childhood memories when AJ's groupies interrupted me. "Sorry Jason. We were all your mother's students and she was our favorite Professor. We meant no disrespect. I guess we all needed a distraction after today."

"Oh, so I'm just a distraction now?" Said AJ in mock distress.

"AJ, come on let's give Jason a break," Renee said. I was impressed with her but the others seemed dim, heartless; interested only in sipping Krug with a handsome star athlete as if AJ, one of the biggest Lotharios in the NFL, would stoop to give any of their 9 to 3 butts an opportunity. He just didn't do normal women. He was notorious for dating models, porn stars and skanky minor pop artists, that is, when he wasn't trolling around in the finest Brazilian bordellos.

The teachers were pretty, to a degree, but not nearly enough to justify the negative energy that they produced. Nor were they so bright or engaging that a man would assume that the sex or the prospects for stimulating communication would be worth the time.

They were the kind of women that could literally talk themselves out of potentially meaningful relationships only to complain about how men are afraid of commitment. I wanted them out of my house.

"*I did think the Mayor was good today Wolfie!*" The commotion was now coming from the kitchen and Aunt Sara was making a vain argument. My father hated the Mayor.

"Fuck that milquetoast *sonofabugger*! I would just as soon slap him as to shake his hand" my father shouted.

"Now Wolfie, your language. I know he's not your cup of tea, but he did do a nice job eulogizing Rachel."

"Jason eulogized Rachel! Reverend Davenport eulogized Rachel. In every tear I shed last week, I eulogized Rachel. *That* little bastard gave a speech. They told him that he had to be there and they got somebody to write a reasonably effective political speech, but that doesn't mean that I am beguiled or beholden. There were points to be scored at that church today, he's got his little white boy Callahan running to succeed him and among people like you, I guess he scored those points."

"Wolfie, that is uncalled for!"

"I didn't even invite that punk and did you see Callahan there sitting in the back?"

"You don't *invite* people to a funeral Wolfie. Try to be more charitable. He was paying his respects on behalf of the city and the announcement that he was submitting legislation naming the Liberal Arts Building at UDC after Rachel was just wonderful."

"Just a goddamn ploy to win over the feeble minded. He's against everything we stand for but this is a quick win for him. He'll get a lot of credit for doing something that doesn't cost him anything of substance. It's good politics, nothing more."

I made it back into the room in time to see my father lighting a cigar from the box of buttery CAOs that AJ had given us, something he never would have done in the house when my mother was alive. He was perspiring with anger and I saw the same look in his eyes that had me questioning his mental state before.

"What's going on Pop?" I asked.

"Your loving aunt is arguing with me son, on the day we buried your mother."

"Unfair, Steppenwolf. That's simply unfair," said Aunt Sara, who was his younger sister and a formidable force in her own right."

My father cut her off. "Look, Sara, in the final analysis we are obliged to be realists. These people have become an occupying force and any kindnesses extended by them have to be understood in that context.

What happened today was essentially part of a hearts and minds campaign. It's propaganda. I know a little something about this. They've been trying to close or compress UDC into a junior college for years but we've stopped them. Now, they name the building for my beloved wife but they'll close it down and blow it up a few years later. We'll be left with nothing, neither a school nor a name. Who's the winner in that scenario?"

Steppenwolf Diggs was always right. For 30 years, UDC had been a beacon of hope for thousands of Black DC Public School graduates who didn't have the money or the grades to matriculate anywhere else. Through that school, the only urban land grant university in America, both good and marginal students alike, became highly regarded lawyers, teachers, nurses and public administrators.

The powers that be had a different vision. A public university was no longer important for a city, which had all but abandoned the concept of developing, uplifting, or maintaining a black middle class. The new agenda hinged on attracting new residents—*DINKS* they called them, *double income no kids*, which should be read as *transplanted, Caucasian, professional and gay*. They didn't need a UDC.

These newcomers paid heavy taxes and required little in the way of city services. The tax money pours in and city coffers swell to the brim, while austere social welfare budgets keep it that way. Those most in need wither on the vine.

This is how the technocrats that now ran the city, men and women hopelessly devoid of personality or political talent, were building their machine. With only a micro constituency to satisfy, there was the bright illusion of success when in reality, they were simply eliminating everyone else.

My father continued his diatribe, leaning back in his chair, as he did in his classroom, "They don't want a university for the uplift of our people, they want Starbucks, gourmet shops and luxury grooming parlors for their Golden *damn* Retrievers. And what do we get? The low wage jobs that go with them!"

"Steppenwolf Douglass Diggs, I will not be lectured to like this on the day of my sister in-law's funeral. I won't stand for it!"

"Look, I don't think you understand. They know I hate them and the feeling is mutual. They see me as an anachronism. Hell, they're waiting for me to keel over *too*, so that they can have their morbid fun by naming a street or a ball field after me, in hopes that some—what do they call it now...street credibility, might rub off on their hind parts at the ribbon cutting!"

He shook with anger. But I watched him control it. He was calm when he continued.

"Now the boy here, thinks he can turn things around, redeem his old man by running for Council next year. That's laudable and I will do everything in my diminishing power to help him, you know I will, (he was looking at me) but the lessons of warfare dictate that it's hard to retake ground that you've already lost. Sometimes it's easier to open a new front."

"New front?" I said.

"Never mind, I'm just rambling now, but Sara..."

"Enough!" Aunt Sara screamed. Tears ran down her face and she was trembling in anger.

"Jason, I am going home, call me if you need anything and I'll be back for the food platters in a few days."

"I'm leaving for the Vineyard tomorrow. You'll have to call Pop." My father left the room.

"Then, I'll wait until you come back. I will not be insulted again."

"He didn't mean it. He's hurting."

"So am I, we all are, but there are limits Jason. You just don't treat family like this. We're all he has now."

"I know. I'll talk to him."

"We both know it won't do any good, baby. He's mourning and that liquor's got him too."

As I walked my Aunt out to her Lexus, I looked back at the house and caught a glimpse of my father peering through my mother's bedroom window. I knew he was upset, but in all my life he had never exploded on a relative like that before. He had also never expressed any doubt about my political plans. Over the years, they had frankly seemed more his plans than my own.

"Just pray on it sugar pie, the Lord will make a way," she said.

Again, I felt the tears welling, but repressed them. They would wait for me.

Aunt Sara and the rest of the family drove away and the women from the living room were also preparing to leave the house. With a well-practiced insincerity I thanked them for coming, even Jennifer, the eerily quiet one. Through Renee, they again expressed their condolences for my loss and their apologies for upsetting my father. But, as the rest of them remained riveted to AJ's every move, I somehow doubted their sincerity.

"It's okay," I said, ignoring for the moment the inconsiderate AJ, "my father's angry at the world right now". As they got into Renee's black Jetta, doors thudding teutonically all around, I turned away to find her phone number, neatly scrawled on a torn off piece of my mother's funeral program. She had pressed it into my hand at the end of what had been an unusually long hug goodbye. I considered then, two separate but essential truths. I *could* have her and my father *was* angry at the world.

SEVEN
Vineyard Calm

"Serenity is not freedom from the storm, but peace amid the storm."

Unknown

With the house empty of all the guests and my father sulking in his bedroom, AJ stayed in attempt brighten my mood. "Now it's time to do some real drinking." He said, and produced from his black leather messenger bag, a bottle of Remy Martin XO. It was a manly gesture, like his gift of the CAOs and I appreciated it just as much.

He was scheduled to accompany me on my hastily planned trip to Martha's Vineyard but a call from his theatrical agent changed that. We hadn't vacationed together since an earth shattering Miami trip several years before and since then, our lives had taken radically different turns. His was the lifestyle of a modern day Pasha; private jets, porn models and movie stars. I lived the life of a political soldier, a trained practitioner of the game of politics.

Politics *is* more game, than art. Artistic talent is innate, a gift of divine benevolence. But, at it's most basic levels politics can be learned by anyone and many of the best aren't naturally endowed. It is a game of the mind and closer to chess or poker than basketball or tennis—but if it is perfected, stardom awaits. Most people couldn't name the best chess players in history, but Arthur Ashe, Wilt Chamberlain and Los Angeles Mayor Tom Bradley had celebrity in common.

The Vineyard trip was to be a welcome catharsis for us both. It was a chance to leave the real world behind, for a moment. To allow the ravenous tears, which ripped my eyelids like wildcats, to escape.

For AJ, it would be an opportunity to escape the paparazzi and the hangers on and enjoy a new experience; for in all the years I had been visiting the Vineyard, AJ had never gone. He'd claimed one poor excuse or another for over a decade.

We planned to do some serious porch drinking, introduce ourselves to some of the Brazilian women who worked at the island restaurants, go fishing, play golf and courtesy of the loan of AJ's agent's house, spend a day or two integrating Nantucket. Again, it was not to be.

A cameo role, on some forgettable sitcom beckoned and AJ was off to L.A. to learn his twelve lines of dialogue, shoot his scene, workout, hang in trendy lounges and go to bed with strange women. In other words, he was going back to his regular routine.

We sat down in the kitchen with our snifters, lit cigars and a couple of cold Heinekens and for the first time that day I began to relax. I planned on getting fucked up on the hardest day of my life.

"Why don't you take your Pops with you?" He said, in a tone that came remarkably close to reasonableness for AJ.

"He'll be grading finals."

"He can't do that there?"

"You know how old school he is. He still believes in giving the test himself. He reads and grades each paper in his office in Douglass Hall the same way he did 30 years ago. He used to smoke his pipe in there and play Coltrane while he worked but Cole's no smoking policy stopped all that. Now my father just plays Miles and broods while he grades. You know, it still smells like pipe tobacco in his office and its been two years."

"Yeah, but wouldn't it be better if he just went away and got his mind off things?"

"Well, that's what I'm doing, but my father has always had a different process. Naturally, he hasn't been himself lately, he's been saying crazy things and his routine with Ma is all broken up."

"Routine?"

"That's right, you haven't been around. For the last week, he hasn't had to cook for her or take her to the bathroom or bathe her or any of the million things he had to do for the last 10 years. He just sat in his study chain smoking the CAOs you got us and blasting *Bitches Brew* on that old stereophonic in there. Then—he just erupted, nearly cussed out his own sister."

112

" Yeah, I heard him."

"You couldn't help but hear him.

"Hey, remember when he went off on that recruiter from Miami, senior year?"

"Yeah, he wasn't even mad, he was just fucking with the poor man."

AJ's father routinely asked my father to sit in on the recruiting visits that had begun to mount up as AJ rose in all the national recruitment newsletters to within the top ten high school receivers in the country. Mr. Johnson had risen to the rank of Captain on the force on native intelligence and grit but wanted his son to have the best education possible.

With my father as advisor and *grand inquisitor*, he hoped to navigate AJ through all the well-practiced salesmanship, into the best academic program he could find. My father was a willing accomplice.

I remembered the recruiter from Miami, a young Black defensive backs coach, going on and on, about football statistics. He was ill prepared for that particular recruiting visit.

"We've been to Bowl games a number of times recently and we feel like we're only a couple of years away from competing for a national championship."

My father responded, "Yes, but can they read—*brother*?"

My father used the word *brother* as punctuation, ironically. Such casual and ethnically identifiable language was never expected from him, and it would have been more likely, given his appearance and reputation, for him to have said something like *my good man,* in it's place.

The recruiter's response was weak and unimaginative. "About as good as I do, I guess," he said laughing nervously, frantically scanning the room for affirmation. It was not forthcoming.

My father's reaction was merciless. He stared at the recruiter and said, "I'm afraid that won't be *well* enough for young Mr. Johnson, sir. Have a good evening."

"Your father's a tough old dude Jason, he'll bounce back. Your campaign will give him something else to focus on."

"I guess so, but I don't know if *I* can take it that long. He's starting to get on my nerves."

"Then going by yourself is a good idea. It'll give you both some space."

"That was my thinking."

"Alright mothafuka, seems like you're back to normal already."

"Not quite."

"What year is she?" he said, standing bow legged in shorts, hairy legs only partially obscured by knee socks and boots. The three days growth on his face and the baseball cap neatly positioned atop an untrimmed mane made him look like a refugee, from a depression era *C.C.C.* project. His white Steamship Authority shirt had been soiled to a melancholic shade of grey and had the name *Frank* stitched over the left breast pocket.

" She's a '77," I said flatly.

"Fiat Spuy-dah right?" he said with a Massachusetts brogue, that would have made a Kennedy green with envy.

"Yes," I said.

"Great cah."

"Thanks Frank," I said, as I drove down the ferry ramp.

"Name's *Bauby, naht* Frank."

Confusion over nomenclature aside, I loved receiving complements on my little car. It was a monument to my college days when I never seemed to have any money but had a sexy car. My father helped me buy her over my mother's objections.

Her name was Fifi and the man who apparently was not Frank, had just proved that she still turned heads. The fact that I still owned her and that she still ran well, was a miracle amid my tragedies.

I'd finally left for the Vineyard three days after the funeral, to lament my mother's loss. As expected, my father plunged right back into work. Finals were upon him and in his words he had "responsibilities." I, on the other hand, was running for my life.

I had taken the 6:00 a.m. ferry, which arrived on island precisely at 6:45 and after the brief dockside exchange, took my usual route past the Black Dog Bakery and the ancient but serviceable A&P. Then left, through the quaint clutter of bike rentals, fishmongers and real estate offices and on into Oak Bluffs.

I was in serious need of comfort food after my eight-hour drive and breakfast at Linda Jeans was imperative. My trips to the Vineyard had rules demanded by tradition, regulations that I whimsically promulgated after the first few visits in an effort to preserve my idealized view of the place. The rules were sacrosanct and rigorously imposed and I enforced them on my travel companions as strictly as I did on myself.

Rule One: I never flew to the Vineyard. I thought it both boorish and irreverent to simply hop on a turbo prop at DCA and materialize at MVY in less than two hours. The Calvinist in me considered the Vineyard so idyllic, that it was right that you should work for her.

Unrelenting peace awaited you on the other side and it was proper that a person suffer to attain the peace that harbors there. Eight hours driving straight through was how one gained the keys to joy.

Rule Two: I only drove at night and would only stop once, for gas, fries and coffee at the rest stop in Darien, Connecticut. You can make better time while marshalling an army of thoughts to fuel your journey.

Rule Three: I always played the same music. Initially on cassette, then on CD and as technology advanced, iPod; but even as the delivery system changed, the music never waivered. On these cathartic treks, the songs were like stalwart compatriots in battle, bolstering me through the long solitary hours.

As I left D.C., I'd set the dial to Howard University's radio station—WHUR, enjoying the classic soul ballads of the Original Quiet Storm until the signal faded just past Baltimore. Then, Earth, Wind & Fire, Joe Sample and Al Jarreau would join the fray, until I reached the New Jersey turnpike.

Cassandra Wilson would grace my journey, ensuring at last, my escape. Her voice was a recurring blessing that never failed to console me. I her met once in a Greenwich Village jazz club and as the turnpike led me past New York, I thought warmly of her at her home in Harlem, my sweet comfortable friend, who visited me on disk, in times of greatest need.

New Haven meant, Return to Forever's Romantic Warrior, Joe Sample's Carmel or perhaps Kind of Blue with Miles and Coltrane but the finale of the rite was playing Seal's debut album, from Providence to the Cape, which I sang in a full throated glee, knowing that in an hours time, I would make Woods Hole. I sang the words lustily, *"Bring it on...don't wait until tomorrow..."* On a dark highway among the truckers, the lonely and the lost, I boldly imagined a peace that only dawn could bring.

I had been off the ferry seven hours when the Vineyard began to wrap me in its calm embrace. After a comforting breakfast of

Linda Jean's best and most ironically named omelet, *The Mess*, I parked on Seaview Drive and dozed on The Inkwell. It was warmer than I expected and I was soothed by the cool ocean breeze and uplifted by the azure sky. Gulls hovered overhead.

By late afternoon, I had unloaded my bag and showered at the familiar old house that I rented in Oak Bluffs, a majestic pink Victorian on the corner of Pequot Street and Naumkeag Avenue. I stayed there frequently and had come to associate it with the serenity I felt on the island.

As I emerged onto the wraparound porch, a crazy man was yelling in the grassy, median that bifurcated the passable areas of Pequot Street. I couldn't see him, but any cottager within a five-block radius could hear him. It was a guttural yawp, dangerous and unsettling.

I had never heard such a thing on the Vineyard, a place with so much peace embedded in its sandy soil but this crazy man and I had something in common. We were both confused.

I was far too anxious to sleep and decided to drive around, curious as to what I'd see so early in the year. I shopped for the week's essentials—a supply of good cigars at Trader Fred's in Edgartown, looping back to Jim's Package Store for bourbon in Oak Bluffs. With this important business aside, I settled down to eat steamers and chicken wings at Coop de Ville on the Oak Bluffs Marina.

I was in a reflective mood, ignoring the raucous noise coming from patrons watching a Red Sox game and after lingering there for hours, I decided to venture toward the jetty to take in the view. I planted myself on a park bench there, watching boats return to harbor as night began to fall.

Tranquility arrived with the sound of waves caressing the hulls of well-moored boats, nautical bells ringing submissively as they undulated with the current. The glow of a waning sun hanging low in cloudy skies made me feel at peace for the first time in many weeks.

The beauty and pain of my journey moved me to tears as I struggled against the breeze to light a cigar. I had no care for what was happening in D.C. They were on their own and so was I.

"Jason Diggs!"

The sound of my name startled me. I did not expect to see anyone I knew this early in the year.

"Jason Diggs, is that you?"

I was enraged by the intrusion and saw a man walking toward me from the other end of the pier.

"Yes, I'm Jason Diggs," I said tentatively, dabbing at my eyes.

"Hey there young fella, they told me you visited the Vineyard, but it's kind of early in the season isn't it?"

The Vineyard season begins jubilantly on Memorial Day ending abruptly after Labor Day, creating a bulge in the year. Homeowners open their highly coveted island homes for the summer and perennial renters, like me, after waiting through the winter for the season to begin, book their Vineyard weeks with the regularity of Swiss watches. At the end of the season, arctic air begins the periodic forays that end in persistent numbing cold by November and the cycle repeats itself.

In early May, there were few souvenir shops to plunder and the movable feast of house parties and cookouts, the living mucilage of Black visitors to the island, had not yet begun. So it was strange so early in the year for me to encounter a stranger, who somehow knew my name.

He had the slick, confident bearing of a member of the political tribe back home, and this was precisely why I wanted to disappear into the weather-beaten planks of the dock. I wanted to push my crimson fraternity cap over my eyes, hide behind my three-day-old whiskers and simply fade away—but it was too late.

Despite my normally effervescent public persona, I cherished my private moments and often ducked behind the coat racks in department stores or, into men's rooms to avoid unwanted exchanges. This time the terrain offered no such retreat and I didn't consider the ocean to be a suitable alternative.

Instinctively, I turned it on. The disarming smile, the aura of graciousness but beneath it all, I hated the intrusion. I was on an inward pilgrimage and coveted my seclusion.

"How are you sir?" I reluctantly replied.

"Barkley Taylor, chair of the Ward 5 Democrats, and you don't have to be so formal man. Call me Sarge," he volunteered.

I knew the name, but was not impressed. Despite his age, he was a relatively new player on the scene and as one of the last Black Ward chairs in the city, he was an anomalous by-product of the short lines to leadership created by gentrification. The real players, the gamers, wanted nothing to do with the state party.

Party leadership was no longer an option for African-Americans in much of the city despite the relative impotence of a party apparatus with no legitimate competition. While Democrats ran the city, *individual Democrats* ran the city, leaving the party apparatus as nothing more than a political elevator—and one badly in need of inspection at that. The Democratic State Committee became a surrealistic assemblage of young gamers on their way up politically and wounded warriors on their way down.

Taylor was dressed from head to toe in fashionable black golf attire topped with a Tiger Woods logo'd cap. It was an ensemble that seemed far beyond his sartorial reach.

He advanced with an athletic spring that was surprising for a man who appeared over sixty and inclined toward me slowly, like a cold war spy novel might dictate, as if to share a crucial piece of intelligence.

Thoughtlessly, he maneuvered himself to within a hair of my personal space and I smelled on his breath the inelegant pairing of cheap cigarettes and rotgut whiskey. It gave me a headache.

"Jason, uh, let me, uh ha, ask you something," he said, in that impish, *half talking, half laughing* delivery that black men of a certain age so often employ.

"Yes?"

"You Married?"

"No, but I came close once."

"Well, I hope you brought a little gal up here wit cha because man, I been here for three days and damn if there ain't shit around here to look at." He laughed with the hearty growl of one who'd smoked entirely too many menthols in his life.

He was a soldier, a functionary, not a principal. Someone else called his signals. I'd been trained to notice such things.

Taylor's presence was already an irritant. Because of this encounter, I could assume that the city would know my whereabouts, both friend and foe.

"I'm not planning on being here that long, but you're right, the Vineyard isn't exactly Miami Beach this time of year," I said.

I played along with just enough enthusiasm to make him think I gave a fuck, but not enough to convey any familiarity between us. He might have been a political enemy, one of Terwilliger's guys. How was I to know?

I laughed insincerely. The toss of my head, twinkle in my eye, and flash of my dimples were automatic. They were intuitive mannerisms that had once identified me as a prodigy in the game, but were now, through overuse, cynicism and outright boredom, compelling evidence to me that I was becoming a caricature of myself. I was not yet forty, but I was old in the game.

Taylor grabbed my arm and imposed himself upon me with almost military precision. His quickness was astonishing.

"Look Jason, in all seriousness man, you look like a comer to me; a lot of us think you can get that Council seat next year and then run for Mayor. We've got to stop Callahan, after one term, if he wins."

"Thanks," I said, puffing hard, in a futile attempt to rescue the light on my cigar.

How presumptuous, I thought, to assume that I wanted the headache of a Mayoral campaign, especially when I had not yet won the tough Council race that was to come. *This guy did get in the short line*, I thought.

"You don't call him *DC Four?*" I said.

I really didn't call Dexter Callahan by that name—it was a head fake, a test. To my mind, Callahan didn't deserve endearments like the technocratic politician they called Bow Tie or the political Janus they named Blackberry, but I wanted to keep the man guessing and find out who was calling his signals.

My father always said, "Never let anyone in politics know what you're thinking," a *Godfatherism,* which to my mind added credibility to the message. So, I didn't call Callahan *Four* or *DC Four* or any of those ridiculous variations of his slogan, as if he were my *homeboy* and I was tagging him with a street sounding nickname out of love or respect; no matter how many logo'd hats, tee shirts and short sets he ordered from the city's venerable houses of street fashion: *Madness, Shooters or We R One.*

Callahan was white. An At-Large Councilmember who had been elected in the previous political cycle. He was from Topeka, Kansas—a most inappropriate birthplace for a Mayor of Washington D.C.

"That's some bullshit!" growled Taylor. "That motherfucker been in D.C. all of five minutes, and now he's got all these nicknames and running for Mayor?"

Callahan had run a clever campaign for Council and he was sure to use similar tactics in his Mayoral race. He ran as a faux Black candidate in a field of four authentic ones, doing all the things Black candidates had done by rote for years by copying the *Poker Game's* playbook.

He hosted crab feasts for the seniors, went door to door in Black neighborhoods and he played basketball with the kids. (As a former Kansas Jay Hawk point guard he possessed an effective, if mechanical cross over and predictably, his three pointer was pretty much automatic.) *All white basketball players can hit the three; it's their raison d'être.*

Callahan's record since being on the Council was consistently left of center. He voted with the *east of the river* delegation most of the time, especially in hopeless causes.

He got credit with most Black people and progressives for being on the *right* side of an issue, without ever running the risk of casting the deciding vote on anything that might run afoul of the Board of Trade, the Federal City Council or the newly reactionary D.C. Chamber of Commerce. "Say this for that white boy, he knows how to count votes," Lock had once said in his defense.

Once in office, he'd likely run for Mayor as a mild critic of Terwilliger's conservative reformation even as he benefited from the incumbent's support. He'd repeat his famous line that, "there is no black or white way to pick up trash, or keep water safe to drink, or provide excellent education for all of our children."

He would expand Terwilliger's rightist policies, rapidly accelerating the gentrification that had already begun. Like so many successful politicians before him, he would be a hypocrite.

"So you came here to unwind before the elections?" said Taylor.

"I'm only here for a couple of days," I said non-responsively.

Taylor nodded and eyeing the dock, began needlessly prolonging the conversation.

"You're Greek huh?"

"Kappa, as you can see," I said pointing to my hat. "Morehouse, '84 spring."

"I won't hold that against you he said laughing in mock derision. I'm a Que, Morgan State, fall '65."

"You have my condolences," I said, with a contemptuous grin.

It was always fun to spar with members of rival Black fraternities and Taylor's membership in another *divine nine* organization, added some excitement to our exchange. The members of these historic organizations had done yeoman work in navigating African-American's through the difficult period following slavery but we had vastly dissimilar approaches. We often engaged in good-natured mocking for these differences. It came with the territory.

"Well I've got a few minutes to kill before my wife and her sister get back from Nantucket. I hate it over there, clam chowder and white folk, so I went to Mink Meadows and played nine holes instead," he said with a snicker.

"I haven't played in a while, no time," I said vainly trying to end the conversation. "I've got a new set of *Callaways* gathering dust." I continued.

"I guess you wouldn't have the time, since you're getting ready for a campaign and all. I'll be here for a week, helping my sister-in-law open her house. Maybe we can play at Farm Neck sometime?" He offered.

"I don't know. I didn't bring my clubs and I hate renting them, the feels all wrong. I'm just here to sleep and think really," I said.

126

"Well, hurry back. Day by day we're losing that city. We need you," he said, his muddy eyes fixed on mine.

I thanked him and we shook hands. I walked down the pier and back to my car, lost again in heavy thought. I planned to do some porch drinking, smoke a few cigars and watch the rabbits dash across the lawn at the house on Pequot street.

EIGHT

The Sanctuary

"Certain questions answer themselves by being asked."

Leo Trotsky

Solitude can be blissful, if you like yourself. As an only child, the circumstances of my birth endowed me with the ability to block out the world and all its vexatious inhabitants. I needed those qualities on the Vineyard, to refocus and relax but never more so than then. I took on a quiet intensity then, a somber focus that was more reminiscent of my father than myself. It felt like the end of youth.

After the family viewing, on the day before my mother's funeral, I asked my father, how he was managing. He'd lost so many people in his life and we had both just seen my mother laying dead in her favorite blue Chanel dress.

The decision to bury her in her pearls was mine. She was rarely seen without them.

I kept it simple, as I passed him a flask of cognac in the funeral home limousine. "Are you okay?"

It had to be overwhelming. My mother died at a time when most of his dearest friends, lions of progressive politics, were passing away. Morton Birnbaum at Columbia, Ben Colson, at Lincoln and Guy Mann, at Fisk had all succumb to various illnesses in the previous months; only Lucrezia Hegamin, the cherished grand dame of Black politics, was still around, vibrantly teaching and writing at Spelman at nearly eighty.

"The stress catches up with you. It shows up in strokes and cancer and heart attacks and such." He answered.

According to my father, it was the accumulated stress of living through the sixties. Of vicious beatings and dodging bullets on the front lines of the civil rights movement. Apparently, the sedentary life did little to alleviate the mountain of dread created by having had daily fisticuffs with evil.

"Think about it son, what happens when the greatest thing you'll ever do is over before you reach middle age? Teach, write, go into business? Take it from me, after changing the world, all of those things appear empty."

"But you taught people that went on to do great things. You wrote three books." I said.

"Marriages crumble, friends float in and out of your life and the relative fame born of youthful heroism do not sustain you in the end. It seems only politics has the capacity to complete the soul's itinerary. But even that is elusive, it's predicated, in the main, on pure dumb luck."

"How can you say its luck when you've been getting people elected for 30 years?"

"That's precisely why I *can* say it son. Our political system is based upon a relatively static set of facts. If the facts change, the system fails, and then you're out of luck."

I was becoming depressed by all the talk of lost, lonely men and decided to talk about my impending trip to the Vineyard. I'd always wondered why my parents had never taken me there as a child, when they had gone so regularly before I was born. I had asked both of them many times before and received no satisfactory answers.

"I'm going to ask you again. Why'd you stop going?"

"You don't want to know son," he said dismissively.

"What happened?

"Well," he said, his pipe emerging, as if under its own control, "that is better off left for another time."

As I sat in Oak Bluffs, remembering all of this so near the sea, I felt that somehow this might be just a prelude to much larger truths hidden beneath waves of time. But, I couldn't be concerned with that.

This trip was about regaining the strength required to wage a battle that many thought I couldn't win. It was certainly not about unraveling old family secrets. Secrets killed campaigns and winning would be hard enough without my whinny ruminations.

I was chased off the porch by a storm, which rose suddenly off the Massachusetts coast. Trees swayed as rain began to hit the windows of the house. Inside, the candles, glowed dimly and swayed as if they were a living barometer of my mood.

I liked these moments alone but they would be short lived. Valor was to join me for the weekend and she would arrive on an 8:00 P.M. flight the following night. I would have one night alone to weep, to hurt, to pray, to reminisce and then, hopefully, to begin. Valor would help me sort things out. I would not miss AJ.

She couldn't make the repast, there was a mandatory meeting in Baltimore and she couldn't explain an absence at such a critical time. She said she would be at the meeting and she always kept her word. I was beginning to feel remorseful for being unable to keep mine to her.

Seeing her at the church, stalwart, in her elegant black suit and pearls reminded me of how striking she was—she so reminded me of my mother. Although she was closer to my ideal than any woman that I had known, her tendency to over analyze my behavior and her penchant for non-conformity always seemed to tip the scale against her. Nevertheless, I concluded when she blew me a kiss during my eulogy of my mother, that on some level, I loved her.

The services were more state funeral than *Homegoing Service*. All of my father's *Poker Game* comrades were present as were the elected officials they had elevated to power. Lock Smith, Langston Davis (the election day sound man) and former Councilmembers Frank Wilcox, Al Hubbard and Bob Parker each served as Pallbearers. Prince Hall Masons all, they looked the part in Black suits, white shirts and black ties and their unspoken loyalty was the most impressive thing I had ever seen.

From the day of my mother's death, the men surrounded my father, fed him, anesthetized him with cognac and pipe tobacco; then at the proper time, they doused him with coffee and prepared him for his official duties. The selection of the casket, her burial clothing, and financial settlements fell to me, but I could not have performed my task without my father's silent but steady presence. His comrades stabilized him, enabling him to support me.

After the service, Valor said goodbye as I helped my father into the limousine. The procession was about to begin.

"Hey Diggs, how you holding up?"

"Hanging in there, girlie."

"Did she show up? I didn't see her?"

"No."

"Her mama didn't raise her right."

"I guess not."

I didn't want to have this discussion. My life was complicated enough without

Valor dredging up old memories. But, she had to have her *I told you so moment.*

"Did she at least send a card, flowers?

"No," I said lowering myself into the limo. The air was suddenly warmer than it had been at any point that entire year and I wanted the air conditioner.

"Her ex-fiancée's mother passes and she can't even show up to pay her respects? Aren't you glad you didn't marry that nasty heifer?"

"It's probably for the best Valor, my people aren't very fond of Mrs. Desiree Pitchford Bradford. My mother called her a *loose woman.*" My father remained silent on the matter, which was itself a rebuke.

"Was it any better when she was the future Mrs. Desiree Pitchford Diggs?"

"No, but Valor, I'm actually about to bury my mother. This is not the time."

"I'm sorry Jason, I just can't believe that she wouldn't have come. It's so disrespectful."

"You knew she wouldn't come!" I said, and shut the door. I lowered the window and said, "If I see you on the Vineyard, I don't want to talk about this again!"

"Okay, I'll see you in a few days. I'm sorry." She was contrite which was a rare sight indeed; like my father, Valor Abernathy was always right.

"Goodbye Dr. Diggs," she said to my father. "I am so sorry for your loss."

"Thank you my dear, you're very kind." Said my father.

" Jason, I'll call you later."

As Valor walked away, the procession slowly crawled down D Street and toward my mother's final resting place, the historic Lincoln Cemetery in Suitland, Maryland. As was fitting, she would be buried with the luminaries of Black Washington.

My father was tired and leaned his head against the limousine window.

"What was the meaning of that?"

"Nothing Pop. She can be that way sometimes."

"That's the one you should have married."

I closed my eyes and we rode to the cemetery in silence.

For years I wondered what *would've* happened if I had married Desiree. My mother had always been civil, as was her way, but they never bonded. Ma possessed inbred suspicions about Desiree's background that would not yield.

"You can't trust those people."

"What's wrong with her? She's beautiful, bright, wealthy—not that it matters, and most importantly, she loves me."

"I just don't like her for *you* Jason," she'd say.

There was something about *"those foreigners"* that she was leery of and she kept her distance—even rejecting foreign-born home heath aides, creating an impossible personnel challenge for my father and me. It was an old D.C. thing that had, once upon a time, also applied to people from the Deep South—*"those southerners."*

When my mother was a child, some *colored* D.C. natives railed contemptuously about how they'd *"like to stand at the foot of the 14th Street Bridge and pick those southerners off with rifles as they came across."* Or so the story goes. These sentiments were later modified in deference to reality—the Great African American Northern Migration had left southerners the conspicuous majority among African-Americans in the city. The natives felt threatened.

As brilliant as she was my mother had an uneven record in discerning character. With Desiree, her instincts proved right, while Valor's southern background seemed to disprove the axiom.

"Now, I like that Valor Abernathy. She's sweet." She told me.

"Sweet Ma? Really? She has many redeeming qualities but sweetness is not one that immediately comes to mind."

Valor's assertions at the funeral had their origins in her longstanding feud with Desiree over my time. Thankfully the graveside service took precedence that day or we would have no doubt fallen into our usual pattern—an endless battle of wits where Valor offered evidence of my numerous errors in judgment.

Ironically, it was this pattern that caused me to reject her in the first place. I wanted an intuitive marriage based on love, shared values and complementary talents. One-upmanship would have no place.

I wanted peace. Daily arguments were not included in that calculus. So it was Valor that helped me to define what I didn't want in a woman, ultimately dooming any potential marriage between us.

⸸

I phoned my father on that first night on the Vineyard and found him in his office, immersed in grading essays. He assured me he was fine, but his sagging tone oozed like tar through the receiver. I was concerned that he might never be the same, might never return as the avenging hero of my youth.

I'd moved back into my old room at the Hillcrest house the night Ma died to keep my father company, but his comrades spirited him away each night and it was I that was left alone. Friends called but I refused their visits, choosing instead to smoke cigars, drink up all the single batch bourbon and read from my mother's favorite books, Baldwin and Hurston and Angelou among them. She'd left me a wonderful collection, many of them signed by the authors.

I was entirely focused on my grief. The rage, truth and understanding that I gleaned from my reading were a comfort. It was a week that seemed to exist in the cracks of time.

The repast reset things, re-launched reality and my father and I could again face each other without interference. AJ left the house drunk around nine and I finally went upstairs to find the lights on in every room and my father pacing angrily in his bedroom.

Entering my father's room was like entering a timeless realm. You were instantly transported back to a time when men wore ankle garters and Windsor knots and smelled of Bay Rum.

I'd always been struck by the painstaking way in which he organized himself. Socks and pocket squares neatly folded in drawers, white tee shirts and boxers pressed and ordered according to age.

In the walk-in-closet were his suits from the Georgetown University shop, Raleigh's, Britches of Georgetowne, Brooks Brothers, and J. Press. Like the pre-fusion Miles Davis, my father dressed in a slightly edgy 1960's Ivy League style and was always the most dapper man in the room. He always smelled like Black Cavendish pipe tobacco and *Eau Sauvage*.

"She's in the ground Jason."

"I know." Other words escaped me.

"It's rather anticlimactic, don't you think? A brilliant, beautiful, woman with the soul of a saint, gets stricken with a horrible disability in her prime, becomes progressively more incapacitated, her care becoming the central focus of her small family, and then one day she dies in her sleep. What are we supposed to do with that boy?"

I hated when he called me boy, but I did not argue the point. The words oddly formed a kind of crutch, helping me to bear the weight of the intolerable and unfamiliar territory into which we had crossed.

I broke the silence after what seemed like hours.

"She'd want us to go on Pop," I said, immediately sickened by the disgusting taste of Cole's words in my mouth.

"Oh, Cole tried laying that nonsense on me earlier."

"Yeah, he got to me too. I'm sorry, Pop, it just sort of came out."

"Nothing to worry about son, we're all turned inside out right now. It's hard to reconcile it in your mind. She was sick for so long and did not want to go into a nursing home. Her illness and the fear that it caused her, created a level of myopia. I suppose she never considered the impact it had on *us*. We will never get over this."

My father did say these things but there was no fiercer defender of my mother's honor. For years he juggled the management of home health aides and his work at Howard, limiting his professional advancement in the process. It was my mother's illness that denied him the chairmanship of the Department; he hadn't published in years and served on none of the committees at the university, which led to such things, but he never said a word.

Before I moved out I pulled all nighters to take her to the bathroom or bring her sodas or change the sheets or roll her on her side or find the television remote. Later, when these duties involved dressing her for doctor's appointments or after she had soiled her gown because she could not make it to the bathroom, I knew I had matured. I'd found a strength that was just this side of madness.

This is the duty that breaks your heart, ages you beyond what you ever thought possible. Wisdom resides in that place, understanding far beyond the five senses. Broken hearts have keen perception.

My father took a long drag on his cigar and said, "Do you know what's sad? We have become conditioned to a life we no longer have."

"Like the slaves that wouldn't leave the plantation after receiving news of their freedom."

My father laughed, for the first time in a week. He liked my sardonic wit. He liked to say that it was the only thing about me that reminded him of him.

He was tall and I was of average height. He was ruggedly handsome and I, like my mother, had a softer, some said, cherubic countenance. He was a curmudgeon and I was jaunty. But the wit, we shared in equal measure.

"Exactly right son," he said laughing. "Exactly right!" Then he stopped abruptly and stared despondently into space.

He went to bed at 11 PM, which was still quite early for me. AJ was off in a limo to the VIP section of the Foxtrappe club or some other nightspot, but I was in mourning and family tradition prohibited socializing at such a time. I had few options, if I didn't want to be haunted by the people on the hallway wall.

I hadn't had sex since before my Atlanta trip and the imaginary romp with Valor in my office didn't count. I yearned for female companionship but I didn't feel like debating anymore. I wanted sex in all its simplicity, which meant paying a visit to Liz.

I called her, changed into black jeans and a black polo shirt and was in Alexandria in about 25 minutes. She met me at the door clad only in the faded Howard Law tee shirt that I had given her to sleep in, the night we met. She was the first I'd taken home after Desiree, when the mystical pleasures of drunken sex were all that I desired.

The shirt didn't cover much, which is probably why I'd given it to her. It gathered on her full hips, giving only passing acknowledgement to her butt. To my alcohol strained eyes, she was perfect.

Ignoring protocol, we went directly to bed; her vanilla scented candles burning and smooth jazz on the radio. She offered me a glass of the *Fonseca Bin 27*, which I'd left there sometime the previous winter and except for the three shots I'd had then, it had remained untouched.

I used it creatively, licking the sweet heavy wine from between her shoulder blades and subtle upturn of her ass. When I turned her over, her navel became a tiny loving cup, holding the reserve.

I made love selfishly that night, ferociously bringing her to climax. I slept satisfied, happy that I came.

The next morning the room was adorned in the kind of glorious sunlight that drove night people like me crazy. My eyes fluttered opened and I became aware that I was not in my own bed, but was instead in an unfamiliar King sized contrivance that smelled of port, cheap perfume, and sex.

My mind was slowed by the hard drinking of the previous day and was of almost no aid to me as I tried to determine where I was *this time*. *I have to stop doing this*, I thought. *What if I made a critical mistake, what if the condom slipped?*

Shit. I always feel so badly in the morning. Why can't I just be a friend to these women? But that was no longer possible.

I hurried to the bathroom, got my bearings and at last understood with whom I had spent the night. Liz tilted her head from her pillows and asked plaintively, "where you going baby?" *Home*, I thought, *getting the hell out of here*.

"I'm sorry but I've got to go check on my father and wrap some things up at the house before I leave for Massachusetts."

It was reasonable, kind and terse, my foolproof method for getting out of such prickly situations when the desires of the night were over. It had worked for over a decade.

"You going to miss me baby?"

"Of course," I said from the bathroom, my voice amplified by tiles. "I always do."

"You never come to see me. It's been months since we've been out together." It was a familiar sentiment.

"I know, but Ma was so sick."

"I'm sorry I had to work yesterday Jason. I never got to meet her." Which was by design. I had arranged for only two women to meet my mother in 10 years, Valor and Desiree and after Desiree, I vowed that no one else would, unless she was *the one*.

I emerged from the bathroom relatively refreshed and rushed over to the bed to give Liz a kiss goodbye: form over substance, the flimsy trappings of affection, if not the reality of it.

The sex was always above average with Liz and she sometimes made smoked oyster omelets afterwards, but a woman with only a high school diploma, an Administrative Assistant for the U.S. Department of Energy, would never do for a future Mrs. Jason Diggs. My family's need to rise, one generation above the next, would make such a pairing impracticable.

I was out of Liz's apartment in less than ten minutes, beckoning the elevator door to open before she came into the hall offering coffee and breakfast; and I was quickly in my car. The SAAB was parked on a terribly inconvenient and almost inaccessible back street. Discretion was always a watchword in the often-conjoined worlds of illicit sex and politics.

The tires reported loudly as I plunged my foot to the floor and only the punctuation of black lines, which lay like exclamation points on the street and the musky aroma on Liz's sticky sheets, served as evidence of my presence there. I never saw her again.

NINE
Potomac Apartheid

"In all things that are purely social we can be as separate as the fingers, yet one as the hand in all things essential to mutual progress.

Booker T. Washington, 1895

The June sun tore violently through my bedroom shutters, signaling morning. My eyes stung for lack of sleep and I tightened them in a vain attempt to dampen the pain, which brought forth a tear.

I had been home from the Vineyard for two weeks, recuperating from the excessive rest and beginning to digest the piles of policy material that I needed to master before I announced my candidacy that September. I had already used my bereavement leave and had gone on annual leave for an additional week.

In a few months I would take an unpaid leave of absence—from which I had no intention of returning. A return would mean a

144

loss, an unacceptable outcome for a member of the *Poker Game*.

My calling tugged at me relentlessly during those days, my flesh burning from ambition. In the interest of preserving my sanity, I focused on mundane tasks like going to the cleaners or shopping for groceries at the newly remodeled but ancient Safeway on Kentucky Avenue. Still, the fire was strong and palpable, serving its own mysterious ends.

I didn't have long to master the material. There was the recently passed D.C. budget, Ward 6 neighborhood crime statistics, and position papers on everything from best practices on public service delivery and community based policing to progressive education policy.

I was committed to it. Public policy was a fungible commodity in politics. It was the game of politics itself that was immutable.

Most candidates for City Council in D.C. or anywhere else did not take such a daunting task upon themselves. Rather than becoming subject matter experts on important issues they relied on the amusing sound bite, the well-timed quip and the tawdry artifice of inflated biography; in other words, bullshit.

In this, like so many things, I was different. During my long apprenticeship I had proven myself equal to the task of being both the face and the brain of the campaign. It was time to prove it under live fire.

I had the education and the training to master the issues and the imagination and experience to develop reasonable solutions. I had been in political war rooms my whole life and I had written policy speeches and drafted legislation for successful politicians for a decade.

This was my edge in that campaign, a political birthright; but the little world of D.C. politics had changed since the glory days of the *Poker Game*. Congress had created the District of Columbia Financial Responsibility and Management Assistance Authority in 1996, when the bottom fell out of the city's budget, and imposed an austerity plan that might have made the IMF envious. As a result, many of the traditional political and social foundations of D.C.'s Black community had been incinerated.

Elected leaders in the city were made largely ceremonial and *The Great Man*—the former Mayor, he of the video, my father's friend and greatest disappointment, was reduced to running the recreation department. The elderly, the young and the poor, once the central focus of the city's safety net and the centerpiece of the *Poker Game's* program were dispensable under the Control Board. They were simply left to wither of their own accord. The District of Columbia was being rebuilt on very different grounds.

The policies enacted by the Control Board and its functionaries hastened the exodus of those African-Americans with the financial wherewithal to voluntarily cross the eastern borders of the city into Prince Georges County. Potholes filled the streets and services were reduced to nothing. The Black middle class abandoned the city in search of an aluminum sided Promised Land and

146

Chocolate City succumbed to its own luminescent heat.

Congress promptly created incentives for first time homebuyers to purchase in D.C. and the Control Board ran national TV ads coaxing homesteaders from Middle America to repopulate the city and restore its tax base. It worked and by the time I stood ready to serve my city, our once vaunted Black majority hung on solely through the grit of senior citizens and the presence of the grandchildren they were raising.

"Looks can be deceiving folks. On Election Day, D.C. is becoming a moderate to conservative white city," said Lock Smith during my first campaign meeting. "This ward, nearest the Capitol, has become one of the whitest and most conservative," he continued. "This going to be a hell of a fight." He added.

It was true. In the wake of the fiscal upheaval, D.C. began to appear more like Indianapolis or Phoenix politically than like Atlanta or Detroit. The effect on low and moderate-income residents was devastating.

There was more. African-Americans naively divided their votes among the multitudes of Black candidates, as they had always done in Democratic primaries but with a larger white population and fewer African Americans voting, the white or most conservative candidates usually won. This created an electoral checkmate and by 1998, the majority of the D.C. City Council was both Caucasian and non indigenous to the city.

My candidacy was to be a restoration, an appeal to remaining progressives both Black and White alike, to hold fast to the dream. I targeted families with children in D.C. Public Schools, tattooed Grunge music lovers and the organic food and Birkenstock crew. There weren't many of them.

Some liked me, if only a little condescendingly. They'd wax on for thirty minutes at a time about the critical importance of *cross cultural interaction* and *racial reconciliation*, as if there could be any remaining racial or cultural diversity in a Ward whose present leadership was hell bent on white homogeneity. Under these difficult circumstances, I, like so many before me had to be twice as good.

Damian Patrick Brennan was the first white Councilmember ever elected in my Ward. Like many of the nondescript thousands now overrunning the parks, shops and Bistro's of Capitol Hill, he was a Midwesterner. He had come from Chicago in the mid 1970's to attend graduate school at Georgetown University and never left. He never finished his Master's but got a job with the Feds at the Department of Health, Education and Welfare under Joe Califano.

Brennan met his wife Nancy Ann at the Department and they settled down just blocks from HEW headquarters, on 5th and D Streets, S.E. They had children, were active on the PTA and the neighborhood watch, and he became the Advisory Neighborhood Commissioner for the area immediately surrounding the Capitol—all the while gathering friends and supporters.

Brennan waited patiently until conditions were right. The couple both left the Federal government, to avoid the Hatch Act (the federal government's ban on political activity by its employees). They planned their assent.

He landed an underwhelming middle management post at some national association and his wife, a high paying partnership at a law firm. They even served on *The Great Man's* first Mayoral election committee—*it was all the rage back then, racy, radical—everybody (white) was doing it.* It was *chic* one might say.

It was also smart because it gave them access to the new power structure without being overly obtrusive. In the District of Columbia of the late 1970s they were, in a manner of speaking, invisible.

Vashti Jefferson was the only Councilwoman the Ward had ever known and she was getting older. At seventy she was considered vulnerable. Rayful Edmonds, the biggest drug lord the city had ever seen, was based only blocks from Vashti's home and effectively controlled the neighborhood. Vashti was helpless—anti-crime legislation is no match for AK-47s.

By 1998, *The Hill Dwellers*, a virtually all white community group dedicated to reducing crime and increasing home values was at odds with Vashti over her failure to stop the violence spilling over into Capitol Hill and bring about long awaited increases in their real estate holdings. In spite of their professed liberal leanings the *Dwellers wanted* Nixonian law and order. They wanted their *own* Councilmember.

The dry run was in 1994 when the *Dwellers* successfully elected one of their own, Fran Damon, a single hill staffer newly relocated from Arlington, Virginia, to the faltering Board of Education. It was widely understood that the next time, Brennan would take on Vashti for the Council.

The Democratic primary was a free for all in '98. Ten candidates, only two white, added ballot confusion to the many problems experience by Jefferson. Vashti had had clearly lost a step politically since her heyday in the 70s. No longer the attractive, tough talking middle-aged firebrand, now she was just a little old lady.

With a white unified front, a black campaign manager imported from Ohio and an unusually heavy turnout in the already gentrified precincts of Capitol Hill, Brennan squeaked out victory by a mere 160 votes. It was a political earthquake.

With an unassailable Black majority in place, race had almost never been a factor in D.C. elections. Marion Barry handily won the white vote in his first three elections for Mayor, although by diminishing numbers. Dave Clarke, an ultra-liberal white native Washingtonian, routinely won nearly uncontested citywide elections for Chairman of the City Council. But that was the old order and this was something new, a campaign deliberately designed to turn a city council seat from Black to White.

"Well, I guess I'm retired. The handwriting's on the wall," Lock Smith said to my father and me as we sat in the knotty pine basement. He had been Vashti Jefferson's campaign manager.

"It's *The Plan*...they've started," he said head in hands.

And so they had. It was the first time the *Poker Game* had ever lost an election.

I chose a cream linen suit, white shirt and crimson tie and was out of the house by ten. It was already 90 degrees.

I had an important meeting scheduled at eleven that morning with some community activists from Near Northeast; a sliver of the ward that despite its proximity to the United States Capitol had more of its share of drug related crime. Under Mayor Terwilliger, the neighborhood had seen none of the public investments made in much of the rest of the city.

It incensed me that in some sections of the ward, there were two Starbucks, a large Supermarket (and plans for more), dozens of restaurants and fashionable garden shops but there was nothing of the kind to be found in Near Northeast. Many Senior Citizens were forced to do a week's worth of shopping on the bus or buy their vegetables from the paltry pickings at Murray's Steaks.

"They're starving them out," my father used to say; which was true on many levels. Trash was not picked up and rats ran rampant. Children went missing and the searches would be both clumsy and attenuated.

The intersection of 10th and I, N.E. had the highest murder rate of any intersection in the nation and aside from a few spotlights, deployed courtesy of the D.C. National Guard, there was never resolution. The children were simply gone.

Orwell wrote of "undergoing poverty" as if it was some form of state imposed oppression from above. I don't know about him, but surely the people of Near Northeast were having these conditions imposed upon them. Surely, I thought—as I drove to the meeting with my gourmet coffee—these people were *undergoing* disenfranchisement. I decided that my mantra that morning would simply be: I will *represent* you.

The meeting had been arranged a few days before by Laura Gordon, an Advisory Neighborhood Commissioner representing about a third of the Near Northeast neighborhood. Laura ran her neighborhood with her heart and kept people in line with a mother's toughness. She was a short, prim, fiftyish woman, whose dark skin and precise mannerisms echoed an 18th century schoolmarm. The wire rimmed glasses that she wore perched on the tip of her nose completed the anachronistic visage.

She was the emotional leader of two thousand voters and it was certainly in my interest to court her. For months we'd talked casually about the community, I attended her meetings religiously. Finally, the week before my mother died, I slid delicately into recruitment mode.

"Laura, it's about time for a new Councilmember."

"I know that Jason."

"I'm thinking about running."

"Everybody knows that Jason."

"I can't run without your support."

"Never heard that before."

It had probably never been true before either, but Laura had become a power player, although genuinely unaware of it. Her innocence was remarkable but quite reasonable under the bizarre milieu of our balkanized Ward. Councilmember Brennan had all but ignored her.

"Well, I can't run without you. You're they key to securing a base and since I haven't lived in the ward very long, I need a Rabbi."

"A what?"

"A Rabbi, someone to guide me and vouch for me in the community."

"But—I'm not even Jewish."

We laughed and I reveled in her homespun wit. She was a good lady and wise. One of those ageless, single Black women with hard-pressed hair who, even without formal education are instinctively competent at whatever they do.

"I want you to co-chair my campaign."

"Well of course I'm flattered Jason, but I don't know much about you. I know you're a lawyer and work on Capitol Hill somewhere, used to work for Councilmember Wendell before the Control Board and your daddy is a big time professor at Howard."

"Well, Laura, there's more to it than that. My family has been involved in every election in D.C. since the beginning of home rule."

"I know that Jason, you think I never heard of *Steffawoof* Diggs. You're daddy's almost a legend in this town, him and Lock Smith. What I'm saying is: who are *you* and what are *you* about?" she said.

She was pleased with herself—her chubby face was relaxed and her luminescent eyes assertive. Her eyebrows, thick with eyebrow pencil, rose in Socratic challenge.

"I appreciate what you said about my father," I deferred, "but I need you to understand that I grew up in D.C. politics and I have been involved at a very senior level at a very young age."

I missed on that one. I was too academic, too formal and too arrogant.

"I get all of that, I think you're qualified, that's not my problem. What I want to know is what are you going to do for my community. People are hurting and then here you come offering them something different; only they may not be able to hear you because they've been so hurt by all the other folks who came through here offering something different. What are you going to say to them? What are *you* going to do about that?"

She had a very profound point. I stopped talking and started listening, nodding my head in contrition.

"Know what they're saying about you?"

"They're talking about me?" I said.

"They're saying that you're *bougie*. That you're just one of them rich folk who moved into the ward to be closer to your big job in the Senate and that you won't be able to connect with regular people."

I couldn't believe it. Through my father, I was only a generation removed from abject poverty, so what the hell were they talking about? I was my father's son, I wasn't weak, and I damn sure wasn't a member of the African-American subculture of the city, although I knew and liked most of them socially—the women in particular.

The Subculture had been an entrenched part of Black Washington society since the 13th amendment was ratified. They *were* Black Washington society.

It began with mulattos and house Negroes, who after the civil war mimicked the white elite for whom they worked. Hair texture—straight or wavy; skin color—the lighter the better. In addition, an aquiline nose, thin lips and an education were the keys to entry but as time progressed, wealth or celebrity became a suitable proxy.

The D.C. subculture centered around two institutions, Paul Lawrence Dunbar High School and Howard University. Many who attended these schools established themselves in education, in letters, in medicine and in the law and then went on to world prominence as *credits to their race*. By the 1970's everyone had heard of Benjamin O. Davis, Sr., Dr. Charles Drew, and Sen. Edward Brooke, alumni all.

Black folks with college degrees were successful in pre-civil rights era America; if not in the larger society, certainly in the Black enclaves. It wasn't considered acting white to get good grades and become a professional. It was expected.

Then there were the fraternities, the sororities, the clubs, and the neighborhoods. You could say that by the end of the first World War, huge divisions had been erected between what some considered the dark, uncouth, unschooled, unkempt masses who had migrated from cotton fields and lived in near squalor in alleys and tenements—and the good people of Howard, who had settled in grand townhouses and Federals in places like LeDroit Park and the exclusive pockets of Black wealth near the U street corridor.

Most members of the subculture knew little of the D.C. that I was defending—that I feared would pass from the scene. Aside from the kids that braved the Go-Go's, at the Capitol City Pavilion on Georgia Avenue, known to all as the *Black Hole*, or *The Paragon Too*, on Wisconsin or the *Chapter III*, there was little cause for the subculture to venture beyond their invisible walls of privilege.

While the men seemed empty, gray and effete, the subculture was chock full of beautiful women with intelligence, style and savvy. That one from UVA is married to Congressman this or former undersecretary of HUD that or this lawyer or that doctor and sits on these Boards. The other one from Spelman is Vice President of this Company and has her MBA and PhD degrees from these schools and all the while, the children—alumni of TIKES Day Care Center and duly *Jack and Jilled up*, were backstroking in the primordial soup of the Black elite.

Educationally and socially there had been points of intersection between the subculture and me but there were ideological rifts that would forever distinguish me as an outsider. What a man cherishes dictates his course and what I missed about the city were the simple vulgarities of common life.

D.C. was a city that ran, but not too well, a place that was clean by some urban standards but not excessively so. A place alive with the happy sounds of the dispossessed, the syncopated and entirely African sound of Go-Go music wafting several decibels beyond the legally accepted limits from wreck cars with illegal paper tags. A city where laughter could be heard from the open windows of row houses on hot summer nights, and booty shorts and short sets seen at backyard spades or bid whist tournaments.

A tough environment, where it was commonplace to see armies of hyper-vigilant young men leaving any one of a dozen illegal afterhours spots at sunrise. A city in which the grass field at Anacostia Park could literally catch fire, as if the dancing feet of Black people set it ablaze. Though I wished to improve some of these things because it was time, they remained iconic images that *I* would miss and the subculture would not.

Struggle bids humanity to create and evolve. Hardship challenges people to fashion safety from peril and beauty from painful experience. As the city exchanged my cherished reality for the sterile dystopian one that arrived with the newcomers, more and more I believed that nothing would live there. That nothing of lasting value would be produced except the soulless, malformed spawn of a place irradiated by an alien ideal of perfection. I had to keep these burgeoning thoughts to myself as I began my run for council.

The narrative that Laura described had me all wrong. I wasn't a member of Jack and Jill as a child. That elite bastion of African-American juvenile privilege was a mystery to me.

I had no annual summer treks to Camp Atwater, in Massachusetts. No fond memories of having a first kiss in a pond with Judge so and so's daughter. *I didn't even know if they had a pond.*

In fact, none of the traditional seasoning of the Black elite had been inculcated in me during childhood. My father, Dubois/Robeson Socialist that he was, would have nothing of it. Of course, by college, when I began to understand all the prestige and lifelong friendships and pretty girls that I had missed for the sake of ideological purity, I regretted my lack of commerce with the golden future leaders of *the Race*.

During law school, it seemed that many of these elect of our people had descended into *ne'er-do-well-ism*, living handsomely off of their family reputations but contributing little or nothing to the upward climb of *the Race*. Only then, did I feel secure in the relative egalitarianism of my upbringing—for through it, I had amassed the strength to preserve my family's legacy.

"Who's saying that about me?" I said in a tone which I believed was firm but did not give away my anger."

"No need to get mad Jason, it's what they're saying that's all."

"Who are the they?"

"Brennan's *people*." She whispered.

I was unable to grasp how this Caucasian first term Councilmember who'd played the race card to win a razor thin plurality in a majority Black Ward, could seriously make the assertion that *I* was a gentrifier. And make it stick. He was trying to build and early lead through lies. This was a new politics in D.C.

There where many such meetings with Laura after I came back from the Vineyard and I found out, much to the detriment of my wallet, that Laura loved to eat. We took what amounted to a Zagot tour of every four or five star restaurant on Capitol Hill, severely damaging my credit limit. But by the end of May, after scores of lunches and dinners, I convinced Laura that I was the only person capable of waging what had become an inevitable war for her community.

At the end of our last dinner meeting at *Charlie Palmer's*, she finally admitted that she had been with me all along and just wanted to watch me make the arguments and display the compassion that would be necessary to sway her people.

"You're a good man Jason and you're head and shoulder's above Brennan. He hasn't been in my neighborhood for a year—stay's over there on the Hill." She said pointing up the hill at the Capitol.

"So, you're on board?"

"Been on board. You didn't know?" I did not; I hadn't pierced her earthy veneer.

The 11 o'clock meeting was to be my coming out party, a gathering of Laura's inner circle plus a few from across the Ward that I had been cultivating, like Kelly Veney a bright young teacher from Southwest who was active in the teacher's union. Derrick Watkins like Laura, was from Near Northeast and Larry Reed a retired D.C. government worker from the treacherous Rosedale area, near Benning Road.

It was a team of regular people. native Washingtonians, citizens, who had tragically and inexplicably, become outsiders in their own community. Adding the *Poker Game* to a group like this would make a potent mixture, I thought. Teeming aggrieved masses led by an intrepid intelligentsia had always been at the vanguard of a successful revolution or so my father taught me.

160

BOOK TWO

TEN

HOPE RUNS

Hope is the worst of evils, for it prolongs the torments of man.

Friedrich Nietzsche

T he arc of history can be disorienting. By the 1980s, the local political structure that my father had played such a pivotal role in creating, was crumbling from the weight of its own success. I emerged into manhood during these troubling times.

So much had changed since I left D.C. for Morehouse College but I hardly noticed. Like all college students I was self-absorbed. The focused escapism of Homecoming pageants in King chapel and my low budget dates with beautiful Spelman women were my priorities.

Student government elections held my attention, not Council races in D.C. I couldn't see my future ending.

While I gorged on stuffed pizza at *Upper Crust*, drank unlikely frozen concoctions at *Fat Tuesdays* and partied till the wee hours at the *Excelsior Mill*, the first mini mansions of P.G. County were under construction. Aluminum sided split levels and town houses in places like Tantallon and Lake Arbor began wooing young professionals away from the crime ridden and infrastructure deprived neighborhoods. Tax revenue was beginning to wane as a result of the exodus and the city was on a respirator.

In the vacuum, an invasion was begun. But, I was oblivious in my college cocoon, dancing to Go-Go on a box at the first *Freaknik*. Stepping so, so smoothly on Spelman's campus. *Running the yard*.

"I liked segregation—," my uncle Joe (my mother's brother) famously said in the late seventies at one of my parent's barbecues. "—White folks knew their place." All of us laughed, but the adults did so wistfully, understanding both the irony and the pain in his words.

His comments were prescient because the '80s brought a white incursion; which began with real estate speculation in depressed neighborhoods and a growing immigrant population, which ballooned as a result of proxy wars, induced famine and staged unrest throughout the world. New people slowly took a stake in the future of D.C. as well as laying claim to the past.

The Ethiopians walked with a street toughness that rivaled what one might see in the deepest corners of Southeast. Even the most hardened thug from the projects of

164

Simple City, Barry Farms or Condon Terrace might be obliged to grudgingly tilt his head in acknowledgement of their swagger. African but influenced by Italian occupation, they wore their capacity for brutality, with élan. U Street was not yet theirs, but it was certainly no longer ours.

Koreans cornered the market on corner stores, Salvadorans owned the world of construction and building maintenance, West Africans and Indians were flooding into the professional schools at Howard but seemed to resent the sweat equity stake that African-Americans had in the United States even as they belittled us a slaves. East Africans established a death grip on the parking operations in town—a gold mine in a smallish congested city without municipal parking lots.

Then came the whites, pouring in like ice water after a spring thaw, crashing into old neighborhoods, which had fallen on hard times. They quickly enveloped nearly everything in sight.

First the gays, brave urban pioneers that they are—always the shock troops of gentrification. Then came the eager young settlers with their bird dogs, running shoes and their luxurious Maclaren double strollers—demanding special attention and accountability from a government that had never countenanced their arrival in the first place.

By the late nineties, the economic became the political and long-term status in D.C. was no longer valued in the halls of power. Native Washingtonians becoming pariahs and people who had come to the city a

165

day before, stood a better chance of landing a high paying government job or being appointed to a Board or Commission.

But, in the eighties D.C. had yet to succumb to its wounds. It was rife with broken glass and graffiti—with the arcane, *Cool Disco Dan,* spray painted all over town. Suzuki Samurais dominated the entry-level drug congested streets and Nissan Pathfinders hugged the middle ground.

There were the first tentative sightings of the newly urbanized Timberland boots. Mini dresses were back in fashion along with fades and waves and asymmetrical hairdos. *Riverfest* was the place to be, Black boaters cruising in the channel shirtless, adorned in various lengths of gold chains, the masses downing succulent crabs and barbecue grooving to smooth funky music and *The Great Man* himself, holding forth at the Chanel Inn like a modern day Pasha in a Captains hat, an open collar and a three piece suit.

There was much to recommend D.C. before the fall. Sugar Ray was the victorious hometown boy made good, there was the sheer comedy of the Bullets' endless losing streak countered by those joyous Sundays when the Redskins won and won and won. D.C. pride was at its zenith.

There was a Black Super Bowl quarterback, Black D.C. Council, Black Judges and a Black Mayor. How fitting for our Black city. As we might have said then in classic

D.C. style, *we were the most thorough city in the world; we was tight like that youngin.*

The summer of 1985 was a wonder. I had a freshly inked college degree from one of the most prestigious institutions in America. Morehouse had produced Dr. King, Julian Bond and Maynard Jackson and it had now produced me. Howard Law School was now to become the platform for the life I had chosen.

I wanted to be a Senator, a tough task for a kid from a city without congressional voting representation. It was a lofty goal, even by *my* Olympian standards, but in those days I specialized in lofty. I had won the Presidency of the Morehouse Student government on themes, which echoed both King and Kennedy and I governed as I imaged Malcolm and Mandela would, if they'd had the chance.

On a college with less than 3000 students, that was fairly lofty, but my alma mater was the ideal proving ground for me to practice the progressive politics that I had learned in my father's knotty pine den.

I planned to further perfect the formula and unleash it on an unsuspecting city when the recipe was right. My confidence in my inevitable success was on a par with the knowledge that there are 24 hours in a day and that the sun rises in the east. Certainty is often the first casualty.

I entered Howard Law exited about the intellectual ordinance to be acquired for the battles to come. I had studied ancient leaders; Philosopher Kings ruled the world and warrior poets defended it. I wanted to govern that way.

Alexander studied under Aristotle. *The pure warrior has first trained his mind.*

I walked in awe among the portraits lining the walls of Howard Law, of the legendary men and women that built the law school into an academy of liberation for a people and a nation. I would be there soon enough.

I was happy to be back home and debated my father for the sport of it, a young lion challenging for leadership of the pride. It was an opportunity to sharpen my fangs.

"This is an anti-intellectual era," my father would opine.

"But as it is my era, it's one that I fully embrace." I would counter.

"It certainly is yours but it is historically inadequate for the social progress that must be made," he would say.

"Is that more Marxist dogma Pop, or is that how you really feel?"

"I am not under the spell of Marxism son, it has proven as flawed a system as all the rest, but I am clear on the existence of an arc of history. This era contributes nothing, though it may be a bridge to another that will. I believe that we're resting as a people. After a tumultuous century, I think we are all just tired."

"Those of us who weren't around for all that marching aren't tired. We're just trying to interpret things for our time, planning the next move." I said this, but I honestly didn't know. Most of my peers were apathetic or selfish. To them, I was a radical.

My father had long resisted the entreaties of his friends to enter government. He refused to run, even though the Poker Game had offered him the Council Chairman position. He refused, even more vigorously, the chance to become the Mayor's political General Assistant or the more administrative position of Chief of Staff.

"Why the hell would I do that, I'd only become a creature of the Mayor and give up my role as his friend. I have more clout outside the government than I would inside and I am not constrained by any conflicts of interest. I'd be a staffer for God's sake and subject to MB's whims. I'm familiar with that man's capriciousness, his narcissism and the last thing I would ever want to be is subject to them. "

As committed as he was to the life of the mind, he was without question a man of action. He had transferred his athletic confidence to politics and the academy—and made a niche for himself in the altered reality of the smoked filled room. In all of these places, he dominated.

My father wore his authority gracefully, as if born to it; and he was. The dirty D.C. streets from which he emerged gave him an intrinsic understanding of the city that even the transplanted civil rights veterans in the *Poker Game*, lacked.

He wrote like an 18th century Philosophe and drove bargains like a twentieth century Mafioso. He was the arch protector of those with weaker minds. Many within the *Poker Game* thought that it was he that should have been Mayor, but my father voted him against himself on the night the matter was decided by the Poker Game's Executive Council.

To be raised by such a man was a privilege. He never fawned over me; he simply presented himself as he was and expected me to have the wisdom to heed his call. I intuitively understood what was to be gained.

There were no conflicts, even in my adolescence. I would never dare to break ranks with such a man as he. In meetings, his stare alone could break the strongest of men.

Steppenwolf Diggs remained his own man, but his lack of official status presented a dilemma. He couldn't directly affect the policies enacted by the politicians that he brought to power. Two of his former students were on the Council and four more individuals owed him their seats, but once there, they often abandoned their earlier stated goals, tilting, as politicians often do, more in the direction of heavy hitting contributors and lobbyists than toward his sage (and usually spot on) advise.

This hurt him terribly. He despised the perks that were showered upon him; the low numbered tags, the exclusive tickets to

170

sporting events and lavish parties. He saw them as affronts, when he could no longer get a bill passed by the late nineties. Yet, he looked at the situation philosophically, the way he looked at just about everything else.

"That's politics," he would say, shrugging his gargantuan shoulders. "Most politicians have a healthy dose of hubris. They do what they want to do and rarely what people need them to do."

Nevertheless, he continued to help the ungrateful lot. "Can you imagine the alternative? We still have the city, so we still have hope."

The best form of hope comes from having a tragic sensibility; from that vantage point, hope is all that's left. So it would be left to me to mine that well of hope in the midst of the impending political turmoil. I was determined to use both my head and my heart when I got my chance to lead.

Law school was the first milestone in that quest and my first year began with the usual core subjects that are known to most through television and movies. They were subjects, which make or break you as a law student: *Contracts, Torts, Property, Civil Procedure and Criminal Law*, the red meat of law school.

There, at the peak of my educational pursuits, I soon discovered that law school was awash with smart, attractive, sexually available women. It was in that environment that Valor argued herself into my life.

Evelyn Birch was a 2nd year student from North Carolina. A woman more provocative than pretty, she was giving remarks to my first year class perched on a professor's desk, her legs seductively crossed in purple spandex tights when she uttered the words that sent shockwaves throughout the school.

"There are a plethora of sexual opportunities to be had here at the law school," Evelyn said to a surprised audience. "I urge all of you to take advantage of them." She drawled. *Rumor had it that she had significant experience in the matter.*

Very soon I was following her advice. The Rathskeller was a sub-basement in Houston Hall that was located right off the small but serviceable law school cafeteria. It served as student lounge, temporary sleeping quarters and the center of political debate and trash talking. It was also a place where love could blossom, if only to get through final exams.

I saw Valor for the first time in the Rathskeller or *the Rat* as we called it then, deeply in discussion on the subject of an arcane principle in torts, known as intentional infliction of emotional distress. She was arguing the merits of such a cause of action in a wildly imagined fact pattern and Jerry Betancourt was the unfortunate soul on the other end of the debate.

Valor had him from the start. I watched her entangle the poor fellow in his own argument and like an anaconda, crush him without mercy. Law Students can be far crueler than fourth graders in a playground brawl and laughter rang throughout the room.

She was from Atlanta, a Pitt graduate, and irascible as a motherfucker. I was as enraptured by her logic as I was her beauty and within weeks we were both study group partners and lovers. I wasn't one to pass up such opportunities.

"I like you Diggs, you take yourself seriously but not too much so."

"I like you too, Valor. You have a lot of spirit."

"You know what I really like about you?" she said.

"What's that?"

"You haven't tried to get me yet."

"Tried to *get* you?"

"Yeah, get the goodies."

"I've certainly thought about it."

"What have you thought, exactly?"

"That it would be nice."

"It would be nice."

"Think so?"

"I'm certain of it. You're just my type. No Jheri Curl, nice dresser, cute, bright, funny."

"Why didn't you say something before? And by the way, I haven't seen *any* Jheri Curls here at the law school."

"And thank God for that. But Jason, I wanted to see if you would try to ruin it by *bum-rushing* me. You had the good sense to take it slow."

"I didn't want to kill our friendship, that's the most important thing, wouldn't you say?

"That's sweet Diggs."

"Yeah, I can wait. I have three years to get that ass."

"Goddamn men. I knew you couldn't hold it." We shared a laugh.

That night, when I dropped her at The Woodner Apartments, one of those large affairs on 16th Street, she invited me up for a drink. The wine wasn't even half gone by the time we found ourselves in her bed.

She was an astonishing lover, the smart women usually are. Sex had been a mechanical act of conquest before Valor, but after that night it was like life itself. I couldn't imagine how I had missed out.

With AJ playing pro ball on the west coast, I was without the counterweight to those old conservative habits that I fell into so easily. Valor became that counterbalance. Her irritability prevented desire from turning into love, but with sex, law and a love of politics in common there were no complaints.

It went along like this for the rest of our first year of law school and through half of the second. It was an open relationship, which gave me a freedom that most men dream of but I generally chose not to stray.

I had all I needed, a study partner, a friend to have a beer with after class and a ferocious and beautiful lover that did not cling. If I wanted to go out clubbing with some of my Frat brothers or to a Redskins

174

game, Valor never dissented—she had her own life beyond me, until I met Desiree.

Valor and I were enjoying a break between classes at the *Vie de France* cafe on Connecticut Avenue, when I told her. I'm not sure why I did; perhaps I wanted to test the limits of my freedom. It was a fateful decision.

"I met somebody last night."

"Who?" She was in the middle of devouring a cheese croissant."

"A woman, of course."

"I'm not enough for you?"

"We're just buddies."

"We weren't just buddies on Saturday night or all the other times. Shit, I'm still sore," she said mischievously.

"You know what I mean. We don't have a romantic relationship. We just sort of *get together*."

"It's good though right? You *do* appear to enjoy it."

"Sure, but whenever we've discussed formalizing our relationship, you tell me that *we're just special friends, that you want to keep it loose*."

"Yeah but that doesn't mean I want you sleeping with other women."

"That's a rather unreasonable position don't you think?"

"It all depends."

"On what?"

"On the kind of relationship you want with these other women. Sexual relationships can get complicated."

"Ours isn't."

"Until *now*," she protested.

"You know I want to start a family early since my parents did it so late. I guess I feel an obligation to let them see their grandchildren since I never met my grandparents."

"How does that affect what we're doing?"

"I'll never settle down if people think I go with Valor Abernathy. You intimidate the hell out of most women. Whenever I go out with someone and they find out about you, they immediately want me to clarify details of our association. It's just not sustainable. I can't let you have your cake and eat it too."

"You have for a year and a half." She said with a smirk.

"So, you've been getting over on me?"

"Not in so many words, but you're safe Jason. I want to keep you that way."

"I don't think I like being considered safe. Safe from what?"

"From yourself."

We argued for hours, only breaking periodically for class. I made it clear that I was going to continue to see this, as yet unnamed woman, and that Valor was free to do what she wanted. From that moment on, Valor's detested the very concept of Desiree.

176

ELEVEN

The Viceroy

"If by the mere force of numbers a majority should deprive a minority of any clearly written constitutional right, it might, in a moral point of view, justify revolution"

Abraham Lincoln

There's nothing like the swagger of an old Black man. It's a strut that says he has survived a world that was dead set against him. His bravado, rooted in that understanding, is worn as comfortably and proudly as an old baseball cap. Lock Smith was such a man.

To the average person walking through the streets of D.C., Lock might have appeared to be just another slouchy old Black man. But, those in the game knew him to be the Viceroy of a dynasty.

He was an irascible, cigar chomping, scotch swigging cherub of a man and I loved him. It was affection like one has for a favorite uncle, love in the way men revere mentors who guided their path to manhood.

Lock had always been part of the family. He'd been an older student, a 25-year-old engineering student at Howard, who'd taken my father's Political Science 101 class as an elective. Soon my father began to advise Lock and his friends in the Nonviolent Action Group, which had begun pushing civil rights issues on campus and throughout the city.

Through that association, my father became a faculty observer in Raleigh on that fated Easter weekend in 1960, when Martin Luther King, James Lawson and Ella Baker spoke of transforming the social structure of the South. SNCC was born that weekend and by the end of 1961 the freedom rides had pushed the struggle to a fever pitch.

The carcasses of burned out buses on the side of the road were stark evidence of the violent reaction by the racist south. Lock, like most of the NAG group members, including his associate Stokely Carmichael, quickly got swept into the struggle. Lock left school, moved to Atlanta and ended up along with Lonnie King, Ruby Doris Smith and Julian Bond, becoming a fixture at the SNCC office led by James Forman. It was there that he learned the organizing techniques that he would employ for the rest of his life.

My father became an important advisor and wordsmith within the movement, joining Howard Zinn of Spelman and Robert Brisbane of Morehouse as academic advisors to SNCC. He had assisted SNCC president John Lewis in the composition of his original speech at the March on Washington in 1963—

the controversial speech Lewis was convinced not to give.

This was dangerous work. The Howard administration was reasonably concerned about protecting its unique status as a Federally chartered university.

It was on the basis of his forty-year friendship with my father that I went to see him in the spring of 2000. I was going to tell him that I running in the upcoming Ward 6 Council race.

Lock lived at 13th and Taylor Street, in a semi-detached row house in the Brookland section of Northeast Washington. Bordered by an alley, the house stood as a monument to an old way of life, of a time when people weren't digitized but were smarter, smaller, and more frugal. It was made for him.

Brookland was a quiet garden filled neighborhood near the center of the city and was anchored by Catholic University and a working class spirit. It looked much as it had for my entire life, solid, steady and still, despite a few recent incursions by newcomers, predominantly Black.

I arrived to find the house, as it appeared when I was a child, a wreck. The porch still had lawn signs stacked upon it from a campaign two years before. Inside, the house was cluttered with loose papers and stacks of books and its walls were adorned with the campaign posters from his many victories: Julian Bond in 1965, Richard Hatcher in 1967, Marion Barry in 1978,'82,'86, and '94 and even the Presidential campaigns of Shirley

Chisholm in '72 and Jesse Jackson in '84 and '88.

In the corner of his tiny living room rested a small desk, which held the same typewriter that once pumped out press releases and policy statements going back to the days of SNCC. On the floor there lay thousands of yellowing pages, which he hoped would one day congeal into his memoirs. *Opening Doors by Lock Smith* was his working title.

Lock was single, "a mistake of history," he always said. He'd followed Stokely into the Panthers when their new harder line broke SNCC apart and then toured revolutionary capitals as his emissary.

Sporting his leather jacket and beret, he went to Cuba and later Algiers, where he met and befriended the exiles Robert Williams (with whom he talked strategy and smoked cigars) and Eldrige Cleaver. Like Malcolm X, the CIA likely tracked his movements abroad.

Somewhere along the line he had taken the first of two African wives; Cherotich Murumba, a Kenyan—but the marriage didn't last. "I was too damned American, she was too damned African and the marriage was just damned," he always said. "But my God Jason, that woman could fuck."

In the early 1970's he had gone to Guinea Bissau to meet Amilcar Cabral, the leader of the revolutionary movement against the Portuguese and returned there many times, finally taking another wife, Ana Maria *something*, a beautiful Cape Verdean. Ana Maria had long black hair with skin the color

180

of cardamom. She had the most surprising blue eyes.

A picture of Ana Maria backed by a sea as blue as her eyes still hung in his bedroom. "She died too young," he told me when I had asked about the *pretty lady* as a child.

"Lock I'm running." I announced, shortly after my arrival at his house.

"From whom?"

He laughed from his considerable belly and walked to the refrigerator retrieving two gigantic bottles of *Tusker*, a Kenyan beer.

"You know what I mean," I said, pressing ahead.

"Yeah, I know but what I don't know is why you would ever want to do something like *that*. You're a young, good-looking kid. You got a good job, making a little bread, got all them young gals you run around with. Shit, why would you want to jump into a hell pit like that?"

"You know why. It's what I've always wanted to do and it's partially your fault. I think I can help the city to --"

"Help yourself Jason! You don't want to end up like me or some of the other brothers do you?" he interrupted. I knew to whom he was referring. Anyone would.

"What do you mean? You're fine and you've probably got close to a million dollars stashed in Africa somewhere from all the campaigns you've run over the years. You must. You live like a pauper here and don't spend any money."

"Do you see a beautiful woman here, making my meals, massaging my feet or reciting French Socialist poetry?"

Most of the women I dated were devoted careerists with BMWs who rarely cooked and didn't read anything beyond Lucky or the Oprah's magazine. Desiree and Valor were the only two exceptions but even *they* didn't recite French Socialist poetry.

"No," I continued, "but you could have gotten married again," I said.

"Don't get me wrong, I have lady friends, but I wish I could have had children. You don't want to end up like that." He said wistfully.

"How would I end up like that simply by running for office?"

"Politics is like a beast from hell. It feeds on itself and consumes everything around it. It'll consume you too if you let it and the worst thing is that you don't know its happening to you until its over. You'll look at yourself one morning and you're bald, forty pounds overweight, have permanent circles under your eyes and a hangover that never goes away."

I just looked at him unable to believe what I was hearing. This was a lion of D.C. politics, of Black politics that was going on like this. It certainly wasn't the answer I'd come for. I expected unqualified support from my father's oldest friend but instead received only sour discourse on the perils of electoral politics.

"Jason," he continued, "what I've learned in forty years is that this life is for people that are in need of something. The reluctant politician is a thing of the past. Statesmanship is over. This is a time of avaricious leaders who are nothing more than gatekeepers for that old political beast.

They get a few scraps from what the beast leaves over and are happy with that. It completes them, adds credibility to their goddamn mediocrity. You're *not* average, what do you need? You should do something with your life like your father and mother did. Raise a family. Take vacations to that beach on Martha's Vineyard that you like so much. Just live, man. Live your life."

"I've already decided Lock. I just wanted to know if you're with me?"

"Now, I'm *always* going to be with you, you know that. You're a *poker player* now, so I have no choice in the matter. I'm just giving you my best advice. I saw what it did to our dear friend; the addictions, women, power— you think you're impervious to all of that?"

I started to joke. "Well the women, not so much—but the other stuff..." He didn't laugh.

"It only gets worse once you're in there Jason. It gets easier all around, that's what that old beast does; it seduces you, breaks you down."

"I can handle it."

"I hope so."

I understood his point. Politics did cater to a life of excess. There were dinners and fundraisers and parties and women and hotels and after parties and the unprincipled, custom suited lobbyists ready to satisfy every desire. You had to be superhuman and learn to focus in an environment in which it was impossible to do so.

As a council staffer, I had already been wined and dined by those eager Ferragamo clad lobbyists in the finest restaurants in the city. On a nightly basis it was *The Palm, Morton's, Capitol Grille, The Prime Rib*— wherever I wanted to go. Bottles of the finest wine flowed all night; Cabernet, Petite Syrah, the finest scotches—whatever I wanted.

Then the ladies would arrive for after dinner drinks. *I hadn't seen them on the menu.* Followed by lounge hoping until late into the evening. For my trouble, I gained a raging hangover the next day, as I prepared for budget meetings or the Council's legislative session.

I knew what Lock was saying was true, but I was in control. I had a calling. "I can handle it Lock and I need you."

"Okay, then you got me."

I left that day both energized and a little chastened. Perhaps it was a congenital weakness instead of a calling, a defect of the blood.

Call it false heroism, a need to lead lost causes, epic quests eternally doomed to failure, an inability to master the mundane, a short attention span even as I reigned over the broad and complex. This was a curse, not a calling.

My mother had always handled things for us. Paying bills, shopping, picking up dry-cleaning. After her illness, life disintegrated. DISINTEGRATED. Millions of details became a maelstrom that couldn't be tamed, at least not by me.

Valor might have been right. I should have been an academic and kept the family tradition; or perhaps a writer pontificating on my ideas but I would have rather pontificated from the floor of the Senate than in some book any time. I had to be in the thick of things.

I could have been a journalist or a litigator, but I wanted to make news and write new law, rather than simply reporting or practicing it. I thought I'd be forgotten if I failed and above all, I did not want to be forgotten.

TWELVE
Before The Storm

"you have set up
a colorful table
calling it life and
asked me to your feast
but punish me if
i enjoy myself
what tyranny is this"

Rumi

With my mother's death occurring near the end of the semester at Howard, my father had some time to gather himself before my campaign. Lock pulled double duty as my campaign manager and as organizer of the *Poker Game*, which had resumed weekly meetings for the first time in nearly twenty years. I was about to regularly enjoy the advice of the most seasoned political minds in town.

"We'll bring you in when we finish the campaign plan," my father said just after I'd returned from the Vineyard. "Just work the community, get yourself out there."

186

He had become something of a recluse the summer before I announced. I couldn't get him on the golf course anymore, not that I had time myself and although we used to go to dinner once every few weeks at one of the cigar friendly restaurants in town, he refused my invitations insisting, "candidates don't go to dinner, they work the streets and eat bad takeout."

In mid-August, I finally succeeded in getting him to go to *Les Halles* for a late dinner and cigars. I enjoyed sitting outside facing the old Post Office on Pennsylvania Avenue. It reminded me of my childhood explorations of downtown with my mother.

I voiced my concern as soon as we were seated and our menus were in hand.

"What's up Pop? I haven't seen you in weeks."

"Which was by design. You should be working that Ward like I told you. I'm pulling things together for you on my end, there's no need to worry about *that*."

"There's more to it than that." I said flatly.

"Well, I am having trouble with some of the usual donors. They don't seem to think that they need to support us anymore now that the place seems to be under new management. Even our old friend Dr. Thurman is starting to equivocate."

"I'm not talking politics Pop, I'm talking about you. The family's worried and they're all calling me. Nobody's seen you."

"I'm alright, I just needed some time alone in that old house. The walls have memories; we were simply sharing a few anecdotes about Rachel."

"Don't tell anyone else that, they might try to put you in St. Elizabeth's."

"They could try," he said ominously.

We talked for a while and I became convinced that while my father wasn't as fit as he reported, he was certainly better off than I had expected. After a time, the conversation drifted, as it inevitably did, back to politics.

"Remember how Terwilliger won last time and didn't even have enough petition signatures to make the ballot."

"Yeah, I guess those things happen if you don't have any real local base of political support to help you get the names on the page. It would be like if Jacques Chirac had to get signatures from the people in St. Martin, way out there in the Caribbean, in order to continue running that Island—hell, he's probably never even been there."

My father looked up from his menu and said, "Son, that's the heart of the argument against colonialism, whether it's here, in St. Martin or any other place in the world. Terwilliger still needs a map to get around and he's been Mayor for two terms already. Without his security detail, he'd be asking for directions all over town—and he calls himself a Mayor. Without an organic base of political support, an incumbent Mayor forced to run for reelection as a write in. How pathetic and how telling."

"Yeah I remember when he first got elected and he thought that the Brookland neighborhood in D.C. was Brooklyn, New York instead of Ward 5. He even tried to crack one of his dry ass jokes about his *jurisdiction not extending that far.*" I added.

"It was an embarrassment to the whole city that we could have elected such a person. These technocrats or whatever they want to call themselves, make the simple things seem so hard. Blasted city planners and transportation experts trying to run a city? At a minimum you should *know* the city that you purport to govern."

This is why I revered my father, his unwavering heart for the common people, for justice. He always taught me that authentic leadership is about being the living embodiment of the people that you seek to represent.

He once held out a bold example to demonstrate his point on a magical late summer evening at my Aunt Sara's place in *Highland Beach.* Highland Beach had always been a magical place to me. For years I was transported *downthebeach*, as I called it, my no speed bicycle carried lovingly in the hold of my father's black 280 SEL.

The city boy was transformed *downthebeach.* I caught tadpoles there and learned to swim, rode mini-bikes, went crabbing and even chased young girls. I was folded into the flanks of my cousins like a fourth brother. I was the youngest brother, the slightest, more bookish brother, but a brother nonetheless and that was the magic.

189

Just before I left for my senior year of college and my term as Student Government President I had driven to Highland Beach to say goodbye to my parents, who were *downthebeach* for a week.

"Be like Gandhi son," my father said. *"Although he was an accomplished barrister, he had the courage to lose his frock coat, spats and British affect and proceed in swaddling clothes for the rest of his life. In him, the people saw an idealized version of themselves."*

I drove to Atlanta with that image in my mind. I had already finished my course requirements for my political science degree and so I recognized what my father said in the way La Guardia embodied depression era New York in all its toughness, pride and pain. I realized that I'd already experienced it in the way *The Great Man* led D.C. with solicitude and savvy, daring, and verve with my father and the rest of the *Poker Game* smiling approvingly off stage.

"This is how a true leader comports himself," said my father those many years ago by the Bay, *"and he never asks anybody for permission to lead."*

"May I offer you some wine with your dinner?" said the waitress. I didn't see her approach but there she was standing attentively in an apron. She was blonde and judging from her accent, it was quite possible that she was actually French.

190

"A bottle of the *Gigondas*." I responded. Red wine on such a warm night was not the usual thing to do, but I knew my father. Like some medieval King, he only drank red wine and cognac.

"*Gigondas*. Yes sir. I will return in a moment."

She turned abruptly and I watched her little butt twitch vigorously as she walked away in Levi's. I seem to remember the stings from her apron moving out of sequence with her cadence.

"You should stop doing that," my father said.

"I can't *look*?"

"No," he said calmly. "They still love to play that *he's after our women* crap on our young men," he continued.

"I'm just looking Pop, things *have* changed a *little* since the fifties and sixties."

"Less than you think son. The sexual terror routine still works but they only pull it out when they really need it. It's a Hail Mary."

"I'm not officially running yet." It was a few weeks before my announcement.

"Yes but you'd better believe they're watching you already, believe that. According to me, what are the five words of political awareness?"

"Come on Pop."

"Indulge me."

"Alright, power concedes nothing without a demand, Frederick Douglass."

"That's right! And there is magic in those words. I need you to rid yourself of optimism son. Realism empowered our people before and it's the only way we'll get it back."

"What are you saying exactly?"

"I am saying that these people waited and planned 30 years for this moment. They finally have the power and they are disinclined to give it back. They won't give it up because you're smart, or because you're well educated or because you have a winning smile. They won't give it up for anything because this has become tribal. You aren't one of them and you never will be—unless they make you into a sycophant."

"So you think this thing is entirely racial? I mean, there *are* still Black people on the Council; and what about the Black folks on the Federal City Council and the Board of Trade?"

"Black elected officials only represent the Wards that *they* can't win yet and the remaining Blacks in those other organizations are merely ornamental—they're powerless."

He had a pained expression, on his face and was clearly burdened by what he knew. He loosened his tie and regarded me over the top of his new wire rimmed glasses. He was beginning to look his age.

"The people running this *thing* aren't afraid of us anymore. We can't disrupt their meetings like Marion and Lock used to do in the seventies or block streets with a couple thousand people like in the old days. Rank in file white voters, *are* afraid and they'll use that against us in every campaign from here on out."

He was referring to *The Plan*; the ancient bugaboo that had haunted the good Black citizens Washington for decades. The abbreviated version went like this: *one day in the future, it would come to pass that the whites will take the city back; permanently disenfranchising and displacing Black folk in the process and returning them to servitude.* But, far from a horror story—it was now a public policy initiative.

How do you change a city from Black to white when the Blacks own the dirt? In D.C., it was done through a subtle change in tax policy.

Property taxes had been calculated on a triennial basis for decades in the District of Columbia, which meant that any incremental increase in property values would not be reflected in the tax assessment for three years. Homeowners relied on this system and had budgeted their lives around it for years.

But at the start of the new millennium, when whites flooded into the city enticed by a national marketing campaign, backed up by gratuitous tax breaks for transplants, a rash of condo development resulted, which rapidly increased property values in the targeted neighborhoods. The City Council, at the urging of its most senior white member, seized on this and voted to annualize property tax assessments. They wanted to cash in now.

The natural result was that long term residents, especially senior citizens living in the most desirable neighborhoods for speculators, were instantly hit with up to 100% increases in their property taxes. Most were unable to pay them.

Some immediately lost their homes. Others succumbed to predatory lenders and lost their homes to foreclosure when the usurious balloon payments came due. Black bastions like Columbia Heights, Capitol Hill and Shaw plummeted in population and *the Plan* had its first casualties. A vacuum was created and whites rushed into the breech.

"Do you think Brennan will get the signatures?" I asked.

"Naturally, he has precinct 89. He can get all he needs in that one precinct in two or three days. They all sit at home listening to Wagner and sipping Riesling all day anyway." He had a wry smile.

"Come on Pop. Its not Greenwich, Connecticut over there."

"It's not the Rhineland in 1936 either but it might as well be with the paltry number of votes coming out of there for any candidate who happens to be Black. Remember when we helped Jesse win the D.C. primary for President in 1984?"

"I wanted to come home to help but you told me to say in Atlanta to help get out the student vote on Super Tuesday."

"Right. Well Jesse won D.C. but you'll never guess who won precinct 89?"

"Mondale?"

"No, Gary Hart. They didn't want Mondale, they clearly wanted new blood, but even as Jesse was winning all over town, 89 couldn't stand the thought of him. See my point."

"I liked Hart, brilliant guy. I heard him speak at Emory during that Super Tuesday campaign. I got a chance to meet him afterward."

"Old Hart. He could have been President in '88, would have beaten the hell out of George Senior, but he just couldn't *keep his tally wacker stowed.*"

I laughed. My father sometimes let loose with highly dramatic rhetorical flights of fancy, as if he were reciting a Gilbert and Sullivan libretto or something. I think he did it to surprise, which he often did, but it was also what passed for humor for him. He was almost back to his old self.

"Jason, I don't want you to waste your time on any petition challenges, you're going to have to beat that *sonofabugger* fair and square."

"I know but –"

"There *are* no buts, anything else is a distraction. Focus on running your race."

He was right, of course, but I naturally held out hope that my opponent might be as inept as Terwilliger had been. I needed to find some advantage.

"What do we know about Brennan so far?" I asked. What's our opposition research showing?"

My father looked up at the restaurant's red awing as if somehow accessing a database. I thought he would beg off, claiming that his secret team of operatives had insufficient time to accumulate any data or some such rationale but the old man was always on his game at campaign time.

"Brennan has twin daughters at Northwestern, both lesbians although they have not yet what's the term? —*Come out* to their parents yet. His wife is a pretty good-looking middle aged white girl. She's had a little work done, like they all do; eyes and chin. She has a personal trainer, went blonde to hide the gray. "

"How did we get all that?" I said dumfounded. He ignored me and continued.

"She's General Counsel at PBS, came into a trust fund a few years back and works the congressional reception and embassy party circuit as if she wants an upgrade to Brennan—poor bastard. But, who can blame her; he's still got that midlevel staffer mentality. He's got no style, no personality. She's having sex with every European military attaché on Embassy row.

Brennan is forced to allow the Capitol Hill real estate barons to fill his legislative dance card. They make him take reactionary positions on every issue before the Council except the gay rights thing—they're good paying customers. Brennan is diddling his Legislative Counsel, that big boned German girl, and he lacks the intellectual curiosity to be concerned about a *damned* thing else."

"Okay, I get it."

196

I wondered how my father came by this information, intimate details about the private and political life of Councilmember Damian Brennan, but I had learned years before not to ask. The *Poker Game* had methods and practices that were as proprietary and secretive as the CIA's.

"There's one more thing," my father said pausing, as the wine was being poured. "There's a 14 room fully furnished house in her name in McLean, Virginia, which of course, is not listed as their primary residence. Even for people like these it would prove hard to serve on the D.C. Council when you live in Virginia. I would imagine that for public consumption, they're calling it a weekend retreat."

"Can't we bring that up? Who retreats from a six room Capitol Hill townhouse to a 14 room mansion in the rolling hills of Virginia, where you're neighbors with Ethel Kennedy?"

"You're wasting your time again son, stay focused! You would need the press to launch an investigation on something like that and they will not. He has backers, the bastard, and he's a racist; too many people have heard the word nigger come out of his mouth when he thought he was in the company of fellow travelers. He uses it casually, like he doesn't care who knows it."

"I get it."

"What do you get son?"

"My opponent has never been Damien Brennan."

"Now your thinking," said my father, his face brightening. "You *will not* be running against Damian Brennan, he's a game piece. You're running against *powers and principalities.*"

"If the real estate interests provide Brennan's muscle, then we're going to have to wrangle support from his natural enemies. Doesn't the rest of the Council hate him?"

"Yes, they do, but they're irrelevant. Brennan has too much power for any of them to feed him to the wolves. Brennan is owned by the wolves."

"Machiavelli."

"Machiavelli indeed. They will come after you with the full power of the Washington establishment. Nothing this transformative occurs in this town without Federal involvement. I have recently come to understand that we only had the city at their pleasure. We can presume that they want it back now."

He took a gulp of wine and seemed in deep contemplation of the bottom of the glass before he continued. "This is going to be the hardest thing our little *Poker Game* has ever done. If we fail, regardless of the odds, history's judgment will be that the city was lost on our watch."

"I don't know if I want all that responsibility Pop," I said.

"You have no choice son because you're all we've got left. It's what we've been preparing you for." He managed a smile.

198

He had a way of making difficult points and then easing the pressure with his smile. It was a talent acquired over many years with my mother.

We both ordered *steak frites and salade* from the menu, an inexpensive but substantial meal, which had always been one of my favorites. During a lull in the conversation my eyes wandered. I noticed the young couples, European tourists, and lawyer types that surrounded us on the patio.

Pennsylvania Avenue loomed before us with the U.S. Capitol to our left and to the right and completely out of sight, stood the White House. In between stood the Wilson Building, our City Hall and the object of my quest. I was nervous.

I wasn't nervous because of the difficult path to victory—I had calculated all of that. I could see that my father was approaching my campaign as some final act of redemption and that was the troubling thing. I didn't want to let him down.

My father was never one to speak in absolute terms; as an academic he generally operated with a certain sense of ironic detachment. But I could now see his pain in having to watch the city turnover in his lifetime.

"It's going to be fine Pop," I said, trying to believe my own words. "We have a great campaign team coming together, we'll just out work Brennan. The message is right, we'll have enough money and I have meetings next week with some of Brennan's people that sound interested in going against the grain."

"I love your optimism, reminds me of your mother, God rest her soul. But we're realists now, right? The question we must answer is whether at the end of the day, that is enough anymore."

I took a long sip of wine while I thought of an answer. When nothing came I continued to drink.

†

I drove my father back to Hillcrest after dinner and we were enveloped by a city transformed. Downtown had been reworked in a mere four years by Terwilliger's skeletal hand.

It was a typical August night in Washington and the humidity was suffocating. The top was down on the SAAB and my father marveled at how much downtown now resembled parts of midtown Manhattan. I watched him silently rally himself for the coming fight.

We turned east on E from 12th Street, and hit a traffic jam as the newly opened ESPN Zone and E Street Cinema released their patrons into the street. It was 10:00 P.M. By the time we reached 9th street, we were again stopped by a flock of young white and Asian women who by virtue of their tiny bra like blouses and *Daisy Dukes* were no doubt in route to the new row of nightclubs on F Street.

Seventh Street offered even more congestion, as smartly dressed people dining elegantly in trendy restaurants settled gaudy checks over espressos, and as MCI Center—the new jewel of downtown, sent happy concert goers into the confusion of the night. This was the change that my father said we had to overcome. This was the change that I knew we could not.

For decades the saving grace of any who wished to preserve the city's identity was that the white people were afraid of being caught in D.C. at night. Washington became D.C. after dark and it was dark. Just for laughs we called it *Dark Continent* and it became *Dodge City when the murder rate rose.*

It was dangerous too. You had to watch your step. In all its ghastly connotations, it was an impenetrable, unknowable, frightful place to all but its inhabitants. Just the way we liked it.

As teenagers, AJ and I would laugh at how the whites would haul ass by the thousands across 14th Street Bridge and every other major artery, frantic to make it back to Virginia or Maryland before sundown. They evacuated to their home improvement projects, manicured lawns and Labrador Retrievers. They were airlifted to their ice cream socials and chili cook offs, soccer games and swimming pools as if escaping a city of vampires, a city of the damned.

Despite my denials, the brief journey through downtown that night made it patently clear that my father was right. They were no longer afraid.

Amanda was already at my house when I got back to Capitol Hill. I parked behind her and approached her car.

"I was about to call you on your cell Mr. Diggs."

"I'm not late."

"Yes you are, exactly nine minutes. You have to do better, a candidate has to be prompt."

"Never stopped Bill Clinton."

"You're comparing yourself to him?"

"The traffic held me up. Did you know that D.C. now has night time traffic jams?"

"It's becoming New York."

"Over my dead body," I said.

"You can't stop progress. It's a natural evolution."

"As far as I'm concerned, it's neither natural nor an indication of progress. You're originally from California right? You can't understand how catastrophic this is for native Washingtonians."

"I think I get the picture. All the diversity and congestion that it brings is a problem for you."

"It's deeper than that. When I was a kid, we basically had two flavors, Chocolate and Vanilla and only a swirl of that. We didn't have but a few dozen Chinese people in Chinatown, it seemed to me. The rest had already moved to Virginia. All the Latinos in town lived in Adams Morgan. You could drive the whole city in about forty-five minutes. Now it's like the world is upside down."

"Seems like progress to me."

"It's not progress, its greed. They extend all these incentives to folks building condos and opening restaurants and clubs but there's no money to create more municipal parking or no effort to change the stop light patterns to allow more cars to flow.

"That's a little too far in the weeds for me."

"Sorry. No municipal parking means that Terwilliger's buddies in the parking industry contribute more to his boy Callahan's campaign for preserving their monopoly. The people who refuse to pay twenty dollars to park for four hours on a Saturday night and risk parking illegally, are ticketed and towed to P.G. County and can't get their car until Monday morning. Then they need $150 plus the amount of the ticket to get their car back. These people are destroying the city."

"The city is making money right?"

"—And there are still not enough supermarkets in the city and no publicly financed recreation activities for kids after six on weekends, no public hospital and no affordable housing worthy of the name anywhere in town."

"What's your point?"

"What's all this development for? Tax revenue to what end? Who are the beneficiaries? Certainly not the people that live here now, that's my point."

"I see you're ready for the debates, she said."

"I've been ready my whole life."

She smiled like a ten year old with her small teeth. Her lips were inviting, sweet. I wanted to kiss her, but that could wait.

She got out of the car and hugged me. When we broke, she got up on her toes and kissed me softly. This is why I waited. I was a counterpuncher.

"The party started at ten, shouldn't we go?"

"It's black folk Amanda, we'll be right on time."

It was eleven and it would take twenty minutes to get to our destination. I'd already been drinking so I got in her car. A candidate couldn't be too careful.

Rick Donavan was having a get together, one of those soirees that urban Black professionals liked to have in summer; white linen, candles, good wine, upscale women, hip-hop and acid jazz. Rick's house, passed down to him by his grandfather, was newly renovated, an 1880's townhouse in the District's Shaw section, an old Black neighborhood just north of downtown, which was named for the White officer that led the famed 54th Massachusetts colored troops during the civil war.

Rick was one of the few remaining Black homeowners on his street, as the change had affected that old bastion of colored pride as well. As dozens of newly renovated million dollar homes stood opportunistically in the midst of evaporating history. Newly laid cobblestone walkways and discarded packing boxes casually pointed the way toward confrontation.

When Amanda and I got to the party, people were noisily hanging off his porch just like we used to in law school, their linen outfits blown by fans. *I wonder how long before the police arrive?* I thought.

It was going to be one of those parties. Light banter, witty conversations. Biggie Smalls and Sade, crab dip and fried chicken, pate and ribs. Brand New Heavies, Tupac and A Tribe Called Quest with Moet toasts at midnight.

Later it would be men on the porch smoking cigars as they talked about women, politics or the Redskin's newest draft picks *"man, that new receiver out of Texas is a beast!"* The women would all be in the kitchen talking about sex, the merits of cross cultural adoptions or Afro-centric education and how cute Arleta's new leopard skinned Manolo Blanik's are. *"Guuurl, they're the bomb!"*

I liked Amanda Richard. She was a producer for Meet the Press and was eccentric in a way that did not diminish her sexuality. We met on the beach in Negril two years before. She was at Hedonism II and I was at Moon Dance Villas. She was golden, topless and wearing a black thong. She was almost pretty.

I said, "I have to know your name." She said, "Why?" I said, "because life's too short to see that much of a person and not know their name."

We had lunch together at Rick's Café after we discovered we both went to Howard and both lived in D.C. (she lived in Silver Spring, Maryland). We made love quietly in my bungalow and we vowed to keep in touch. We didn't. Schedules.

It wasn't until she heard that my mother died (she had read the fairly good-sized appreciation written about her in the Washington Post) that we finally reconnected. She called to give her condolences and to ask if I needed anything. At the funeral, she insisted that we get together "real soon now."

I had almost forgotten that she was sexy. Her hair in was an explosion of twists and swirls and she had big round eyes the color of sandalwood, which created very little contrast with her skin. She was a thick woman and had the look of a lioness.

Admittedly, She was more AJ's type than mine, as I still tilted toward the petite and the pretty, but in all matters sexual, I had learned never to discriminate on such a minor point. She would do.

After navigating around the porch crowd, we wondered around the house trying to find Crazy Rick. He was the anchor on the local cable news station, *News Channel* and it turns out we both knew him at Howard, me from the Law School, she from their undergraduate days in the School of Communications.

Snoop Dogg's Gin and Juice was blasting through Rick's impressive sound system as we carefully climbed wooden stairs lit by tea candles. I lingered behind Amanda to catch the view, fashionable white linen shorts imprinted with the inverted delta of a thong, nicely lotioned legs with well toned calves—and she had on a white sleeveless top.

"How did Rick get the name Crazy Rick?" She asked, smiling, awkwardly twisting around to talk.

"Oh, it's a story from law school. He had been pulling an all-nighter in one of the classrooms, studying for a mid term, and for some reason he liked to take off his shoes and socks when he was studying. At some point he fell asleep and a 3rd year came along and took his shoes, socks and his backpack. He didn't wake up until the following morning when folks started coming in at 8 o'clock for the test.

So there he was bleary eyed with no shoes, no socks and no backpack—not even a pen to write with. When the Professor came in to administer the test, Rick was frantic. People were laughing hysterically. Finally, he just looked around and said *Rick ain't crazy, somebody just took my shit!*"

She laughed freely as she turned the final landing of the stairs. At the top we ran into the man himself, Crazy Rick, bouncing to Go-Go music with a girl that looked half his age.

"What's up Rick?"

"Jason Diggs!! Is that Mandy on your arm?"

"Mandy?" Amanda buried her face in her hands with embarrassment.

"That's what we called her at the School of Communications. This dude was on line for the Alphas and they made him stand outside her window at Truth Hall and sing that Barry Manilow song Mandy about a million times until she finally looked out the window."

"Oh, hell no," I said bursting into laughter.

"It was just so embarrassing", said Amanda, hand over her mouth. "They called me that for years."

"Oh Mandy, will you hold me and stop me from shaking..." Rick sang out, arms swinging out theatrically. He wore a white linen tunic and faded jeans with black leather flip-flops, which was quite fashionable for Rick.

His voice clashed violently with Lil Benny's Go-Go performance on the stereo and we all laughed. It was my last party as a civilian and I needed to laugh.

"Hey, Rick, what's up with the 200 people and the food and the loud music? I thought this was going to be *a little get together.*" I said.

"Well Ramika here thought that I should just *jiggy* the thing on out, you know. Do the damned thing. Crank it on up! So she invited a few folks," said Rick. "Ramika, these are my friends, Jason Diggs and Amanda Richard. Jason here is going to be the next member of the City Council. I can say that —- I am at home and not on the air."

"For *reeeaal*?" Said Ramika. "Damn, you squeaky clean like that?"

"Well I guess so, I mean I have tried to do things the right way." I wondered who she was.

"That's *ah-ite* boo. Good luck and shit." Ramika said.

She was what AJ would call a redbone—a freckled product of antebellum miscegenation who was light enough to give the whites on the Metro, who were usually clueless about such things, some reasonable doubt as to her racial background. Black people would implicitly know her as member of the tribe.

She was tall and willowy with long blond braided extensions and large breasts that were almost implausibly squeezed into a mini dress. She was quite beautiful really, a ghetto flower, with knowing eyes; eyes that probably had seen years of roach infested apartments and dustbowl courtyards, eyes that had never seen the staid utility of a SAT test center or the nuanced queries of a college final exam. In another world, she might have been a supermodel.

Rick chimed in, "Ramika is my new lady, ain't you baby."

"Yeah whatever man; psyche, you know you my boo. I love the shit out of some Rick Don-o-van." She hugged him.

She was drunk and happy, smiling with uneven teeth.

"I seen him on TV right," she continued, "and I said damn, that big chocolate thang is fine as shit, right. Then, later—I was at the 9:30 club for the Tupac Go-Go *re-spec-tive…*"

"Retrospective baby,"

"Yeah and they had the Word Messengers and Piggly Wiggly and the Ass Worshipers right? They my favorite Go-Go bands."

I was a fan of classic Go-Go. *Chuck Brown, E.U., Trouble, Redds and the Boys (I'd seen them at the Atlas Theatre in '83 over Christmas break).* I even liked the suburban guys, *Shady Groove* but I'd never heard of Ramika's folks. I was clearly getting old.

"Anyway, who was the MC? My baby," she said, leaning in to hug Rick.

"It's true, she found me in the VIP and whispered sweet nothings in my ear. We had three or four bottles of Moet and we've been inseparable ever since. She's moving in next week." Rick said, grinning mischievously.

"My baby ain't had no-body like me before. I be showing him my 'preciation like nobody never done, right baby?"

"Right baby," Rich blurted out. "Look at my Black Barbie-doll. You might look at us and say that we're not compatible but she's really smart. She's kind, generous and, well she's 25, the sex is *off the chain*. Sorry Amanda."

Amanda looked stunned and I was too, but happiness is a rare commodity. I couldn't judge the man; I was still in search of.

"Yah a couple?" said Ramika, looking in Amanda's direction.

"Well, no --", said Amanda nervously, "it's only our second date in two years but I'm having fun so far," she said looking up at me.

"I know that's right. He fine too, look at them dimples." Ramika said, as if I wasn't there. "Where they be hiding these cute ass mah-fuckas? I didn't see nothin' like them growin' up round my way."

"Where did you grow up?" I said endeavoring mightily to change the subject. She had the tale tell drawl of the northern most outpost of the state of North Carolina: Washington, D.C. It was distinctly southern, but more stylish, decisive, knowing; an accent of the streets.

Many people thought it was the authentic D.C. accent; and there was much debate about it. Most of my classmates in undergrad and law school didn't believe that I was from D.C. due to *my* accent but as fourth generation Washingtonian, I sounded like I was from generic America, with a little crab cake, sweet white corn and mambo sauce mixed in to spice things up a bit. This was the real D.C. accent and it too was becoming extinct.

Ramika's accent was probably from Southeast. I knew that accent best; Anacostia, Barry Farms, but it could have been Potomac Gardens. She had a project affectation, the speech pattern of the working classes, the first and second generation Washingtonians.

"I was born at D.C. General, grew up in Kentucky Courts then me, my muhva and sista, right? We moved to Capitol Heights. I live in Suitland now, but not for long." She said, kissing Rick on the mouth.

Capitol Heights was in *Ward 9*, that mythic ward which had been facetiously adjoined to the city's official complement of eight. P.G. County, the final refuge of the city's marginalized and displaced—the new middle passage.

"Oh okay!" I said with feigned enthusiasm.

We went downstairs together and drank a fruity rum concoction from a punch bowl. "Ramika made it!" Rick said. The heavy sweetness of the punch was devious as it slithered around my brain. I soon understood Ramika's inebriation, she had probably only had one drink before we arrived.

In the midst of about eighty happily sweating guests, the four of us danced loosely in a kind of rum enabled circle. The DJ played all the classics, guaranteed party starters: Parliament Funkadelic *"flashlight -- neon light..."* EU, *"...doin the butt..."* Chuck Brown, *"I feel like bustin loose, bustin loose"* and we danced absently, our cups refilling as if by magic. I needed that night; it had been months since I'd enjoyed myself.

At 1:00 A.M. I got a nudge from Amanda. She whispered that she had to be at work in six hours and that "Tim don't play." I understood and we quickly said our goodbyes, dancing our way out the door and into the sweltering summer night.

"Can you believe Rick?" Amanda said as we walked to her car. The haunting sound of *Always And Forever* wafted behind us from

212

Rick's house. The obligatory late night slow dragging had begun.

"Yes I can." I said.

"But she's--"

"Ghetto fabulous?"

"Yes," she said in disbelief. What was up with the little sheer white slip dress?"

"Hey, she looked good."

"I know but that's a little trifling when everything is on display. She really could wear some panties."

It worked for me and later it would work for Rick, I thought. Her body was as defined as the finest Greek sculpture. Her breasts were firm; her ass was high and tight. Such a body should be seen and admired. I considered it a privilege to have done so.

"But you know," I said.

"What?"

"He's happier than I have ever seen him."

"You know, you're right. He has a right to be happy. She *is* cute."

"Yes, she is."

When Amanda dropped me at my house we had a short kiss in the car. We promised to get together *real soon* and I never saw here again.

THIRTEEN
The Announcement

Tyranny, like hell, is not easily conquered; yet we have this consolation with us, that the harder the conflict, the more glorious the triumph.

Thomas Paine

I
t was Indian Summer when I announced and after a lifetime of preparation, the day was as anticlimactic and deflating to me as my mother's death. In the reception hall of my ancestral church, about fifty of my nearest and dearest, their ranks augmented by the stalwarts I'd recruited over years of quiet politicking, made eighty-five souls standing with me that day.

It was a full year before the D.C. Democratic primary and my campaign committee members proudly wore their red "I Digg Diggs" tee shirts. I appreciated the risk that many of them were taking as I grimly processed the anemic size of the crowd. The powerful real estate interests in the Ward had already ostracized them since Brennan's rise

214

but failure to win, meant political death. For me the stakes meant the collapse of the *Poker Game* and the end of Black politics in Washington. I understood this as I took in the crowd's brave applause.

The program had gone largely according to plan. My Minister gave a rousing invocation that quoted from 1 Chronicles 18:14 *"And David reigned over all Israel; and he executed Justice and righteousness unto all his people."*

Next came my most visible and ardent white supporter (although he like me was part Cherokee) Clark Harrison, a retired journalist and former hill staffer for John Lindsay who rallied the crowd with kind words about me: *"Jason represents the kind of progressive political vision that I haven't seen in this town in years."* Clark was followed by the church's dance ministry, a new contrivance, in which modern dance is performed to Gospel music. Alvin Ailey meets The Richard Smallwood Singers

There was something about full extension ballet leaps being performed to gospel music in a church fellowship hall that epitomized the inimitability of D.C. politics. It was a natural expression of an edict that had been passed down from the sages that founded our political traditions (my father and Lock among them); *in D.C. politics, there was no separation between church and state.*

By the time I announced that I was running for office, there had been three ordained ministers elected to the Council in the 28 years of home rule. Since 1968, a Catholic priest had once been elected to the Board of Education and several protestant ministers had served as well; and of course, Rev. Dent, was in Congress.

But there was more than that. Nearly every successful politician from 1974 to the early 1990s seemed to have prayer breakfasts as a part of his or her electoral repertoire and these breakfasts competed against each other so fiercely that they probably raised the city's cholesterol count by half: Sausage, bacon, salmon cakes, fried apples, grits, eggs and biscuits being favorites. Later, the victors would scramble to sponsor additional prayer breakfasts as part of their inaugural activities and the process would begin anew.

As a testament to the centrality of religion in D.C.'s political life, much later in my campaign, I actually had my feet blessed by a priest from an Afro-centric Catholic denomination so that I, in the words of the priest *"may walk these streets in righteousness, speak truth to power and meet with no harm."* Thus, the location of my announcement and my decision to be preceded on the stage by praise dancers was an ode to a venerable tradition and a signal to those that watch these things that I wasn't anybody's technocrat but a paleo-progressive D.C. pol.

Brennan's early decision to misrepresent my background and challenge my authenticity, made me, much to my father's delight, abandon my plan to run to the center and compelled me to challenge black people to support their own interests. It was the last reactive decision I would make, until I did it again. But it was necessary to hold my base.

216

When I previewed the speech for my father on the night before, he leaned into me, the smoke bellowing from his pipe like a steel mill on a production deadline. When I hit my biggest applause lines the smoke filled the room, only dissipating as he concentrated on the composition and forensic merit.

"You write like I did thirty years ago," he said when I had finished. "I didn't know you were so angry son." I'd earned his highest complement.

"I wasn't—until I walked Near Northeast and Southwest and talked with the seniors and-"

"And what?" He said, with the same bemused look that he wore when he saw me play football in the street as a child or when I told him I was pledging his fraternity and when I was sworn into the Bar.

"I wasn't angry," I continued, "until I heard what Brennan said about my authenticity!"

"That's a pretty sophisticated word for a street level politician."

"Yes," I said gathering my papers, "I suppose it is."

I began the speech slowly, lovingly mimicking through years of practice, the infectious cadence of the Black Church:

I would like to thank those stalwart souls who started a movement early this spring. These municipal patriots—committed to their city, their Ward and their community took a chance on someone new and suggested to me and to this community that I might be of some service to our Ward from the Council of the District of Columbia. Will the members of the Diggs for D.C. Committee please stand? These are the true visionaries of our Ward; please honor them with your applause.

Special thanks also to the brothers of Kappa Alpha Psi—I wasn't born with brothers but through Kappa Alpha Psi, I have them nevertheless. I love you brothers...give them a round of applause.

For the last several months, I have undertaken a bit of a quest. I wanted to understand what makes our Ward tick. In that process I have questioned, talked and listened in every corner of this Ward. Many of you have been witness to this process and I can tell you it has been among the most rewarding experiences of my life. This is what I discovered on that quest:

Number one, we have a tremendously vibrant Ward with talented people, strong businesses, wonderful churches, great neighborhoods and courageous community groups. We also have a problem.

No, it's not a financial crisis and no it is not a crisis involving human carnage of the kind that we experienced when we were the murder capitol, but my friends we are in crisis nevertheless. The crisis of which I speak is one of the failure of civic vision and the absence of social cohesion. It is a crisis of the heart. We have managed to get the trains running on time as a city, but we don't know where they're going.

218

My friends, the city is divided, and despite our intrinsic greatness, our Ward is the most divided Ward in our city. Some of you are thinking, Jason that's a rather extreme statement. And I say, yes! But these are extreme times.

This division manifests it's self in very insidious ways. We are divided racially which should be patently obvious to all of us; we are divided geographically, our neighborhoods and quadrants often at odds – causing paralysis in the development of a unified civic vision. We are divided chronologically, with many of our seniors cloistered away from the life of our Ward— forgotten assets in our struggle to build community.

Many of our young people live on the edge of our civic life, finding more joy, liberation and solace in the streets and in carousing on the steps of closed schools, than they do inside those that are open to them. We are divided economically—we have million dollar homes and dilapidated crack houses coexisting within easy walking distance of each other— and the inhabitants of both are not exactly on speaking terms.

Political cronyism and gamesmanship has all but obliterated the formation of community consensus on issues in our Ward. Where democracy once reined treachery has taken root.

It is now clear that the problems in our Ward are far too great to be bridged by false compromise and handshakes and far too serious to be assuaged by the political tools of scoundrels: overt political intimidation and cash filled brown paper bags delivered at midnight.

There—is my friends, no poetry being spoken from the dais of the Council on behalf of the citizens of our Ward, no vision displayed, no wounds salved, no hope created, no leadership shown. Too many promises have been broken, too few have been kept and the trust of the people has been violated.

But it wasn't always that way. I remember growing up in this city in the 1960's. We were a strong community. We didn't have home rule, no delegate to Congress but we had each other's back. Children were the shared responsibility of the neighborhood. Education was the number one priority in the community and the most exalted title that a person could have was teacher...I should know, I am the son of college professors.

People took responsibility for their neighborhoods—you couldn't just come into a person's block and reek havoc because the community would rise up to defeat you under the leadership of home grown Napoleons, who would rally the community in defense of neighborhood values. I should know, because my father, Steppenwolf Diggs, is one of those pillars of the community—standing often in defense of neighborhood children, neighbors' property, the aged and our way of life.

Let me tell you something! Community cohesiveness is our birthright in this Ward, it is our soul, it is our spirit and I believe that we can reclaim it if we only have heart! People have a right to expect that their elected leadership will have the same civic passion, creativity and sense of inclusion that they

220

possess. We can and we must make that a reality again.

"The circumference of life cannot be rightly drawn until the center is set", said Dr. Benjamin Elijah Mays. But how is this accomplished?

My friends, on the not to distant horizon, I, see a gathering storm, a storm of hope, a storm of determination, a storm of courage -— a cleansing storm that will leave in it's wake a renewed civic spirit that will cross the divide that has been created in our community, that will destroy the false idols that pit neighborhood against neighborhood— community group against community group and citizen against citizen.

My dear friends, notwithstanding our recent urges to come together as a nation in the face of the recent horrors of 9/11, as so we should— in recent years, in this community, we have allowed ourselves to become victimized by the politics of fear; the politics of bitterness and the politics of malign neglect.

As a native of this great city, I cannot and will not sit this one out.

When I see the look of children without hope and low and moderate-income citizens increasingly unable to afford a home in D.C. it gives me great concern for the future. When I see the look of fear in the eyes of our most vulnerable citizens who are afraid of the loss of an effective safety net in our city and when I see cars vandalized or stolen in front of my own house and all over the Ward, it lessens my optimism for the present.

When I see citizens locked in epic struggles all over this Ward, against unwieldy, unnecessary and potentially destructive development projects, while other citizens cry out in despair due to the lack of rudimentary commercial services and economic development in their neighborhoods, in the words of another native Washingtonian, Marvin Gaye, "it makes me want to holler".

When I watch the Council on television or attend community meetings and see my Councilperson being blatantly duplicitous on issues of public concern or more interested in appearing clever and appeasing the powerful than in solving the problems of real people, it moves me to action!

Action is what is needed now in Ward 6; stronger, more energetic leadership to represent the hopes, dreams and aspirations of the residents of our historic community. In my travels throughout our Ward I have found that people are tired of having to fight so hard to maintain the quality of life in their neighborhoods -- they wonder what the person they elected- is doing to defend their interests.

People are tired of having elected officials twenty paces behind the curve; testing the wind to find where the people are on the issues. People are tired of elected officials joining in futile protests, just for the photo op, rather that proactively legislating to prevent unwanted incursions on the community.

Thomas Paine said: "We have it in our power to begin the world over again." And so we must in our little corner of the world. Friends, we have been governed by fear for too long;

We have been led by suspicion and negativity for too long; we have been manipulated by malevolence for too long; and now it is time to regain our course—our spirit—regain our soul and regain our heart.

And so let us begin. In the face of the politics of division, let us begin. In the face of the politics of distrust, hidden agendas and bitterness; let us begin and offer to our neighbors something they haven't seen in a while, the politics of open dialogue and unity, politics of reconciliation and community empowerment. We will offer, the politics of love!

Therefore, today I announce my candidacy for Ward 6 Member of the Council of the District of Columbia.

We will seek to engage in a conversation with the people of this Ward about the issues that confront them in their everyday lives. We will engage the people in a discussion about the future of our Ward and our city---and where they fit in that future. We will seek to build bridges across all the divisions that we now endure and to put in place, with the people of our Ward, a blueprint from which to repair the breach in our community. We will build a winning team from every corner of the Ward. From Near NE to SW from Capitol Hill to the Navy Yard from Penn Quarter to the Sursum Corda projects.

And I need your help. It will not be easy— there will be many early mornings and late nights and many miles and doorsteps in between. I will need all of my friends on my flanks in this bold endeavor. I'll need your time, your prayers, your advise, your home cooked meals at times—your encouragement and your money.

And so I ask you, who will work with me, who will fight with me for the future of this community! Whether you live in this Ward or work in the Ward or go to church in the Ward or have friends or family in the Ward—which of you will work to build community with me?

I have faith that we will construct a team that will ride that crimson storm to victory for the people of this Ward.

.... And when we do, when we have built a sturdy ship to ride that storm... The Ward and the city will be changed... and changed for good.

Thank you, God Bless you and God Bless this mighty Ward!

The crowd cheered when they were supposed to and clapped solemnly when appropriate. Some yelled out the time honored "that's right!" and "come on!" that made for good call and response. It was African in rhythm, it was visceral in tone and it worked.

It was a thematic speech and actually wasn't one of my best. It was exceeding low on specifics but full of hopeful vision and harsh polemics about the present leadership. But what it lacked in policy prescriptions it made up in tactical precision.

It was definitely the speech that the *Poker Game* wanted to hear and a clear signal from me that pedigree aside I was their guy. If Brennan wanted a fight, it had begun.

FOURTEEN
The Notion of Regret

"I've looked on many women with lust. I've committed adultery in my heart many times. God knows I will do this and forgives me."

Jimmy Carter

I hated funerals, especially after my mother died, but much to my chagrin, funerals like campaign announcements, victory parties and birthday celebrations were among the most important rites in politics. Attending the funerals of political figures or of humble constituents with large families is an important tradition of long standing. People kept score.

"I didn't see you at Buddy Wright's funeral" or "You should have seen the line to view Hilda Shorter's body, took me over an hour," were not so subtle abasements hurled at the unfortunate politico who chose to disregard the rules of the game.

In D.C. attending the funerals of murdered youth had almost become a profession in itself—so many had fallen since my own high school graduation. Almost weekly, the T.V. news would flash the picture of a smiling, unsuspecting teenager who had sadly met their end through violence, sending the political tribe into immediate action—descending upon the grieving family at light speed. The tribe would then dutifully express heartfelt condolences dispensed with easy grace and well-practiced solemnity.

The Monday after my announcement, I paid my political dues at the funeral of Antonio Brown, a 16-year-old football star at Eastern High School who was shot to death in my Ward on the corner of 17th and Independence Avenue. He was found in the backseat of a blue 1996 Acura Integra with two bullets in his head.

As I stood in line at the church to view the slain boys corpse, a thin man wearing a Metro Bus uniform and reeking of cigarettes, said "if all these politicians was doing they job instead of *comin* to these funerals, less of *dese* kids would be getting killed out here."

Both Mayor Terwilliger and Councilmember Dexter Callahan were in line just ahead of me and must have heard it too, but despite the well-placed jab landed by the bus driver, they just stood there impassively, their upturned faces set in pious contemplation.

I shared the man's point of view but not being in attendance at these services was considered evidence of not campaigning hard enough; which would undoubtedly reach the

226

self appointed arbiters of who was worthy of campaign cash. A political career could be scuttled in an instant from such an oversight. Damien Brennan did not appear.

Early on, I had decided to pen a series of OP/Ed pieces to get my message to the people. The old rules were not working anymore, we were losing ground and someone needed to be the first to say it. The first of my pieces was called *Conventional Wisdom* and I had begun working on it earlier that morning. It read in part:

Conventional wisdom has left us weak and rudderless in our public policy prescriptions. The new politics has produced little more than a tracking system through which to measure our failures.

We have abandoned our historic adherence to a politics of communalism where our most vulnerable are prioritized and we are all the worse for that. An investment in neighborhoods, jobs, recreation and education will reduce violent and economic crime, allowing our children to contribute to our future rather than being tragically and prematurely divested from it...

I emailed the draft to the *Poker Game* before heading to the funeral. As I emerged from the church, Lock Smith was the first to approach me.

"Jason, what the hell are you doing? This isn't what we discussed at all."

"What do you mean Lock? I'm being aggressive. We certainly discussed *that!*"

"It's too philosophical for the grassroots and too radical for the media. It just ain't gonna work."

"I'm not going to dumb myself down and I'm not going to be handled. I told my father that before."

"Yeah, the Wolf said you said that but he also said you wanted to win. I'm here to help you do that, but you can't just go flying off the handle like this."

"What do you suggest?" I said.

"Hug the center Jason."

"What?"

"The center man. It's the only way."

"I thought you guys hated that middle of the road crap? In fact, I know you do."

"It's about getting elected, you can preach on your own dime."

"It doesn't make sense Lock. They propose fiscal policies that will reduce tax revenue because they're catering to business, shifting the tax burden to the middle class. Then they pay lip service to the need for sweeping social programs that you can't pay for because the money isn't there and publically ring their hands when drug addiction skyrockets along with AIDS and kids like Antonio in there, die on the streets. I'm not running on that!"

"Yes we are, because that's the formula for victory these days. I know it stinks but that's it and unless you get on board, well, it's going to be a long campaign."

"Lock, you can't guarantee that I will win even with this watered down bullshit!"

"No, but your chances improve dramatically. This is scientific Jason. It's worked in the last three city elections. The one's we've been losing."

"But isn't Brennan running on this shit?"

"Yes but he's taking it further to the right, he takes a tougher line on crime because of all the hill staffers that used to get jumped coming home from work. There have also been a lot of car thefts, he's responding to the fear that's out there."

So are you, I thought.

I went home disillusioned about what I had gotten myself into. I decided to take off the uniform (blue suit, white shirt, red tie) and go out for the evening. I was ordered by Lock to keep my night wanderings to a minimum during the campaign but after Desiree, a level of recklessness had crept into my personality. I was not the earnest young kid anymore.

Before I was a candidate, I used to engage in hunting expeditions in the clubs and lounges around town. It almost wasn't fair, slip dresses and pumps, nicely oiled legs, blouses that plunged in the front and dipped in the back, beautifully coifed hair and manicured nails were the fashionable camouflage employed, because in D.C., *men* were the hunted.

Like an Impala, I meandered through vast savannahs of urban sophistication, but was fully aware that I was in the cross hairs. I understood the game. I could see them, see me coming and it was fun that way.

I put on my nicest pair of jeans, a red long sleeved polo and a black plaid Burberry sport coat and drove to Ozio, a cigar lounge at Connecticut and M that I had frequented for years. It had recently abandoned its traditional 1940s elegance for a trendier vibe and become the hunting ground of choice for some of the most exotic international woman in the region.

I ordered a double shot of bourbon at my favorite upstairs bar, lit a CAO torpedo and watched football highlights on ESPN. AJ had apparently made one of his crazy catches for a touchdown against Denver for the win and I made a mental note to call and congratulate him.

I pretended not to notice the bevy of beauties congregating at the tables behind me. *Make them wait*, I thought.

After an hour, I felt a tap on the sleeve of my jacket. All I saw were eyes.

"Hello, are you alone?"

"Yes, but I wouldn't mind changing that situation."

"Good, I would like to join you then."

She had an accent, slightly British— African I suspected.

"Where are you from?"

"Kenya."

"Oh interesting. I have a dear friend that was married to a lady from Kenya."

"Oh really, where is she from."

"I'm not sure but she's deceased now."

"I am so sorry."

"I never knew her."

She was a flawless picture of African beauty that made me understand why the Europeans wanted the continent and *its people* so much. Her tiny Afro and enormous silver earrings completed the picture. *Miriam Makeba*.

After talking for hours she suggested that we go to Adams Morgan for a nightcap and by that time I was in no position to disagree. The huntress had bagged me.

We partied at some African club that sat atop one of the better-known restaurants on 18th Street. I had never seen it before. She danced vigorously, thrusting and wheeling even jumping in my arms, demanding that I twirl her around the dance floor. She was slight and strong and willing. I wondered if I would get to go home with her.

We left at midnight and went to a Kenyan club on Georgia Avenue where she introduced me to her friends. Kenyans are energetic friendly people and while she reflected this lineage, she was also clearly on a mission.

I would find out some time later that her paperwork wasn't quite right. A quick marriage to an American lawyer might make the problem go away.

At 24, she still carried the tattered passport through which she had gained lawful entry into the United States when she was nine years old, but by then the visa and the passport had long since expired.

At 3 A.M. we arrived at her apartment in lower Shaw. It was an area where prostitutes, both male and female still practiced their ancient art and where you could still get an apartment, for less than $2,000 a month. She opened the door to her unit and I walked into the smallest efficiency that I had ever seen. She instantly removed every fiber of clothing that adorned her sprightly figure.

She peed loudly in the bathroom with the door open, an invitation to casual intimacy if I ever heard one, and then hopped into bed. A massive mattress that encompassed over three quarters of the available floor space dominated the room and an equally gargantuan television set sat against the wall on parson's tables, her priorities obvious to all that entered.

The kitchenette was a closet, which had just enough room for two people to turn around. The bathroom was gritty but functional. She was clearly on the edge.

"Well, are you coming baby?" she said from the bed.

"Uh, sure."

I scrambled out of my clothes and stood naked in front of her. I imagined cameras outside when I left.

"You're beautiful Jason."

"Thanks, so are you."

"Join me."

Join me, a phrase laden with possibility and danger. I didn't know this woman and I was naked in her apartment. *This is something AJ would do*, I thought. But I was up for it, ready as it were. Fortunately, I had retrieved the condom that I usually kept in my glove compartment, lessening my anxiety so that early that morning, I could put aside my candidacy for city council, and fuck an illegal alien until the sun came up. It was the best sex I had ever had.

Later I asked myself, how many undocumented people walked the city in the shadow of the INS, the Justice Department, and the FBI, fully comfortable in their illegality. Blending into the mass of blackness and brownness, knowing that discovery was unlikely.

She had a cell phone registered in Ohio and was otherwise off the grid. Her apartment was rented, so she said, in the name of an uncle that had returned to Kenya two years before. She had no other legal attachments, except for her job at an African restaurant, which paid her off the books and school, a junior college in Virginia that had somehow failed to ascertain her murky status.

"Baby, I need to get my stuff straight." She said weeks later, as we lay in her huge bed after another remarkable night of sex. She had a throaty African voice, tinged with a dramatic British inflection.

"Yes, you do, and I want to help, but its tough. You're already illegal. They'll probably deport you first and you'll have to reapply for entry. The fact that you overstayed won't help. In the current climate, you will probably be denied." I said.

She cried. "I don't want to go back, not until I'm a nurse."

I held her. "I don't have any friends doing immigration law, but I'll check around."

"Can't you do something more—immediate?"

I was taken aback by the formality of her speech. *The British had done a number on these people but then again, I had to reflect on equally transformative history of the African American experience. At least she could speak African languages, her father was Kalenjin and her mother was Maragoli and naturally she spoke Swahili. She could still prepare Kenyan food, like Ugali, a porridge made from millet flour and Sukoma Wiki, which was a hodgepodge of greens onions and tomato which she told me literally meant — to stretch the week, which she had made for me in her microscopic kitchen.*

Valor was still busy with the doomed Project Kujichagulia freeing my nights to explore Africa. I suppose it was a way to rediscover that part of myself, with so much of the city no longer resonating with the aura of Blackness.

I kept coming back for weeks, slipping away after campaign events and into her gigantic bed. She was a runner like many Kenyans, small, sinewy and agile. Her flat stomach was a marvel to me, so many of the woman I had been with had a bit of a pouch. I would run my hands over the smoothness of her dark body, absent of body fat, tight and lithe like a dancer. *I could stay here forever, I thought, stay here and father AFRICAN American babies, a new tribe of political athletes who would win Olympic medals before running for American governorships or President of Kenya with their dual citizenship.*

The girl was a sexual prodigy, knew all the tricks but I began to believe that I was one of them. Was she a prostitute? Now, that is a relative term in the third world, where survival dictated a more flexible moral scale. What was becoming certain to me was that I was not the only one she was spending time with and that put me at significant risk.

One night at a club on U Street we were dancing when a white man tried to cut in.

"Serah! Serah Kuttuny!"

I ignored him as she did and kept dancing.

"Serah!" he said and bumped into me. He was drunk and in light of the fact that I should not have been there in the first place, I handled it differently than I would have ordinarily.

"Excuse me, can't you see that we are dancing here?"

"I was just trying to get her attention."

I looked at her but as usual, she appeared lost in her inebriation.

"Look man, just go on, she clearly doesn't know you.

"Oh, she knows me alright."

I could have destroyed him, he was my size and drunk; but I was a candidate, couldn't fight or make a scene. To top it off I had a debate the next evening. Fighting him might destroy me.

I decided to take her hand and leave. It was the first time I remember ever backing down from a confrontation. I was my father's son.

Later in the car I asked her, "who was the white guy?" When she didn't answer I repeated the question. I repeated it a dozen times in the ten minutes it took me to drive to her apartment but she never responded.

I tried another approach and stated something that had been on my mind for weeks.

"I wish you wouldn't party so hard and focus on studying."

"Oh gosh Jason, its all in good fun."

"I know baby but I want you to get out of this legal situation. Being focused would help you to get there."

"I know, your right."

Serah worked, binged, fucked, danced, ran and studied in a cyclical routine that made me understand that she was not the kind of person that I could ever keep discreet. Our trysts were not sustainable. I had been seen in too many African clubs and restaurants and she was too beautiful and was far too demonstrable, as she hung all over me most of the time. I was becoming an easy target.

The incessant kissing and rubbing and provocative dancing was, of course, too much but the incident with the white man was the last straw. It had to end.

That night I gathered the incidental items that had accumulated in her apartment and told her to call me when she got herself together. I did this knowing that she would not, which was what I wanted. No regrets and one more beautiful dangerous distraction out of my life.

FIFTEEN

The Former Love of My Life

"It is with our passions as it is with fire and water, they are good servants but bad masters."

Aesop

I was never overly moralistic, which perhaps is obvious, given my choices. But, I was ethical and lived my life within the boundaries of a well-designed plan. My relationships with women followed that pattern.

For most of my early life, due to a series of dating mishaps, I forced myself to exist within a zone of romantic indifference. But, as I entered my mid twenties I acquired a surprising ability to attract and convince. These charms suited me well as I began relationships with more beautiful women than was ever conceivable in my lonely and uneventful childhood. Perhaps this was my calling perverted for purely personal use or maybe it was simply my latent Grafton family courtliness coming to the fore, but whatever

238

the case, it was fully present when Desiree entered my life

She was tall; a dark chocolate marvel of a woman, who at 5'9" was nearly as tall as I was. She had shimmering brown eyes, luxuriant brown hair and the confident swagger of an athlete.

When I first saw her she was wearing tight faded blue jeans and an even tighter red cashmere sweater. Her sweater was mercifully short and I glimpsed, at her waist, a flash of smooth black skin.

"Excuse me, would you mind watching my books while I use the ladies room?" she said. The words surprised me not only because I was trying feverously to get my mind around the various exceptions to the hearsay rule, not only because of the candor of her crisp southern New England accent, but principally because I had somehow failed to notice her at the end of the large oak library table where I had been sitting for three hours.

She had mysteriously appeared from behind a mound of Property hornbooks, Torts casebooks, and a large Chanel tote bag. When she asked her question, it was not lost on me that I was the only other Black person sitting there.

"Of course," I responded, "but with a small caveat."

"Which is?"

I took my best shot. "Take a coffee break with me in a half hour."

"That wouldn't be a coffee break, that would be salvation."

Laughing, I snatched a mediocre response from the jaws of my moderate success, "salvation?"

She gave me a pass, "Let me get to the *ladies* first, then we can debate the finer points of my choice of adjectives."

"What's your name, I should know, if I'm to be the custodian of your professional future?" *Better*, I thought, as the 12 others at the table looked on with distain.

"Desiree Pitchford," she said.

And before I could summon another witty Diggs rejoinder, she was bounding gracefully toward the ladies room at the Georgetown Law Library, her round ass swinging like a battle flag—full, high and proud.

During my first year at Howard Law I acquired three new habits rooted in necessity and convenience; drinking coffee, studying in anonymity at Georgetown Law School and Valor. But when I met Desiree, I had a new passion that I was free to pursue without reservation.

Coffee turned into a midnight dinner at Bistro Francais in Georgetown and by the time I stumbled into my parent's house at 2:30 am, I knew that I had met *the one*; the image that I dreamed up at twelve years old to describe the girl who had the tools to occupy both my mind, and my sexual appetites—the one girl that I would never have to shrink myself for.

In my teens I actually complied a list of attributes for *the one* and hung them on the wall next to my bed. A litany of requests to the Almighty, a selfish entreaty that would make my life complete, if fulfilled.

After six hours I knew she was that fulfillment incarnate. First of all, she had the most remarkable hindquarters that I had ever seen. It was curvaceous, full and tight, with tremendous depth and volume.

As we walked through the restaurant to our table, I noticed that all the men and quite a few women had difficulty staying focused on their dinner conversations as they beheld it. It was if it had its own center of gravity, drawing eyes and attention from far and wide.

I called AJ immediately after dinner about her and he was infuriated—

"Man I have practice in 5 hours. We're playing Dallas this week."

"And I have school."

"Man, I get fined if I'm late."

"And I fail law school."

"OK Matlock, I know you have an answer for everything, what's so important."

"I met her AJ."

"Who?"

"Her."

"Who her?"

"The One."

"Oh that her. You sure?"

"Yeah man, she's it. Beautiful, body, brains, personality—everything."

"Everything? None of these biddies have everything," he said.

"Look man, no bullshit. She is brilliant and she is beautiful. I don't mean cute or pretty, this honey is bad. She's a JD/MBA candidate at Georgetown; she's also a reasonably successful model locally. We actually saw her face on the side of a Metro bus in a DC lottery Ad as we left the restaurant tonight.

"Not one of those Jason." He had seen his share of models, mainly from Playboy and Hustler.

"No man, she's witty. Know what she said?"

"No, but of course I will in about 10 seconds."

"She said, *that it was a fun shoot, the photographer was pouring Moet all night.* So I said you can drink while you're working? And she said, *its modeling not heavy construction.* Isn't that funny?"

"Oh man, you're whipped and you ain't even get none yet."

"She is fantastic AJ; I can't wait for you to meet her. Plus, I found out that it all comes naturally, as if by any other means right, but her Mother represented the Bahamas in the Miss Universe Pageant in 1964 and her father was the second Black Vice President of a Fortune 500 company, he was named Vice President of Connecticut Amalgamated Insurance Company in 1972. He just retired."

"Rich honeys have problems," he said.

"Shit AJ, middle class women have them too and poor ones but I haven't dated any since high school." I remember the girl's face but not her name. I'd cook her steaks at my house after school and with my parents still at work; she'd let me fondle her breasts while she ate.

"Just be careful Jason, is all I'm saying, man. Keep you're head on a swivel."

It didn't take long. Desiree and I fell into an instant and comfortable rhythm. By that point in my life, mid twenties and a man, I had grown at ease with women and no longer accorded them the mythic status I applied to them in my youth. But, Desiree had nearly resurrected that kind of magical deference in me. I assumed for the first time in my life that this was the one that I would one day marry.

I fell hard and painfully. So hard that I could hardly stand to be apart from her and I started losing study time to drive from Hillcrest to her Foggy Bottom Apartment to take her to National Airport for her weekend photo shoots in New York.

On very rare occasions I would go with her, but she was working and I was more of a distraction than anything else. Besides, in order to go to New York, I had to miss my weekly trial advocacy class, which met on Saturday mornings. I couldn't keep doing that, even for love. I had a calling.

We had become a team and together dreamed of Desiree as the high-powered fashion executive and me as the United States Senator, a power couple of historic proportions. The covers of People, Fortune and Ebony beckoned, as far as we were concerned.

Despite the fame and glamour that we believed awaited us, the time we spent together was simple, perhaps even a bit mundane. A typical Sunday morning, when she was in town, would find us nude in her rather opulent King sized bed with the Washington Post, New York Times, law books and outlines, drinking mimosas until the hard and serious work of becoming who we wanted to be, gave way to frantic lovemaking far into the afternoon.

As a rule, sexual aggression in women is a double-edged sword and Desiree was the most sexually aggressive woman that I had ever known. She'd initiate sex at odd times, like when we were at the mall or buying groceries at the *social Safeway* in Georgetown.

At her frequent urging, we'd find ourselves semi-nude and going for it in parking garages, bathroom stalls and even the narrow passenger seat of my Fiat. My fundamental conservatism and sexual naiveté had worn away like rocks against a relentless tide and soon the sex depicted in porno movies was less spontaneous then we were.

There is a bedrock principle among men that women have an unerring propensity for the dramatic, to make the simple complex and to rattle the nerves of the most emotionally self-contained of men. It seemed to be their fundamental purpose; but not Desiree, at least not that my lovesick eyes could see.

She appeared to be a drama free female and that was a cause for celebration among my friends. Most of them had never heard of, let alone encountered such a phenomenon.

Despite my torrid love affair, life was not some carefree stroll through some preverbal field of daffodils. My mother's illness was in, what I now know to have been it's final stages. She had been able to get around some in the earlier years and had attended my college graduation, though in much diminished condition; but her care began to become more of a burden on my father and me. My father retained a housekeeper to help us keep the laundry and basic housework under control. My free tuition at Howard was a blessing.

Law school, which started with such anticipation, had bogged down in a torturous ebb and flow. For the first time in years, I was not academically sure. My mother's illness had taken its toll on me.

I could not devote the time to school that it required and lacked the luxury of academic isolation. I had passable grades by third year, but I was no longer studying with conviction. For me, success bred remarkable achievements and mediocrity bred distraction and confusion.

During these days Desiree was helpful to my mother in the unique ways that women can aide their own in times of incapacity and despite my mothers skepticism this was indeed so. I cannot honestly attribute this to compassion or sincere emotion or an obligation born of love, it is more likely that her support at that vulnerable time was a means to an end and that is the great uncertainty that still endures.

Desiree gave me Martha's Vineyard on Fourth of July weekend 1989. I had just finished law school and had been furiously studying for the bar since May.

"You need a break Mister," she said stroking my month old growth of beard.

"I'll have one after all this is over."

"No, you'll go crazy first and I have too much invested in you."

"You're sounding like an MBA."

"I am an MBA now, and I'll be a lawyer next year, but I love you now and forever."

"I love you too girlie, but I really need to stay on pace with these Multistate practice exam questions. I need to do at least 5,000 to be in the comfort zone before the test."

"Who says you can't do them on the beach?"

"It would be a distraction."

"No more than when you take a break to, what do you call it, *come holler at me*, or when you have to take care of your mother."

"You've got a point there."

"Come on babe, it'll be fun, you'll meet the gang and it'll reduce the stress."

She was very persuasive. We were on the road by midnight and were in Woods Hole catching the ferry by eight the next morning. She'd already made the reservations.

I had a number of preconceptions about the Vineyard before I arrived. Though the island's history was undeniable, what was it, an island enclave for upwardly mobile Negroes or a proving ground for African-American greatness?

King and Malcolm X visited the place. Adam Clayton Powell and other luminaries had homes in Oak Bluffs and of course, there were my parent's visits in the 50s and 60s that were established family legend.

I found out that weekend, ensconced in a suburban style townhouse in Edgartown, which was hidden from the road by a dense grove of wind-tortured trees. We shared the house, as I learned was the custom, with four of Desiree's friends who'd come up from Connecticut, New York and Atlanta respectively.

After unpacking and changing into the Vineyard uniform of tee shirts, shorts (over our bathing suits) and flip-flops, we headed to South Beach to find out who was *on island*. I drove down a road that looked both coastal and agrarian, with cows and horses on the inland side and brief glimpses of sparkling blue water on the other.

There were Llamas grazing on the grounds of an ocean front mansion. I was instantly at peace.

We parked and walked toward the beach to find over a thousand people reclined in beach chairs, playing beach football and enjoying a sense of relaxation that I would come to know intimately in the years to follow.

"Hang a left," said Desiree.

"Are your people down there?" I asked.

"Well, yes; but all the Black people hang a left on South Beach."

And sure enough, as I looked toward the broad expanse of sand, with the exception of the odd interracial couple, sprawled carelessly on beach blankets every person—out of nearly 700, was Black.

"What's up with that?" I said. "Self segregation?"

"I guess you'd call it that. It's been like that ever since I was a kid."

I was amazed but also a little bit proud. Black folk had established their own tradition and our own place on this island. Later, I found that this was a pattern and Black traditions and establishments of position were to be found all over the Vineyard.

That day on the beach we drank champagne and ate Desiree's favorite snacks of Grapes, Brie and water crackers with a few young Wall Streeters, a cute young Judge and her husband from Boston and Brittany Booker, Desiree's childhood friend from Hartford, Connecticut who was just finishing up Med school at Columbia.

We listened to acid jazz on boom boxes and posed for pictures with members of our respective Greek organizations when we identified them on the beach.

I even played wide receiver in one of the football games, reprising my childhood talents and caught a game winning fifty-yard bomb for a touchdown. I celebrated by running straight into the frigid Atlantic.

The coldness of the water shocked me as I was used to the much warmer Chesapeake Bay waters off my aunt Sara's house in Highland Beach; but I enjoyed a nice toweling off and an even nicer kiss from Desiree. It was the kind of joyous moment that you wait your whole life for and I savored it like a dying man.

An hour later, on the way back to the house, I began to profess my love for the Vineyard.

"Oh, wait, you can't say that yet," said Desiree. We're going to the AC tonight."

"The AC?"

"Yes, it's the only nightclub on the island, everybody is going to be there. It's really fun but just wait until then."

We arrived dressed in linen at nine after a great seafood dinner at the Navigator restaurant on the Edgartown harbor. The lobster was the finest I'd ever eaten.

"Isn't it a little early to go clubbing?" I asked.

"Not on the Vineyard. It's going to be over at midnight."

"So soon?"

"It's a small town in the middle of the ocean, it's not D.C."

"Oh, right." I said a bit embarrassed.

I paid at the booth and we climbed the winding narrow stairs to find our housemates drinking and dancing by the bar. Many of the people from the beach were grooving on a fairly small but adequate dance floor below.

The DJ was a heavy set Black man who wore a Boston Red Sox cap and the away version of the New England Patriots jersey, as he spun an imaginative blend of house, hip hop and Go-Go music. His jersey was so drenched with sweat that a small puddle was forming at his feet and the club had only been open an hour.

The Go-Go made me feel at home.

"Rare Essence on Martha's Vineyard?" I said to no one in particular, but loudly enough to be heard above the bass.

"They got it going on huh?" Said our housemate Chuck, a BET account executive from New York.

We danced almost non-stop that night between periodic forays to the bar for my Remy and Heineken *set-ups* and Desiree's vodka and cranberry's. By closing time, with our entire group now just as soaked with perspiration as the DJ, the women adjourned to the ladies room to make themselves more presentable. Their wet linen and cotton outfits clung and revealed and it was on that night I discovered the popularity of thongs.

Desiree, who wore a nautical navy blue outfit that night, was the first to emerge and we walked hand in hand to the front of the club where I witnessed yet another Vineyard tradition in action. It looked like a fire drill; all of the patrons of the club were in the middle of the street.

Desiree again grabbed my hand as we plunged into the midst of the undulating mass of Black people and the few whites that crowded Circuit Avenue, Oak Bluffs' main drag.

"What's up with this?" I said.

"They're exchanging numbers and getting the schedule of house parties for the weekend. Lets walk," said Desiree.

As we wandered through the crowd, Desiree announced casually (she seemed to know everyone) that we were *"having a party tomorrow night to celebrate my boyfriend's first trip to the Vineyard, just bring wine."* It was a fact that she hadn't shared with me yet.

We made love vigorously that night as we always did. The lights were on and the windows were wide open—Desiree's own unique peccadillo. Nighttime temperatures of under sixty degrees added a bracing chill to our exercise.

She took me in stride, as usual, but graciously never complained. "You fuck me with you're mind," she said. It'd been a constant theme from the beginning of the relationship and it was the thought that bound me to her. The mind is a sexual organ, the heart is it's willing accomplice.

When we finished, she took a gentle sip from her glass of cabernet on the nightstand, then abruptly leaned forward to hug me, nearly spilling the wine. For a model, she was always a little bit ungainly.

"Okay, now you can say you love it."

"I already said it."

"Say it again."

"I did."

"Say it!"

And so I did, tipping my cognac snifter toward her as I uttered the magic words.

"I love the Vineyard and I love you."

"I just knew you would," she said and turned off the light.

SIXTEEN

The Apprentice

"A valet, of stealthy step, thence conducted me, in silence, through many dark and intricate passages in my progress to the studio of his master."

The Fall of the House of Usher

Edgar Allen Poe

A beaux arts building thick with cobwebs and rats; gloomy, dark and forbidding like a castle keep. Desolate even when engorged with people. A disaster. Yet, despite its frightful veneer, it was neither prison, nor garrison; the District Building was my second home, D.C.'s seat of government.

I'd been visiting the building my whole life. Taken to meetings by my father, drawing quietly on sketchpads and reading books like *The Red Badge of Courage or Last of the Mohicans*; while he huddled with the Mayor or Councilmembers or attended

Democratic State Committee meetings in the Council chambers.

I was twelve when the *Hanafi Muslims* took the building in 1977, in retaliation for what they deemed the government's failure to properly investigate the murder of five Hanafi children by a rival sect. Kareem Abdul Jabbar owned their compound, as he too was Hanafi.

I was in room 312 at John Philip Sousa Junior High, learning state capitals and oblivious to the mayhem occurring downtown. I also didn't know that the *Poker Game* had gone into a failsafe mode for the very first time.

I was an adult before my father told me that the *Poker Game's* leadership had been sequestered that day and that contingency plans had been activated. The assumption was the *Poker Game* was under assault by enemy forces intent on decapitation.

The plans were highly specialized and had been quietly and expertly put into place after the death of Dr. King. They had learned hard lessons on that day.

When Councilmember Marion Barry was shot in the mêlée following the Hanafi assault, my father and mother were quietly whisked from their respective universities, directly to my aunt's home in Highland Beach surrounded by highly armed off duty Metropolitan Police Officers loyal to the budding dynasty and pledged to defend them with their lives.

Apparently, my father *was* the failsafe. If Barry had died, it would fall to my father to take his place as the public face of progressive change in Washington, D.C.

A message had been sent to Sousa within minutes of the attacks, that I was to be released to Lock Smith as soon as the lockdown of public schools had abated. Lock's instructions were to get me to Highland Beach, which, per their plans, was being converted into a government in exile for the *Poker Game*. Had Barry fallen, the Democratic State Committee would have appointed a successor to the At-large seat on the D.C. City Council and the Poker Game's machinery was already being oiled to secure the seat for my father.

Later, the already famous *Poker Game* campaign apparatus, would have stirred to life, insuring a Diggs victory in the 1978 Mayoral primary just as it had for Barry. *How things would have been different.*

It didn't come to that. Barry's uncanny ability to survive a bullet lodged so close to his heart saved my father from a public life that would have likely paralleled Barry's own meteoric rise, while saving the city from certain, embarrassments. For while Dr. Steppenwolf Diggs and the Honorable Marion Shepilov Barry, Jr. were on the same team, time would reveal that they had far different playbooks.

Nearly twenty years after this secret history, I entered the District Building as Chief of Staff to one of the steady hands of the *Poker Game*, Ralph "Horse" Wendell. He'd been in the knotty pine basement since the beginning and had watched me grow up.

A Howard Law alumnus himself, "Horse" was at the start of his final term as an At-large Member and after four distinguished terms, was ready to retire. After the untimely death of his long time Chief of Staff, a woman of almost legendary tact and political skill, it was decided that my apprenticeship in the game would begin with him.

"Has he paid his dues?" "How did he get to the front of the line?" "I thought he'd be taller." "I know his father is Wolfman Diggs but—." This was the water cooler conversation at the District building that heralded my arrival.

I was just out of law school and up until that point had only volunteered, principally under my father's supervision, in the policy end of the *Poker Game*—writing brochures, policy papers and speeches for backbench candidates during their inaugural runs for office. For a few years, during my undergraduate days, I was lent out to Lock Smith, during the long hot D.C. summers, who schooled me in the arcane arts of political field warfare. The hard work was a welcome distraction as my mother's illness was beginning to take its toll.

I learned about the city's precinct structure, about campaign finance procedures and the importance of displaying the union bug on literature if one wanted to be blessed by their weighty endorsements. I was taught the black arts of opposition poster removal and push polling.

256

I loved the game and was proving to be a natural. Soon I was leading my own strike teams, garnering petition signatures for candidates, door to door canvassing and directing motorcades.

My advanced studies were under my father's leadership and he revealed to me the mystical arts of policymaking and political communication. I learned to highlight positives and downplay any potential negatives in a prose so sparkling and pithy that even Madison Avenue might have to take notice.

I began to understand urban policy in a way that connected the academic and the practical and wove them into a belief system that bordered on the spiritual, a social gospel that I carried with me the rest of my life. To have knowledge directly conferred upon me by the city's best political minds was intimate and humbling and the process brought us closer together.

My father was a race warrior of the old school and I was beginning to understand that his steely reserve, his nearly patrician carriage was armor, which veiled from the world the ancient rage that drove him. I was also beginning to understand more about myself.

I matriculated in this gritty school of practical politics as the 1950's era scion of a manufacturing company might once have apprenticed in the corporate mailroom and the shop room floor, before receiving the key to the executive washroom. Middle management was always envious of this practice and similarly envies were generated when I moved into the office of *Horse Wendell's* late Chief of Staff, Sue Mason.

After my arrival, I noticed most members of the staff eating breakfast at their desks every morning, well after the start of business hours; they went around me directly to the Councilmember, taking advantage of his jovial nature, to lollygag in his private office, while there was important work to be done.

Phones went unanswered and petty nonsense flowed continuously through the office. Lunch breaks were excessively long as were the cigarette breaks and no one seemed to be able to compose a letter in English.

I was miserable and in my personal life, Desiree's carefree worldview began to grate against my reality. We argued frequently and often broke up, only to reunite out of need. *Wasn't she the one?* I couldn't stand to be around someone whose happy disposition seemed so unaffected by the vicissitudes of life. I was affected, as was everyone else I knew. It was the curse of the *subculture.*

One rainy Friday night in April, instead of joining Desiree and her friends at *Club VIP,* I went to Hillcrest to search for answers in the midst of my father's knotty pine. It was always a touchstone, a place where confusion seemed to melt away, but since my official initiation into the card game that winter, (a simple matter of drinking cognac and playing the dozens) it was also a place of business.

As I came down the stairs into the den, my father was sitting comfortably in his favorite wing back chair in pressed khakis and an exquisite cream-colored Kappa sweater, which despite its obvious age, was in pristine condition. I had never seen it before.

His stocking feet set upon a stack of books he'd recently acquired. He seemed to be enjoying himself, which was, in and of itself, a rarity. I hated to interrupt him but as his only child, I felt entitled. I needed his help.

"Pop, it's a nightmare, they're all idiots. How did *Horse* last so long with a staff like that? I thought Sue was one of the best, how could she have tolerated that?"

"She didn't. They're just not working for you." He barely looked up from the biography of Ho Chi Minh that he was reading.

"They're making the Councilmember look bad. Don't they understand that?"

"No, they're making *you* look bad. You're being hazed—surely you can recognize *that* when you see it. *You're* doing *their* work, cleaning up *their* mess, so that *Horse* doesn't look bad. Ten, twelve hour days you're pulling right?" I nodded yes.

"—You're going to wear yourself out before you get started boy." He let out a little chuckle, either amused at what he'd said or frustrated at my naiveté. Probably both.

"You set me up!"

"Not as such, but you're going to have to learn to be a better political practitioner. You're not at Morehouse or Howard law School anymore and the District Building is not a courtroom. There are many other kinds of people in the world that you're going to have to deal with and they're not limited to the best and the brightest or those that always put their best foot forward. You're going to have to find ways to earn *their* respect."

"Respect should come with my title. I can fire them."

"You can't fire your way out of this one son. *Horse* would fire you before firing any of those people. They've been in the foxhole with him. You just showed up."

"Shouldn't they just respect his choice? I mean he did hire me?"

"There are probably three people on that staff who thought, rightly or wrongly, that they should be moving into your chair. You probably already know who they are. You need to cull one from the heard and make friends with the other two. That will buy you some time and gain you some respect."

"You think that will do it?"

"Not entirely, there's one more thing you have to do. After a few months bring in your own people to replace the two that you have befriended."

"I though you said I couldn't fire myself out of it?"

He retrieved two long maduro cigars from his humidor, handing one to me. "That's not firing. Firing is a blunt instrument. This is stagecraft, artful manipulation."

"When the remaining staffers see how you went about your business, I can assure you of their full cooperation," he said, his dark eyes widening to emphasize the point.

"They'll know that you aren't to be fucked with, understand? If you do as I say, they will know what it means to have you as an enemy."

He approached the basement door, which led to the lower patio of the house, and opened it. There was a loud *ping* as he popped opened his Zippo and began to light his cigar.

"Now go upstairs and see your mother." The rain had stopped.

I followed my father's advice to the letter and by November, the result was as he predicted—the office was mine. Not only that, the old Councilmember, who had constantly been written off as being out to stud, was reinvigorated. Suddenly *Horse* resembled the hard charging champion of his youth. He again was introducing socially resonant bills and conducting oversight of the Judiciary Committee with vigor.

My reputation soon began to rival the best hands in the building. It was now *Jason's Office and* I became one of the go to people on legislative drafting, office administration and day-to-day politics. Horse involved me in all the back door political wrangling and internecine wars in the Council, using me as one uses a Knight or a Bishop in chess—to slash, control and intimidate opponents, while he remained the stately King.

These were the nineties and my days were filled with the legislative back and forth, working the media and power lunches at the Palm, and Prime Rib. My nights were often booked with lobbyists, drinking with friends or socializing with Desiree at Takoma Station or T.J. Remington's.

What U Street had been to my parents, *The Station* was to us. It was a headquarters for our dreams. It was the venue to exchange information, meet prospective lovers and renew the culture. There were remembered faces and the familiar comfort of a living room.

The station carried the zeitgeist between its polished brick walls. There were the wing baskets, (chicken wings and French fries drizzled with Old Bay Seasoning) a shabby chic delicacy for those of us reveling in our newly minted status as young professionals. There was the hum of ardent conversation accented by the best in live Progressive Jazz; and there was plentiful alcohol—while I stuck to Remy and Heinekens, the specialty of the house was an unusually potent Long Island Iced tea.

On any given night, Bernard Shaw could be found seated comfortably at the bar in subtle decompression from his daily role as the world's griot on CNN and the occasional black Hollywood actor might be found meeting and greeting among the city's up and comers. This was Takoma Station in 1993.

My fondest memories were there, surrounded by friends collectively enraptured by our privilege to live in such a place and in such a time. We were arrogant in our youth and beautiful in our limitless potential. Even the waitresses, ravishing lovelies meticulously recruited from Howard's quad, went on to dance in music videos, star in never released television pilots or anchor newscasts in secondary markets with perfect diction.

But, I needed to escape from time to time. In warm weather, I would hang out with Valor at her Waterfront Condo in Southwest. There we'd laugh and share a bottle of wine on her patio.

She was quickly becoming an amateur sommelier and in those days, I was a willing guinea pig. It was during these sessions that I decided that my favorite wines were *Nero D'Avola* from Sicily and *Amarone* from Verona, both Italian reds. I was my father's son.

Over time, drinking bottles of wine as Valor lounged in silk camisoles and panties proved too much. My mounting frustrations with the course of my relationship with Desiree slowly evolved into a re-exploration of what I'd shared with her when we in law school.

It seemed innocent at first. We'd sit on her balcony for hours looking out at Haines Point, scanning the horizon for the Spirit of Washington as she went out on her evening cruise.

"I want a boat one day," I said one evening.

"That would be nice."

"Yeah, one big enough to take into the Atlantic. No river cruising for me."

"Could I come?"

"I wouldn't think of bringing anyone else. Just bring wine."

"You're just going to stay cute aren't you Jason Diggs?"

"Nice of you to say, but I'm not feeling very cute these days."

"You just need to relax, I can help you with that."

"You *know*, according to Desiree, we're getting married next year."

"According to her?"

"I haven't bought a ring or proposed or anything."

"*Hmm.*"

"I'm not sure what I'm going to do."

"I think you *are* sure, that's why you're here with me."

It would be easy to impute a mythic quality to my relationship with Valor. Over the years she'd blossomed. No longer simply the sexy, trash talking tough girl she was in law school, by her thirtieth birthday, she had become quite startling in her refinement.

She'd joined a small law firm and within a year had become its star litigator. (Howard lawyers know how to fight) Professional success had brought her certain ornamentations—a Rolex, fashionable designer glasses and a beautiful wardrobe, which she'd accumulated on numerous shopping junkets to Paris and Milan.

Valor had become comfortable with herself in a way that radiated beyond these

264

recent trappings. Her power was in this and her soul stood bare, basking in the glow.

This was what I found missing in her before, the reason I had not continued my pursuit and moved on in favor of Desiree. Her truculence was an inconvenience.

I sought her for her scintillating intellect and her perfect form. I wanted her loving companionship not her accusations and polemics, but there had been something deep inside of her that had violently resisted a life of escapism and repose.

Valor and I were enjoying a renaissance of sorts and our wine drenched encounters continued unabated for many weeks. We were again having sex and it was good.

With Desiree, I would chalk up the time to poker games with my council staffer buddies (a study in the ironic). In my mind, I'd reconciled it to a need for a last hurrah before my final entombment in Desiree's world of prefabricated phoniness—*one far more moral and uplifting than bachelor party sex with a professional.*

I was becoming increasingly less committed to the concept of life with Desiree by the day. I hated the group behavior of her subculture friends, which included the recurrent line *"oh we're all going to..."* I detested the gratuitous destination dropping in their conversations, *"oh remember when we all decided to go to the Black Enterprise Tennis Weekend instead of Sag Harbor? Wasn't that just awful?"*

Most of all, I hated the general presumptuousness of the group, *"Jason I want to be pregnant by July so that we can show off our baby on the Vineyard the next summer. Think of it, my Mom and Daddy can babysit for us so we're free to party."* I HAD NOT GIVEN HER A RING!

At the end of his term, "Horse" retired. His successor, the young and virtually unknown Ahmed Mitchell, hired me to guide his office. Before long, it became clear that I'd made a mistake in accepting.

Mitchell was a phony. His speech was inelegant, he hadn't studied *the game* with anything approaching the depth that I had and despite my skillful authorship of most of his public statements, his lack of sophistication was often embarrassing.

Why was he on the Council when I was still staff? *His timing was right; he slipped into the short line.*

"Don't worry son, my father told me. Mitchell's a run of the mill transactional politician. He fit our current needs, so we put him in as a placeholder. He'll have a few terms, probably run for higher office, when his seat is safe and embarrass himself due to incompetence. Left to his own devices, he'll sit there stroking his own ego until we find a suitable replacement or the people discover what he is."

"But doesn't this prove that I should run right now? That I could win?"

"No son. We're preparing you to be a transformational figure. You have natural talent, a fine education and vision. Sometimes it takes longer for the people to recognize that kind of leadership—They're so accustomed to the transactional kind (*I thought of Lincoln*); but when they do, the support you'll receive will be for a lifetime. Your time will come. You'll know it when you see it."

I was questioning myself and believed that both the calling and the *Poker Game* had led me into the wilderness. But, Valor kept me grounded. She seemed to reaffirm my pain and in 1996 I was beginning to love her for it.

SEVENTEEN
Friends and Strangers

"In the end, we will remember not the words of our enemies, but the silence of our friends."

Martin Luther King, Jr.

The Palm Restaurant is as iconic a place in Washington as the Lincoln Memorial only with better cuisine. Tucked almost clandestinely on 19th Street, in a canyon of grey, mostly humdrum office buildings, it's gravity for the powerful was legendary and its walls, festooned in caricatures, documented for posterity all those in its eminent constellation.

Several weeks after my 2002 campaign announcement, I entered the restaurant in search of the political credibility that simply being sighted there could magically bestow. Merely having lunch in the place could generate a blurb in the Washington Post's style section, if you lunched with the right person and wore the right suit.

I wore the right suit, my favorite blue pinstripe three piece. It was K Street with a Southeast swagger. It said power with its lapelled vest and its luxurious super 130's fabric. I accessorized with a three-pointed white linen pocket square, a French Blue, French cuffed shirt with both white collar and cuffs.

I finished the look with a red tie with blue polka dots and black deerskin oxford shoes, which had been shined to glossy perfection by one of the guys in Union Station. *They literally melt their polish onto the shoe with a hairdryer.*

Earlier in the day, I paid a visit to my barber, Arthur Grant, whose shop in Fairfax Village had become legendary the day Doug Williams received a crisp fade haircut there, about a week after his record setting exploits for the Redskins in Super Bowl XXII. I received my fade, again in expert fashion, amid questions about my campaign and promises of volunteers.

Like all barbershops in the Black community, *Clipper Cuts by Art* was like the town square. It was a place to buy socks, movies, stuffed animals, and second tier designer shoes. You could also get a damned good haircut.

It was primarily a place to exchange information but on that day the reports seemed more like ghost stories than casual barbershop conversation. I listened carefully.

"Man, yesterday I saw a white girl in hot pants and a big floppy hat riding a bike up Benning Road."

"I gotcha beat. I saw a white couple on a Vespa. They was riding across Sousa Bridge—and they was headin east!

Then Art chimed in, "yah ain't said a word. A white dude just moved next door to me and I live right there off of Good Hope Road! You heard me? He got a big ole German Shepherd too."

From the moment I walked in until the moment that I got out of the chair, I heard them share stories about their ever-increasing encounters with white people. The sightings were becoming more numerous by the day and what began as curiosity was beginning to turn into alarm.

Given the city's recent history, the locations of the sightings, deep in the heart of Black neighborhoods where even some Blacks feared to tread were a shock to the system. Most D.C. natives never thought they'd see the day.

I noticed it too. I began to see more pickup trucks in the city, more bicyclists and even people on motor scooters. The daily line at *Horace & Dickies*, home to the best-fried fish in town, had gotten shorter and for the first time in recorded history, did not extend beyond the door during lunchtime.

I took it all in but left the barbershop upbeat and ready to achieve my goal. *I didn't believe in ghosts.*

⸶

A common misconception about campaigns is that money is dispositive but the *Poker Game* had long since disabused me of that amateurish thought. "You only have to have enough money to work your plan," Lock had always said. "Money is a tool, fundraising is tactical and not strategic," my father had always preached.

In a perfect world, we only needed fifty thousand dollars, at a targeted vote of nine thousand. It worked out to fewer than six dollars a vote. It was a conservative plan and assumed a large turn out for the historic mayoral election year that was brewing and a high hit rate with my door to door canvassing. The campaign limit per person in a Ward race was five hundred dollars, so bundling contributions from the well heeled was the historic road to victory.

Life could be hard for challengers in the political fundraising game. Incumbents, as a rule have almost insurmountable advantages. Lobbyists' plowed cash into the coffers of Councilmembers with whom they often had significant disagreements because they subsisted on access. Having their name appear on a challenger's financial report was a cardinal sin punishable by *the death penalty—*

official banishment from that member's offices.

Even the business of scheduling appointments, a massive undertaking in any Councilmember's office, was often performed against contribution logs lovingly kept by the Chief of Staff. I had done it myself.

Most of the city viewed my opponent with contempt and I wanted to present myself to the moneychangers as a viable and reasonable alternative. In my suit and celebrity haircut, I was going against the grain.

I was meeting Chad Highsmith, a top city lobbyist who had gone to Georgetown law school with Desiree. I met him in the years that Desiree and I were together and followed his career with interest, as he became the preferred lobbyist of Mayor Terwilliger.

The Mayor was funneling business his way by not dealing with interests that didn't hire him. In eight short years, he had amassed an impressive fortune and brokered power like a man twice his age.

Chad didn't have an office and didn't play golf, an oddity for a top lobbyist. The Palm *was* his office; his sport was politics.

He was short, blond and mannerly and his folksy manner was either born of a genuine generosity of spirit or of veiled diabolical intent. I hadn't decided which.

He wore his custom made suits like a man to the manor born, despite his humble upbringing in the mountains of North Carolina. After graduating from Appalachian

State in finance, he talked his way into Georgetown Law. *At least that's what he said.*

He told the admissions committee that his father died in the eighties during the Marine Barracks bombing in Lebanon and the Jesuits admitted him. He lied, the Highsmith in question among the casualties was only a 3rd cousin once removed, that he had never met, a foreshadowing, perhaps of his future profession.

He told me this story in the opening minutes of what promised to be an opulent lunch, a ploy no doubt to gain my confidence. "Order what ever you want. *Whaddyagonna* have?"

He went on about his supposed exploits before lobbying, going on to claim that he had once done contract work for the CIA.

I didn't believe it but it certainly made for good conversation. There was some mystery to him though. Rumor had it that he'd been banned from Federal lobbying as a result of a FEC scandal.

After 30 minutes of coaxing, I broke the first rule of campaigning and shared a remarkable bottle of Chardonnay with him that cost more than my shoes. I was trying to show him that I was a regular guy and didn't mind sharing a drink with him. He no doubt, was trying to get me loose enough to see the real Jason Diggs. I'd seen that trick before.

A half-hour into lunch, after talking about the recent 9/11 attacks and the impending war, I popped the question over appetizers of Calamari and hearts of palm salad. *Enough with the niceties,* I thought.

"Chad, I need your help raising money. It's obvious that Brennan is going to out spend me but I need to keep it respectable."

"I understand your dilemma," he said leaning across the table."

"I am going to need thirty to win this race," I said purposely low-balling the figure. I realized that I couldn't trust him yet, if at all.

"Can you win?" he said in his Asheville drawl.

"I'm going to win!"

He smiled, pearly white veneers confidently glowing at me. *Must have cost him a fortune*, I thought.

"I'm not going to waste time asking you how. Your father, Lock Smith and the gang have a record that's hard to beat. I'm sure they have that well in hand.

"Well, they haven't even given me the full strategy yet. They even went so far as to say that it's my job to execute the plan, not to know it."

He laughed, teeth shimmering, his tie casually flipped over his left shoulder. He looked like my idea of Jay Gatsby, Robert Redford notwithstanding. His eyes were a nearly colorless shade of blue. He had no lips.

"Okay, lets cut to the chase. How much do you need from me?"

"Ten is fair for a man of your unique station in our great city."

"Hey, I'm just a little redneck from Asheville," he said disarmingly. His famous charm was wasted on me but I appreciated the effort. He was billing someone a fortune for this meeting.

"That may be, but you're a rich one and you control the Mayor's money."

"My complements."

This fact was not widely known but had been supplied to me by one of Lock's key operatives. Chad funneled money from various associates throughout the country and maintained several front corporations, holding companies really, to launder the cash to the Mayor's campaign committee, constituent service fund and pet projects. The actual donors were in the shadows. Though technically illegal or at least inconsistent with the spirit of the law, it was a tried and true method of getting large sums of money where it needed to be and later extracting the desired political results.

After the contribution landed where it was supposed to, Chad became the point person for these hidden interests in the city. In land write downs, where the value of city land was officially lowered and then sold; or in sole source contracts, the parties paid Chad to lobby the city after they had already bankrolled the Mayor, through Chad, to do their bidding. *The mafia would be proud.*

"I like you Jason," he said. "I always have. I was very sorry to hear about you and Desiree— I mean, that it didn't work out. You made such a great couple. She would have been a big help to you now."

"Well, thanks. That was a long time ago. She's moved on and as you can see, I have as well. A lot of other people are being helpful now and I hope you'll be too."

I was trying to get him back on the subject. The specter of Desiree always seemed to come up when I was moving on with my life.

"I understand. I've had my issues with women too. I just pay them up front now. Saves me time."

He started to grin again but I interrupting the process. "Will you help me Chad!" I have a goal of raising at least fifteen by November. I want to look good in the December 10th financial filing."

"Oh, I get it, you don't want anyone else in the race. Trying to keep 'em out are you?"

"That would be helpful, I think. Don't you?"

"Well let me think about that."

"You have a slight demographic advantage but a huge electoral disadvantage. You need to hold the black vote in line and turn them out but you want to suppress the white vote as much as you can and possibly win over some converts by running more to the center than you might ordinarily. Tough task I think. Especially with Callahan in the Mayor's race."

Chad was smart or his people were. He'd seized upon the underlying political realities of my campaign. He'd been briefed for this meeting.

"It's a tough task," I admitted. "But it becomes much more manageable with proper funding.

Then the check came. He quickly snatched it up, took a glance and set it down. I've got this buddy. You're a candidate." We hadn't ordered our entrees. With some imperceptible signal, he had cut our lunch short. *The Palm was his office.*

"Thanks Chad. What do you think?"

"Let me make some phone calls and I'll call you in a few days."

"That's fair, but I'd like to have you with me on this one. We're going to shock a lot of people."

"Oh, Jason, I don't think so Bubba. Here's a gift and you didn't hear it from me. I had a question about you dropped in the Mayor's most recent tracking poll and apparently all that door knocking you've been doing is starting to work. You're name ID is at 60 percent. Your favorability rating is already 4 points higher than Brennan's and he's the incumbent. You're doing well enough in the early going to be dangerous and people are concerned. You know what that means?"

"Keep it up?" I said eagerly.

"No, it means you're a legitimate threat. Not someone to be ignored, but someone to be eliminated."

"You mean beaten."

He leaned in again, this time with a strange intensity. The boyish charm was gone.

"No, Bubba. I mean *eliminated.*"

I had never processed fear well, not during Southeast street fights or the pledge process or even law school exams I hadn't studied for. I had to be sure of what he meant and decided to be direct. *Elimination, even for the heartiest of souls, is difficult to stomach.*

"What are you talking about Chad?" I kept it open ended, he could still help me, no need to burn down a bridge that I hadn't even reached yet.

"I think you know. Conservatively, there's about twelve billion dollars in development slated for your Ward in the next 5 years; condos, new single families and luxury apartments but not just residential. They're talking mixed use retail and possibly a new baseball stadium."

"We don't have a baseball team."

"We will. You saw the movie, *build it and they will come.* Football too, the Redskins will come back to the RFK site if we give 'em a reason to, they're leaving too much money on the table out there in the boondocks. Most of the city's scheduled revitalization is coming your way and people want to make sure the ground is level before investing that kind of cash."

"That the ground is level?"

"Sorry", he said smiling again, "I still have the Carolina's in me. What I mean is that developers and their investors are generally risk adverse on these kind of speculative projects. They can handle the usual market fluctuations but they don't want any big surprises, most of all political surprises. Surprises like, upstart Councilmen talking about smart growth, stopping gentrification and mandating inclusionary zoning while they're trying to get their deals done. No hills to climb. Level ground."

He might as well have been reading directly from my website, in fact he probably had. I had made all of those issues the centerpiece of my campaign, although I had used the positive phrase, maintaining *economic diversity* instead of the politically charged, *gentrification*, as part of my play toward younger whites. I was still trying to keep one toe in the center.

"I'm not anti-development Chad. I've even proposed a tax free zone on H Street to spur development over there."

"Yeah but they don't like H Street yet. There are too many legacies still."

"Legacies?"

"That's what they're calling your friends in Near Northeast and that's the nice version."

"What's the not so nice version?"

"Holdovers."

There. It was in the open. My father, Lock and even Valor seemed to have gotten it right and I had been very wrong. *The Plan* was more than operational; it was in its final phase. I thought we had more time.

"What I'm telling you Jason is that you need to modulate your tone a bit if you hope to stay out of these folks' way."

Modulate my tone? Who the fuck was he talking to? Strange that a man who made his living off the backs of Black people could think that way, I thought. Then I caught myself. Wasn't slavery based on similar cognitive dissonance and irrationality?

I wanted to knock the aura of white privilege off his smirking face. Perhaps it was the wine but he'd allowed his mask to slip and I'd glimpsed on his face a look, which said: *Fuck you; my whiteness trumps your brilliance.*

Keeping a cool exterior was proving difficult. It required all my inner strength but I was fortified by words my father drilled into me since those carefree days on my *no speed* bicycle: *Anger or fear in the presence of an enemy is weakness and above all show no weakness.*

In difficult situations, I liked to think of what AJ might do. It helped to lighten my mood since we took such vastly different approaches to life.

I had a good sense of what he would do in this situation—he *had* chosen, as a profession, a game, which celebrated violence. I mustered a smile then responded.

"I'm not in the way, Chad. I am standing in the gap for people who don't have a voice. I'm trying to save D.C. before it becomes Seattle or Boston or San Francisco."

"Those are all nice places, what you got against them?"

I didn't like facetiousness in people I didn't know very well, it smacked of condescension. There was something about a white man from the south taking that tone with me that hit me deep in my DNA. I looked around the room to gather myself again and saw Bob Schieffer come in with Carville.

"Nothing," I said. "They're just not D.C. We shouldn't try to mimic something that we're not. We're not about trendy lounges and sushi bars...we're not even about cherry blossoms, although they're nice. We're about crab feasts and Go-Go music, hand dancing and Heinekens on a humid summer night, BYOB cabarets at the Masonic Temple and Frankie Beverly and Maze at Constitution Hall. That's what I'm fighting for."

Chad leaned in again, as if sharing a secret. *I could see then that this was a tactic of his.*

"Jason, how's that old saying go? You build on people, and you build on mud?"

"It's from Machiavelli's *The Prince* and the actual quote is *he who builds upon the people builds upon mud*," I said.

"Right, right and that's the point. There's a big mudslide happing in the city right now. You're going to want to be on the other side of that, Bubba. You don't want to be washed away."

"I studied Machiavelli Chad. I just don't happen to agree with him on that point."

I stood up and thanked him for lunch, such as it was, and shook his hand firmly. I didn't bother to ask when I could expect his call because I understood then that he was just a messenger and this had been a friendly warning. I had just broken bread with the enemy.

The room was buzzing with high-powered luncheon activity, deals were being cut, secrets exchanged. I walked past the bar and toward the series of doors to the street and Chad called to me from the table in order to get the last word.

"Hey Bubba, by the way, nice suit!" His crab cakes had arrived, along with another bottle of Chardonnay.

EIGHTEEN
The Enterprise

"I am and have always been your friend."

Star Trek II, The Wrath of Khan

I t's hard to think of the neighborhood that I grew up in as being in a major American city. A jaded New Yorker would call it the suburbs. Trees dominated the landscape as far as you could see and great hills, small mountains really, were the dominant feature there. Old stately houses with perfectly groomed lawns peppered the scene. It was an oasis in a turbulent time and a Black oasis at that.

Hillcrest and Penn Branch were Far Southeast's outposts of Black success. Unlike their gold coast counterparts of Shepherd Park or East and West Beech, the hard working people who settled in my neighborhood were neither lions of politics nor high chiefs of K Street or even business tycoons.

They simply saved their money and achieved the all-elusive American dream. It was D.C.'s Silver Coast.

In the 1970's, deep in the recesses of these nearly unknown neighborhoods, young simbas were nurtured for the future; and we fully expected that a future would exist for us. In my neighborhood, AJ and I were leaders of this pride of young lions—initiating trends, approving the slang and setting the pace on fashion. As disparate as our tastes were, we were the arbiters of what girls were or were not desirable.

While AJ leaned toward the precociously developed, pretty faces and keen intellect, moved me. At least in that regard, not much changed over the years.

It was the 1970s and we had mostly intact families then. Life was a slice of Americana, from a decidedly Black perspective. In our Afro's, bell bottoms and knit shirts we roamed our territory with confidence riding ten speeds and racing home fashioned go-carts down the undulating hills of Southeast Washington.

We fashioned homemade guns from six-inch wooden boards and rubber bands and with soda can caps as ammunition, patrolled menacingly as if to protect our adolescent fiefdom from certain invasion. We were prescient, if premature in our vigilance.

With my father busy both at Howard and with the ongoing development of our political system, and my mother newly installed as Chair of the English department at the newly consolidated University of the

District of Columbia, I was often left to my own devices. After our violent introduction, AJ had become my best friend.

At 14, Girls were enigmas, reflections of a dream that I couldn't remember, unfamiliar and untouchable. To AJ they were the punctuation in a well-written sentence, necessary and intimate. Boys always seemed to always lie where their penises were concerned, but as far as I can tell, AJ never had to. He appeared more sexually experienced than many of our college age neighbors and he spoke of the alien terrain as a boy who'd been there.

AJ's edge was confidence. He was never reticent about talking to girls, while the rest of us stood at mirrors reciting well-practiced lines that we were often not bold enough to employ. He laughed heartily with the girls as they giggled at our pathetic attempts.

Yet AJ was not as expert as most of us at negotiating the mundane life of middle class teenagers. Principal among his faults was his hatred of school. He just couldn't abide 8th grade English and basic geography and never really tried.

"I go to school for lunch, to play basketball and because my Papi would kick my ass if I didn't," he would say.

I was devoted to the academic aspects of school and decided to intervene in his cause. I felt I owed him, he had taught me so much.

I explained that Calvin Hill, his favorite running back had gone to Yale and that Alan Page, was not just a Purple People Eater for Minnesota's defensive line but was also a lawyer. He got the message but still resisted.

"I ain't you man," he would always say.

"Your a good looking motherfucker, you're a fast motherfucker and you're a smart motherfucker. I'm just, good looking, cool and fast. That's all I got."

I was strange to see the normally confident AJ in such a state and I felt badly for him. It was clear that beyond his bravado, AJ was just as unsure of himself as the rest of us.

"Look man", I would respond, "You're smart too, only in a different way. You're funnier than the rest of us. You talk to girls better than all of us and you're drawings are cool; nobody can draw superheroes like you do. I'll help you with your work, but you have to do it yourself."

"I don't know man," he said.

"AJ, we both like Star Trek right? Looking at Uhuru in that red mini?"

"Yeah, she got a sweet ass."

"Well, you know how Spock helps Kirk out with things he doesn't understand?"

"Yeah, Spock *ah-ite*. I like how he be choking them aliens out."

"Well you're Kirk and I'm Spock. Kirk kicks butt and has all the women and he's smart too, but Spock has special powers and makes Kirk a better Captain. Think of our friendship as the Enterprise."

For weeks after that we shared information at warp speed. I loaned him Tolkien, Twain and Orwell and he introduced me to the prettiest girls at the parties we attended, often using the fact that I was going to be a lawyer one day as my calling card, as if that made any difference to a twelve year old girl.

I worked with him on integers, though I didn't fully understand them myself, and he gave me fashion tips, like where to buy those sporty Italian soft leather shoes (at Iverson Mall) or how to go to Cavalier at 10th and F to buy the flowered shirts and polyester pants that were the height of fashion at Sousa Junior High in the fall of 1977.

The Enterprise was a success over time. By Christmas time AJ had become a C student and I could comfortably talk to girls. By the end of the school year, he had a solid C+ average and I was considered cool, if a little too bookish. By the time we were about to leave for High School, AJ was a B student and I had nearly become his match on the social scene. I left my former walk partners from the honor roll to their reading in the scholarly section of the lunchroom, while I held court within the clubby confines of the party section.

We were free in that summer of 1978 confidently walking our neighborhood like heirs to an empire. There were recreation room gatherings to listen to the latest Parliament Funkadelic or Cameo albums and the more adventurous among us had taken the first tentative musical steps toward the jazz-fusion of Return to Forever and Weather Report. We would ride our bicycles to Ft.

DuPont Park on hot and humid weekend nights, to hear among the multitudes, the legends of jazz and R&B—a thousand bands of sweet burning incense rising through the oaks like the ghosts of a forgotten age.

These were like AP courses in progressive Black coolness as Afro's gave way to Shags and inevitably to waves, if you could get them. These were the days when the Afro pick was replaced by the stiff bristled brush. This was the summer of Carine Clarke and my sap was rising.

My education under AJ's tutelage was complete and I had emerged independent in my ability to solicit a girl's telephone number but I had never fully tested my newly acquired powers until a shopping trip for school clothes in August of 1978. It happened at Iverson Mall, just across the Maryland line and I was with my mother in the ladies section of Woodward and Lothrop department store.

"Jason, I am going to try this on."

"All right Ma," I said.

I almost never complained on these shopping sprees, I had been trained as her shopping companion since birth, but now there was an added incentive to accompany my mother on these forays. Beyond the wonderful lunches at the Hot Shoppes Cafeteria or an abundance of nice purchases in the bag for me, there were Girls!

I suddenly noticed that there were hundreds upon hundreds of girls at the mall. They were different girls than the ones in my neighborhood. Tall, short, pretty, big boned, small boned. I became quite a compliant shopping partner.

I first saw Carine at the register, giggling with her sister. A lady, obviously their mother, was paying for a dress. I smiled at her and she smiled back beneath her open hand.

Later, I saw her again downstairs at Orange Julius, alone at a table. She was adorable—long hair in braids, light brown skin and petite. She was wearing a pink and white shorts set and pink Candies.

My mother was in the ladies room and I made my move.

"Hi, my name is Jason."

"I'm Carine."

"I'm not going to take the chance that I won't see you again, so I'd like have your phone number."

Amid the giggles of her 11-year-old sister, who'd suddenly arrived from the hot dog line, Carine scribbled her phone number on a damp napkin in girlish purple ink. I had gotten my first phone number.

I called her for weeks and convinced of my love for this tiny doll of a girl, visited her on my bike one week before my 15th birthday. She live in Penn-Branch, just down the hill from me on Nash Place and it was there, under her parents' carport, that I had my first kiss.

I loved her sticky, candy stained lips, which tasted of watermelon *Now and Laters*.

We were boyfriend and girlfriend within days but by Thanksgiving, it was over.

My heart was broken for the first time. Adolescent love, like all love, can be ephemeral but the experience was pure, the intimacy real and the memory eternal.

Days after we began talking on the phone and many months before our break-up, Carine asked me if I had a nickname. The question made me feel awkward because although I didn't have one, I felt that she wanted me to. I gave a quick response.

"It's Kirk."

NINETEEN
Desiree

"The hottest love has the coldest end."

Socrates

Sexual relations with Desiree Pitchford was an intoxicant. It carried both risk and reward.

The after effects of encounters with her were akin to possession—no, addiction describes it best, for there was nothing remotely spiritual about our association. It was ultimately a carnal and base affair.

Our sexual exploits weren't as avant-guard as one might, expect, and were firmly with the realm of decency that I'd experienced with other women. *Although there had been Desiree's two-month fascination with anal sex, but that developed an irksome quality over time.*

Desire was mildly sadomasochistic and believed that good sex was based on primeval notions of desire, power and control. Spirited and intelligent as she was, Desiree longed for a man to control her entirely and this herculean labor, this solitary province of the gifted, fell to me.

It seems I'd unlocked her. Command of her robust sexuality was only to be achieved through mastery of her amoral, compartmentalized mind.

The realization that that I could control her empowered me; but it was like playing with dark matter and just as dangerous. Her physicality could overwhelm.

She had a disquieting mouth, which teased with perpetual moistness. It was fragrant, delectable—unchaste, like ripped open citrus.

She had boyish narrow hips and she was strong, stronger than many men, almost as strong I and in every position she tried to dominate. Even with her voluminous ass raised submissively in the air, she'd happily devour everything thrown at her.

With Desiree you did not conquer, for fear of becoming lost in her sexual and intellectual snobbery. To emerge victorious you surrendered, not losing your manhood in the process, but in fact, gaining it in the knowledge that you had harnessed such a rare and magnificent creature.

So it was the challenge of her mind and body that was addictive. Fearsome and sweet like the Roman goddesses that drove men mad and madness was my fate for daring such intimacies with such as she.

Several years had passed since she'd first brought me to the Vineyard and in the years that followed the trips became as anticipated as the springtime after the bitterness of winter. We adored the cocktail parties in rented houses, the stylish friends encircled on the beach; it was like a familiar dark rendering of a Fitzgerald classic.

We craved the fresh air during Circuit Avenue strolls, long naps taken naked on rainy days and meaty lobster rolls with toasted buns eaten as impromptu afternoon snacks. We'd make up-island runs to Menemsha for fresh steamed lobsters at sunset and to Aquinnah for *all over* tans—the weak New England sun bronzing our precious melanin to perfection. In the end, there was always hot sex on cool nights—windows open, the gooseflesh rising on our quivering bare skin.

The Vineyard was the plumb line for everything we experienced in our lives. We oriented our lives around its unerring tranquility; needing all we saw and all we did to conform to *it*. But nothing *did*. Nothing could.

In 1997 boredom set in. Even as our course toward marriage remained true, we began to argue over minutiae. I endured an endless stream of *subculture* events as lifestyle concessions to her, which blurred into a series of farcical vignettes. I suggested alternatives but she was committed.

Desiree's friends weren't dumb just blasé and effete. With the exception of the unmarried women in attendance, I was always the most motivated person in the room.

There was a permanent absence of substantive dialogue within the group and I feared for the city when I realized one black tie New Years Eve that these people would one day, if only through attrition, become the leaders of the African American community.

Most of them already had low tags and were on the right lists. Half of them had familial or social ties to the present leadership, Councilmembers, Board Chairmen, law partners and heads of surgery.

I was sick of the whole thing. Even as a Diggs and a City Council Chief of Staff, I never fit in, never had the social currency. But my disillusionment with the *subculture* was only a proxy for my disgust for the permanent ennui that I was convinced I would suffer upon my marriage to Desiree.

I cringed at the thought of giving up my Hillcrest progressivism for what I saw as the relative conservatism of Shepard Park. I knew well that with Desiree, anywhere we lived would be transformed into a dreary *subculture* outpost, but I continued the relationship out of loyalty to a swiftly fading conviction; *she was The One, we were perfect together.*

People wanted to know why the engagement was broken off only a month before the wedding and how it was that Desiree moved out of town so fast. They were even more eager to know how she met, got pregnant and married another man in less than five months.

My stock answer was that she was motivated. Apparently, there was trust fund money coming to her if she married and I had called it off.

I shared the true story on only two occasions. Possession is hard to overcome. Even now I can visualize Desiree's body, long and feline like a panther, swaying toward the bathroom after sex. Time heals, but it does not erase.

In 1999 we had been on a short winter vacation in Miami with AJ and his girlfriend of the moment, Li, as she liked to be called. Li was an actress who was a rising star in the porn industry and had her own voyeuristic website. She was 6 feet tall with flaming red hair and green eyes. She was African-American.

The Pro Bowl had just been played but for only the second time in his career, AJ had not. He decided to treat us to a Miami getaway as consolation and a premature marriage gift, generously flipping for a two-bedroom suite at the Savoy Hotel.

I had always been reluctant to accept the largess of my friend the pro athlete. I feared the negative repercussions of public partying and drunken high-end mayhem on my then far-in-the future political career.

I relented at Desiree's insistence. "Oh, we simply have to go." She said. One time couldn't hurt, I told myself that it was just a long weekend with friends and we'd be careful.

The weekend started, in fine fashion, on an eighty-degree February day. The ladies were gorgeous in their bikinis and AJ was armed with what seemed like a lifetime supply of Cuban Montecristo #2's which he carried in their own padded stainless steel suitcase.

I carried a small travel humidor of my mainstay CAO Brazilia cigars. They were better for me, just in case a photo surfaced later and for flavor I found they more than held their own with AJ's stash.

We had a Rolls Royce and driver at our disposal and beautiful women on our arms. We had partying money the likes of which I had never seen, as AJ's season bonus had just hit his bank account.

"Jason, I got a 2 million dollar bonus for going over 1000 yards."

"What?"

"They didn't think I could still do it. They were underestimating my *skill sets* brother." We had a good laugh at his spot on impersonation of me.

"Well you did have an off year last year."

"But I still made the Pro Bowl last year and got the best deal of my career, four years, 10 million. I didn't make it this year but I'll live with that. I *am* 36 years old."

"Hey man, the whole city is proud of you, H.D. Woodson's own."

That evening we feasted for hours at Joe's Stone Crab and spent the night partying at *Nikki Beach*. AJ adding admiring fans (mostly women) to the entourage as we went.

296

By 4 AM we'd returned to the suite with a dozen people collected from the club and AJ had several magnums of White Star and a few bottles of Patron brought up.

I decided that I would rather walk on the beach with Desiree and smoke a cigar, than party into the wee hours of the morning with strangers.

We walked barefoot in the sand and talked about the future, while we waited out AJ's groupies. The slight breeze on the beach barely moved the thermometer; *the next day will be even hotter than today,* I thought.

I told Desiree that I wanted to make love as the sun came up. She said it was a wonderful thought on a beautiful night and I began to feel remorseful about the ill feelings I'd been harboring toward her. I wanted to make this work. We'd been together for almost ten years and it was time to consummate matters.

She'd wanted to get her career of the ground and she had, as a manager in one of the smaller agencies in D.C. government. It was a job in the Office of People's Counsel that my father wrangled for her. It was far from glamorous and she wasn't happy about it.

Desiree and I returned forty minutes later to find the room in a state of orgy. We found AJ in the bedroom with Li and a very attractive Latino woman was very much engaged with both of them. I was aroused and naturally stayed close to Desiree.

"We should join them," said Desiree, finding my eyes as she did when she was happy.

"That's a little wild don't you think?" I said.

"I know, but just look at them," she said, excited by the debauchery. She wasn't reticent at all and seemed to consider it as harmless as leaving the lights on or opening the windows.

I had to acknowledge that it was a titillating sight. Li was in her natural element with naked men and women in sexual frenzy, all to the weird sound of muffled house music. It was exactly the kind of gross indiscretion that I had avoided my whole life.

I couldn't even afford to have pictures or eyewitnesses to my presence, let alone my participation in something like this. I was making my move politically and this was the kind of thing that ends it for you.

"I see them," I responded "maybe we can go somewhere else, get another room, you know I'll *holler* at you as soon as we're alone." I smiled.

"No, here babe. I hoped this was going to happen, I mean with AJ and Li—I was going to tell you. Don't you want to fuck Li, I do—she's gorgeous isn't she? AJ is too."

Perhaps I was naive but I was surprised when my fiancée (who still had no ring) spoke of pulling a foursome with my best friend and his porn star girlfriend. I was even more startled when she took off her blouse and pulled down her skirt before I could answer.

She was wearing one of the dozen Cosabella thongs that I'd given her for

Christmas and the room noticed immediately. Soon a young blonde woman, who had been ogling us from the corner of the room, sauntered over and began removing Desiree's bra.

I will admit that I became aroused when they began kissing and even further aroused when Desiree took my hand as she walked the three of us toward our bedroom. Three Latino men were taking turns doing a pretty Jamaican girl with a Hottentot ass.

Desiree saw them too, but I did not pull her away, deciding, due to my preexisting ambivalence about our future to let her go her own way. She would have to make *that* decision just as *we* would have to live with the consequences.

Naturally, I was surprised when she released my hand and continued with the blonde into the bedroom. What did she expect me to do? Was she aware that she was crashing through thin ice into an abyss? I have always assumed so, just as I assumed that she expected me to follow.

The steps Desiree took, she took on her own; perhaps it was she that was getting rid of me. I simply closed the door, selected one of AJ's Montecristos and walked away.

I wasn't angry or hurt. I just needed to think. It had been a very long day.

I left early that day after maneuvering through the naked masses to pack. Desiree was still asleep, wrapped in a twisted heap of humanity.

AJ later told me that Desiree had been one of the stars of the show. He'd watched her have sex with both men and women that morning; including the girl with the Hottentot ass. "I'm sorry, but I told you to keep your head on a swivel man." He said.

Apparently, true to her word, she'd even propositioned AJ, who but for his friendship with me, would have surely been amenable. When pressed, he could neither confirm nor deny whether Desiree and Li had gotten together. "I was kinda of busy at the time dude."

Desiree denied these facts upon her return to Washington, in spite of what I had seen. It was as if she was trying to will a different interpretation into existence.

"How can you believe him over me?"

"That's an easy proposition. I saw what I saw and the rest can simply be inferred." In the end, it was irrelevant. As much as it pained me I had closed the door.

The events of Miami had been charitable; they left no outward scars. I appeared as I always had, except for a moderate tan from my 24 hours in the famous Florida sun. The damage, if you could call it that, was to my state of mind.

I alone recognized it. Others simply viewed my manic moments as the natural response of a public man who realized too late that the love of his life was possessed of more libertine sexual mores than he imagined.

One of my fraternity brothers put it another way: *"maybe she's one of those very exotic women, but you want your wife to be your mistress, not everybody's whore."*

For Desiree, there had undoubtedly been other times. One does not make their first solo flight in a 747. There must have been hundreds of hours logged in on a Cessna.

The incident manifested itself within me as a frosty cynicism about the utility of romance and a cold-eyed skepticism about love. Women had been toppled from the ivory pedestal I'd erected for them in childhood.

I began to recruit women to my bed with the regularity of the seasons. But the sex did not heal. It was only recommended by the lustful satisfaction it supplied.

Valor had once again gone off the grid, only to return after a year with budding dreadlocks, a renewed social conscious and a new job lobbying for the NAACP. I was growing impatient with my job at the Council; I was working for a fool.

I began to seek new horizons. Change was all around me at the end of the Twentieth Century but for the moment, we still had Chocolate City.

TWENTY
Drop The Bomb

"The only thing I know is that I know nothing."

Socrates

There is really only one rule in politics: things never turn out as you plan them. Several months after my announcement for Council, I abandoned my fundraising plan and made the painful decision to dip into my inheritance from my mother to keep the campaign going.

By then, I had lived for five years in my uncle's Winston's house at 600 A Street, N.E. It was a house that he'd left my mother and it was now four short years later, it was mine.

In the earlier days of the arrangement, I demanded to pay rent on the property as I had for the random series of apartments that I rented since law school, but my mother insisted on putting the money into an account—the corpus of which I never expected to see again. Her round the clock care had generated many expenses.

"Jason, I'm not using this money, it's your nest egg. Your uncle Winston's house was paid for over thirty ago. I'm only paying the taxes."

My mother's health care needs were so severe that the house into which I had been born, long a rental property adding to the family income and which had helped my parents pay for my college education without student loans, had already been mortgaged to fill the gap. But, even though the exchange of family wealth for peace of mind was tragic, it was worth it.

600 A Street was small but dignified. It would have fit comfortably within the Hillcrest House at least three times but it was enormous by Capital Hill standards. Its neat brick structure was set horizontally upon a small hill in the heart of the Northeast end of the Capitol Hill Historic District.

Its dense emerald lawn set it apart from the adjacent houses, which primarily had yards of mulch and haphazardly arranged wildflowers. My Uncle Winston's House possessed its own attached garage and its driveway provided the house with the most coveted of Capitol Hill amenities—off street parking. Above the garage rested a small deck, which I often used for small cookouts, daytime reading and seasonal cigar smoking.

The interior was immaculate. It had pristine floors of Georgia Pine and a working marble fireplace. In winter, Desiree and I would cuddle before it. Later, I brooded before it, alone.

I never lit the fireplace when Valor came over. We normally went to bed straight away, toting glasses and a good bottle of wine.

Stacks of books lined my walls, mostly unencumbered by bookcases. Several pieces by Black artists were staged at pivotal points throughout the house, pieces by Varnette Honeywood, who'd I collected since law school—inspired by her vivid Cosby Show displays and Andrew Turner, for his brawny and colorful depictions of black men working.

Most of my money was in the books and in my sound system: Nakamichi components with remotes and JBL speakers. Assembling that tour de force was a labor of love and essential for the jazz influenced soundtrack, which accompanied my life. Brothers like me need theme music.

I filled my house with Mission Furniture from Crate and Barrel. It was economical, sturdy and masculine. I kept red carnations in a green vase. I had a Brown bed with white sheets. It was clean. I had a humidor. I wasn't there much.

In desperation, I was using my former rent payments for Uncle Winston's House, my "nest egg," to finance my campaign. It was surprisingly substantial, about $30,000 and I instantly understood that my mother had given me a gift that could never, however hard I worked or tried, be repaid.

My father offered to loan me ten thousand dollars—royalties, which to my astonishment still came in from the sales of his books to colleges and university libraries. I refused. He was very near mandatory retirement age at the University and needed his money to live on.

"Keep it, Pop. In a few months, after this is all over, you should take that trip to Cuba, you haven't been anywhere since Ma got sick."

"Are you now my travel agent?" he responded.

"That might not be such a bad career after all of this is over, I said."

We had a good laugh. His humor was back. There was hope in his eyes.

Rain is the mortal enemy of fundraisers. People tended to stay at home or go to the mall or do almost anything instead of eating Costco hors d'oeuvres and contributing their hard earned cash to a political campaign. That night, I was losing an ancient duel with human nature.

Only a dedicated few had battled the elements to join me and by 8 PM it was clear that we wouldn't even break $300 on the night. Before I decided to run, I had been pledged enough money by inside players and in-kind support by the gamers and soldiers that victory seemed inevitable. I knew better, but I continued to smile with appreciation for contributions that would never come.

Trey Cobb, a diminutive utility executive and member of the subculture, urged me to take on Brennan. Pumping my hand in his microscopic mitt, he described how I could win on my *"youth, D.C. roots and passion for the city."*

Craig Stone, a former Councilmember and latter day lobbyist told me fervently that, *"I had the goods"* and should I decide to run, he would be *"with me all the way."* These men were not unique in their early professions of faith—nor in their failure, following my announcement, to return any of my telephone calls.

With so intimate a crowd at my fundraiser at the trendy *Café 202* on Capitol Hill, it was understandable that the discussions among those assembled might turn from my political dreams to the realities of the day. Just before five that morning, a luxury condo under construction on Florida and New York Avenues, near the future site of the headquarters of the Bureau of Alcohol Tobacco and Firearms had been leveled by an explosion. People were scared.

I had been preoccupied with my quest and not very interested in headlines but this was post 9/11 and the anthrax attacks had already occurred. Roadblocks had been set up throughout Capitol Hill and palpable fear in the streets. Now another terrifying event had the city reeling.

No one claimed responsibility and the authorities were baffled. The site was without any discernable political significance. Without any answers fearful people stayed at home, out of the rain.

✝

That morning I had been uptown at People's Congregational Church. I had not gone to pray, although I needed every entreaty of that kind that I could get. I was there to meet with Reverend Richard Clarke about receiving his endorsement.

Clarke was an old mainstay in D.C. politics and while he shaded toward the conservative, he was honorable and clearly had the city at heart. Receiving a nod from him might loosen up some of the 16th Street cash that had eluded me up to that point.

People's Congregational was in Ward Four but the luminaries that were parishioners there wielded citywide influence. Judges, Doctors, Law Partners, retired city officials from the days of Walter Washington—the city's first Black Mayor. Much of the Old Guard sat in those pews and they had resources.

My father and the *Poker Game* had done battle with Reverend Clarke dozens of times over the years, and had defeated him in every skirmish. They'd elected SNCC alumni and their acolytes to office over those golden scions of Black privilege that Clarke doggedly promoted.

I was relying on the good Reverend's piety and his willingness to turn the other cheek. I needed him in my gambit to retake the Council and the meeting bore fruit.

"I like your background and you're a passionate young man, very impressive. You're a native Washingtonian, a Morehouse Man, a Howard Law Man and you have a good head on you're shoulders. I'll need to poll the Trustees but I don't think we're going to have a problem."

I knew he controlled the Trustee Board of his Church and so the poll was a mere formality. I had appealed to his sense of vanity because no one in politics considered him a power anymore. In a weird twist of fate, my father had done more to diminish his reputation as a kingmaker than anyone, but I needed help from wherever it graciously came.

I was grateful and promised to be at his church on Sunday for the announcement. "If I am blessed by your support sir, I won't let you down."

I'd given him my stock stump speech, full of lofty platitudes about uplifting the downtrodden and preserving our way of life. Told him that I stood on his shoulders and that of the thousands that made D.C. what it had been to so many. That, "we can't afford to lose what so many had fought so hard to attain."

We knelt in prayer at his insistence and after an unusually long 5 minutes, I arose refreshed and hopeful that this could be a turning point. I left the church pleased that someone was willing to back what was increasingly becoming a herculean trial.

I had prayed not for victory but for something more powerful. Salvation.

Brennan was raking in the cash like a Lincoln Heights drug dealer. His last report showed him with fifty thousand dollars cash on hand with over sixty-five thousand raised and we hadn't even had the first debate yet. I on the other hand was running on fumes. The money I had loaned the campaign was gone; used to pay for posters, phone service and to keep our little storefront campaign office open on H Street.

I walked deep in thought and prayed again for a good showing at the fundraiser that night. I knew there'd been some kind of explosion on the edge of the Ward that morning but there was no further information. At that point I was more concerned that the weatherman had called for rain. I knew what that meant.

"Jason, Jason!"

I heard a woman calling me. The voice sounded sweetly familiar. I squinted into the afternoon sun smiling the candidate smile, the smile that said *I'm approachable, even electable. Give me some money, please!*

Persephone Randolph was shouting from an extravagantly accessorized Mercedes S Class that was idling parallel to my car on 13th Street. Consumed as I was by my campaign, it did my heart good to see that a woman who had once shared my bed was still willing to call my name these many years later.

She was radiant, even in jeans and a weathered '93 Black Dog tee shirt. I felt it instantly. She was *the one that got away.*

"I saw the signs on the car and I decided to wait to see, you know, if it was really you," she said.

"Well here I am," I said, now giving the *please come to my fundraiser tonight smile.*

"I heard you were running. I always knew you would."

The trees on that part of 13th street are old and lush, harkening back to the days when Washington was called *the city of trees.* The big elms framed her as she emerged from the car to hug me, reminding me of a Labor Day weekend when for two days we had become lovers on the Vineyard.

I met Persephone during one of my many break ups with Desiree, who in order to avoid seeing me over the long weekend, had gone to Sag Harbor with her modeling friends instead of the Vineyard.

"You look exactly as I remember you," I said.

"And you are just as charming as you were then. So, what are you doing up here in the middle of the day? Aren't you running down on Capital Hill?"

"I had a meeting with Reverend Clarke, I think he's going to endorse me!"

"That's great. I've gone to this church since I was a baby. I was Christened here and my mother is on the Trustee Board." *Another break.*

"That's a coincidence. I had no idea." I said. "The Reverend is going to bring up my name at the meeting tomorrow, he's looking for the Board's support of his endorsement of me. Would you mind talking to your mother about me?"

She laughed.

"And what am I supposed to say to her? That Jason Diggs deserves the support of the church because for two days he rocked her daughter's world, like nobody ever has and then never called her again?"

Women have elephantine memory's when it come to sex. They literally internalize it.

"Okay you've got me. I was in a bit of a funk back then," I said trying to recover.

"Hey, I'm just joking man, chill out. I know what happened and I'm cool with it. Consenting adults and all that. Did you and Desiree ever get back together?"

"We did and then three years ago it ended for good."

She looked at my left hand.

"Still not married?"

"No, you?"

"Divorced."

"I'm sorry, were you married long?"

"Not really, only four years and don't' be sorry, he was an ass. It just became final last month. Don't worry, he wasn't one of your Frat brothers."

"Excellent. He didn't ruin things for me then," I said. She laughed.

Persephone was a graduate student in international relations at Johns Hopkins when we met. She loved my Fiat—her black wavy bob blew wildly as we drove up island to Menemsha for lobster. In her sunglasses, she looked like a brown thirties era starlet.

She was also a sweet girl, a pretty girl with a wonderful sense of humor. She'd attended Yale as an undergraduate but of all the women who had come into my life, she reminded me most of the Spelmanites, with whom I'd begun my romantic career—so grounded and full of class.

But I wasn't ready to reengage so soon after that break up with Desiree. If I had been, I would have avoided many hard days.

"You seeing anybody?" I said.

"Are you kidding? I'm seeing *everybody*. I'm enjoying my freedom."

"I can understand that."

"You?" She said smiling.

"Well, lets just say that I have a few friends, but no one in particular. This campaign has all my time now."

"Well, we should get together when you have time. I am leaving for South Africa tomorrow and won't be back until October but when I get back, I'd like to *see* you Mr. Diggs. Hopefully, you'll be the nominee by then."

"Thanks. But, South Africa? Wow, that's great!"

"I work for TransAfrica now as a senior policy analyst. It's business."

"Wow, I was going to invite you to a fundraiser that I am having tonight at 202 but that might be a bit much with your schedule."

"Oh, I wish I had known, but I will write you a check. I'll drop it I the mail before I leave."

"That's nice of you. I really would like to hook up when you come back. It would be nice to get together."

"I think so too—but do you still have a sheath of granite around your heart?"

"What?"

"That's the last thing you told me when you dropped me at the airport on the Vineyard—that you had—let me get this right—a sheath of granite around your heart and that it would take a while for you to fully open up again."

"Well, I think you could say that that situation has been addressed. It's been a long time."

"That's good to hear Jason. Really. So, what ever happened to that cute little white car? Fifi right?"

"I still have her."

"Oh, that's wonderful Jason."

"I'll give you a ride when you come back."

"I can't wait."

I could imagine spending time with this woman who, like me, had a classical sounding name. I'd never really given us a chance; I might have missed a chance at happiness with her. *I was going to stop running the streets when I got elected.*

"So what do you think about this bombing? Who do you think did it?" I said.

"Well no international terrorist organization would bomb a condo building a mile from the Capitol. It has no strategic or symbolic value. They'd just try to bomb the Capitol, wouldn't they?"

"So are you saying its domestic?" I asked.

"I'm saying its local. Somebody is trying to make a more parochial point, using this new war on terror as cover."

A storm was expected and the wind blew her ribbons of wavy hair. Wisps of it stuck to her freshly applied red lipstick. *I'm going to call her in South Africa, I thought.*

She tossed her hair to the side, delicately dislodging the stuck sticky strands. *It was provocative and was perhaps an invitation.*

"This is all very disturbing," she continued. "You're probably going to get asked a lot of questions about this, I mean, about what the response should be."

"That's for sure. I hope I have some answers." I looked at the ground, as if searching for them.

"Hey, lets exchange information, I know you have to go and I have a ton of

314

running around to do before tomorrow." she said reaching for her purse.

I handed her one of my campaign cards. All of my numbers were on it.

"Very efficient Mr. Diggs."

"Just a little something-something, you know." I said laughing.

She laughed and handed me her TransAfrica business card:

Persephone Randolph-Bennett, PhD

Senior Policy Analyst, South Africa

She'd crossed out, *hyphen Bennett* with red ink.

"Very nice *Seph*. You've done well for yourself, girlie."

"It's important work and I enjoy it. I get to meet with Mandela quite a bit."

"Wow! That's alright." Is this cell number good in South Africa?"

"Yes, but just remember the time difference. I need my beauty rest." She smiled freely, enjoying the irony. She knew that she was beautiful.

We hugged again and I kissed her firmly on her cheek. I walked her to her car.

"I'll call you this time," I said with a wink.

"You'd better," she said, hopping into her car. And off she went, driving in style past the lush old elms on Allison Street.

TWENTY-ONE
The End

*"Every great dream begins with a dreamer.
Always remember, you have within you the
strength, the patience, and the passion to reach for
the stars to change the world."*

Harriett Tubman

What is it like to tilt at windmills in the modern age? My quest took on a decidedly urban patina. We were being hopelessly outgunned financially and I had no more money to loan the campaign.

My personal finances were in shambles but despite Brennan's propaganda we'd caught fire in the streets.

The whole city was abuzz with talk about the sea of red posters on lawns and shop windows throughout the Ward which were defiantly emblazoned with the words:

Jason Diggs, Our Next Councilman.

Defending the Future of Our Community

I highlighted the theme at the end of my stump speeches:

And so this campaign is dedicated to the hopes, dreams and aspirations of every man, woman and child to whom this place is more than a way station or a temporary government posting but home. Home, the place from which we sprang. Home, a place where the very ground is fertilized with the bones of ancestors who scratched their way up from bondage to stand as freemen and women in this shining Capitol, and building better lives for their children.

Ladies and gentlemen, these lives are now in peril. Help me to defend the future that our grandmothers and grandfathers fought and died for. Help me to ensure a future in which our children and grandchildren are partners in our city's progress and not just the help—one in which they are property owners-not just groundskeepers, a future in which they are they educated to the fullest extent possible and not simply in the employ of those who are. Join me in defending a future, where our children are not at the mercy of anyone, but retain all the blessings of citizenship; rights that were purchased with the blood and sacrifice of the fallen.

Join us in protecting a future that can be enjoyed by all, to the benefit of all. A future of shared burdens and shared rewards—and with your help, we will build the Ward that we always deserved, in a city that belongs to all of us.

I had a fine line to tread in my rhetoric. I couldn't come off too stridently for fear that Brennan would tag me as divisive which is the word that white demagogues use to describe a Black person who is pro-Black.

He had still not set foot in the Black areas of the Ward, hadn't suggested any Black people for appointment to the vaunted

Boards and Commissions that lent prestige and authority to ordinary citizens. He had espoused policies that hastened the loss of Black population and had been openly dismissive of the interests of the poor, the Black and the disenfranchised and for this, he was praised by the powerful. *And I would be painted as divisive?*

I had to employ a finely crafted code to make my points, points that if said outright, would give Brennan ammunition to caste me as some wide-eyed radical, ineligible for leadership. *I had to change the rules of engagement.*

Guerilla campaigning is a largely lost art in the days of online fundraising, media buys, polling and focus groups. But perhaps it is not so much lost art as abandoned. It is a hard and often painful practice but now my early training bore fruit.

It was a tremendous grind. My whole campaign was bus stops and front doors, churches and grocery stores. Naturally, I was exhausted and the pressure was enormous. Every day I had an encounter, which strained credulity but was a very real testament to the height of the mountain I had chosen to climb.

The petition process was over. I had submitted three thousand signatures of registered democrats in the Ward, when only five hundred were required. You always needed a cushion and the process was good politics.

Brennan's people had begun tearing down my posters and replacing them with his garish gold and blue standards. Homeless and halfway house residents were paid, one hundred dollars a night, to physically and symbolically destroy the only real hope they had. It was classic Brennan.

Upon learning this, I decided to take my anger out on a few blocks of doors. I always felt better when I went door to door because in the precincts so precisely targeted by Lock, I was rarely rejected.

The first house was on 11th and Florida Avenue, N.E. across from Gallaudet University and I approached the door confidently. The procedure was to give a few bullet points from my platform, interwoven with my biography and then ask if I could place a lawn sign in the homeowner's yard. I proceeded as usual.

"Hello sir, my name is Jason Diggs and I'm a candidate for the city council for this Ward.

"Who you running against?"

"The incumbent is Mr. Brennan, but I am running for the seat that will be vacant in January.

"Oh, you running against that light skinned dude."

"Well, actually Mr. Brennan isn't light skinned in that sense. He's Caucasian."

"He white?" I always thought he was just real light skinned. I didn't know he was a white man?"

"Yes sir, but that's not really the point. (As far as this campaign was concerned, it really was the point) I am running to provide better representation, better advocacy, and to defend the neighborhoods against the kind of development that is likely to push us all out. I think our community is worth saving don't you?"

"Yes I do," he said.

"Then I need your help on September 6th because we need to reorder our priorities in this town. Remember when kids had a place to play other than in the street, when schools produced people like Dr. Charles Drew and Denise Graves, the opera star. We can do that again if we stop subsidizing millionaires in their downtown developments."

"Man I like the way you talk. You got my vote. These people are moving in and destroying this town, I was born here, right in Freedman's Hospital, lived here all my life and now it seems like the place is getting so that I don't recognize it anymore. It *kinda look like* we're an endangered species."

"You make a great point, sir," I said. That's why I want to institute some protections for long-term residents of the city. Development shouldn't mean displacement."

I was tired and my mind had been playing games for weeks. Then and there, I wrote a satirized television spot in my mind.

SAVE THE BLACK PEOPLE

THEIR NATURAL HABITAT IS BEING ENCROACHED UPON

SAVE THE BLACK PEOPLE

THEY ARE BEING ATTACKED BY PREDATORY LENDERS AND REAL

ESTATE SPECULATORS FOR WHICH
THEY HAVE NO NATURAL
DEFENSES

SAVE THE BLACK PEOPLE

PUPPY DAYCARE LOUNGES AND
COFFEE SHOPS ARE REPLACING
THE CORNER STORE

SAVE THE BLACK PEOPLE

THEY'VE OUTLAWED SINGLE
SALES OF BEER — 40s ARE GOING
THE WAY OF THE DINOSAURS

ONLY YOU, CAN SAVE THE BLACK
PEOPLE

DIAL NOW 202-555-SAVE

WE TAKE DEBIT POKERS, SOCIAL
SECURITY CHECKS; SECTION 8
VOUCHERS, EBT CARDS,
UNEMPLOYMENT CHECKS AND
CASH.

DIAL NOW, BEFORE IT'S TOO LATE.

"Do you mind if I have one of my volunteers come by a place a lawn sign in your yard?"

"Go ahead."

"That's great sir. If I could just get your name so that we can contact you before Election Day?"

He gave me his name, Leroy Day, along with his address and phone number and I thanked him profusely for the support.

These interactions were effective but inefficient and I often found that our supporters weren't registered to vote. My spirits slowly started to waver.

"Remember Invictus! Hold on a little while longer son," my father told me one particularly disappointing day.

I had awakened to find all the new posters that we had placed on Massachusetts Avenue torn down. The homeless had been laying in wait for us. Misery loves company.

"Look, Lock's people will do the follow ups, you just continue to make contact. You are becoming a very accomplished retail politician, far better than I'd thought you'd be."

"That's a backhanded complement if I ever heard one."

"Well you have your mother's refinement. I didn't know how that would play over there." *Like he wasn't refined, with his bespoke suits and nearly British turns of phrase.*

"So you agree with Brennan?" I said feigning outrage.

"No, I just didn't know how tough you were. You never know that about a man until you see him in a fight. Now I've seen you take a punch and fight back. I'm proud of you."

"What did you expect, I'm a Diggs."

"Yes you are, a damned strong Diggs at that." We laughed together, united in struggle.

These moments were few, for my father was not a man who was given to sentimentality. I learned to cherish the glimpses of paternal love that I so rarely received. He was all I had left and I knew in my heart of hearts that after my mother's death, I had only gone through with the campaign for him.

†

There were parts of the new D.C. that still retained glimpses of what I had always known. As I rode in the weekly Sunday motorcade that Lock insisted that I do without fail, I waved my hands frantically and with increasing desperation.

Griffin Ferris, my most loyal volunteer, was on the microphone heralding my arrival and smiling at the people, hopeful that they understood the urgency. In the crowds I saw the ancient traces of our lineage, the people possessing Mandinka physiques or Bantu eyes that populated our city. I could close my eyes and imagine coursing through the crowded streets of Lagos or Accra in another time, preaching a message of liberation instead of one of restoration.

It was on the back of my convertible, Griffin inching along so that I could be seen, when I first grasped the futility of what we were trying to do. White people had made a choice in the dark, about the future of Black people, which had now come to light. Hundreds of thousands of people, had been deemed insignificant and as my campaign struggled to awaken the victims of this final judgment. Time was running out. We needed a miracle.

Brennan was confident. He had raised one hundred thousand dollars, was being endorsed by almost every major player in town and maintained his façade of universal appeal. He hired Black people to stand in manufactured crowds. He paid Black people to spy on our activities.

Like a colonial governor general, when called to account for the sad state of the divided Ward, he accepted no blame. In turn, he accepted all the credit for any positive developments. He was a competent, if lackluster politician.

Every day, in the face of all this, it became harder to arrange that look of humble confidence upon my face. Every night, it became harder to limit myself to only one glass of bourbon. More and more people who had been so eager to pledge support became scarce in the face of battle and my little cadre of believers grew closer as we faced the bitter inevitabilities.

Griffin Ferris and Bobby Phillips were ANC Commissioners who'd signed on to the campaign early and stuck it out to the end. I remember sitting in the campaign office with them about 4 AM after a full day of campaigning; cold beer and cigars a fitting reward for noble work.

We were tired, weary like Carthaginian Generals after months of moving men, materials and Elephants across the Mediterranean and through the Alps, only to be met with an improbable and impenetrable resistance.

"We're doing good, huh man?" Bobby said, endlessly up beat. It was his stock line after a night of hard work. They were short, stocky, tank like men and they lent their strength of heart to me as it waivered.

They both reminded me, one light brown skinned and the other much darker, of younger versions of Lock. They were bright, fearless and loyal to a fault and I indulged myself with the notion that I might lead my own version of the *Poker Game* one day.

"We got 'em running scared", said Griffin, the more pugnacious of the two.

They both looked at me and I couldn't find it within me to tell them my true assessment of the situation.

"We're going to win fellas!" This was my standard operating procedure, *rally the troops in the midst of disaster, and remain upbeat while all around you is going to hell, the true test of leadership.* "We have no choice but to win, consider the alternative." I continued.

It was a lie. Despite my best efforts at moderation for so many months and sustained attempts to build a winning coalition across racial boundaries, it was not to be. I learned that certain interests couldn't be coalesced.

My message was job training, jobs and neighborhood development to blunt crime and blight. We'd follow this up with educational investment and recreational enhancements to address the issue of delinquent youth and a strong good government package, which included better constituent service and neighborhood advocacy.

The silence was deafening in the enclave of Capitol Hill. No more than a few had requested lawn signs and only three Caucasians had volunteered. Valor had been right, it was too late. Now it was about family pride.

BOOK THREE

TWENTY-TWO
Balancing the Scale

"A mind may not be changed by place or time. The mind is its own place, and in itself can make a Heaven of Hell, a Hell of Heaven."

John Milton

The *Capitol Hill Dwellers* were spewing gallons of personal and political misinformation about me and Brennan's campaign was comfortably holding his home base. As a result, I was being greeted in the white areas of the Ward, as at best, a curiosity and at worst, someone from whom they should hide their children.

For those keeping score at home, I was getting my ass kicked. My door-to-door campaign bogged down on Capitol Hill, which limited my effectiveness to the Black sections of the Ward. As if this weren't enough, there were more bombings.

Every week a newly renovated house was burning on Capitol Hill or a condo garage mysteriously exploding in the newly pioneered areas around Massachusetts Avenue. Even D.C. government buildings were not immune. The D.C. Department of Housing and Community Development had been damaged by a car bomb, blowing out car windows as far as two blocks away and scaring people to death. Surprisingly, no one was injured.

But Black folk do chaos well. There's a curious benefit in times of uncertainty to have endured four hundred years of abduction, slavery, terrorism and murder. *The runner that trains at high altitude receives a benefit in a sea level race.*

The majority of African-American neighborhoods throughout the city handled the disturbances with the same bluesy fatalism and faith with which they had abided everything else. But mounting hysteria in places like Palisades, Georgetown, Dupont Circle and Spring Valley prompted Channel 5 to revive its old *City Under Siege* program for expanded coverage of the crisis. Violence sells ad time.

As fear gripped much of the city, the Hill residents seemed to primarily be afraid of *me*. I had underestimated the depths of the transformation. After one hundred years, Capitol Hill was lost.

It was evident by then that the *Dwellers* were, in fact, a crypto-fascist hate group, masquerading as a civic association. They were the modern day equivalent of the White Citizens Councils, a more elegant face for the

Klan. They had receptions, coffee klatches and garden committee meetings but also ran a contemptuous list serve as a forum for *last-ditch* racists to anonymously spew racial antipathies.

The public face of the organization was the very essence of propriety until they testified before the Council that summer. They wanted increased police patrols in order to physically remove Black youth, who lived in the housing projects encircling the Hill, from the streets. It seems that the sight of these children had disturbed some of the Dwellers as they enjoyed bad food and microbrews in the dive bars lining Pennsylvania Avenue.

Perhaps they were oblivious to the white congressional staffers, who drunk from a night of revelry, routinely vomited and peed in the nearly perfect English gardens of Hill residents. Maybe they didn't hear them screaming slurred profanities into the night only to repeat the process with ever increasing intensity during St. Patrick's Day, the World Series and the Stanley Cup Playoffs.

No, it was Black children who were deemed a menace, a danger to hearth and home. It was they, whose forbearers had lived there for generations,that were sure to drive down the property values in the increasingly white enclave.

In response to the uproar and the accompanying list serve chatter, Brennan sponsored legislation to have the projects closed down, literally disposing of the problem. It quickly received Mayoral support.

The political craftsmanship of the decision is not in dispute. The legislation solidified Brennan's base and his backers had been rewarded; but now my eyes were fully open. It was the rotten afterbirth of a new age and augured the end of the city that I knew.

The story of the impending project closings went largely untold. While the mainstream papers had broader issues to cover, the small papers had another agenda.

The D.C. *Pulp was easily* the most ridiculous paper in town. It was free, like the old *Village Voice*, only without the award winning journalism, the political cache, the intriguing style, the integrity and the worldwide audience.

The Pulp's two claims to its minor local fame were the relentless crusade it had waged against *The Great Man* in the eighties and early nineties and its shameless cheerleading for the onward march of gentrification. It was clearly not in *the Pulp's* interest to report on the closing of public housing projects in anything but a celebratory way.

The neighborhood papers, should have jumped at the chance to get a scoop, but the nugatory headlines of the *Capitol Hill Pages* usually related to more mundane pursuits, like: which dog won the ugly dog contest at Eastern Market last month or who won the *Hill Dwellers'* annual house beautiful event. There was little substance to be had in the paper, except for the ninety-five percent of it, which consisted of paid real estate advertisements.

The *Pages'* Black-Italian soccer playing publisher was LaDante Montefiori, a man who's mysterious mien gave one the dubious impression that Italy had once colonized a Caribbean island whose descendants exist today in a micro Diaspora which apparently includes Washington, D.C.

Montefiori was a tiny brown man with a small child like face. He was fit from the weekend soccer matches he played on the Mall with his bleach blond dreadlocks blowing in the wind. Year round, he wore silk lounging wear and open toed mules and looked like he was conducting a never-ending series of mathematical computations in his head, his heavy eyebrows permanently furrowed in contemplation.

He was never to be found in the large suite of offices that his paper leased on H Street, N.E. near my campaign headquarters because he was always wandering the streets of the Ward, greeting people by name like the Mayor of a small Italian village. Most people thought him a nuisance and therefore, paid him no mind.

One day I watched as he began his routine outside of my office. I came out to ask him why he had not reported on the closing of the projects. "This is the biggest story this neighborhood has had since the closing of D.C. General Hospital, but nobody's touching it. Why didn't you?" I asked.

He nodded contritely as if I had uncovered some horrible indiscretion from his past, then said in his Italian patios,

"Look-a. Jason-a. I'm going-a to balance tha' scale-a. I'm-a going-a to treat-a your campaign-a fair-a, full-a coverage-a of-a your campaign-a."

I was still not encouraged. Montefiori was notoriously subservient to his wife and Editor in Chief, the ironically named Ava Braun, a large blond woman who was known by all to be the actual proprietor of the *Capitol Hill Pages*. Needless to say, with the paper completely dependant on real estate advertising for survival, in the weeks that followed, the scales never balanced and *the Pages* never reported on the projects or me at all.

TWENTY-THREE

Woke Up This Morning

"Think. The big fucking picture."
Tony Soprano

Jocamo "Jock" Andruzzi was the Mayor's fixer, brought in from Bay Ridge, Brooklyn for just that purpose. Tall and stocky on a nearly bovine level, his New York accent was unmistakable. I heard that accent one morning late in the campaign when I was trying to sleep off another late night poster hanging session.

"Jason, Jock Andruzzi; nice to finally talk with you. I've seen your fieldwork, lawn signs and what not. I've done some polling Jason; you are running one fine campaign there my friend." I thought I was having a nightmare until he kept talking.

"Thank you Mr. Andruzzi." I didn't know him but I was aware of him. Everyone in the game was. *Keep it professional, I reminded myself.* It wasn't lost on me that he didn't know me and yet was already on a first name basis. *Are the rules of etiquette really different for these people?*

"Hey, call me *Bull,* everybody in politics does."

"Bull?"

"Yeah, on account of my size. I don't mind it really; it's a pretty good calling card in my business. That Jock business is for strangers and after this campaign Jason, you're no stranger.

"And what is your business exactly?" I knew of course, but I was probing for advantage.

"I'm like OPEC, only I trade in information instead of oil. This town runs on information, so that's what makes me powerful see."

"Are you some kind of detective?"

"Let's put it this way, *nothing happens in D.C. without I know about it.* I'm like a mechanic for a finely tuned automobile and I am a very good mechanic."

I noted his crass braggadocio. Jocamo *Jock* "The Bull" Andruzzi must have only recently been promoted from soldier to principal; he hadn't the style of a person accustomed to wielding power.

"Jason, I'll come right to the point. You realize of course that you are not going to win this election." *A statement of fact more than a rhetorical question.* He went on, "most of our people don't know you, although Chad says you're a nice guy. I got no reason to doubt that about you and I appreciate the way that you're keeping a lid on all the racial stuff—very honorable. But, pleasantries aside, you're going to lose this one."

I was not a morning person. My eyelids felt like shutters that had been pulled down and then tied off on a hook. I struggled to open them and sharpen up.

This was a gut check, one of those times when your manhood was on the line. Silence was weakness and he'd be checking for that. I needed coffee.

"Well there are a number of factual inaccuracies there, *Jeff*. I don't know where to start." I was stalling for time as I ran down the stairs to start the coffee maker.

"You were very kind to complement my field operations, I'm very proud of it. My campaign manager has won more races in this city than anyone, so I am pretty confident there."

"Yeah, I know about Mr. Lock Smith. He's got a hell of a reputation down here. I've even heard of his other work around the country, but he's lost a step don't you think? This ain't the eighties."

"Actually, I don't," I said. The water was starting to boil. "Now as for who knows me, I am a fourth generation Washingtonian and I even seem to remember the Mayor coming to my mother's funeral last year."

"Yeah, you have my condolences, I actually suggested he come to that. I have always believed that you never lose by being respectful to an adversary."

"My point is that I am fairly well known in the city. My family is quite well known and the support that we've gotten in this election is further evidence of the strength of our message. So, while I appreciate your call, I think I'll just let the people decide."

"Jason, no need to get all puffed up here, it's too early in the morning. I have already said that I respect you, but this is business. I said *our* people don't know you, the guys that really run this little town of yours. Decisions have been made Jason about who's in and who's out. You're not in our plans right now."

The coffee was ready in the French Press and I quickly poured it and took a sip. Black, no sugar, there was no time for the accoutrements.

"What's all this about. I'm sure this isn't some courtesy call to let me know that I can't win because I haven't been signed off on by your powerbrokers. If the result is predetermined, then this is a waste of both my time and yours, right? If you're right, then I should get off the phone and get back in the streets." The coffee was kicking in, doing its job.

"Nice Jason, I'd heard you were a glib little prick. Heard that you've been bustin' Brennan's balls in all-a tha debates too, good for you." *I had. Brennan's stiff delivery and rote presentation was no match for me. He had started to back out of the contests and I, in turn, debated an empty chair.*

"My associates are very concerned about these bombings Jason," he continued. "This Urban Underground group that has taken responsibility for this stuff is causing people a little heartburn. A lot of money is going up in smoke and residential real estate sales are suddenly down city wide and I mean by a wide margin."

" I see your problem but what do you expect me to do? I'm going to lose right?" I was not aware that a group had taken credit for the bombings. He had inside information, which he had just deliberately leaked to me.

"We'd like your help on this. We know you're close to the Chief of Police and we'd like you to try to broker a deal with these U.U. people to end this insanity before somebody get's hurt."

It was clear to me ever since the bombings began that if they wanted to hurt people they would have done it already and if their tactics included inflicting casualties, they probably couldn't be stopped.

"Let me make sure that I understand you." I said for effect. *Let him feel some of my anxiety.*

The call was probably a head fake. He was probably in his K Street office drinking espresso and eating biscotti with a tape recorder running, ready to catch me saying something that could be misinterpreted as an admission of involvement and I'd hear it run over and over again in 30 second ads for the next two weeks on every radio station in town.

They'd have six hundred thousand people thinking that I was the bomber and I would never recover in time. *Ballgame.*

"Do you people actually think that *I* know who is doing this?" I said. "Don't let your paranoia land you in court *Jeff.*" I used the lawyer voice, even though I had never litigated a case.

"Name's Jock. But look, I'm not saying that you know Jason. It's actually a complement. Our folks think that you are uniquely positioned to handle this for us. Not even Jesse Jackson or that *Louie Farra-can* guy are set up to do this, but you are. We think these people would listen to you."

"What makes you think that this is an African-American group?"

"Jason, the name of the group is Urban Underground. It sounds like a fucking rap group for Christ's sake."

"It could be a white rap group. It could also be a group of white terrorists that would like the world to think their Black; basic misinformation. They could be like one of those anti-globalization groups that tore up Seattle or a right wing hate group."

"We don't think so for a variety of reasons but anyway, we would like your help."

"Why should I trust you? You've already indicated that I am your adversary."

"Don't trust us, trust your long time family friend and neighbor Chief Johnson. He'll be calling you later today with this very request."

340

"Maybe I'll call him first."

"I wouldn't advise that. He doesn't even know he's going to call you yet. The Mayor hasn't spoken to him. He'll know only a few minutes before he calls you."

"Very manipulative," I said.

"Jason, the man is the Chief of Police, he responds to the Mayor or he's not the Chief of Police anymore. He's been due to be replaced for a while now, but we're letting him beef up his pension. It would be bad press to fire him during a crisis, his son being a local football hero and all."

I interrupted, "—And of course you people own the Mayor."

"That's what *you've* been saying on the stump. What do you think? Just look at it this way, this will further your political career. We would look upon something like this very favorably. You could get a paid city board seat out of this, something to rest in before we green light another campaign, a *sinecure*. I love that word, *sinecure*. The Mayor laid that one on me, ain't it great?"

"Oh, so then you'd own me too."

"Not me Jason, I'm just a working stiff doing a job. Later on, with our help, you would only have to be responsive to *them* on the development issues and tax policy when you're on the Council. On all the social welfare stuff, you'd be free to go your own way. You do have that issue with your car loan, we could be helpful with that." I heard him take a sip of something; maybe he did have espresso or something stronger.

"What makes you think I have an issue with my car loan?" I tried to sound unfazed by the personal intrusion.

"You should shred your business correspondence Jason *before* you recycle."

Now I was concerned. They'd gone through my trash?

"So this is how it's done. I've read about this stuff."

"C. Wright Mills, The Power Elite?" he said to my surprise.

"No!" I said. Mario Puzo, *The Godfather*!"

He laughed it off, but I'd stung him.

"Jason, Jason I would consider that racist if it wasn't you, said it. Just think about it, Johnson will call you tonight. Your meet and greet in Southwest should be over by then."

"How did you know about that?"

"We know a lot. What's that Cathy Hughes says on WOL? Information is power?"

The world was small in D.C. politics. He even knew what was being said on Black AM radio. It was his job to know. I had a grudging respect for the fat Italian. *He would make a formidable enemy and I needed to be as well.*

"We don't know everything though," he continued. "That's where you come in. I understand you consider yourself as some kind of D.C. patriot. Well now's the time to show it. See, if the city doesn't solve this shit and I mean yesterday, the Feds are going to impose martial law or some other over the top crap. Cheney is a mean *sonofabitch*. They'll start setting up additional roadblocks, really locking the city down. You know who gets hurt the most in *that* scenario."

I did know, people with bullshit outstanding warrants, expired licenses and unpaid child support. People dependent on public transportation would be delayed for spot checks and traffic snarls due to the checkpoints. It would be an inconvenience to everyone in the city, but it would be a nightmare for Black people.

Andruzzi let the reality set in and continued. "I'll be in touch. Be like your fellow Morehouse guy Spike Lee and do the right thing, *brother*."

The phone went dead, preceded by the clearly identifiable sound of laughter.

TWENTY-FOUR
Canine Politics

Blamed by the gods for stealing a dog made of gold, Tantalus's punishment was to stand in a pool of water beneath a fruit tree with low branches for all eternity. Whenever he reached for the fruit, the branches raised from his grasp. Whenever he bent to drink, the water receded.

Greek Mythology

S uddenly I had a pet. Musa was an Akita named for the legendary African King, Mansa Musa of Mali. My father bought the dog as a companion for my mother just before she died, but she had a strange aversion to his fur and couldn't stand to have him around. She'd acquired a similar phobia of her own mink coat, which had been placed in cold storage at a furrier in Chevy Chase.

Musa had been in exile with Aunt Sara in Highland Beach and as the campaign wore on I asked my father if I could have him. He reminded me of my mother, he used to lick her feet.

"You should keep him Jason. Those Hill people love dogs; all those dog parks over there are great places to campaign. I'd rather you have him have anyway." He was still angry at his sister from the argument at the repast. It had been over a year.

So I inherited Musa, picking him up from the beach during a dead spot in the schedule. By then he was no longer a puppy. He was quite large with flashy black and white markings.

He regarded people suspiciously with his bear like face, his tail curled menacingly over his back like some primordial angel of death. At 120 pounds he was a very impressive animal and knew it. It was doubtful if Andruzzi and the boys would try snooping through my house with him around. Musa was a potent deterrent. *Fortunately, he remembered me.*

After my conversation with Andruzzi, I walked Musa to Lincoln Park in a white, 1994 Black Dog tee shirt, sunglasses, baseball cap and madras shorts. I was working hard for anonymity.

I carried my mother's old volume of Langston Hughes's poetry. It was a habit from childhood, reading Hughes when I was under pressure, and God knows that I was under pressure. The meter calmed me and I was uplifted by the wit.

It was warm and the park was once again adorned with women in lotion, rolling in the sun. The smell of suntan oil was carried on the heavy air and reminded me of the beaches that I missed that summer as I toiled in the furnace of D.C. politics.

As I sat on the park bench near the iconic statue of Mary McLeod Bethune with Musa laying at my feet, a parade of women clicked by. *Where are they going*, I wondered.

They wore pantsuits, dresses, skirts, jeans their panty imprints heaving dramatically into round hips and the pleasing curve of their bottoms. Oddly, the flatter the ass, the more violent the imprint—counter intuitive, *interesting*, I thought.

I understood what was happening. I was without *the voice that had carried me through my life with such focus and determination*. Due to mounting pressure, the calling and maybe even my sanity was slipping from my grasp.

How long had it been, days, months? I was unmoored, drifting. This was why I sat idly, my dog at my side, inspecting panty lines on a park bench.

"For the first time in my life I don't know what I'm doing Musa." The dog looked up from his nap as if he knew what I should do, but had been sworn to secrecy. Perhaps it was true. *You need to fight, bite the shit out of them. That's would I would do*, I imagined him saying.

I needed the distraction of the park, of its women, its nasty exhibitionist sunbathers. I had not seen any of the women in my life in weeks, determined to fight without self-compromise.

Valor had disappeared again, abruptly quitting the campaign after the bombings proved too much for her to handle. *I couldn't keep her in my life it seemed.*

"This is getting too scary for me. I'm going back to Atlanta," she said abruptly.

I was surprised by her skittishness, she had always been so unflappable, but she *was* always a little capricious. Her job had been phased out, as she had feared and Project Kujichagulia was abandoned due to lack of community interest. The little house in Petworth that she had purchased just two years before, like so many around the city, stood with a for sale sign swinging in the yard.

"You're still my Chief of Staff when we win this thing," I said at the passenger drop off zone at National airport. *No self respecting D.C. native had ever called it Reagan.*

We hugged for ten minutes, waiving off the newly vigilant security guards. To my surprise, she cried.

I wanted to call one of the women, any of them—perhaps even Serah and forget for awhile. But I couldn't do that; Andruzzi's phone call had made such an indulgence impossible unless I wanted to see it on the front page of the *Pulp* complete with pictures. DIGGS DATES WHILE CITY BURNS.

I read for an hour, receiving sustenance from Hughes' words, *"LIFE AINT BEEN NO CRYSTAL STAIR"* and then called Dalton West. West, an old comrade from my days as President of the D.C. Young Democrats during the eighties was my host for that evening's *meet and greet* and he had promised 150 people for the event. With so few of the people who should have been at my side, actually standing with me, I was especially thankful when anyone stepped up and lent a hand.

"How do we look, West?"

"I am at Costco now getting the platters."

"How many again?"

"A hundred, hundred fifty."

"Okay. Thanks man."

"No problem Jason. From what I'm seeing out there on the streets, you're going to win this thing."

I walked back to the house with Musa, getting the occasional glance from passers by. I smiled my dimpled closed mouth smile; the earnest one, the one that said *I'm not going to talk to you but I'll be pleasant.*

Then it began.

"Hey dog." "Hi puppy." "What's going on there, pal?" All directed of course at Musa. Most of the white people never even looked at me as they fell over themselves to talk to my dog—as if I wasn't there! Some even reached down to pet him, to give him a treat; actions to which both he and I took offense. *Akitas don't like people less dignified than themselves.*

It occurred to me that by acquiring a dog on Capitol Hill, I had somehow been given the power of stealth. As Ellison wrote fifty years ago, *did they still not see me?* The dog's leash must have been floating in mid air. I guess Musa was walking himself.

This caused me to think of all the other indignities, which build up over a period of years in a gentrifying area as the change sets in. Of how I was always assumed to be a deliveryman when I was double-parked in front of my house.

"Oh, honey we can get that space, this guy is leaving, he's delivering to that house." *The logical precision of these people was amazing— a deliveryman in a red SAAB Convertible, wearing Ralph Lauren?*

"No actually I'm not leaving, I'll be parking here and then I'll be walking into MY HOUSE."

Or when I did yard work and people would ask me how much I charged. "I work for free but I get to live here and sleep in the master bedroom."

Once I overhead the Black woman, who lived next door with her Norwegian husband, elegantly dispatching a white woman who erroneously thought she was nanny to her own blond haired blue eyed infant:

"You're so good with him, so loving." Said the white woman. "Do you need more work?"

"No, thanks," my neighbor said. "The Justice Department's *Civil Rights* division had plenty of cases for me to try, the last time I checked. But, since you're so kind, I'm coming off of maternity leave next month and I'll be looking for someone to babysit *my* child here. Are *you* available? I'll need references of course.

Then at the Stanton Park Civic Association dinner, early in the campaign, I was parking and a woman runs out frantically saying "Oh, good. Are you with the band?"

"No I'm not," I said.

"Oh, then you *must* be Mr. Diggs."

It was only later that I discovered that the band consisted of one African-American member, the drummer (who had been late for sound check). *I don't look like a drummer; I'm more a lead singer or keyboard player type myself. Sadder still was how the immediate alternative to my being the drummer was that I must be DIGGS! Not so much anticipation as forewarning.*

Three weeks before a gay white ANC commissioner who I tried to convert to my side (my intrepidity and desperation were astonishing even to me) informed me, over coffee, that the assumption among the Brennan camp was that I was renting my house from an out of state white person. It was thought and that I would be moving back east of the river after I lost.

The Commissioner had sandy hair and wore jeans and a pink polo shirt that was virtually indistinguishable from his skin. From the waist up he was monochromatic.

He also needed a shower. It was only 9 a.m. and he reeked as if he had just spent the morning working a Skipjack out in the Chesapeake Bay. *He's pink and he stinks*, I thought. I played such mental games to get through the difficult days.

"Do you own your own home Jason?"

"Yes I do?"

"They think your renting."

"Why is that?"

"The house is recorded in the name of a Winston K. Grafton."

"Yes."

"Yes, well it does seem to prove their point." He sat back in his chair—wide know-it-all eyes looking into the middle distance, self-satisfied.

"Well I am sorry that I have to spoil the fun, but Winston Kenneth Grafton was my deceased uncle. He owned the house, lived there for forty years." I paused, sipped my coffee, then I said channeling my father, "I've recently inherited the house, so I won't be going anywhere."

"They have no evidence of that."

"I'm sure you can understand that since the house has been in our family for fifty years, there's really no hurry in changing the name on the deed. My mother was ill and didn't get around to it. Now, it's mine."

I thought to myself, *they're checking our land records?* Then, *of course they would, they're a bunch of real estate agents.*

The look of shock on his pink face was more than enough to compensate me for all the coffee and pastry the man devoured, but I was beginning to understand what Chad had told me at the Palm; I was considered a holdover too.

Lock tried to settle me down when I told him the story. "The thing to remember

Jason is that this is not reality. Look around, how could it be?"

At six in the evening, after being threatened by a gangster then ignored while my dog was greeted like a foreign dignitary, I had implausibly gotten my swagger back. I bounded into my fundraiser with my usual verve.

I worked the room, a condo party room with a beautiful view overlooking the Southwest waterfront, shaking hands, answering questions and talking policy to the awkward accompaniment of a 1980's Trouble Funk P.A. tape, until it was time for the speech.

It went off well despite the sparse but enthusiastic crowd of 47 that attended. The spirit in the room pleased me, but we raised little in the way of campaign funds. I would never be able to pay for an election eve campaign mailing, like that.

We did sign up twenty new volunteers and it occurred to me that this was how I could still win. We'd live off the land, campaign by word of mouth and lock down votes through an underground railroad of barbershops and beauty parlors, car-detailing operations, hand dancing contests and carry outs.

We weren't done yet and we were still winning the battle of the streets. I drove home that night with the top down, Earth Wind and Fire on the stereo and my red posters dominated the Ward. *Could I still win in spite of everything?*

When I got home, I walked Musa round the corner, poured a Jack and Coke and tried to relax. A candidate rarely has free time when he is not being watched.

I cherished the midnight hour, when I could grab a cigar, listen to Cassandra Wilson or Coltrane and relax over a shot of bourbon. These were personal moments, time to reflect on the day and critique my performance.

The whiskey took hold quickly and I dozed, lulled to sleep by Charlie Parker's strings album. I awoke with a start to the sound of the phone and stumbled awkwardly to answer it.

I had almost forgotten the Andruzzi conversation and Chief Johnson's voice reestablished it in my mind. AJ's father had been Chief for four years but still maintained a casual approach with me.

"What are you, sleep? He said with his usual jocularity. "You can't win a campaign in the bed, no wonder you're behind in the polls."

"I see you don't know my reputation with the ladies."

He laughed.

"I see Eddie Murphy ain't got shit on you, huh."

"What's up?" I said feigning ignorance. "Its what, 1:30 in the morning?"

"There was just another attack, that makes ten," he said grimly.

"What, where?"

"They hit Barracks Row, down on Eighth Street."

"What did they get?"

"The whole damned thing. It happened two hours ago, somehow they were able to set charges on that new brick sidewalk. They blew the whole thing. The storefront and restaurant windows were smashed—glass went flying everywhere. Even in front of the Marine Barracks."

"Anybody hurt?"

"Cuts mostly, a few contusions from people falling on the ground, but no one was hurt seriously. Seems the charge was set to blow inward toward the buildings and most of them were empty. The shock wave still reached the street though, about five cars were totaled."

"Shit."

"That's an understatement. They've gotten more sophisticated. We're not going to be able to keep the Feds out of this one. It was too close to a military installation."

"Whoa."

"I know. This is a worst-case scenario and with the Mayor's boy running, he is breathing down my neck. He called me earlier tonight about you, but I had to handle this new thing."

"He called about me?" *Andruzzi wasn't bullshitting.*

"Yeah, he wants me to get you involved in finding out who is doing this. My guess is that he will have more of a sense of urgency about that now."

"But he can't stand me."

"Hizzoner believes that you have credibility with whoever is doing this because of your platform. He thinks that you can engage these people and get them to stop for the good of the city." *Stupid*, I thought. *If they cared about the city, they wouldn't be bombing.*

"Why me?"

"The profilers think that these folks are politically motivated. They believe that this group is trying to send a message about the Mayor's development policies and all this *regentrification* stuff."

"Its gentrification Chief, I don't want you out there getting *that* wrong, you know what they say about you Black people screwing up the King's English." The Chief was silent.

"Anyway, since you have come out against development in your campaign, you might be able to talk them down," he continued.

"How am I supposed to talk to them when we don't know who they are? I've already issued a statement against all the bombings and toured the damaged sites in my Ward."

"What we want you to do Jason is call them out. We want you to go on TV and ask for a meeting; we'll set it up. It should actually help your campaign. You can't pay for that kind of publicity." *He was right, I couldn't pay for any publicity.*

"You think that'll work? If they are as smart as I think they are, they'll smell a trap *off-the-jump*."

"Not if you offer yourself up. Say that you'll agree to be picked up, kidnapped, blindfolded, the whole nine."

"And I should do this because?"

"Because the Mayor asked you to."

"Try again Chief."

"Because I asked you to, then."

"Chief, I'm in the last two weeks of a campaign. It sounds like the Mayor, who does not support me by the way, wants me out of the way. He wants me running around on a wild goose chase, after some crazy ass urban terrorists, while the clock runs out on the election."

"If this works, you're a national hero. Who wouldn't vote for you then."

"In this Ward? You'd be surprised. Ask my father about precinct 89."

"Jason I don't have time for—"

"You know, if I did this Chief, you'd probably have an opportunity to dust off your dress blues for my funeral."

"I don't think they have any interest in killing you Jason. We think they consider you as one of them. Only they use explosives and you use words."

"I never quite thought of myself as a terrorist, Chief."

"They probably don't see themselves that way either. Anyway, just think about it. I have a meeting with the FBI joint task force tomorrow morning at eight. I'd like to float the idea then. It just might stave off martial law for a few days. This administration already has its hands full with 9/11, the war, but they certainly aren't going to let anybody blow up D.C. one piece at a time either. The National Guard is now federalized, as of 30 minutes ago."

"Tanks in D.C., like in the sixties?"

"That's how it's shaping up. It wouldn't be so bad if all this shit weren't happening on Capitol Hill, but with the Capitol, the Supreme Court and all those Congressmen and Senators living there, my position isn't as strong as it could be."

He was going to retire and this would leave a pretty ugly stain on what had been a remarkable career. He'd been elevated to Chief during *The Great Man's* last term and served 25 years on the force, the last six of them as Chief. There had even been talk of him running for Council in the old neighborhood a curtain call for the *Poker Game* after my victory. Now, all of that was very much in doubt.

"I'll think about it but this is crazy." I said

"I know, but we are running out of time and options." His voice sounded heavy, he'd probably been up for days.

"Have you talked to AJ?" I said.

"You know him the week before training camp. Radio silence."

"Yeah, I haven't been able to reach him on his cell. If you talk to him, thank him for the contribution, it helped."

"I will Jason. It's his last season. Let's get you to some games."

"That would be nice." I said. "It's been a while."

My friendship with AJ had drifted, propelled by the weak inertia of personal history and no longer by any conscious affinity. We were no longer boys and as men we make different choices.

"We'll talk in the morning," said the Chief. "And Jason, I don't need to tell you that this is confidential. No press, no campaign staff and no talking to your father."

"Not at all?"

"Not about this. If you want to go forward, I'll tell him about it once you're inside."

I told him I wouldn't and not to worry. I had always been good at keeping secrets.

I climbed the stairs to the bedroom, Musa dutifully following behind me, panting hot breath at my ankles. *This is crazy*, I thought. *Who else had to negotiate with terrorists to win a local council seat?* Then I thought, *isn't that what I had been doing for over a year?*

TWENTY-FIVE
Lost and Found

"Ever has it been that love knows not its own depth until the hour of separation."

Khalil Gibran

As deputy campaign manager, Valor had been responsible for implementing the *Poker Game's* campaign plan. At this stage of his career, Lock was more strategist than day-to-day administrator and Valor ably filled that role. She was the person on the ground, the eyes and ears of my trusted advisors.

Lock Smith, the best political tactician in urban America was training her, which was perfect preparation for Councilmember's Chief of Staff. I'd come up with the idea myself.

She had been stellar in her role, dealing with the press, the printers and other vendors, acting as coordinator of fundraising events and comptroller of our meager but precious campaign funds, organizing the volunteers and perhaps most importantly—keeping me on schedule. She woke me up to wave to passing motorists and shake hands at the Metro stations at 5 A.M.; a responsibility made easier by her occasional presence in my bed.

She would block out time for me to sleep and protected me from unnecessary intrusions as I prepared for a debate. I was a better candidate when she was around but like always, she was essential and then she was gone.

I pressed on in her absence. Funds needed to be raised and I had to do it. I still had friends who had not weighed in, had not supported me. I had nothing to lose, so I decided to call them all.

After eighty phone calls, I had only four positive responses but I set appointments for pick-ups nevertheless. Sometime before the call from Andruzzi, I'd met Steve Ross, another old law school classmate, at *Stan's* on Vermont Avenue. I ordered a club sandwich and a Coke. His lunch consisted of three Grey Goose and tonics and a basket of wings.

Stan's was underground, dimly lit and always smelled of the cigarettes that chain-smoking regulars puffed at the bar. It had been around for years, kept open primarily by a crowd of middle managers, lawyers and *Washington Post* reporters, who appreciated the stiff drinks and fifties era bar food. Even in the changing landscape of Washington it had it's own niche and would probably never close.

"What's been up? I had to look you up in Martindale-Hubbell to find you," I said.

"Nothing man, just working, nothing exotic."

"Somehow that doesn't sound like you. I remember you always talked about going boating in the islands."

"Yeah, I talked about it. Now its just billable hours, wife kids, billable hours, repeat."

"I hear you, but having a family like that, has got to be rewarding. I wanted to have a family by now, but things never quite worked out."

"It is great to see your children running around and everything but it can be a grind."

"Where are you living these days?" I said.

"I Just bought in Tantallon North, it's a big ass house, something for the kids to grow into."

Steve had gone the way of so many, lured by the trappings of suburban success. I imagined that his house was easily worth a couple of hundred thousand dollars less than mine with nearly triple the square footage—a devil's bargain. Steve was always trying to get over; earlier in his marriage he'd been spotted outside of Hogates at happy hour, trying to proposition women. There was a car seat in the back seat of his Volvo.

"Get a good deal?"

"Hell yeah, but I'm going to get killed on the resale. I'm in for the long hall on this one. The wife is complaining about how far she has to drive to shop for good clothes, but this is all about the kids."

"Did you ever consider moving over in my old neighborhood, you know, Hillcrest, the values are still relatively good over there I understand."

"Tammy's from California and is terrified of Southeast."

"Did you ever take her over there? Most people don't believe its Southeast when they actually see it."

"You don't know Tammy, she would have divorced my ass the next day if I tried. It would have made my life easier too, believe me, the commute is killing me, but in my case it wasn't workable."

"I bet. Well as long as you're happy."

"Happy wife, happy life."

With all the liquor he was putting away at one in the afternoon, I doubted that his life *was* happy (the car seat incident being only one example), but he'd accomplished something that I had only dreamed of, raising a family. I couldn't fault him for his choices, I had made my own.

We said our goodbyes and promised to get together after the primary. We went our separate ways and it was only after I'd turned the corner onto K Street, that I looked at his check. It was for $25.00. He'd spent more than that on his liquid lunch.

TWENTY-SIX

Rivals

"The ordinary man is involved in action, the hero acts. An immense difference."

Henry Miller

Security had the area locked down. A helicopter was in the air, containing a sharpshooter for the Mayor and his protégé's protection. It was a pre-electoral made for television, production, which was designed to prove that the Mayor had the emergency well in hand and that his heir apparent, Dexter Callahan, was up to the task.

My favorite Starbucks was in ruins, its sign, completely intact, was in the pocket park across the street. The whole neighborhood smelled of burnt coffee.

Bricks from the sidewalk were tossed like leaves in every direction. No glass windows survived.

AJ's father was there with several other high-ranking police *white shirts*, the Director of the city's office of emergency preparedness, FBI officials, Dexter Callahan who was hugging dutifully to the Mayor's coattails, and my nemesis, the less than Honorable Damien Brennan. I didn't want to be there.

I imagined an alternate reality in which I was at home reading and smoking a cigar. Valor, who was only just a little fleshier than she was in reality (and all in the right places), was in the kitchen preparing a down home Georgia Thanksgiving supper, something with collard greens, yams, mashed potatoes, home made biscuits — the comforting scent wafting tantalizingly into the den.

In this reverie, we lived in a small college town. There were children, our children — cute, well-mannered intelligent children and Valor had her own small law firm and I was Dean of the local university's law school and the prolific writer of legal treatises and literary fiction.

That was the dream but the reality was that Dr. Cole was standing amid the rubble on the corner of 8th and Pennsylvania Avenue, frantically waiving me over to the Mayor's delegation.

"Come on over here Jason."

I didn't know how long he'd been calling; I had been entangled within the warm, inviting folds of the dream.

"Jason!"

Cole stood arrogantly amid the chaos of Terwilliger's throng, pointing at people officiously, trying his best to look important. He wore a black suit of cheap construction and unfashionable design—a discount warehouse job that was probably pasted together by a twelve-year-old sweatshop worker in Myanmar.

The seven-button suit, which he wore with a white shirt and lime green tie, was too modern for a man of his advanced years and looked like the costume of a third rate hip-hop impresario.

His sparse straight hair was dyed an improbable shade of black, huge flakes of dandruff dusting his jacket like a late spring snow. It dawned on me that his face had the narrow lupine ferocity of a German Shepherd.

I reluctantly fell in with the group of political men, smiling and greeting each in turn. They returned the gesture. The protocols of politics required practiced grace and feigned cordiality.

"What are you doing here Jason?" asked Cole. I could have asked the same thing of him, but had no interest in prolonging the conversation beyond what was necessary.

"Just getting a cup of coffee," I lied, As *if I needed a reason to be anyplace in my Ward at any time of any day.*

"Didn't you her about this? The Starbucks has been destroyed! Isn't it terrible?" said Cole. I hated his dour expression and his fake concern. This was a political goldmine for his patrons Terwilliger and Callahan. Under such conditions Cole could continue to rise.

He went on, "You know as Chair of the Mayor's Economic Development Task Force, this really hurts. We were already seeing increased foot traffic and new business start-ups on this corridor. We invested over twenty million dollars into this streetscape. Authentic gas streetlights, period brick for the sidewalks, even mock hitching posts to line the streets. All gone, it's a tragedy; thank God no one was seriously injured."

It was the first I had seen of him since my mother's funeral, a lapse in time for which I was grateful. My father told me about how Cole had manipulated his way onto the Howard Expansion Task Force or *HETF* and how he had pushed poor Darnella Henson, the Dean of the School of Business, out as its Chairman, despite her twenty-five years of community development experience with D.C. government. He skillfully made these things appear independent of his agency.

The *HETF* was a largely ceremonial outfit, as the university had retained experts in the field to indentify properties of opportunity in the LeDroit Park and Shaw neighborhoods for possible purchase and to plan for future growth. The early success of the plan was widely heralded due to the silence of those being targeted for displacement. They simply had no idea. Cole was given credit for this.

The Mayor had relied on the mythology of Cole's success and Howard's status as one of the city's largest employers, when appointing Cole to his economic development Task Force. The Mayor was an outsider and having Cole carry some of his water lightened his load.

As my father explained to me many years before, "In politics, a good but undeserved reputation is always superior to one's actual ability. Good press is superior to good works. Ruthless self-promotion trumps a visionary's selflessness just as a well-connected man of average ability will usually rise above the brilliant man who has only his talent to recommend him. The brilliant man always has enemies that he didn't know he had."

"He got in the short line", my father grumbled when Cole was announced as Chair of the City Task Force several years before. We were watching the news with my mother and he couldn't contain himself. "There is no stampede among any brothers and sisters that I know to stand beside that man and support the implementation of policies that are designed to wipe out our communities. What they're doing is ethnic cleansing, its Rwanda but more artfully done, absent the blood." he continued.

"Who says it's bloodless—," my mother said, temporarily relieved by medication, of the worst of her Parkinson's symptoms. "How many have died in transit, since they closed D.C. General Hospital? The next closest hospital is almost thirty minutes away."

My parents always agreed on the subject of Cole. He had never published anything of any note, certainly not enough to rate the Chairmanship of the Department. But, he did play tennis on skinny legs with the Howard President's brother.

Cole was on television earlier that morning discussing the bombings, smiling halfheartedly with his ratty little mustache. I saw him pompously employing his desiccated humor as a shield against a more thorough investigation of his credentials. There he was, recondite terms strung together as if they were medals evincing intellect rather than the rehearsed regurgitations of an inferior mind.

"And he can't even dance," my mother said after a faculty Christmas party many years before. "He looked ridiculous, like a big blue heron getting ready to fly, arms flapping, knees bending off beat, to the music." This was another thing to cause distrust—for who in the world had ever heard of a *Black man* that couldn't dance.

I remembered all of this as I stared at the man. In Cole, the Mayor had bought a native Washingtonian, to add gloss to what most Blacks considered an illegitimate rule. The dismantling of the city that the *Poker Game* built was going full throttle and my feeble efforts had been exposed as a mere stalling action; the fierce engagement by a truculent rear guard to slow an advancing assault.

"Jason, have you considered the Mayor's idea?" said Cole.

The depth of the conspiracy was astounding to me. Cole clearly knew about it and was probably, one of the architects of the scheme.

"Who else is involved with this thing?" I said without even a hint of diplomacy.

"Well of course the Mayor has shared it with his most senior advisors," he answered.

"So Brennan knows." I looked in my opponent's direction, finding him laughing it up with some reporter from The Pulp, which had just made its expected early endorsement of Brennan in that morning's edition. The front page was dominated by the sensationalist headline, **Beirut on the Potomac!** A large picture of the bombed out D.C. Department of Housing and Community Development building was superimposed upon it.

"No, you have it wrong Jason. This is an executive branch operation. We knew you'd be sensitive to that and I insisted that Damien not be brought into the loop on this." Cole responded. If he only *taught* at Howard, why was he so involved?

"The Chief didn't propose this?"

"Well, of course he was supportive of my position on this but ah, it was I that demanded that it be made a ground rule."

The pompous ass was grandstanding, trying to play the hero. His duplicity knew no bounds. I was sure that by insulting my intelligence, he knew that he would never have my trust, which was perhaps his purpose. Maybe he was trying to get me not to go along with the plan. Another head fake.

"I see." I responded coolly.

"Time is of the essence Jason. We can't wait for another incident to occur before you make a decision. After all we've done to get the Federal Government out of our affairs, we can't appear to be inept in handling this situation. What in God's name are you waiting for? We're talking martial law here!"

His temper was legendary but raising his voice was not the way to get my attention. It only stiffened my resolve to be cool.

"I'm a candidate for public office in the Ward that seems to be bearing the brunt of these attacks. The many people that support me believe that my candidacy may be their only hope. My first responsibility is to them."

"Yes, well I'm sure we're all very impressed with the job you're doing, but there is a higher value here."

He was trying to lure me in with his usual pseudo intellectual babble. Offering a simple prescription for a complex dilemma. It was an old game. *If the square peg will not fit neatly into the round hole, then just imagine the peg to be square. There, all solved.*

He continued, "You have strong support in *certain* neighborhoods over here, I've seen the polls, but the safety of the city and preserving home rule should be of paramount concern. You can help us bring this unfortunate episode to a close. You'll live to fight another day."

"That's assuming I live, of course."

"Oh Jason, these folks have no interest in hurting you, you've become a symbol. A more effective one than their barbarism has been, I might add."

Two things struck me. First, everyone appeared to have seen polling data on my race but me (my dear friends who urged me into the race had ensured, by their conspicuous non support that I could not afford to do any polling) Second, no one seemed to believe that I would be martyred in the scenario, an odd conclusion to make given the obvious violent intent of the Urban Underground.

I thought about this predicament as I joined my strange bedfellows before a bank of microphones and added my voice in condemnation of the attacks. I was angry at the depth of Cole's presumptuousness of his smug suggestion of cowardice on my part— but what he didn't know was that at six that morning, in spite of everything, I'd told Chief Johnson that, I would do it.

TWENTY-SEVEN
Make Your Play

"The Black man is forever caught between a sort of heroism and just being a nigger."

Prof. Gerald Early

My terms were simple. I would make the taped statement immediately but would not surrender to U.U. until after the election. They seemed to have settled into a pattern of one bombing per week, toward the end of the week. Presumably there would be time after the election and before the next event to broker a deal.

I also demanded protection for my father. I didn't want him endangered as I went off to play secret agent. I had already lost one parent and I wasn't about to lose another as a result of my foolishness.

"You know he won't accept our protection Jason. He's not that kind of brother." The Chief had said.

He was right. My father would no sooner allow himself to go into the loving arms of the police as jump off the Woodrow Wilson Bridge; but I had a solution for that too.

"Place him under surveillance. You guys can do that right? Watch him discreetly, so that he doesn't know he's being watched?"

"We'd need special permission to do something like that, a court order."

"Well Chief, I guess you need to get on that then. I'm not doing it any other way. I'm rusty on this area of the law but if you say it's a matter of national security, my guess is that the world will be at your feet."

I was feeling a familiar sense of confidence. I was dictating terms to the Chief of Police; my voice was back.

Watching the sunrise over Washington from the top of an aluminum ladder is an experience that few have ever had. Even during the pitched battle for a community it was peaceful there, a reminder of what we were fighting for.

There was still an election in a few days and we were making final preparations, as is traditionally done, by hanging our remaining posters on the streetlights and telephone poles nearest the voting precincts. It was two days before the vote and we knew that in all likelihood they would be down by

Election Day but by then, we were specialists in defying logic.

It was all about positioning. The earlier you hung them, the better the sightlines for the voter, but they were more vulnerable. In the end, we opted for location over sustainability.

For the entire campaign a proxy war had been waged over signage. Ours had come down by the box full and Brennan's too in retaliation but his superior cache reduced our counterattacks to petty harassment. Even our lawn signs were disappearing. Brennan's hired thugs continued to trespass in my supporters' yards to get at them.

I knew that Griffin and Bobby were *my* covert operators, but I never inquired and they never volunteered their involvement. I had to maintain deniability in the gutter level politics that Brennan's actions necessitated.

Occasionally Griffin would hint at his activities. "Man, did you notice that all of Brennan's signs in Southwest came down?" I would say, "Yeah I saw that this morning on the way to the Waterside Mall Metro stop."

"It's something huh?" he would say.

"Sure is." I'd respond.

"Yeah, who ever did that knew what they were doing." Griffin would say, an impish grin on his face.

"Obviously the work of experts, I'm sure glad they're not working against us."

We were mixing it up with the most powerful business and political interests in

374

town and holding our own. We never backed down. We were waging a guerilla war on the streets of Washington, D.C. and I know my father was proud.

One morning, sometime in the late sixties, I was riding in my father's old Mercury when a very large white man rear-ended him at a stoplight. My father emerged from the car in his grey flannel suit to confront the man, who clearly hadn't bothered to check whether the light had turned green (it had not).

I remember the white man, who was wearing the stained overalls of a mechanic, jumping out of his car and calling my father a nigger. Hearing this my father said, *"My son is in that car and might have been hurt by your recklessness. If I'm such a nigger, then you make your play."*

My father balled his massive hands into fists and waited for the man to strike. Under a minute later, the white man lay bleeding on the ground. My father had caught him with a vicious right cross to the nose.

It sounds apocryphal but its true, a cornerstone of my childhood memories. I must have been four but I never forgot my father's words, *Make your play*. It was an invitation to battle. He was saying, you're wrong; *I'm ready*, so *make your play*.

After we were safely in the car and on our way, the man still rubbing his nose on the ground, I asked my father, "Daddy, why did you beat up the white man? Huh? Why'd you beat him up? Huh? Why?"

"Always remember *this* boy." He said. "A man's got to do what a man's got to do. If a man calls you a nigger, you make damned sure the he remembers the experience as long as you will." He hadn't broken a sweat.

✝

I was feeling more and more strident as the campaign wore on. One evening Griffin and I were out hanging posters on 3rd and Pennsylvania Avenue just blocks from Brennan's house. I decided to place signs closer to the Capitol. There were Library of Congress employees, many of them Black residents of the Ward that would see them there.

Twenty minutes later Griffin called me on my cell phone to say he needed help. I saw a squad car with its lights whirling and a white police officer emerging from it. I ran down the street hoping that nothing terrible had happened to my most trusted field operative and newest friend. Since the beginning of the campaign, he had always had my back.

Griffin was a poster child for the concept of rehabilitation; an ex-felon who had completely revitalized his life through education and entrepreneurship. He co-owned a small auto repair shop and operated a non-profit dedicated to assisting ex felons like himself. We'd bonded through battle and I wanted him for my Constituent Services Director if we won.

"Jason, this officer is telling me that we can't place these signs here."

"That's correct sir," said the Officer.

"That's actually *not correct*. I am a candidate for the Council of the District of Columbia legally registered with the D.C. Board of Elections and Ethics, notice the disclaimer at the bottom of this poster." I pointed out, line by line, the public disclaimer required by the office of campaign finance, then continued, "I am entitled to place signs here."

The officer held his ground, "That's not what I was told." Do you see that sign," I said pointing to a Brennan poster, "that's my opponent. Why is that sign permissible while mine is not?"

"I'm just telling you what they told us at roll call sir, no red signs here in the First District."

"How can you enforce that when it's not a law?"

I was teaching legal methods now at three in the morning, living my alternative reality as a law professor. Teaching *Street Law to a cop.*

"It must be a new rule or regulation or something?" Said the Officer.

"No, it's more like official intimidation Officer, I'm aware that the FOP endorsed Mr. Brennan, they always do, never even sent me a questionnaire to fill out. They had a citywide endorsement meeting to which I was not invited. "

Such hypocrisy was not unusual in the new D.C. The Gertrude Stein Democratic Club a gay constituency group within the D.C.

Democratic Party had done the same; endorse Brennan without even giving me an invitation to speak. *"We weren't aware of your candidacy,"* they said, despite my announcement almost a full year before. Odd for organizations dedicated to justice, public safety, human rights, civil liberties and fair play to pull up the ladder once they're over the wall. *Gentrification makes such strange bedfellows.*

I kept at the cop, ignoring years of conditioning about dealing with white policemen at night. I was empowered by my law degree, the truth of my argument and the futility of my campaign. In the end, I was amazed that it had boiled down to whether I was even allowed to put up signs in this new D.C.

"I want you to understand something Officer—" I leaned in to read his nametag. "— McCrowley, I will continue to place signs in this Ward and I will not be intimidated by you or anyone else. Now I'd like to ask for your badge number and first name but that would be escalating matters wouldn't it. I'm pretty sure my best friend's father, Chief Johnson, would like to know what is going on in this District, behind his back."

"No need for all that Mr. Diggs, I've been working a couple of power shifts this week uh maybe I misheard that SOP this evening."

"Perhaps you did."

TWENTY-EIGHT
Vicissitudes

"To ravage, to slaughter, to usurp under false titles, they call it empire; and where they make a desert, they call it peace..."
Tacitus.

The rallies were over. Balloons lay airless and torn in empty church halls. Motorcades that once coursed gallantly through every artery of the electoral battlefield, speakers amplifying our message of love and change, had transformed into a funeral procession for the life that I always believed was mine by right.

I suppose you could say that I had had a meltdown. It is not enough to have been on the precipice of personal greatness or to have been the son of legends. We're measured by our own achievements--if only by ourselves.

I was staring forty in the face without having made a mark on history, which is not a tragedy for most people, but for me it felt like I had wasted my time. Everywhere I turned there were the reminders of failure; reminders that my life as I had planned it so long ago, was at an end. Even my campaign posters, once fiery banners of defiance glaring their message of hope, faith and love, now seemed to sag wearily in defeat; as if they knew that the noble cause that they represented failed to win the day.

Seeing those proud emblems in such a state sealed my decision to head north again for consolation. The old folks say "it's a poor rat that only has one hole," and maybe they were talking about me, because for there was nothing else to do but retreat to the Vineyard for a prolonged investigation of time.

My return to Martha's Vineyard was the kind of bittersweet moment about which poets write and the soulful long remember. The course of my life made the Vineyard inevitable as the vessel that was my life seemed to run out of navigable sea. I'd often sought sanctuary on that tiny rock in the ocean, my refuge in times of trouble and those were such days.

That first day back, I sat alone on South Beach and the salty Katama breeze tossed the smoke from my cigar like a ship in a tempest. I could not help wondering what had happened to the long promised support when my hearty band of insurgents was engaged in a sleepless battle for a community. I refused to construe this as self-pity. In light of all that had happened, sober empiricism dictated that the fervor of my supporters was misguided. Misguided for reposing their most precious hopes in me.

I never believed in the good fight, the selfish sacrifice of the charge of the light brigade. Winning was everything, a city was at stake and ultimately I had failed the cause and the people to whom I had pledged my love and fidelity. I left the scene, for good, I thought and began to write.

I did not anticipate that the video taped message to U.U. that I recorded in late August would generate a response. It had been broadcast on the day of the election and I'd quickly forgotten about it.

I was boxed in. I concluded that Brennan, Terwilliger and Callahan would leak any refusal on my part, to the media, pegging me a coward or in league with the conspiracy or both. So what did I have to lose?

Brennan's next move was surprising. He knew of the plan and soon began to deride my rhetoric as the cause of the violence. In every newspaper and every piece of campaign literature leading up to Election Day he called me dangerous and irresponsible. I simply lacked the means to respond.

I was always aware that leadership requires sacrifice; my parents drilled that into my brain during my formative years just as they did my phone number, my address and my ABC's. What I didn't anticipate was an attack not intended to stun or incapacitate, but maim and destroy.

Back in Oak Bluffs for the first time in over a year, I was uneasy about many things. At the house on Pequot Street, I lay in a hammock dappled in sunlight amid heavy stands of trees, but did not find peace. I was there to assess the wreckage of my life, search for the black box and arrive at causation. From there, I could restart my journey and get on with my life. But it didn't happen. There was no Vineyard calm.

I had watched the election returns alone. I took a long hot shower, removing the stress of the long campaign and slowly put on the black Ralph Lauren suit that I would wear to my victory party. My mood was calm, introspective. I had done all that I could do. "Leave it all on the field," AJ told me when I finally caught up with him in Bermuda. And I had.

The first call came from Calvin Crenshaw, an old associate from my earlier flirtations with the subculture. He, like so many, had contributed little more than kind words to my campaign, neither sweat nor treasure, oblivious to the war for survival being waged in the streets.

"Congratulations."

"What?" I said.

"The News Channel has you ahead by 19% with 20% reporting.

"I was shocked. I'd believed that the events of the year had made me immune to emotionalism but for a moment all had been redeemed.

I hadn't indulged myself with the possibility of winning in many weeks. I was too busy campaigning and making deals with the enemy to think of victory.

In the last two weeks of a political campaign a candidate simply executes. You're too tired to innovate. It's too late to issue an earth shattering proposal that might cause an electoral earthquake; the famous October, or in this case, September surprise, which might force voters to cleave along radically different lines.

My entire strategy after the call with Andruzzi, was to get the turn out in the majority Black precincts up above 50%, in an effort to equalize the electoral playing field, leaving the race to a competition for white liberal swing voters who might be persuaded to choose me in spite of tribal allegiances. It was Valor's plan, the one that I had upbraided her for more than a year before. In the end, the *Poker Game* had completely agreed.

What Calvin was telling me was that our feisty little ground campaign might well have done the trick. I held my breath for news that might vindicate what we had done. I had to see it for myself so I turned on the T.V.

"If these numbers hold, this would represent an historic upset."

Crazy Rick Donavan smiled proudly into the camera, as he said it. I ran down the stairs and sped all the way to Eastern Market and my victory party.

As I drove I prayed like I never had before, trying to summon my maternal Grandfather's Grafton's spirit and resurrect his mighty faith. I prayed to bring a victory into being and find a way out of no way. But by the time I entered the North Hall of the Market, the numbers had suddenly reversed and the election had been called for Brennan.

My speech was short and off the cuff. I abandoned the camera-ready remarks that I had prepared in case of victory. I thanked the contributors and volunteers. I thanked the two unions that had endorsed me, the hundreds of church people who worked so hard despite their Maryland residency. Lastly I thanked the ACORN members who had bolstered our ranks and fought for me down to the last man and woman.

While it was far from a landslide, I had lost. Some in the room urged another campaign in four or eight years, *you're a young man*, they said. *There's plenty of time*, they said. Just like Randall Reilly thirty years before, it was over, before it started. The Poker Game had come full circle in my lifetime.

My defeat hurt all the more because I knew that Andruzzi and Terwilliger, Cole, Brennan and Callahan now had free reign to finish what they started. Callahan had won the democratic primary for Mayor with nearly 65% of the vote, which in the District of Columbia was tantamount to victory in November. I was angry for missing the futility of the effort from the outset.

The people, who really run this town, as Andruzzi put it, were prepared to do anything to consolidate their victories in the city. They used the false prosperity of tax base and business growth to replace the older virtues of community and safety net. A process so old that it's got moss growing on it and I remembered from college Political Theory that Tacitus said it best.

I wandered the room as the surroundings lost focus. There were hugs and handshakes, reassuring pats on the back, which coagulated into one excruciating vision.

"Jason, you're shaking man," Griffin said grabbing me by the shoulders.

I was. I felt the anger radiating from me like a strange heat. "I'll be alright I am just tired and angry." I said.

Griffin had a strange smile on his face. In his time, he had seen far worse.

"I'm pissed too, but look here man, we gave it our best shot and they got it. But they didn't get nothing see, because they already *done* ripped the heart out of this place. Don't worry they ain't get shit man. Nothing."

He was right. The conquest of Chocolate City would be nothing more than a pyrrhic victory. So much of the city's spirit was already irrevocably diluted. But there was more. While, I always knew that the real D.C. existed beyond the monuments, it was only then that I understood that it also existed beyond the neighborhoods.

D.C. as I knew it, was more than a physical place and much more than an idea. It was a belief system, a set of principles and a way of understanding the world. We were the fortunate ones who'd experienced it in its halcyon days. We'd known the pungent odor of the wharf during summer, known giddy nights at the Carter Barron Amphitheater grooving to gaily-costumed crooners. We knew the intoxication of life in a Black city led by rugged kin who loved you.

Those of us who lived this cannot be dispossessed. We walk with it now. It's a part of us.

In the midst of this suddenly gloomy gathering, I spoke to Tori Boone, a young newlywed and a Howard graduate who had reported to our campaign office each and every day to answer the phones. She had waited in line respectfully most of the night to speak to me deferring to people who in my estimation had done far less for the cause. When it was her turn to hug me, she cried.

"Jason", she said sweetly. "Nothing in D.C. will ever be interesting again."

I smiled at her, momentarily lost in her innocence as anger again rose inside me. It had finally come together in my mind. I knew the purpose of Urban Underground and I believed I knew who they were.

The final results, Brennan's 8,152 to my 4,482, were not close but respectable, if you factored in his incumbency, the huge financial advantage that Brennan enjoyed and the mountain of dirty tricks. Nixon would have been proud.

The pre-electoral redistricting run to devious perfection in the majority white Council had lobbed off the politically sophisticated middle class Blacks in the east, of my Ward's map in exchange for the poor and disenfranchised Blacks in the projects north and south of Capitol Hill. It was technically legal but my true base of support was gone before the first vote was cast.

Reports were also coming in from all over the Ward that cash filled brown paper bags were issued as bribes throughout the low income Black precincts. Unlike in previous races, when the *Poker Game* ran things and people voted their interests, these ghetto power brokers kept faith with their illegal bargains—their ignorance and short-term memories a feature of their impoverished neighborhoods and depraved souls. *They will, I am sure, burn in hell.*

Comatose Black senior citizens in nursing homes somehow voted for Brennan, as did the homeless who lived in the famous shelter that Mitch Snyder built. *Did they know Brennan wanted it closed?*

It was a wonder that we were able to win the four precincts that we did. Nearly every house surrounding my old family church had a Brennan lawn sign. It was their neighborhood now.

The bombings hadn't helped. They seemed to have galvanized the white vote in favor of both Callahan and that steady hand and arch protector of white citizens everywhere, Damien Brennan. Even the tofu eating set, were scared out of their minds by the explosions and though fascinated by me, Lock calling them *Diggs curious*, they could not bring themselves to support someone who according to Brennan's whispering campaign, *just might be behind all of this*.

The claim was ridiculous on it's face. I had neither motive nor opportunity and we did not exactly have bomb-making classes as electives at Howard Law School.

I concluded that the bombings were the work of far more sinister forces and as I watched the hope drain in teardrops from Tori Boone's eyes, I realized that in order to elect a white successor and complete *The Plan*, the Mayor might be bombing his own city.

TWENTY-NINE
Winter In America

"Winter is a metaphor: a term not only used to describe the season of ice, but the period of our lives through which we are traveling... Western icemen have attempted to distort time..."

Gil Scott-Heron

I s it logical to miss a life you never had, grieve for an existence longed for but not experienced? The essence of what is not achieved can be felt. When a dream is strong enough it lives on in regret.

Councilmember Diggs is alive somewhere, changing the city, saving the salvageable. A beautiful wife and kids to come home to, a legacy preserved. In some alternate universe, in the years that follow, Senator Diggs stands in the well of the Senate, giving the great speeches of the age, removing the veil of ignorance, uplifting millions; the Poker Game now of national scope, the Diggs clan continuing to grow in stature, strength and love through the ages.

My dream lives in that shadow world and I do too, for this reality has been too costly to bear consciously. In the end I fell short of the mark that my gifts might have granted me and that is my great tragedy.

I wrote these words in my journal on a blustery Vineyard beach, concerned that life had passed me by. After all that had happened, a return to the Senate Judiciary committee was impossible. I had been smeared a terrorist sympathizer and that simply wouldn't play in post 9/11 America.

Kelleye's poorly written but politically powerful letter to the Chairman, in which she stated that she *"may have been witnessed to a sexual copulation during the spring snowstorm,"* made my ability to return unlikely. Such an allegation, even a spurious one, doesn't go down very well, even with bourbon and cigars.

I had long ago abandoned any real path to the private practice of law and no longer had the stomach for government work. In the end I was a leader with nothing to lead.

The existential question of what to do with my life haunted me in those days. I called some of the women I had known and got mixed results. It seems my frequent absences from their lives had taken their toll. I called Valor and received no answer from her home in Atlanta.

I decided to purge the detritus from my ruined life and with it, all the phony people of flimsy character and dubious motivations. This included A.J. For the first time since the quiet of childhood, I was almost completely alone.

I received the call one week to the day after the election. The Vineyard calm had been reluctant, but it had finally come. I was leaving Linda Jean's full and reasonably content in jeans and a Morehouse tee shirt.

Earlier that day I decided to grow an Afro and beard and disappear from public life—a last act of defiance, an acceptance that I would never be a Councilmember, let alone a Senator. I committed to write a monograph or treatise, which described the state of the city, thinking that it might provide to some future historian a glimpse of what had befallen our old empire. I would sell Uncle Winston's House and buy an up-island home on the Vineyard, away from anyone who knew or ever heard of Jason Diggs.

I answered the phone hesitantly. No one had called in a week, not even my father.

"Jason, it's Chief Johnson. How are you young man?"

"I'm doing well enough, I guess."

"Sorry about the election. We're all very proud of you."

"I don't know why, but thanks."

"Listen, we got a call."

"From whom?"

"The Urban Underground."

"Couldn't have. I mean, I thought all that was over."

"Why would you think that?"

I thought about telling him my theory about Terwilliger but decided against it, just in case he was involved.

Apparently they hadn't finished with me yet. Defeating me in an election and ruining my life was clearly not enough for them.

"What did they say?"

"They have accepted your terms. They want to meet with you."

"You mean they've accepted *your* terms don't you Chief? Terms, I might add, that I want nothing more to do with now that my campaign is over. I'm going to get over D.C., since its seems she's over me."

"I thought you might have that reaction, but they've promised a bombing a day unless you come back to town."

"How do they know that I'm not *in* town?" *I didn't tell anyone that I was leaving, except my father.*

"They make reference to the fact that they know you are in Martha's Vineyard. They say that you will need to come back immediately."

"Well I'm not interested Chief, as a private citizen, I don't want to do it okay. You're just going to have to solve this shit yourselves!"

"Jason, there's one more thing."

"What's that?"

"They have your father."

"What? You said that you would watch him. This is some bullshit!"

"We had him under surveillance for a few weeks but yesterday, after his three o'clock class, he went into the bathroom on the First Floor of Douglass Hall and we lost him."

"Why wasn't I informed of this?"

"I thought we'd pick him back up, but we didn't. Then the note came."

"Couldn't it be a hoax? I have more than a few enemies out there now." *Including Kelleye, the Mayor, the Mayor-Elect and one patrolman on the graveyard shift in the First District, I thought.*

"They sent a picture of him holding today's Washington Post. It's real Jason."

"I'll drive down tonight." I said.

"That will take too long, they have promised to bomb tonight, if you are not in town by five this afternoon. They say they will know if you haven't arrived."

"What am I supposed to do?"

"There is a two o'clock flight on US Airways from Martha's Vineyard to National Airport. The ticket is already paid for, I suggest that you be on that plane." It was 11 a.m.

"I'll be on it." I said.

"I'll be there to meet you at the airport myself."

⸸

The note was simple:

Message received and agreed to. We know Jason Diggs is on Martha's Vineyard. He must return to Washington immediately. We will bomb each night until he does. Casualties will occur.

We have Dr. Steppenwolf Diggs. He will not be harmed if Jason Diggs complies. Upon Jason Diggs' return he will be exchanged for the Professor. Wait for further instructions.

The Urban Underground

My father looked relaxed in the picture, almost happy in his shirtsleeves and loosened bow tie. I imagined him lecturing his captors ad nauseam with revolutionary quotes from Che, Mao and Kenyatta; ironically he would have in them, a captive audience.

The Chief collected me from the airport, and we immediately went hot; the cruiser tearing across 14th Street Bridge, sirens blazing, like he'd just gotten a report that Bin Laden was on the National Mall. We drove into the city and directly to the impressive Art Deco municipal building, which held Police Headquarters.

A Diggs poster still hung languidly on the traffic light in front of the building. *Insult on injury.*

"What now?" I said.

"We wait for further instructions, like the letter said."

"I can't wait. They have my father Chief, this is not a waiting matter."

"We can't do anything else."

We walked into the building and arrived at his ornate offices. There were awards and certificates and encased in glass were old police uniform shirts dating back 100 years.

"Coffee Jason?"

"Yes please, black with sugar."

We waited for hours and I emptied the pot of coffee. More was prepared.

At 10 p.m., seven hours after my arrival, I was ready to go.

"Chief, I'm going home."

"Jason, I can't take that chance. I need you to stay here, where you're safe."

"My father isn't safe. If I go through with this thing, I will *not* be safe."

"I just can't take the risk that we lose you before the next bombing occurs. You may be the key to saving a lot of people's lives."

"Am I under arrest Chief?"

"No, of course not but I *could* put you in protective custody."

"If you think you can make that one stick make your play, I'm going home."

He considered it for a moment and agreed. "But you're going in a cruiser and the Officer will remain outside your door."

I laughed for the first time in a week. "All that protection didn't seem to help my father." I said.

The Officer, a pious looking young Black man who appeared more preacher than cop, drove to my house and walked me to the front door. He insisted on searching the house first. It was clear, of course.

Two weeks before, I'd placed Musa in one of the local doggie spas for the final days of the campaign and left him there, while I did the Vineyard. The blonde high school aged desk attendant blushed when she found out who I was, even asked me for an autograph.

"What school do you go to?"

"Like, Sidwell? Mr. Diggs."

"Jason's fine, I'm off duty." We shared a laugh.

"So you like dogs?"

"Love them, I have a Cavalier King Charles at home. His name's Oliver."

"Well Musa is more like a bear, think you can handle him?"

"I'll do my best."

"That's all anyone can ever ask."

"If I were old enough I'd vote for you," she volunteered. I thanked her and went on my way. *Maybe there is hope for the future,* I thought.

After the officer went back to the cruiser, I sat at the kitchen table, where I had debated with Andruzzi on the telephone and went through my mail. The phone rang.

"Jason Diggs?" The voice said.

"Yes?"

"This is the Urban Underground!"

"Yes."

"Tomorrow morning. Come alone to the Ocean View Hotel in Ocean City. 4 a.m. No police, no FBI no tricks. Turn off your cell phone and take out the battery, they can track it."

Before I could ask about my father, I heard his voice.

"Jason?"

"Pop, are you okay?"

"Yes son, just tired. They won't let me sleep. They keep asking me things about your campaign."

"I'll be there soon Pop."

"Don't worry about me son. They're treating me alright otherwise."

"Have they hurt you or anything?"

"No, just the incessant questions. I—"

The other voice was back on the phone.

"Read your mail." The phone went dead.

I was already halfway through the week's mail and hadn't seen a thing other than bills and advertisements. Then I saw a plain white envelope with an Oakland California postmark. My heart raced as I carefully opened it. In it was one of the old style hotel keys, with the thick plastic fob on the end. It was green and embossed in white with the words: *Ocean View Ocean City MD.* The key was for Room 66.

I knew I couldn't tell the Chief but I also knew that that police cruiser would follow me to the city limits where I was sure to be picked up by some law enforcement agency, FBI, Maryland state troopers or even PG County police. I had no idea how I was going to drive the 148 miles in time.

I was about to break down and call AJ for advice. He was always the devious one, the risk taker and the one who would know how to escape the police, his father.

Then there was a blast, then another, and another. All near enough to my house that the windows shook. I went to the door and people were streaming into the street.

U.U was easing my escape through a well-timed attack. I saw the cruiser containing *preachercop* go hot and race off toward one of the sounds. I had a chance.

I ran out of the house toward my SAAB, which, as usual, I had left in the city in favor of *FiFi. She had always been my Vineyard car.*

I started the car and considered my situation. I had not informed my father about the plan, a misstep, which might have caused his abduction. I had stripped him of his best defense, awareness.

I didn't tell him because of all the people in the world, he alone could have dissuaded me from making such a Faustian bargain. He alone, at the time of my greatest peril, retained the credibility in my life, to turn me from such a perilous course.

I simply idolized the man. I envied his mind, his ability to instantly draw accurate conclusions when presented with the most limited of information. This episode had proven that I had no such skill.

I imitated him relentlessly as a child. From the way he crossed his legs at right angles to his often-anachronistic style of speech. These things I did consciously but many others came from the kinship of blood. I looked more like my mother's clan, but I was my father's son. I thought these things as I went to find him. He had so much more to teach and I had so much more to learn.

I remember my father telling me that *the definition of courage is to proceed through fear, undaunted by its presence.* Some saw my campaign as courageous, an indication in my mind of the low threshold possessed by so many. Most people had no stomach for truth telling in the face of an emergency. *All I'd ever done was talk.*

I was merely willing to rise in the face of indifference and say what had to be said, speak the names of the forgotten and fight for those that some deemed expendable. *I did what I had to.* I had not done anything that was particularly courageous but what I was about to do certainly was.

I called Valor and again got her voicemail. I had to tell someone what was going on, in case I didn't come back.

Valor it's Jason. I'm going to find my father, the terrorists have taken him somewhere. Ah... I want you to know that if I don't come back, I love you and always have. If its possible, I mean if

I get out of this alive, I will move the universe itself to be with you. I want to marry you Valor. I have been imagining us together, kind of in our own world, unencumbered by all the bullshit and umm making our own reality. It's only a dream, but in spite of everything, I still believe in dreams. I'll call you if I can. I love you.

Then I removed the battery from my phone as I had been instructed. I was tired and it was going to be a long night.

THIRTY
Beach Meeting

"Every time I find the meaning of life, they change it."

Unknown

Route 50 East is beautiful on a cloudless late summer day. When you cross the wide expanse of Chesapeake Bay Bridge, glancing at the water as you go, you can usually see a flotilla of sail and powerboats cruising the wide blue green expanse before you make landfall on Maryland's eastern shore. But, at that hour, the boats were as tightly secured, as I was adrift.

You can find peace on such journeys; white lines and countryside lulling you into a meditative state. But, I would find no peace that night. Something else awaited me.

I drove in an incoherent pattern from my house to I-295, blending in with the mass of cars and took the off ramp to Route 50. To avoid suspicion, I drove sensibly until reaching the Anne Arundel County line, which was where I opened up the Saab. The turbo kicked in and the engine growled. It was half past midnight and I would make it in just less than three hours. With no traffic at that time of night, I might have an hour to spare. They had thought of everything.

I saw myself overcome, flipping the car. A wisp of smoke wafting up from the side of the highway to alert all who passed on that lonely stretch that a damned fool city driver done gone asleep at the wheel and rolled his SAAB. Which would not be how it happened. I was an excellent driver and wide-awake despite my fatigue. No, it would be a conscious act.

The putative cause of death would be my broken neck severing all sensation and electrical impulses from my brain. It would all be finished, the inevitable end of questions—the answers, known but to God.

It didn't happen that way, never could. I was my father's son. I listened to Cassandra Wilson, which made me hopeful that my father and I could somehow emerge on the other side. I now felt that there *was* another side. Valor.

I had been put off for years by her unwillingness to adhere to my idealized conception of the One but she had always been there. Hadn't she? *Life presents certain oddities,* I thought.

I thought, I prayed and I cried, while driving into the night—discarding the emotions that would be of no use at my destination. Once again, I was going to war.

I had no stomach for martyrdom, others had done it so well that it didn't need doing anymore, at least not by me. I did not know what I would encounter in Ocean City, but I had no intention of making it my last stop. Suddenly, I had things to do.

As I approached Ocean City it was 3:15 am and I had a little time to gather myself. I drove the 20 blocks North on Ocean Drive to the hotel and found it on the Bay side situated sideways on the street. I might have missed it were it not for the 1950s era marquee that jutted ostentatiously from the facade, proclaiming to all that passed: *air conditioning, color TVs, Redskins/Ravens Football.*

I could smell the salt in the air and recalled that only hours before I was, hundreds of miles up the coast. I could feel specks of Inkwell sand that were still in my shoes from the previous morning. The situation was surreal.

Soon, the sun would rise over the ocean front hotels and the memories would give way to the reality of my circumstances. *Let's get this over with*, I thought.

It was 3:30 when I walked into the motel. I showered and shaved with the motel's plastic kit. *Let's leave a good last impression*, was my sardonic thought.

I waited.

By 4:30 a.m., I had this notion that it might be all an elaborate hoax, but I remembered my father's capture and was reluctantly forced to disabuse myself of it. I was looking for a way out but couldn't find one. I was there and it was happening to me.

Then the telephone rang in the room. It was 4:45. I must have dozed.

"Jason Diggs?" said the woman on the other end of the phone. *A woman, I didn't expect that somehow.*

"Yes?"

"This is the Urban Underground, welcome to Ocean City."

"Thank you, but I need to know—"

"You honestly don't expect to receive answers do you? Your role is to listen, *politician.*" She said the word *politician* with disgust, the way one might say *asshole or motherfucker.*

"Okay."

"You will be treated with respect and we expect the same. Is that understood?"

"Yes, of course."

"You are to drive to Delaware immediately. Proceed north to the Bethany Beach sign and park at the lot nearest the access point to the beach. Sit in your car and await further instructions. You have twenty minutes. Don't be late."

"But." She hung up.

The woman sounded strong but her voice was calm and strangely soothing. That "don't be late" smacked of a girlishness that I was familiar with, something I knew.

Fear, was my primary emotion as I drove the few miles north into Delaware. I parked and again waited, but not for long. The parking lot was desolate as it should have

404

been just off-season at nearly five in the morning.

There would be no witnesses to what was about to take place there. All the little trinket shops had been buttoned up for the year a few weeks before. No ice cream parlors, no Boardwalk French Fry concessions, not even Seagulls pecking their way through the detritus of a million summer vacationers. Nothing.

A few minutes later a Black Ford Explorer with blacked out windows pulled up beside me. The passenger side door opened and a man in a black ski mask approached me. He looked like an NFL tight end, tall and almost leonine in his countenance. He wore black fatigue pants and I noticed an insignia on his black tee shirt. The letters U.U. were in red, surrounded by green laurel leaves and were superimposed on what looked like a dagger through an outline of the United States. *Extravagant*, I thought. *Elegant, not like the rag tag pictures of the Taliban I had seen on TV over the previous year.*

He asked me to get out of my car and into the back seat of his truck. I complied and was immediately blindfolded by a smaller but equally intense fellow. They told me not to talk as we drove, an easy proposition. I had nothing to say.

After driving for what seemed like an hour, the truck stopped and they escorted me from the backseat. I heard a door open and the sound of muffled voices. They walked me down several flights of stairs and then several more. I couldn't see a thing and by then the sensory deprivation was starting to disturb me. It was completely Black.

At the end of the stairs I was led around toward the right and could tell I was being seated a few feet from where we entered.

"You have requested an audience with central committee of the first cadre of the Urban Underground. The Ministers will be with you momentarily. Would you like something to drink?" It was a man's voice, he had a D.C. accent and so I played my old game to calm my nerves. The accent was old school but was probably from near Minnesota and Benning, *Greenway Apartments*, I guessed.

"No thank you," I said grateful that I was being treated so well. *I really wanted straight bourbon, but didn't ask for it. A clear head would be of value later.*

It did occur to me that these people who had my father and me, were not thugs as they'd been portrayed in City Under Siege. There was a quiet dignity in the way they comported themselves and I suppose that I wanted to maintain the same level of decorum.

A few minutes later my blindfold was removed and I gradually began to see. I was seated about ten feet in front of a long table behind which sat three older, very distinguished looking Black people. I saw another person, seated in the middle with his back turned.

They all wore black suits and black turtlenecks. The suit jackets bore the same insignia that I'd seen on the tight end looking fellow that had brought me there.

"Welcome Mr. Diggs to the Central Committee of the First Cadre of the Urban Underground." *Damn, Black people sure love titles*, I thought.

I didn't recognize any of them but I couldn't see anything too well. The poor lighting cast shadows on their faces, partially obscuring their features. From my perspective, they could have been members of the Deacon Board at one of the churches that I visited so frequently during the campaign; anything but terrorists.

"You requested a meeting?" said the deaconess.

"Yes ma'am."

"Sister!" She barked.

"Yes, sister," I said contritely.

"You may proceed." I felt like I was in Moot Court, in law school again, but the stakes were infinitely higher now. I began cautiously.

"Before we begin, I would like to see my father."

"In good time. He is near." Said the woman. I knew not to press it so I went on.

"There is one question that will determine the value of any continued dialogue. Is your organization responsible for the bombings that have occurred over the past year in the District of Columbia?"

"Yes, we accept responsibility," said the man on the right.

"Well brothers and sisters—"

"Very good Mr. Diggs," they said in unison.

"I am here to negotiate the release of my father and an end to hostilities."

"On whose authority?" Said the woman ominously.

"On my own authority and that of hundreds of thousands of Black people in D.C. who will be victimized as a result of your actions."

"The Mayor didn't send you?" said the man on the right. The man in the middle still had his back turned and had not spoken.

"He's certainly aware of it but this was *my* decision. You may know that we don't see eye to eye."

"We're aware of many things Mr. Diggs, but why do *you* want us to end our offensive?"

"Because it's counterproductive."

"How can you say that when you are not privy to our goals and objectives?"

It was Socratic. I was asking questions but they responded with better ones. There was a disarming gravitas about them, one that demanded respect.

It was the natural dignity of older Black people, the, *I've known rivers* kind of dignity. An *ancient dusky* kind of dignity, like the Pyramids or an old country church and like those timeless structures, they are immovable.

"All I know is that if the tanks start rolling down East Capitol Street again the last vestiges of black control of the city will evaporate," I said.

"Why is that such an undesirable outcome?" whispered the man whose back was turned.

"Because we fought for generations to build a power base in the city. It deserves to be saved."

"Why? It seems manifest that if you can't hold on to it, you probably didn't deserve it. Besides, isn't it already too late?" Said the woman.

Her remark caught me off guard. I hadn't reconciled my own belief that it was too late to save the city with the matter before me, talking U.U. out of doing any more harm and releasing my father in the process.

The woman continued, "While your campaign was quite valiant and your tactics surprisingly effective, in the end, it was a waste of time, wasn't it? You can't rouse, a sleeping giant when it's already dead."

"I think there's a chance—" I was immediately cut off by the man whose back I had been speaking to. I could see that he was a big man, as he stood.

"How does it feel to be an historic figure?" He voice was barely audible. "Gentrification has insured that, your campaign will always be known as the last time a Black person ever credibly ran for Council in your Ward. The city of Washington has elected a white Mayor, who will no doubt respond even more obediently than his predecessor to a corporate oligarchy. With Washington as a beachhead, the reign of the Black man in urban America is over."

I was speechless. He had said what I had been thinking since my meeting with Chad Highsmith. We *had* lost the city and the creation of a Black minority in D.C. and cities nationwide was now inevitable, given the rise of gentrification.

The woman spoke next. "How about some statistics? Did you know that eighty percent of the homes sold in your Ward in the last eighteen months have gone from Black to white ownership? Did you also know that ninety percent of those Blacks selling their homes have moved out of the city?"

The man on the right spoke, "Did you know that the average three bedroom house in your Ward is now selling for over $300,000 dollars? How can you fight that when you couldn't even get elected to the very office that might have mitigated these trends?"

I said, "We can register the people who are left and fight for a seat at the table." I hated myself for saying it. I sounded like a feeble accomodationist. *That's not going to play well with these folks*, I thought.

"Mr. Diggs, we believe that you mean well, but through no fault of your own, you were ten years too late. While you were still singing nursery rhymes, your predecessors squandered their time in power. They were too busy partying and bopping around in limousines with whores. Too busy running

410

around in and out of strip clubs, prison and rehab," said the woman.

"—And, too busy making deals with the devil." Added the man whispering in the shadows. "None of this could have happened if our people hadn't abandoned the city in the first place. The schools weren't invested in and city services became so abysmal that it sent the Black middle class packing. All you have left is rich and poor, nothing in between."

I didn't recognize the whispered voice but I recognized the reasoning. *My father taught this guy*, I thought.

"The man on the right continued, "Your electorate left the city years ago. By 1998 it was over, your fate was sealed. The redistricting that occurred in your Ward was just the icing on a very well baked angel food cake." *He smiled at his own irony.*

"Since this is supposed to be over, your actions are designed to do *what* exactly?" I said, sarcasm being the last refuge of the uninformed.

"We've lost the political battle but we have not finished fighting the war. D.C. was a tremendous symbolic loss but there are other black communities in other cities that might still be saved. D.C has been the test case for *their* concepts and ours," she continued.

The man on the right picked up where she left off. "Culturally, our people are at the lowest ebb since our arrival in chains on these bloody shores. Without a geographical and cultural lodestar, we will be condemning future generations to life as a trivialized second-rate minority—and that's no life at all.

We have been divested of the indigenous ties that undergird a people, like the roots of a tree give strength and depth beyond what is seen. We have suffered the propaganda of those that have exploited our labor our talent and our bodies for four hundred years and now we are expected to function successfully and independently without the self-knowledge that is the birthright of every human being."

I decided to chime in. "I agree that these are many important questions that we did not deal with adequately in the sixties and seventies. I believe that our failure to address them has led to the amoral behavior that we now see being advanced by some hip-hop artists and the degenerate behavior by some of our youth, but what I don't understand is how gentrification in D.C. or in other cities for that matter, has anything to do with that. It seems to me that this is an internal issue."

The man on the right jumped right on it. "Our ghettos are ghettos because our *Black Broadways* died after integration. Our public hospitals are being closed in neighborhoods with a million epidemics. Take your pick, AIDS, homicide, cancer, TB, substance abuse. The generation that won the vote and control of the cities made a big mess of things. They allowed the federal government to walk away from responsibility. We allowed hopelessness to set in for the first time in 400 years. We lost our willingness to fight."

Now, the children of the generation that was bitten, beaten and murdered in the streets is largely apathetic unless a Jesse Jackson or somebody riles them up for a moment and those moments are getting more and more attenuated. They people no longer have staying power; they think freedom is an instant process, that they can simply add water and stir. Now our people, stand half naked on corners, drinking their forties and calling each other dogs, tricks and bitches when their ancestors died for the simple courtesy of being addressed as men and women!"

It was now clear to me that U.U. weren't thugs but an intelligentsia, like the philosopher kings that I had long admired. That's what scared me. I was thinking about how to get out of there when the man in the shadows spoke in full voice. "Jason, we intend to bomb everyone back to their senses."

He emerged from the dark center of the table into the light. His voice had been only a faint whisper but now I heard it in all it thunderous glory. Had he somehow been able to disguise it or had my mind betrayed me. *People tend to see what they expect to see and hear what they expect to hear.*

"What was the first thing I taught you about politics when you were five years old?"

I could hardly get it out, my throat was dry and I had no wind. Then I said it.

"War is politics by other means, Pop."

THIRTY-ONE
War

"Revolutions are brought about by men who think as men of action and act as men of thought."

Kwame Nkrumah

There is no name for the emotion that I felt when I saw my father emerging from the shadows. It can best be described as a mixture of relief, anger and fear.

"You lied to me."

"It was one of omission, not of commission."

"You could have told me something."

"You would have compromised our operations and that couldn't be allowed."

"So you decided to..."

"We gave you a lot of play in the rope. You reeled yourself in."

"Pop, what's this all about really?"

"Jason, the masses of Black and poor people have been lulled to sleep by this convenience store they call a country and in their slumber, they have forgotten that our struggle is not over. We have made many advancements in the last 40 years, politically we've elected Black Mayor's, Congressmen, Governors even Senators and we are clearly destined for even higher office one day, but its lulled us to sleep, made us weak. The irony can't be escaped; we elect Black people to uphold a system that has never been in our interest. A Black warden running the jailhouse doesn't make the wall disappear." My father looked around like a preacher to his choir, receiving nods of appreciation from his co-conspirators.

"We are entering the first post-Black epoch in this nation's history. The Hispanics, the immigrant Russians and the Asians have already overtaken us on many levels; soon we will just be a part of the great American melting pot, the bottom part, the pot liquor."

It was 2002, not 1972 and both Black people and the country had moved on. I tried to tell him this, knowing that I was about 30 years too late.

"Isn't that what we've been fighting for Pop, inclusion, to be a part of the mix irrespective of race and let the best man win?" I slid back in my chair, exhausted.

"That's what some of us were looking for son, not all of us." He was looking intensely over the top of his glasses as he did in his classrooms, lecturing the prized student.

"The rest of us," he continued, "had a more sophisticated understanding of the power relationships at work in this country. We understood that certain people had a 400 year head start on us and that Black Nationalism was a way to even the score."

"But why the violence? They are going to come after you like nothing the Panthers ever saw. This is a post 9/11 world, and this kind of stuff is not going to be tolerated," I said.

"This is asymmetrical warfare!"

The voice had come from behind me and I turned to find him smiling at me. He was wearing the same uniform as the others, but complemented by a black beret. Other than the day of my mother's funeral, it was the best dressed I seen Lock Smith in years.

"What do you mean?"

"Our intent is to signal to our people that the time for complacency is over. We must slow the rate of gentrification in D.C. and the other major metropolitan areas and to establish a permanent strategic base of operations in Africa for Africans in the Diaspora, like the Jews have in Israel. Do you follow?"

My throat was still dry and burned with each word I spoke. My heart was racing and my golf shirt was soaked. I felt like a submarine in this new world, *dry inside, wet outside.*

"I'm not sure."

"Go ahead son."

416

"Bombing the construction sites, real estate and other economic targets on Capitol Hill will get maximum national press. They'll slow down the rate of gentrification by scaring potential new white residents into bypassing the Hill, thereby dissuading new investment and maintaining affordability for our community. We won't be scared off, they will."

"Good," said the man on the right.

"What about the first goal?"

"That one is harder, I suppose Garveyism. *Rise up you mighty race?"*

"We wouldn't expect you to get that one Jason. It's Panther code," my father said.

"As in Black Panther's. You're Panthers Pop?" I stood up.

The tight end moved quickly and soon his hands were on my shoulders, a clear sign for me to sit down.

"It's alright Malik, he's just a little nervous."

"Okay brother Diggs," Malik said, returning to his station by the door. I suppose I could have made it a respectable fight, if it came to that, I thought as I sized him up. His height and reach advantage neutralized by my quickness and tactical mind—yes, just like the campaign, I *would* be able to keep it close, for a while.

"The answer is technically yes Jason, we were recruited into the Black Panthers, but our cadre had a unique purpose."

He could see my confusion and I saw on his face a parental empathy that was as old as time itself.

"Jason, Urban Underground was founded in 1966 by a small group of SNCC members who followed Stokely Carmichael into the Black Panther Party." *I understood the reference, studied it relentlessly in undergrad, I was on familiar ground.* "After it was clear that the Party had been infiltrated through Hoover's COINTELPRO operation, it was decided that we needed to go underground. The design was simple. Several Panthers along with one of our heroes, Robert Williams, were already in exile in Algeria and Cuba and many other places around the world. Many never came back. Urban Underground was established to be in exile right here in the United States, to hide in plain sight, to serves as what they call today, a sleeper cell."

"I thought COINTELPRO decimated the Panthers and all the other leftist organizations back then?"

"The founders of U.U. knew that with the rate of incarcerations, murders and mass disruptions occurring at that time, that by 1975 the Panther's would effectively cease to be an effective instrument for Black liberation in the United States. Ten of us were chosen to form the First Cadre of U.U. We were to disassociate from the Panthers in every way and live our lives normally. A certain confluence of conditions was established as the trigger that would stir the cadre from our hibernation. These conditions occurred in 2000 and we have been operational since that

418

time. Of course 9/11 slowed us down considerably, the Patriot Act was very difficult to work around but we've recovered well enough to engage in limited action."

I was stunned. For years I had painstakingly constructed an image of my father that had turned out to be as fact based as the Easter Bunny. The stodgy college professor, resplendent in his tweed vestments, the D.C. political icon who doted so tenderly on his invalid wife was never what he appeared to be. He apparently was, *I almost could not bear the thought*, a *domestic terrorist* bent on some kind of race war—a left over sixties anarchist, who had the motivation and wherewithal to implement his destructive plan.

"I don't know where to begin," I said. "You spent years getting people elected, that's working within the system right? And you were successful; you're responsible for the election of a dozen different Councilmembers over the years and a few Mayors. Don't tell me all those folks were Black Panthers too."

"Of course not Jason. We didn't know when the confluence of events would occur, or if it ever would. In fact, each of us, in our own way, has tried to prevent it. Remember, no properly led oppressed group takes up arms as a first response. If you're out manned and out gunned, you're usually doomed to failure. We tried to work the system first, influence events from within, through politics, business, and education, even the arts. No one wants violence."

"Then why engage in it?" I said.

"Has anyone been hurt?

"Then all that has been lost is property correct?"

"Yes but ──"

"I thought the law school at our fine University prepared you better than *this*," said my father as he turned and laughed with the others. All but Malik the tight end, laughed heartily at my expense, he remained stoically positioned at the door, perhaps mulling *his* chances in a scuffle with me.

The sun must have been up by now and I thought of the people going about their day unaware of what was happening in an unfinished sub-basement in Delaware or Maryland. *I didn't even know where I was exactly.*

Jason, I realize I have been exceedingly rude. Let me make the introductions. Lock you know of course, he was an original, a founder of U.U. and now serves as Deputy Minister of Defense.

"But Lock…"

"We'll explain all of that later Jason, but I'm glad that you're finally here, it's been a long, hard road but we're finally here," said Lock. I wanted to ask him what he meant by his cryptic response but reserved my comments for later. I sensed that Lock would give it to me straight if my father wasn't around.

My father continued with his introductions, "To my right," he said grandly, "is our Minister of Propaganda, Dr. Cherry Francois". The woman smiled pleasantly as

420

she looked up at my father and then at me. I could tell that she must have been a remarkably beautiful woman in her youth. Even in her sixties, she was a lovely lady.

"Excuse me sister?" I said timidly, "but your *given* name is Cherry?"

"Yes, I was named after the wife of Nat Turner. My parents were educators many years ago in Louisiana and they were what you might call rabble-rousers."

"That's a very unique name."

"Yes well we have a lot a fun with it around here as you might imagine."

"What do you mean?"

"Well, Cherry Bomb for example." Again, the room erupted in laughter.

Jason, my father interrupted, to my left is our Minister of Defense, Joe Underwood."

"Good morning Jason, so glad you made it, I knew you as a toddler," said Underwood.

"Do you mind if I ask a question," I said to Underwood.

"No, go ahead," he said.

As Minister for Defense, you are technically the heir to Huey Newton, right?

"Well yes technically I am, but we have a different hierarchy in U.U. I am not the leader, only second in command."

"Well then who's the leader?"

"Jason, my father said, "I was elected Prime Minister at a Panther safe house in Seattle 30 years ago."

"I remember when you went to Seattle. You came back with all that smoked salmon. I always thought you went for some Black faculty Conference at the University of Washington."

"The Panther's reach was quite broad then. They were able to get a few faculty members to set up a Black studies conference as cover for the founding meeting of U.U. and since most of us were young professors anyway it made it convenient."

"We were chosen because we were from different important regions and fields of endeavor. They selected two physicians, an engineer, an economist, a political scientist, a lawyer, a psychologist, a writer, a community organizer and an actor."

"Why an actor?"

"The Panther's believed that the Arts are a powerful tool for liberation. Art makes great propaganda, and it has the capacity to generate much needed revenue for the struggle," said Cherry.

"What happened to them?" I said.

"The doctors, the writer, the lawyer the economist and the actor all died of natural causes," my father said.

"I'm the engineer", said Underwood "I own the largest minority contracting business on the east coast. We do a lot of blasting," he said with a laugh.

422

"I'm the psychologist," said, Cherry. "I know how to persuade people."

"You know what I am, said Lock looking bored.

"Why are you telling me this," I said.

"Jason, now that you have lost your campaign after giving it everything you had, we believe that you understand as we do, the futility of reforming this system. Gentrification has already begun to erode the political power base in our cities that took thirty years to build; D.C. was just the first large one to fall. Soon we will have no political foothold in this country; it will be like the days of full-fledged gerrymandering where towns with massive Black majorities had no Black representatives. We could literally have a Black President but only a few Black Mayors in less than a decade," said Cherry.

"Let me get to the point, Jason, we want you to join us," said Underwood.

"It is my most fervent hope son," my father added.

"What makes you think I would do this? It's destructive, its illegal, not to mention immoral and—it's suicide." I said.

"My son is lecturing *us* on morality," my father scoffed.

"What do you think made us join U.U. and then pick it back up 30 years later?" said Lock.

"I don't know, the massacre of the Panthers, Fred Hampton, Bobby Hutton,

George Jackson's death, Assata Shakur — you tell me."

"I'm impressed with you knowledge of history Jason", said Underwood.

"He is my son, what he didn't get in school, I taught him," my father said, as if I wasn't there.

"Think about it Jason. It was 1969, give me three things that would turn ten young professionals with reasonably bright futures for that time, into the Urban Underground?"

I thought for a moment and began to think of the things that might have been such a shock to the system as to turn a bunch of young proto-buppies into a violent guerilla movement.

"King's assassination meant the end of non violence. Bobby Kennedy's assassination meant the end of any hope for national reconciliation and the election of Richard Nixon meant the rise of terror. Add the Vietnam War into the mix and you probably thought this country was about to blow itself up." I said.

"That just about covers it," said Lock.

"It radicalized a lot of us," said Cherry.

"But that was a long time ago. What could possibly be as compelling today as those things? Why would I risk going on a most wanted list for some thirty-year-old grievance. Haven't we gotten past this as a nation? My generation doesn't have those wounds."

"You ask what should be obvious?" Said my father.

"I'm sorry but I just don't get it," I said.

"There are times in war when you are forced to salt your own ground and burn your own fields," said Underwood.

"Does the response have to be so extreme? I mean, gentrification isn't exactly the fall of western civilization," I said.

"Are you sure about that? We have seen the return of American fascism—war, the business of war and the human casualties that it creates at home and abroad. Gentrification is only a symptom and D.C. is what it has always been, a test case. It is for them, it is for us." said Cherry.

"I don't understand."

Yes you do son. Its just politics by other means."

THIRTY-TWO

Buffalo Soldiers

I am neither a fanatic nor a dreamer, I am a Black man who loves peace and justice and loves his people.

Malcolm X

My father was a brilliant man, a sober man not given to irrationalism, but I had been confronted with something that challenged everything that I knew about him. It was a sensation that might be like finding out as an adult that your parents adopted you or finding out that the world is really flat after all—a worldview shattered in an instant.

I was allowed to stand, stretch my legs and use the bathroom. What I had not seen locked in the smallish windowless, room was that there were dozens of men and women in the same uniform as Malik, who were lining the walls and huddled at desks with laptops.

There was also a large white board on the wall with the team mascots for most of the D.C. public high schools written on it with dates times and locations. They had used the Knights, Green Wave, Rough Riders, Clerks, Ramblers, Indians, Tigers and Warriors as code names for strike teams in their nightly attacks. *I wondered who had had thought of that flight of fancy. With that device you could plan a bombing over dinner in a quiet restaurant and the other patrons would think you were talking about your kid's game schedule.*

The installation was appropriately clandestine. It was underground but I had no concept of what ground we were under. I saw generators and enough supplies to outfit a small army.

They had executed their plans with precision and I was as impressed, as I was afraid. I was no longer fearful for my safety now that I knew that my own father was the ringleader, but I was concerned for his.

"May I have some water?" I asked. I had been thirsty for some time but I didn't want to show any weakness.

"Of course Jason, but we do have something a little stronger if you want. You know your father, only the good stuff," said Lock. *He'd always looked out for me.*

"Just water, for now."

"Gotcha," said Lock. He nodded to Malik, who immediately ran up the stairs. *I was beginning not to like Malik.*

"Lock, I have more questions."

"I figured you would. We knew it was going to take time for you to get your head around this thing but Jason, we need you to do it in record time."

"What's the hurry?

"I am going to have to let him walk you through that, but its important that you get it in a hurry man."

"Well can I ask you some questions?" I said.

"Go ahead." Said Lock.

"How many people belong to U.U.?" I asked.

"I can't answer that."

"How many cities are you in?"

"I can't answer that either."

"What is the next target?"

"You *know* I can't answer that!"

"I thought you said that I could ask questions."

"Jason, I thought you knew where this was going? What's that old joke, *I said you could ask, I didn't say I would answer.*"

I laughed nervously with him, because I knew he wanted me to. In that environment, I felt it necessary to put *him* at ease. It appeared that *I* was a big operation for them and the outcome was not yet clear.

Malik returned with a bottle of water and I drank it in three or four gulps. I was grateful for it. Concrete floors were usually cooling influences, but it was boiling hot in Urban Underground's bunker.

Minutes later they resumed, but this time the walls were fully lined with U.U. members. Were they there for the spectacle or to rough me up if I asked the wrong question, said the wrong thing or otherwise failed to conduct myself with a suitable degree of deference? I trusted that my father wouldn't allow anything terrible to happen to me, but I had trusted so much about him, things that I would have sworn a thousands oaths to confirm, only to discover that they were a chimera.

"American fascism?"

"You *do* understand the concept?" said my father.

"Yes but I don't know what evidence you are citing of its existence." I actually had a pretty good idea, but I was probing for something to help me through the situation.

I believed my father was referring to the widely held view in the progressive community that the 2000 Presidential election was an historic shift in American history. The basis of that conclusion was that George W. Bush's election (the closest in history) represented a step backward in American democracy, as it was the byproduct of Supreme Court intervention not an exhaustive counting of all ballots cast. It had become a stock line among progressives at the time that Bush had in fact stolen the election and that *President Gore* had been denied an opportunity to serve.

Then there were the urban legends around the actual causes of the 9/11 attacks. Some going so far as to assert that Bush's cronies were responsible, not just by omission, but by commission, with an end toward putting the nation on a war footing; passing reactionary legislation like the Patriot Act as a predicate for fascism.

I knew the line of reasoning, I had heard them in barbershops and cocktail parties and standing in line at the movies, but as sweat beads formed copiously on my forehead, I was also conscious of the fact that I was present in the U.U. bunker at that moment, precisely because of what I didn't know.

"Pop. Can we speak in private for a moment?" I asked.

There was a loud murmur along the wall as the men and women whispered their objections.

"I don't think that's advisable," said Cherry, back to the original formality that had somehow been relaxed during the previous session.

"Oh, I don't think it'll hurt", said a familiar voice behind me. This time, I knew who it was before I turned around and instantly recognized that it was her thinly discussed voice that I had heard on the phone in Ocean City.

"Valor, you're mixed up in this shit too?"

"So it would appear," she said smiling. She wore the same garb as my father and the

430

others at the front of the room, a black beret askew on her brown dreadlocks—but with a black skirt, black tights and boots. *This underground has style*, I thought randomly.

I had gone hours without much sleep and was starting to feel the effects. I was dizzy; my eyes were stinging and probably quite red.

"How did you get mixed up in all this?"

"Later Jason, after you speak with your father. By the way, I got your messages, all of them." She was beaming.

My father nodded again and all the U.U. members along the walls turned and ran up the stairs with a militaristic precision reminiscent of the Fruit of Islam. The others, Valor included, adjourned to the room behind the table.

"Alright, let's talk," my father, said. He led me into a smaller room to the right of the Council table. It was filled with elegant office furniture. A small bar was set up in the corner and I could see a large humidor. It appeared that this was his *wardroom.*

My father closed the door and I began immediately. I didn't know how much time I had and dispensed with all the pleasantries.

"This is crazy Pop and you've got all of these people involved. This is dangerous and people are going to get hurt. How can you embrace all that *off the pig* bullshit now? We have Black Mayors, Councilmembers, and Congressmen. We even have a Black Secretary of State, for the first time in history.

We *are* the powerbrokers in many places, it's not race anymore, its class, education."

"I know that this is a lot of information to absorb in a short period of time, but you're just going to have to do it. Your analysis is too slow and too simplistic."

"Pop, I understand the facts and I think you're acting like a *let loose fool*."

"You sound like your Mother, now."

"Well, she wouldn't like this either. This is the worst possible time to *start* being a terrorist."

"This isn't that *Fight Club* movie that you liked so much, son. We aren't just a bunch of idiots trying to work out our millennial angst. This is not Columbine, we aren't some goofy, white teenaged loners with bad skin; we aren't like the Beltway Snipers—lunatics who went berserk after a bad childhood and a bad divorce.

This isn't like the final act of some bastard who's finally set off because he eats microwavable TV dinners every night and goes to the movies alone and hasn't had sex with another human being in five years. This is a revolution!"

"Pop I worked at Senate Judiciary, remember. I already told you that with the Patriot Act in place and because of all the anti-terrorist activity in the country these days, they'll find you and they'll kill you. Lock, Valor and all of these people will be dead. Where's your revolution then?"

"We have contingency plans."

"So do they. This U.U. apparatus wasn't designed for the 21st century. Can't you see why this won't work? They'll lock down the cities and go house to house until somebody gives you up. Hell, they executed Timothy McVeigh, a blond blue eyed white boy, what do the hell do you think they'll do to your black ass?" *I unexpectedly felt liberated to curse my father out, in the interest of saving his life. I wanted to shock him back into reality.*

"I don't believe I like your tone son."

"How's this for tone, I didn't give a fuck about the bombings, that's what we have law enforcement for. I only came here because I was afraid for your safety, now that I know you are behind this, I'm even more scared for you."

"Think for a moment son. Have you considered that a national state of siege may be exactly what we want?"

"What?" I said as I approached his table.

"Yes, that's what we're counting on. Remember, every major industrialized power in the history of the world has gone fascist after it reached a level of military and economic hegemony. Great Britain under Queen Victoria and Disraeli; France under Napoleon, Japan under Hirohito, Germany under Hitler, Spain under Franco, Italy under Mussolini.

We believe that but for the Depression and the world wars, the United States itself would have gone fascist during the early to mid twentieth century. It had certainly been headed in that direction with the robber

433

barons and the increasing imperialist urges after the Spanish American War."

"But why would it be in your interest to accelerate that process? The very people you want to help would be those most affected."

"It's a simple matter of history, Jason. In each of the cases that I mentioned, the fascist period was followed by longer periods of progressive government. Look at Japan, highest standard of living in the world. The European countries experienced the effect—universal healthcare, proportional legislative representation, free education through college.

Until the United States goes all the way over the edge into fascism, we will never emerge on the other side with the public will necessary to end the destruction that goes on every day in ghettos, reservations, barrios and rural areas across this country."

"So your little group is going to start this chain reaction all by yourselves? What happens when they've wiped you out?"

"We're much larger than you think. Each of the young people you've seen here tonight is being trained to lead his or her own cadre somewhere in the United States.

Already there are young teenagers coming into consciousness through progressive hip-hop music. There are remnants of prison groups that could be mobilized, there are those Haitian groups in New York and Miami and of course there are the gangs and drug crews."

"Come on Pop! Those folks have bought into the American dream more than anybody. The conspicuous consumption, the *bling- bling*; to so many of our people, a set of rims for their luxury SUVs is more important than owning property or buying books and getting an education. Immigrants are more conservative than Ronald Reagan. How do you intend to get across to them?"

"How did you get across to them in your campaign?" he responded expectantly. He had pulled his pipe out of its pouch and was preparing to smoke; relaxed because he knew he had me.

I had hoped to reach the young people by showing them how their lack of participation made them silent co-conspirators in their own disenfranchisement. My relative youth and ability to connect with them on a cultural level would help me gain access. It had been moderately successful. We reached those that were reachable.

"That's not a fair comparison, I said. "I wasn't recruiting them to blow up the city but to help me reform the system."

"They no longer believe in the system son. The kids that voted for you did so because they believed in you, despite your naiveté. There is a whole generation of Black people, Latinos and even some whites who have completely opted out of the mainstream economy and live better than their cousins who still catch buses to minimum wage jobs with no benefits."

He was right. Throughout the nation hardened criminals made fortunes selling drugs to their neighbors and to any white suburbanite who happens by in the family mini van. Many went on to make millions as rap stars. It was a parallel economy.

"You don't expect them to form a voting block do you?"

"So your solution is more attractive?"

"They have nothing to lose son. They have already opted out. You've heard them; they speak a form of patios, which defies the very concept of Ebonics. Look at what they wear, complete devolution from acceptable western attire, they could be in Mogadishu instead of New York, Atlanta or D.C. They are desensitized to violence and appreciate its efficacy. We won't even have to train them on Fanon and Guevara; they live a sort of attenuated version of the philosophy already."

"What about Valor?"

"A warrior that one, she can already make stink bombs, smoke bombs and Molotov Cocktails with the best of them and you should see her with an AA12 Automatic shotgun," he said grinning broadly. "You chose well, it took you too long, but you made a hell of a choice in the end. Congratulations, I'm proud of you!"

"You taught her how to make Molotov cocktails and use assault weapons? Are you crazy? "

"Mandatory paramilitary training son, everyone in the Underground undergoes the training, its necessary for survival. You'll learn too."

436

She told you about my message to her, about getting married?"

"Of course, there are no secrets here."

"How did you convince her to get involved with all of this anyway?"

"It was fairly easy actually," said Valor, who had crept up behind me during the argument. She was always popping in and out of my life.

"You saw it on the streets during the campaign Jason. How many people have jobs, bank accounts, health insurance, their own homes, or even clean police records? Our community is dying. In most neighborhoods the drug dealers hold more sway in the streets than the Mayor. Remember Rayful Edmonds? People bought homes, cars, took vacations, had stable upper middle class lives under Rayful and they all stayed in the neighborhood. All the, what do you call him, *the Great Man's* people took the money they earned from D.C. Government and private sector jobs that he created and ran to P.G. County."

"So now you're saying that we should use drug dealers as role models?"

"Think of what the Panthers did during the sixties and seventies. Free breakfast programs, sickle cell anemia screenings and crime went way down in the neighborhoods they patrolled. We're going to do that again, through neighborhood based businesses and a series of non-profit organizations. We're even opening a charter school system, the Kwame Ture Public Charter Schools."

"Laudable goals, the businesses and particularly trying to educate all the little gangster kids, but what about the violence, I can't believe that you would want any part of that?"

"Has anyone been injured?" she said.

"I see that's the stock answer around here." I said.

"It's by design Jason, we are primarily a defensive organization, like the Panthers. The bombings are a necessary evil, if you want to call it evil. We have got to slow down the exodus of Black people from the city. Project Kujichagulia could have been a solution, but it died for lack of leadership, remember?" Even then she had to get one in on me.

"We have to get their attention. Remember we *want* them to crack down. The inevitable repression will radicalize the people, then we will have their respect and a welcome audience. Think Hamas, or the A.N.C. that's the model."

"Now you sound like him." I said looking at my father.

"That's a complement," she said with a grin. Her smile was perfect. He smiled back at her.

"I can't go along with this."

"Jason, you have to come with us. You're the key to our plans. Who do you think is going to lead this effort into the future?"

"You're kidding right?"

"Why else do you think you're here? You made the decision to come here, right?"

"Under false pretenses and anyway you don't control the Mayor. His people suggested this."

"Yes, after the Chief mentioned the possibility to Andruzzi, knowing that that fat self promoting motherfucker would try to take the credit."

"Reggie Johnson is involved? He's the goddamn Chief of Police!"

"—And my first recruit before we went underground Jason, Reggie is our Minister of Intelligence," said my father. "How do you think he got to be Chief?"

My head was spinning as we reentered the larger room. The others began filing down the stairs as orderly as they had left. The ministers reassembled at the table.

My father continued. "We learned something from COINTELPRO son, we manipulated the Mayor and Andruzzi and we knew that you would be more responsive then because of your vanity."

"Vanity?"

"Yes son, you have always been a little vain. Most people who have the political bug are. But don't worry; you don't have an excessively virulent strain, which is perhaps why you lost. It was your vanity that brought you here. You wanted to be the hero and your vanity convinced you that you could pull it off," said my father.

"So what's keeping me from turning you in?" I said looking in Malik's direction. Malik returned the glance with derision.

"It's a calculated risk Jason, you would never turn in your father," said Valor. "Based upon what we have already done, he could go to jail for the rest of his life, and that's if they don't allege treason. You won't turn me in because you love me and we are finally going to be together now. Also, not a lot of people would believe your story."

"The last thing Jason," said Lock, "is that we believe that you fundamentally agree with us. It's what you have been working toward your whole life, *defending the future of our community*. You thought it was denied you, now we are giving you a second chance."

Valor resumed, "it's allowing our people to exist on this land in perpetuity. Land purchased with the blood and sacrifice of those that have come before. Now darling, I believe I sound like you," she said.

It was late afternoon when I was finally led upstairs. The sight of the sea was refreshing. I'd been in the subbasement for so long. Waves crashed onto the shore, mounds of foam rising as they receded. I was on the deck of an ocean front mansion and more confused than ever.

They were right of course; no one would believe the story. I turned to Underwood who was preparing a large barbeque on the deck.

"I'll have that drink now, and do you have any cigars around? I like CAOs."

THIRTY-THREE
Anthem

*Let me say that the true revolutionary is guided by
a great feeling of love. It is impossible to think of a
genuine revolutionary lacking this quality.*

Ernesto "Che" Guevara

An hour passed and Valor joined me on the deck. The sun hung low over cloudless skies as I considered how to approach her.

My hopes of discovering that it was all an elaborate hoax were dashed by afternoon and I realized that as incredible as it was, the Urban Underground was real and my dearest loved ones were deeply involved.

I decided to make it simple. My fatigue and the alcohol were taking hold.

"I need to ask more questions Valor."

"That's why I'm here," she said.

"Let's start with the operational aspects. I tried to ask Lock but he just told an old a joke and clamed up."

"Sorry about that. Your father hadn't given us the word yet."

"You mean he has now?"

"Yes, an hour ago. It means he believes you're ready Jason. He always has."

"How can he know what I don't know yet?"

"He is your father Jason, he changed your diapers."

"I see you don't know my father very well."

"Well, he knows you, is all I'm saying."

"How long have you been a part of this?"

"For a few months, just after the Council overturned the term limits referendum."

"Why did you do it?"

"It became clear to me that *The Plan* was real. It was not just an old bugaboo passed around card tables or radical meetings by conspiracy theorists. The Council actually invalidated a public referendum to limit their own terms and I think they did it to complete the take over.

They knew that Black folk wouldn't stand for another majority white Council after the referendum limited them to two terms— the city was becoming too politicized with the closing of D.C. General Hospital and with the homicide rate being out of control. There was a chance that one or two brothers and sisters could slip in.

The Council bolted the door with their vote and they did it in broad daylight. It was a gangster move, in your face like they knew they had back up."

I interrupted, "so you're saying that Congress backed them up?"

"I'm saying that they did it under the direction of somebody," she replied. "But, the real power is elsewhere, in the shadows. We think it has something to do with what they're calling the browning of America. What better way to maintain control of a country that you are losing the majority in than retaking the cities? Cities have the infrastructure for command and control and they are usually surrounded by military installations."

"Well assuming you're right, how did your anger over this turn into membership in Urban Underground? I mean, I'm sure you didn't just post an application on some job website in the terrorist section."

"You have jokes Diggs? Is that it?" She edged up to me in her usual seductive way and I felt the normal flush. I really did want her. I held her and she fell comfortably into my arms. *I had wasted so much time.*

"How am I going to get you out of this girlie?" I said.

"How am I going to get you *into* this, she said laughing."

"I'm serious Valor."

"Look Jason, when I became a believer U.U. hadn't surfaced yet. I called your father looking for advice after Project Kujichagulia folded."

"And he just recruited you on the spot?"

"It wasn't that simple, there are old rules at play here. Remember, these brothers and sisters were recruited by people who were attacked by the full force of the United States government. COINTELPRO was no joke, the misinformation campaigns, the phony letters sent to people's wives alleging affairs, fake check stubs slipped under doors implicating people for spying for the FBI. People were being set up, killed and forced into exile in serious numbers."

"The rules are designed to minimize this problem in the future?"

"That's right, it's very transparent internally, communal. There are no secrets."

"So how did it happen?"

"He talked with me for about an hour and asked me what I thought about your campaign, whether I thought you would win? I told him no, because there was too much hatred of you and your program in the white parts of the Ward, that some of those people acted like you didn't even have the right to run."

Your father agreed with me and said that The Plan was in full operation and that only something drastic would be able to slow it down. I asked him what he meant and he said that the group doing the bombings had the right idea and that he thought they were Black.

"So he baited you to find out where you were on all of this stuff?"

"Yes, at first I told him that I was frightened by all of the bombings, that we were all conditioned after 9/11 to think the worst and that since the seventies, Black people haven't been involved in anything remotely like that. Then, I shared with him the frustration that I felt living in a city that had so much wealth—value created by Black folks, with none of it going to benefit the people in the Black community. I told him that I could get disbarred for saying it, and begged him not to repeat it, but that I thought that like in the American revolution, sometimes an oppressed group of people just has to start blowing stuff up!"

"You said that?"

"Yeah, I did."

I saw the intensity growing in her eyes as she spoke. I had loved Valor's mind for years and her body was like a trusted friend, but what moved me on that night was not her mind or her body but her complete commitment to a set of principles that belied her old six figure income, her Mercedes Benz and her fashionable clothes. Her willingness to throw all of that away reaffirmed the love that I had expressed for her just one day before.

"Well," she continued, "over the next few days, your father led me to believe that he knew some students that he suspected of involvement. When I told him that William

445

Kunstler was one of my legal heroes and expressed an interest in representing them on a pro-bono basis if it came to that, he said he might be able to arrange a meeting. He told me not to tell you or the deal might be off." She looked at me embarrassed that she had not.

"Go ahead." I said.

"Okay well, somehow I didn't think to ask him how he could possibly know so much about a terrorist organization on Howard's campus, without going to his friend the Police Chief about it. It was really the question to ask, but you know your father, he's so compelling, this eyes, he way he expresses ideas, his analysis, that voice. You know I only just realized that you have his voice."

"So you've fallen in love with my father, like some 19 year old sophomore," I said only half joking.

"I did fall in love Jason, she said. "I fell in love with the man's cause before I even knew it was his. I got the same treatment that you got today, only he didn't reveal himself until after I agreed to represent U.U. and a privileged relationship had been established."

A privileged relationship, beyond the legal implication, took on a different meaning as I discussed with the woman I loved, her decision to become a terrorist. Privileged: special, exclusive. Relationship: personal intercourse, social engagement. Wasn't that what I was so feebly trying to convey during my campaign about my feelings for the city and how public power should be exercised in respect to it.

446

Common squatters had rejected me in my campaign, as if the city had always belonged to them; as if it was their blood in the streets and their sweat on the wheels of history. I couldn't let that stand; could I?

Surely the fatigue of the long campaign and the confusion of the long night had taken a toll but I told her that I was ready to fall off the world and join them. The city that I loved was no more; I could no longer go back to it.

"How would this work? I mean if I went forward."

"Your father and the other central committee members are better equipped to answer that, but here's what I know. We have weapons and explosives. The original plan from the seventies was to take out strategic targets as a counter insurgency against COINTELPRO, but that plan was scrubbed because of leaks.

When your father and the others were recruited, they were to wait for a few years, rebuild and attack, but the war in Vietnam ended and the glue for so many of the leftist groups was gone. A few hung on, the Weather Underground being the most notable.

U.U. was deep underground at this point, going on with their lives, but waiting for the moment when all the suffering endured by the people could be transformed into coordinated action. The key to the Panther's plan was its activities abroad and it's biggest secret was its alliance with Amilcar Cabral in Guinea Bissau."

"Guinea Bissau? That's where Lock was."

"Exactly. The other leftist groups talked about revolution, but the Panthers actually made preparations for it. They knew that training camps and the propaganda machine would have to be set up outside the United States during a major conflict and Lock was the emissary sent to establish bases and learn guerrilla fighting tactics and bomb making. He fought alongside Cabral against the Portuguese."

"Lock was in a guerrilla war?"

"Fifty-eight confirmed kills," she said coldly.

"What are you telling me Valor?"

"I am telling you that U.U. controls an area the size of New York City within the nation of Guinea Bissau on the west coast of Africa, including one of the four western most islands off its coast, in the Atlantic. We have palm oil and cashew processing plants already in place; we're already making millions annually.

After establishing the cadres in the rest of the United States, the entire central committee and the general staff, that means you and me, will be going to the island of Uno, where our headquarters—the city of Malcolm, has been secretly under construction by Minister Underwood's company for the last twenty years."

"So this is full scale war?"

"Not yet, but we're planning to stir things up a bit."

I hadn't seen Valor this way in many years. She was strong, focused and happy.

Not the scared, confused person who had come to my office all those months ago.

✝

At the barbeque expertly prepared by Underwood and his staff, my father held forth like a head of state and according to Valor, in a sense he was.

I was introduced all around and found out that Malik was Cherry's son. He continued to sneer at me, but I still had a feeling of recognition that I couldn't shake.

"Get used to cooking and eating out doors everyone, that's the Guinean way," he said in his booming voice. He was joyous in a way I hadn't seen him in years.

The food, expertly grilled seafood and lamb, was better than anything I had ever had at the fine restaurants that I once frequented and I was lost in that thought when a saw a familiar face enter the deck.

"Sorry I'm late. I just came back from the Vineyard with my wife for the last time." It was Barkley Taylor, my old nemesis from so many months ago.

"Jason I want you to formally meet our Head of Security, Brother Taylor. I think you've met briefly once before. He and his team have been keeping tabs on you since your mother died. We had to protect our investment," said my father.

The whole thing was amazing to me. I had been under the loving care of the Urban

Underground for over a year and never suspected a thing. They *were* good.

"Jason, I am glad to have you safely within the bond of the Underground. My job is done."

"Brother Taylor won't be joining us on the island, he will stay behind and head our follow on operations in D.C.," Lock said.

"My wife wouldn't understand all of this anyway and moving to Africa would keep her from her Delta meetings," Taylor said, laughing his gravelly laugh.

"So, what is my role in all of this?" I said.

"I want you to be my Viceroy, Jason. You will be my right hand within our little shadow government and then you will succeed me as Prime Minister after four years, or upon my death. The vote has already been taken."

He noticed me struggling with a response and continued.

"I've also appointed Valor here as Minister of the Interior. She will oversee the day-to-day operations on Uno. Supplies, munitions, sanitation, communications and training will all come under her. She will be the Mayor of Malcolm."

"I have a question to ask you," said Lock.

""Go ahead," I said.

"What happens to old revolutionaries?"

"I don't understand the question?"

"It's our security question in the Urban Underground. If you hear that question, the person that asks it is UU."

Revolutionaries rarely reached old age. They were often killed in the struggle, or died of stress in middle age.

Sometimes they devolved miserably into drug addiction or alcoholism, unable to soberly acknowledge the futility of their dreams. Those that escaped this ignominious fate, went on to teach or lead non profit social service organizations dedicated to eradicating the symptoms associated with the inequities they once tried to cure through struggle.

"I'm going to need some time to digest all of this."

"Were going to need your answer immediately because we are making a phased transfer of operations to Uno in January. How does ninety degrees and an ocean breeze in January suit you?" My father said, smiling. I had never seen him so happy since my mother died and didn't quite understand until I saw Cherry furtively holding his hand under the table.

"How long has this been going on?" I asked Valor, pointing under the table. She looked uncomfortable.

"For a long, long time, I think. They met on Martha's Vineyard in the early sixties." she said. I was *definitely* my father's son.

I looked at my father and he did not turn away, he just smiled and stared at me with his penetrating eyes. I guess I had my answer about why he never took me to the Vineyard. It represented another life for him.

✝

My father always said, *"reflection is a leader's closest ally"* and as he always practiced what he preached, he gave me the time I needed. I returned to the city the following day to find a new apartment building smoldering, a construction site for a new gourmet grocery store in ruins and a new office building on M Street, S.E., across from the Navy Yard missing its top four floors.

Chief Johnson smoothed over my disappearance with the authorities claiming that I was emotionally distraught and could not go on with the planned efforts to negotiate with U.U. He soon retired.

My father did the same after reappearing in the same place from which he'd eluded his surveillance team, the men's room in Douglass Hall. He claimed he had no recollection of his capture. He told all assembled at his retirement party, which was gleefully presided over by Cole, that he was going to see more of the world.

Valor and I sold our houses at a loss and I formally quit my job at Senate Judiciary. "Getting married, going into private practice, lobbying" I told them. "Perhaps for a foreign concern."

"Be careful oversees", they told me, "its dangerous for Americans these days."

My departure ended the investigation launched after Kelleye's letter. On my last day, Kelleye sneered her goodbyes as I walked out of the office with my law degree under my arm. There was nothing else to take.

Most of the Urban Underground disappeared from their American lives during the 2002 Christmas holidays and took various routes to Africa. My father booked passage on a cruise ship bound for the Mediterranean. During a day trip to Algiers, he broke off and took an old Panther escape route through Mali and on to the coast. He was officially declared lost at sea.

Lock went the conventional route, directly into Dakar and then a long truck ride into Guinea Bissau. He'd met a Malian woman on the plane to Senegal and quickly married her, fathering three children with her in Malcolm. He lived to be a spry one hundred years old. Lock's last words were: "Home, home."

Valor, always the risk taker, flew to Brazil for immersion having acquired the Portuguese language skills that she would need in Guinea Bissau to assume her duties. She joined a tour group headed directly to the Archipelago dos Bijagoes, where she landed on the island of Caravela, four islands away from Uno, our new home. U.U. speedboats whisked her to her destiny.

I had never been to the Vineyard in January, but was pleased to see it one more time. I had been called in for questioning once Chief Johnson retired because the Federal officials thought it odd that the bombings ended so soon after my campaign—another twist of the wheel from my father, there would be no going back now. I was a person of interest in an ongoing investigation. (Mayor Callahan and his handlers still considered me a threat.) So the Vineyard it would be until a final escape route could be found for me.

January 15th, Martin Luther King's actual birthday was the day of my escape. I was under the ironic assumed name of Malcolm Little courtesy of Cherry and had been holed up for a week in a little room at the Beach Plumb Inn in the lovely little fishing village of Menemsha.

I spent my last days reading, listening to music and taking in the best cuisine on the Island. My nights in deep contemplation of what the future held.

My training under Barkley Taylor in the preceding months had been grueling, a U.U. modified version of the Marine Corps officers training he once administered as a sergeant Major at Quantico. The process changed me.

I'd been a poet. Now, I was a warrior: By the day of my extraction, I was reaching proficiency in both Korean Hapkido and Brazilian Capoeira and could field strip a

454

Beretta PX4 in 4 seconds. I was a marksman with a variety of deadly firearms. The process changed me.

Below my temporary dwelling, rocks rose defiantly from the sea, salt water deflecting all around them as though weightless. What lay beneath the waves: sand and shell and secrets—I understood these things.

On the evening of the 15th, I was collected by my security team, twenty young men fresh from specialized U.U. training whose sole responsibility was my survival. I had traveled so far in four months.

I took one last walk on the beach that cold night, the sun drifting into the sea in an orange blaze. My troop of guards, dazzling in their black boots and fatigues, field coats and Berets, enveloped me at a respectable 20 yards and must have given me the appearance of a rebel warlord on an evening stroll.

I was identically attired and was down to the sweet spot on a CAO X3 Torpedo. It was the last cigar I would ever purchase from Draper's in Washington. Smoking it seemed like the ritualistic end of my former life.

At that time of year, Menemsha was virtually empty and with the approaching darkness, the prying eyes of fishermen would have difficulty seeing the squad, micro Uzi's in their hands, preparing the extraction of their heir apparent.

When darkness fell, I heard the zodiacs roaring in from the cruiser and speedboats about 100 yards off shore. They had prepared a very swift flotilla to get me out of the country.

"Sir, it's time," said the captain of the guard.

"Alright, just another minute."

"Yes, sir", but we have a time window to meet. The coast guard will be changing shifts, we need to slip in between them."

"As fast as those things look I don't think we'll have a problem." I said reviewing the assemblage of *go-fast-boats* that awaited us off shore.

"Yes sir, your cruiser will do over sixty miles per hour and the interceptors will all do over a hundred, even in rough seas. We've also made some upgrades."

"Weapons?"

"Yes sir. 20mm mounted cannons and we have a few Chinese stinger missile knock offs on board." *Close ties to an unstable foreign government certainly had its perks.*

"I feel safer already." I was actually joking, amazed at the irony of the events. My father had given me a retrofitted 58-foot Motor Yacht to serve as my flagship. *Merry Christmas, the palm oil and cashew business must be good, I thought. I finally have my boat.*

"You should sir; feel safe I mean. We're pretty good, you know." He smiled, but not too much, understatement not overconfidence.

"Where you from brother?" I asked.

"Warrior cell sir, your personal guards." *They were all from my old high school.*

"No, brother, where are you from?" *I no longer guessed at such things. I had no time for games.*

"Oh, I'm from Northeast Sir. Mayfair, but I spent a lot of time in Oak Hill when I was young."

At 22 or 23, the look in his eyes confirmed his capabilities. There was a hardness there that could not be simulated. He had spent time in the Oak Hill youth detention center, and might even have killed people in his young life; I didn't want to ask.

"I'm glad you're on my side." I said.

"All due respect sir, you should be, but ah, we have a surprise for you sir." He raised his hand and Musa came bounding off a zodiac at the end of the beach. He was in a full sprint, his coat shimmering under the light of the rising moon. Remarkably, he stopped at my heel, and sat.

"Musa!" I patted his head and rubbed his sides. The Akita let out a howl of joy and recognition. "Wooulf".

He'll protect you too. We've had him trained as a military dog, he'll take out ten men and keep going."

"An Akita military dog, that's scary."

"We've bred him to a beautiful hundred pound female, you'll see his puppies on the Island."

"Thank you, I missed my old friend."

"All Power to the people sir!" He said, as the entire squad raised their fists in the traditional Black Power salute.

Perhaps my father was right, these men, all of them just months out of boyhood, might have been drug dealers or homeless or in jail but they were in fact an elite fighting force dedicated to the liberation of a people, guardians of my life, the shock troops of a new beginning. What was the distinction between these manifestly dissimilar fates? It was simple, but it was everything. These hard men had been touched by the greatest motivation of all— love.

I returned the salute of the Captain and his troops, pleased to have their respect and honored to have a place in leading them. It was then that I acceded to my station.

Hadn't I been raised in princely privilege? Hadn't I been educated and trained in the manner of an heir apparent? The facts conflated in my mind that night. *This is what the voice had been telling me my whole life?* I was Viceroy to the Prime Minister of the Urban Underground/Prime Minister Designate and I accepted it as my birthright.

I would have a long journey to my new home, a reverse middle passage that promised to restore my puissance as a Black man, as an African man in a western dominated world.

We would take the speedboats to Nova Scotia, transferring at sea to an innocuous looking U.U. owned freighter off the coast for the long voyage to the Continent, and then finally our little Navy would round the beautiful face of Africa to the island of Uno.

My guards told me that a large party had been planned for my arrival and that the local matrilineal engagement traditions will be observed. Valor would prepare the ceremonial proposal dish of fish in red palm oil and build an authentic Guinean island hut by herself. *Surely the world is a strange place, I thought, for me to be going to a country where women dominate the social structure.*

We were scheduled, of course to live in the shining new city-state of Malcolm and abide by our own laws, but the local priestess has been an ally and the Central committee deemed it politically expedient to appease her as much as possible. All was prepared.

The zodiacs darted briskly toward my cruiser, the *Rachel (I'd considered Argo for a name but I did have some limits)* and the biting spray in my face was but a small physical reminder of the gnawing thought I had been contending with for months. The man I had been was gone and I mourned his passing. But, I could not yet celebrate the man I had become.

THIRTY-FOUR

Urban Underground

The first lesson a revolutionary must learn is that he is a doomed man.

Huey Newton

A J, later known as A. Juan Johnson, became the second highest grossing Black actor in Hollywood in the years that followed. After early success in action films he settled into character driven roles for which he gained critical acclaim, playing doctors, judges, astronauts, professors, presidents and businessmen. He served for many years as the film industry magazines reported, as the Chairman of the board of the Kwame Ture Charter Schools based in Washington D.C. The school system is unique for its focus on international business development and its Portuguese language requirement. The school's new multimillion-dollar facility is named the Diggs educational center a reference perhaps to a little known political activist who disappeared after losing his only campaign for city council or perhaps his father a Political Science professor of some renown at Howard University who was tragically lost at sea during a vacation.

A building previously named for Dr. Rachel Diggs a former professor at UDC has been raised along with the rest of the Connecticut Avenue campus for the new two billion dollar, Andruzzi Palazzo condominium community. A significant portion of A. Juan Johnson's movie salary, it is reported, has always gone to a little known non-profit organization called the friends of Guinea Bissau.

Eight years after the relocation of the Central Committee of the First Cadre of the Urban Underground to the island of Uno, the census figures for Washington D.C. were released. The document revealed that due to unprecedented migration patterns among African Americans, the city would be majority Caucasian by the next census, even as the United States becomes majority non white. No further explanation was provided.

On the day after his inauguration, Mayor Dexter Callahan's suite of offices on the sixth floor of the John A. Wilson Building was completely destroyed by explosives. No one was injured. No one took responsibility.

The Organization of African Unity, led by its rotating Chairman, the President of Guinea Bissau, protested former D.C. Mayor Alvin Terwilliger's nomination as U.S. Ambassador to South Africa. The nomination was withdrawn in the face of the

461

unprecedented move.   After his defeat, Terwilliger was last reported to be living in seclusion in the Castro district in San Francisco, California.

Professor Cole was removed from the Chairmanship of the Howard University Political Science Department after a routine check discovered child pornography on his office computer. He denied any wrongdoing until his death by asphyxiation in his garage one day before his trial. He was found in his black BMW, with the engine running.

By 2028, the largest palm oil exporting company in the world, according to the CIA fact book, was Anacostia Oil, Ltd based in the tiny West African Nation of Guinea Bissau. It grosses 100 billion dollars (U.S. annually) as it converts most of its raw product to biofuel for use in automobiles, through the community owned and operated plants that it licenses in distressed urban communities throughout the United States. These businesses, which were established under a program known as the Jason Project, has stabilized minority populations in most major American cities. Anacostia Oil is privately held and has a notoriously shadowy board of directors.

EPILOGUE

The credit belongs to the man who is actually in the arena, whose face is marred by dust and sweat and blood, who strives valiantly; who errs and comes short again and again; because there is not effort without error and shortcomings; but who does actually strive to do the deed; who knows the great enthusiasms, the great devotions, who spends himself in a worthy cause, who at the best knows in the end the triumph of high achievement and who at the worst, if he fails, at least he fails while daring greatly. So, that his place shall never be with those cold and timid souls who know neither victory nor defeat.

Teddy Roosevelt

War Anthem:

From The Journal of Jason Diggs

May 2, 2038

This is my war anthem, made sacred by the blood and sacrifice of many. I trust you will see the truth of it and in its truth, hear its music. I do not seek to explain myself, for such would be a vanity to which I am indisposed. Many years have passed since I indulged myself with such an extravagance.

I was the child of a waning sun. I seek only to bear witness.

Valor and I never married. Her duties on the island were far too consuming and delays in our plans were inevitable. But I will say this, I wish I had, she was, at the end of it all my one true love. We simply ran out of time.

I wish I had known that she was carrying our child—conceived in a seaside mansion in Bethany Beach— before we left this country. Perhaps we could have waited, perhaps the baby would not have been in breech so far away from a hospital, perhaps Valor would have survived the tribal caesarian that was administered by the priestess.

I have been to Valor's grave in Atlanta many times since my return; we sent her to her people, we thought it was right. I once slept there, another vagabond with strange tastes in lodging. Who would have noticed, I no longer resemble the earnest young man who disappeared so many years ago.

I've had a fruitful time since I have returned to the Vineyard. I raised my Akitas, read a thousand books and have written twenty more. The rag you hold is but one of them.

Persephone and I live off the fish I catch in these coastal waters and we grow our own vegetables during the short season. It's been a good life now that the wars are over and the good I tried to make of everything has taken root.

In these ending days, I have often wondered what my mother would say of me, if through a conjuring, she could now confess her thoughts. Would she be proud of how I've spent my life? I think her peaceful spirit would be offended at the coarseness of my path, though she would be pleased to know that Rachel Valor, her granddaughter is a beautiful brave woman, who now rules a small African nation with both wisdom and compassion. *She is her mother's daughter.*

Would my mother consider her sacrifices in my cause a waste? Perhaps not, but she did not mince words and I would certainly feel the full brunt of her judgments.

Still, I believe that having given me her maximum love, my mother would even now, find it within herself to wring out more of her tender bounty that it might sustain me. Such was the fullness of her commitment to this imperfect thing she had so selflessly created.

I could have done a thousand laudable things with my gifts but appeared to fail the cause to which I gave my life. Was I my own worst enemy? Assuredly so, but when confronted with such a real thing, what defense has purchase, what evasions have efficacy?

I suffered through a misreading of my purpose, the arrogant voice of self-infatuation, ambition mistaken for a spiritual charge. Was it self-anointing and not divine ordination? God has his own plan for men and my lie has been my life.

I was also my father's son and destined to fight for the recompense of my fellows. The end of D.C. as we had known it set in motion inconceivable events. I did what I could in response and seek no exonerations. Years ago I left the city of Malcolm to the care of my half brother Malik, for he too is my father's son and perhaps even more so.

Winter's coming and I cannot be optimistic about the future, when the world is full of evil and the good are so naive. So I leave the messy business of advancing hope to those still possessed of it.

Capitulate and win the possibility of survival or fight and face the prospect of death; these are the choices of leadership. These are the choices in life.

The heroes of my youth, flesh and blood and full of flaws, all fell in struggle. They were human beings and lived as such in their troubled times. In anthems, portraits and hagiographic books they live on, doubtlessly thankful as they sleep, to be spared the battlefield. Now, their mighty hearts fertilize future dreams.

And what of me? That, I leave to you.

AUTHOR'S NOTE

After spending a quarter of my life working on "the book"—it's finally here! Just a word of caution, don't expect me to thank some literary agent for their "invaluable help in bringing my work to publication" because that would be fiction and this is the non-fiction section of this book. But, seriously, this novel only exists as a result of the mighty agency of God. So, THANK YOU GOD!!!

I would also like to thank God's earthly helpers who either inspired or in some way supported me during a lifetime of writing. There is no War Anthem without you.

My appreciation to my magnificent hometown of Washington, D.C. a magical place about which more should be written. My late aunt Dr. Certeta Perry, who was the first published author in my family and who sadly just missed seeing this product of her inspiration; my cousin Donn Davenport for ties of friendship—beyond

Bond and blood and his mother my first cousin Yvette Davenport Cothran for keeping faith with our ancestors; Ebenezer United Methodist Church, for a strong foundation; H.D. Woodson Senior High School's late and lamented Humanities Program, for encouraging me to write; Morehouse College, especially Dr. Hamid Taqi and the late Dr. Robert Brisbane—high priests of Black political thought who prepared my mind for battle; Howard University Law School, especially Professor Spencer Boyer for requiring me to think on my feet; the late John Gibson for his heart; Mayor Sharon Pratt for giving a kid a chance; Hon. Marion Barry for allowing me to shine in both good times and bad; and the island of Martha's Vineyard for providing me with peace amid the storm—I'll see you soon.

Friends ground and center you and I would like to thank the New York/Vineyard Crew for torrents of laughter—especially the ever beautiful and graceful Gayle Ellis Davis of Harlem USA—proprietor of the best private B&B in America; the lovely and simply hilarious Deborah Whitfield Small, who I still believe is from Connecticut; the fabulous Yvonne Durant of the Upper East Side, writer, raconteur and member of the New York literati (grazie mille); Fred Jewell, enough said; and Tracy Thomas for the very useful concept of porch drinking. The brothers of Kappa Alpha Psi Fraternity Incorporated—especially The Founders, Donn Davenport (yes again) George Rose, Sowande Tichawonna, Ernest Duncan, Barrington "Bo Gigolo" Scott, the late Terry "T— Polo" Hairston, Vinny Latimore, Corey Barnette, Mike Jones, Mike Butler, and Dr. Michael Fauntroy; I waited a decade but it was more than worth it— PHINUPE.

People for Perry were my campaign family when I ran for the D.C. City Council in 2002 and their heart and spirit is in this book. I would especially, like to thank my buddy the late

Advisory Neighborhood Commissioner Gregory Ferrell for his friendship, dedication and unparalleled passion for justice; Commissioner Wanda Harris for believing in me when so many others didn't; my warriors Commissioners Philip Edwards and Lamar McIntyre for the many sleepless nights on ladders; and ACORN, for the soldiers—R.I.P.

There were numerous others that contributed in very practical ways to the completion of this work. They are: the simply wonderful Diane Howell Esq. for starting it all in 1993 and for being my first reader and audience; C.F.—it was stranger than fiction; Ralph Ellison, for setting the standard; Kenji Jasper and Edward P. Jones for giving D.C. a voice; Trey Ellis for *Home Repairs*; Brother Sam Greenlee for his heroic example, Carleen Brice for her gentle advocacy; and Stephen Carter for proving once again that there is a market for African-American literary fiction; Journalist Richard Miniter for his "chaotic" Morton's rant; Jazz musicians Cassandra Wilson, for setting the mood in the middle of the night and Christian Scott, for the title, the music and for giving me my pen back.

My eternal gratitude to The Center for Black Literature, North Country Institute for Writers of Color at Medgar Evers College for confirming and nurturing my talent. Hugs and kisses to my workshop leader, the prodigiously gifted writer Tonya Cherie Hegamin. Thanks for showing me the way home (my island can still beat up your island).

As I completed this novel, I lost my two Akitas to old age. I would be remiss if I did not thank Kuro for his loyal and brooding presence over the years and for serving as the model for Musa and Nikkei for being the best canine editorial assistant that the world has ever seen. For months she stayed up in the wee hours with me, guarding both this manuscript and its author with her life. I miss our walks my friends (fuse, rest easy now.)

To Keith and Taylor, blood of my blood and face of my face. You were both toddlers when I started this novel, proof positive that it is never too late.

Special thanks to you, the reader; please continue to support highly weaponized Black literature.

Finally, I reserve special thanks to my wife Belinda Kittles Perry, Esq. for motivating me as I plowed though multiple drafts of this work. She deserves a medal for her unwavering courage in weathering the vicissitudes of life with me and for keeping it together as I completed this novel.

War Anthem was written between 1993 and 2010 in Washington, D.C., Martha's Vineyard, Negril, Jamaica and Brooklyn, New York—on scratch paper, envelopes, legislation being considered in the Council of the District of Columbia, legal memoranda, napkins, legal pads, Moleskins, shopping receipts, Metro fare cards, the back of my hand, an iPhone and on Sony, Compaq and Apple computers.

September 2010